THE FIRST SECRET OF
EDWIN HOFF

A.B. BOURNE

Watch Hill Books

Weston, Massachusetts

Published by Watch Hill Books.

Printed in the United States of America
ISBN (print): 9780983980704
ISBN (e-book): 978098398071

For Julian

PROLOGUE

The night was still warm, windless, when the man slipped into the black water east of the Lesser Antilles near Venezuela. Stars slid on the ripples he made. The weights led him straight down. With conscious effort, he stretched his ribcage and forced his lungs to suck deeply as he sank meter after meter through the Caribbean.

A mile off the coast of the island of Bonaire, a black inflatable dinghy shifted against its thin anchor line. A parachute, crisply folded, was stowed beneath the seat.

Twenty meters below the surface, the man blinked his eyes in pitch blackness. Then his forked flippers scraped sand. He reached out his glove until it grazed the jagged wall of coral, exactly where he expected it to be. Then the man known to a select few as "Raptor" swam due east, without a light, for 78 minutes. Each ticked precisely in his mind. The luminescent numbers on his wrist would lead him to the break in the coral wall to Krajlendik Harbor and the target: *The Silver*, 48 feet, white sides, black hull.

"Where bad people are doing bad things," Raptor thought. "For the moment." He ran his fingers across the sealed rubber bladder at his belt. The pouch contained an adjustable wrench, two rolls of duct tape and two eight-inch lengths of plastic pipe packed solid with C-4. When triggered, the bars would decompose to nitrogen and carbon oxide gasses expanding at 26,400 feet per second. Enough to demolish a truck or a house. Or a boat. Plenty.

Reflexively Raptor touched his left shoulder, confirming the thick hose still connected his lungs to the square tank on his back. Neoprene wrapped him head to toe, matting down his short black hair. His light green eyes shone through the oval mask. It was the eyes, if they lit upon you, which warned that he was a deceptively agile humvee who could bull through anything, clamber over anything, endure any struggle longer than anyone else. His eyes scanned minute details but gave up nothing about the conclusions he drew. He had instant, photographic recall.

68 hours earlier, Raptor had peeled his orders off the bottom of a condiment shelf at the designated coffee shop. The Dead Letter Drop was a time-worn way to pass secrets. There were newer technologies, but this one worked like a sharp pencil. His orders scrolled in his memory as if playing on a computer monitor:

ASP Operator: *Raptor*
Mission: *Destroy Ricin Manufacture and Distribution Hub*
Date and Time: *July 11, 1999 5:45a.m.*
Special Considerations: *Khalid al Hamzami, cell director, swims daily at dawn. Sunrise is 6:14 am.*
Location: *Krajlendik Harbor, Bonaire, Lesser Antilles*
Site: *The Silver 48' dive boat, white sides, black hull*
Weapons: *Underwater Explosive Device: C-4*

A stocky 5'9" Raptor appeared, at first glance, physically average. This was a covert asset. He was unreasonably strong for his size, and an efficient swimmer. He could cover fields charging low on his muscled thighs, push out of a flying plane through 85 mph of slipstream, or beat the water with extended flippers for miles without tiring. Raptor had excelled during his tours in increasingly elite Special Forces not because of his raw strength, but that together with his sheer determination and uncanny strategic mind – genius, even. With unshakeable focus on his goal, Raptor always won. After twelve years of escalating elite military training – first the Marines, then the Navy Seals and Delta Force - his current official posting was: "Retired."

Raptor reached the jetty at the outer edge of the harbor in total darkness. He swam along the rocky bottom of Krajlendik Harbor for a quarter of a mile to where the mangroves grew thickly at the edge. The black curve of his head and an inch of his mask breached the surface. Ten feet back in the thicket, he saw the black duffel. His exit plan was still wedged between the branches. Now he could begin.

Raptor's eyes swept the harbor. When he flicked a lens over his mask, he could see details on each of the seven anchored boats. Lights were off in all but one boat. Through the powerful night scope he saw a man dangling his feet over its bow, and easily read the nameplate: *The Silver*. In the wide flat cockpit, twelve scuba tanks stood yoked by red line against the transom. Another man stood nearby with a lit cigarette.

"Happy to light up next to twelve tanks?" Raptor wondered. "No fear of a gas leak. But something is worth babysitting." He watched as the cabin door opened. A man lifted another scuba tank and placed it gingerly in the pack.

It was 5:10am. Raptor had 35 minutes. He descended, and then flutter kicked past anchor lines that stretched diagonally off the sea floor in the remote, nearly empty harbor. When he reached *The Silver*, he swam beneath the boat and ran his fingers over the keel. He felt the rows of two-inch thick bolts securing the heavy steel fin to the hull.

Along the edge of *The Silver's* galley porthole, a small round mirror tipped towards the glass. It passed the reflection down to Raptor's mask through a series of mirrors in the handheld periscope. Balancing on his flipper toes in the rocky sea floor, Raptor saw a man with scraggly grey hair and a full beard lying back on a mattress, an elbow over his eyes. His glasses, thick black frames, hung below the kerosene lamp.

"Hamzami is older," Raptor thought. "53? 55 maybe?" He checked his watch. 5:18. Sunrise was at 6:14, but already the ocean was absorbing the predawn grey.

While their leader slept, three younger men wearing thick green hospital masks gathered around the small galley table.. One man scooped a pile of beans from a burlap bag into a large bowl. Black with brown striations, the beans looked like exotic legless beetles.

A second man added a squirt from a bottle. He crushed the beans with a mallet, and then mashed them with his fists. Another sifted the pulp, a powdery residue settling on wax paper. Carefully he scraped the powder onto a funnel that filled a tube leading to the scuba tank. He did this several more times. Then he lifted the tank and put it in the rack on the back of the deck with others just like it.

"Castor beans," Raptor thought. "They're making ricin. The poor man's poison."

The Silver looked like an unremarkable dive boat anchored in a harbor known for the sport. But in its galley the crew mashed beans into a biological weapon, and its cockpit carried now fourteen tanks full of uncompressed air and thick layers of weaponized ricin powder.

Raptor recalled his biological warfare training on poisons. He read the typeset words as clearly as if he held the datasheet in his hands.

RICIN
Substance: *Powder synthesized from mashed castor bean.*
Toxicity: *Lethal if inhaled or injected. Stops human body from making proteins. Organs begin to shut down within 4 hours.*
Symptoms: *Unceasing diarrhea after 4 hours, death within 24.*
Military Application: *Assassination by lethal dart, or mass casualties if released in closed air circulation system, i.e. bus, plane, subway, hotel or mall.*
Availability: *Easy and cheap. Castor beans are sold legally to make lubricants and oil. Ricin protein can be extracted from the bean waste inexpensively, through widely available chromatography separation methods.*

"Fourteen tanks," Raptor thought "already separated into portions, sealed for secure delivery. So *The Silver* is providing means for at least 14 separate attacks. Maybe timed to go off together. 14 malls? 14 planes? 14 buses?"

Raptor felt his adrenalin surge. He had no subpoena. He had no official sanction. But he had a sack of C-4. This threat needed no committee to conclude it was pure evil. This was exactly why, when the ASP made him a proposal, Raptor had eagerly accepted. He was a force to be felt in a larger battle, one unencumbered by politics, process or law. Even if the ASP's contract imposed upon him duties that grew heavier each day.

The green numbers read 5:35 am. He had 10 minutes to deploy the explosives and get out of range, back to his duffel bag and exit.

Through the regulator, Raptor's steady breath washed in and retreated, then rose again. The water made his movements slow and deliberate as he pulled open his bag and withdrew the duct tape, which had a special adhesive on both sides. With a sharp short blade, Raptor sliced a foot long section and wrapped it around the pipes. Then he placed them against the hull of the boat. They held. For good measure, he stretched two more lengths of sticky tape over them. He checked the detonator cap, then the trigger. The blast might wake some groggy sailors sleeping off their pitchers of Dark n' Storrmies. But the island was remote; the harbor nearly empty. One blown out rusty dive boat would be soon forgotten by the few there to notice it.

It was 5:38am when Raptor pressed the detonation timer. The sea was light grey. He had five minutes before the bomb would destroy *The Silver* and its dirty lab. He kicked hard, his long split flippers propelling him like dolphin tails out of the kill zone.

But two minutes later, just as Raptor glimpsed the stone jetty, he heard an immense roar bellow through the water. A tidal surge caught him, spun up sand and pushed him head over heels. The roar continued; it was not an explosion. Raptor surfaced. In the dim light of dawn, what he saw changed everything.

While Raptor had crawled the ocean floor to enter the bay from the east, a city had steamed in from the south. It had entered Krajlendik Harbor just as Raptor deployed the bomb, with its eight stories of cabins, six pools, on board surf pool and 3200 passengers from all over the world.

"This is a non-trivial problem," Raptor said aloud. In three minutes, the explosion would shake the eggs off the early birds' breakfast spoons and scare the moment out of the sunrise yoga class on the Lido Deck. They would breathlessly report their close call to their fellow travelers; the captain would call the event in ship to shore, and report to the travel agents and news outlets at all of its departing ports that the crew had kept the boat and passengers entirely safe during a minor explosion in the harbor.

What should have been just an unfortunate accident on a remote island would become, in two minutes, an international incident.

"The ASP won't go for that," Raptor said. The ASP did not tolerate exposure. The world did very well by the ASP, as long as no one tread on it.

It was 5:40. The bomb would go at 5:42. Raptor snapped his mask in place, bit the regulator and dove. Because he had come to a full stop he had no momentum. But he swam hard, straight into the kill zone with each fierce kick, as time ticked away and the wake of the cruise ship pushed him back toward the shore.

Inside the cabin, the man on the bunk shifted. KAH swung his feet off the edge and yawned.

At 5:41:45 Raptor reached the Silver's hull. He felt for the place where he had secured the tubes of C-4. But they were not there. He scanned the underwater horizon, bellies of boats dangling their fins. They looked so similar. Had he gone off course? Was this the wrong boat? 8 seconds. 7...6....

Then he looked down. Two tubes lay in the sand, a wire emerging from them. When the surge came through, the tape had failed. 5...4...3...Raptor pulled cupfuls of water and beat his flippers toward the sea floor. 2...1...

Thick fingers curled around the wire and ripped them off the tubes.

"Change of plan," Raptor thought. "Now destroy *The Silver* and its 14 missiles without an explosion, within the next 20 minutes, with whatever I can reach."

Fortunately, his next weapon of destruction was at hand in abundance.

"How many?" KAH asked, pushing between the men to inspect the table. It was his plan. His boat. His day. The man whose hands were coated with mashed beans kept kneading the batch.

"Fourteen, so far."

"Good. The distributor will be here at 8," said KAH.. He dropped his underwear and pulled a dingy towel off a hook. Naked, he trudged up to the cockpit.

Raptor counted the pauses between his heartbeats. Years of training told his muscles to pull the trigger offbeat because even a light pulse would jar the sight. This was habit. Now he had no gun. But the practice lowered his blood pressure and focused his mind as he sat on the bottom of the ocean floor directly beneath *The Silver's* swimming deck. His recirculating underwater breathing apparatus was designed to retain and reformulate gasses so it did not release any bubbles. The surface showed no evidence that one of the best trained fighters in the world was kneeling on the rocks below in fifteen feet of water, twisting lengths of dental floss and wrapping the ends of the braid several times around each hand.

Raptor watched for the small red glow of the cigarette as he rose. When the tank guard man shook his ash over the water, Raptor snatched his wrist and pulled him onto the swimming platform. The thick braid cut into his windpipe while Raptor snapped his neck. Then he rolled the body onto his shoulders and sank silently with the load.

Moments later, Raptor was back, peering over the rail into the cockpit. It was empty. The cabin door was still closed. Raptor looked at his watch. 6:10 a.m. He could hear muffled conversation. He had five minutes at best before KAH appeared for his morning constitutional. The priorities were clear.

"First, neutralize the acute threat: the prepared weapons. Then destroy the boat. Ricin is deadly to breath," Raptor recalled. "But just disgusting to digest."

He saw a bailing bucket rolling on the dock. He scooped it full of seawater, and then crouched by the rows of tanks. He unscrewed the first one, poured in the water, and shook it, then put it back in the rack with its cap ajar. Then the second. And the third. Seawater would dilute the ricin powder and neutralize each tank of poison. Eleven to go.

At 6:13am, KAH pushed open the cabin door. He scratched his hairy belly as he walked slowly across the slippery cockpit. He studied his array of tanks and smiled. He stepped blearily to the rail and swung a leg over it to the swimming platform. His foot landed an inch from the gloved finger that hooked through the platform.

Raptor clung to the underside of the swimming deck as the cell director dove in. If KAH opened his eyes beneath the water, he would see the dead body rolled in duct tape and strapped to the black hull like spider prey. Raptor pulled out the wrench.

Instead KAH kept his eyes closed until he surfaced, rolling on his back. The sea was brisk against his bare skin. As he raised each arm past his ears, KAH chuckled.

"Simple, cheap, brilliant! Who will question the contents of a couple of spent scuba tanks?" Then he lurched up. He had seen the fourteen tanks. But no guard. Treading water, he squinted at his boat. Then he rolled onto his belly and slapped the water with one arm, then the other, as he swam several laps around the craft.

The Silver's hull was built from a single cast of fiberglass designed to seal out the sea. Then the manufacturer filled it full of holes, bolting on navigation equipment and other gear that sealed them tight. When Raptor sat on the ocean floor, he counted each plug. Eight bolts held the swimming platform to the transom. The speedometer was a little fan at the bottom of the hull, mounted on a rubber o-ring. The propeller entered the boat through a large hole, sealed with rope made of greased flax. Ten more bolts. And in the transom itself, there was a plug with a simple spring clamp, to drain the water out when the boat was pulled out of the water. The ocean quickly finds unplugged holes.

After thirty minutes, KAH reached for the swimming ladder. But when he put his weight against the platform, the steel shrieked and gave way. Then it sank.

"Piece of crap!" KAH sputtered, shaking water from his face. He tried to reach up to the transom railing. It looked strange without the swimming deck, lower than he remembered, but he still could not reach the railing. He called out. Then he noticed something else odd. The name plate on the transom was tilted so the "*r*" touched water.

"Strange. There's no wind. No tide pulling it," KAH said. Then he heard the sound of water rushing. Continuously. It happened too quickly to stop. He watched in horror as *The Silver* listed to one side, filled with seawater, and sank.

The ricin manufacturing director twisted in the water, scanning the surface for fourteen bobbing canisters. But all that floated were plastic bowls and paper, cushions, and other meaningless refuse. He plunged his face underwater. The salt stung his open eyes. Then he saw them lying askew on the ocean floor, mouths open, and bellies full.

At the edge of Krajlendik Harbor, beyond the stone jetty, mangrove branches scraped Raptor's shoulders when he reached for the duffel bag. He dressed quickly in a pair of faded blue jeans, the right back pocket frayed where two pens clipped the denim. He pulled on a white t-shirt with the logo "D6" in small blue script. Then Raptor grabbed the duffel bag and walked up the beach, a tourist returning wistfully to the real world.

An hour later, Raptor boarded his flight and sat down in business class. It was a Boeing 767-200. He saw its layout and dimensions as if he had clicked on a PDF. The aisle was 28 inches wide. Three feet separated seat backs in Business class, four in first. There were two rows of business class seats, two rows of first class, the closet, the galley. 21 feet between him and the exit. The lever would release if pulled in and to the right.

Raptor looked in the seat pocket. Someone had left a copy of FastWire, the magazine that issued twice a month to report on the buzzing technology industry that was producing IPO's and making millionaires of secretaries each week. Raptor could just see the top of the cover photo, and recognized immediately the thick shock of black hair, and his own bright green eyes enjoying a joke.

"Meet Edwin Hoff," read the cover. "MIT's Next Billionaire."

CHAPTER 1

HUDSON
JULY 11, 10 P.M., CAMBRIDGE, MA

The sidewalks were mostly deserted between the Massachusetts Institute of Technology campus and the office buildings where start-up companies were commercializing classroom inventions. Between a darkened coffee shop and a book store, where red and white t-shirts hung like flags in the window, Hudson Davenport leaned his six foot frame over an ATM machine embedded in the brick wall. He squared his broad shoulders and glanced down the street, but he saw no one. The machine hummed, clicked, and spat out the card.

"Insufficient funds," shone across the screen.

"Not you too," Hudson said, raking his fingers through his chestnut hair. He wore it longer than most sales guys, so the waves began to curl and women could not resist putting their fingers in it. "Not after all we've been through together? St. John…New Orleans…Tahoe…."

Hudson opened his wallet, counting the two bills. "Six dollars. Ouch." He thumbed the row of neatly filed credit cards, extracting the one at the bottom. "How about eighty dollars then? Come on, lucky number seven." He stuck the card in, keyed his password and pressed the amount.

Beep. Whirr. Pause. "Insufficient funds."

Hudson jammed the card back in the machine. Tapped "$20.00." The ATM spun, paused, and then chucked as the rollers pushed out a single crisp twenty dollar bill. He stuffed the bill into his wallet and checked his watch. The plastic band was cracked, but the cheap digital watch told him that his friends from Harvard Business School would be rocking the roof deck in the Back Bay by now.

Most of Hudson's business school friends came from finance jobs and planned to return to them after Harvard. Not Hudson. After graduating from Williams College, he had taught basic reading skills to fifth graders in South Central Los Angeles. But by October, when gunfire outside the playground made them take cover under their desks for the fourth time, Hudson had applied to business school.

The problem was this: his classmates lived like the captains of industry the school promised they would all become. Some came in with assets; others banked on the seven figure bonuses Wall Street would pay soon enough. Networking was part of the education, they said. The school said it too. So, thanks to the upper limits of freely offered credit cards, Hudson took his education seriously and joined in for the weekends in Vegas and New York. And for heli-skiing in Utah and sailing in the British Virgin Islands.

The numbers started to add up. Hudson had no interest in a finance job. Instead he was taken in by the frenzy he read about in entrepreneurial magazines. Every week some new student invented a new way to plant a flag on the Internet's new frontier, raised millions in venture capital, hired hundreds of employees month after month and went public before figuring out how to earn a dime. If Hudson chose the right start-up, the money would take care of itself. And meanwhile, he would have fun.

But the mounting debt still made his gut clench. As he stood by the ATM, Hudson muttered, "A hundred grand in tuition. Six, okay, seven credit cards maxxed out. Sixty thousand and commissions just don't cut it with my crowd. They're earning and I'm burning. I need a raise."

"No you don't," said a gruff voice from behind him. "You'll be rich tomorrow. And you get to change the world." Hudson turned abruptly to face the intense green eyes of a thickly muscled man. He was about Hudson's age, with a shock of short, dense black hair.

"Edwin!" Hudson said, his smile flashing too quickly. Edwin Hoff was the 28-year-old CTO and founder of D6, the company Hudson worked for. "I didn't...you're like a cat."

"To an antelope maybe," Edwin said. "Don't worry about money. It'll take care of itself tomorrow afternoon when we go public."

"You think the stock will really fly?" Hudson said, a grin sliding up the side of his face.

"I know it. Davenport, what we are building is going to change the entire world." Edwin's eyes locked on Hudson's. "Just think what will be possible when our software is out there, everywhere, built into every electronic device that plugs into a wall, transforming it into something that can send and receive data. People will buy, shop, meet, date, sell, stop global warming and robotize appliances over D6 technology. It is the sixth dimension. This is Edison stuff, and you're earning stock in the first light bulb. And – you're helping make it happen."

"Wow," Hudson said. He felt giddy. "When you put it that way…."

"Let me ask you," Edwin said. "Do you believe an idea could ever come out of someone's brain and change the world?"

"Yes, sure, absolutely," Hudson said.

"Do you believe there could ever be a company that created absolutely profound value?"

"Yes of course. Microsoft, IBM, and yeah, like General Electric," Hudson's enthusiasm rose to meet Edwin's.

"Well, that is exactly what is happening here. Now. With our company, D6," Edwin said. "It's the chocolate factory, and you have one of the golden tickets."

Hudson drank the Kool-Aid. "Well, come on then!" he said, bouncing on the balls of his feet. "Let's pop the cork on this thing. There's a party in the Back Bay. It's going to be epic. My friends from business school introduced me to the investment banker on our deal – JD Sullivan. He's sparing no expense. Raw bar. Pretty ladies. Fireworks over the Charles. I heard he even hired a…a…little person."

Edwin frowned. "J.D. Sullivan is obstreperous. And…. I can't. I have to work. That sounds like your habitat. But thanks."

"Work? Come on, Edwin! Have some fun! You're going to be a freaking billionaire tomorrow. You cannot work tonight. I will personally assure you are entertained. It would be my sincere pleasure, sire," Hudson bowed magnanimously. He had cultivated the skill of inviting people to play. He spread it like sugar, glazing over cracks, making everyone feel sweet.

Edwin grinned, and then shook his head. "No. I, uh…I wouldn't know anyone else." He peered through the dimly lit window of the Cambridge Coffee Shop. "I was just going to get a cup of coffee but it looks like…no one's there."

Hudson slung his arm around Edwin's stocky shoulders. "You – of all people – do not need to know anyone. You realize you are a rock star, right? You have done what makes them all sit back and wonder. You built the rocket ship. And we blast off tomorrow! Come on, Neil Armstrong. Don't worry. I'll introduce you to everyone."

Edwin shook off Hudson's arm. "Nah," he said, blushing.

Five minutes later, when Hudson walked through the open doors onto the Red Line train, Edwin stepped over the gap behind him. To other riders, the two young men holding on to ceiling straps looked like peers. But while Edwin bore the weight of the world, Hudson always found a way to dance on it.

As the train rumbled over the bridge, Hudson thought, "Tomorrow the chocolate river starts flowing. As long as I don't stick my head in it, what I have is a temporary cash flow problem." The wash of debt now looked like a rounding error that the D6 IPO would soon wipe out.

J.D. Sullivan was the star investment banker at the firm Dashiel M. Samuels who technology CEO's courted to take their companies public. With each Initial Public Offering, J.D. made for his firm 5% of the total deal – each of which averaged $100 million. Over the past several years, he had had a very, very good run. He lived alone in a Back Bay brownstone, steps from Boston Public Garden, with an unobstructed view of the Esplanade, the Charles River, and just across the river shining back at him, MIT's glistening gold dome.

The private elevator doors opened on to the roof deck. Hudson and Edwin saw white lights stringing the potted trees, bouncing off white tablecloths and glistening on the moist glass bottles and crystal goblets at the bars. The night was humid. About fifty people milled about on the rooftop, some tipping up their chins, mouths forming oooh's, as fireworks lit up the sky over the river. Many of the female guests wore backless tank dresses and spiky heels. Men wore tailored dress shirts with buttonless collars, cufflinks poking beneath blue blazers. A few others wore polo shirts, their bright collars folded over seersucker blazers. "What'll you have?" Hudson said, moving to the bar. When Edwin did not respond, Hudson looked back. He saw Edwin still standing near the elevator, in his faded blue jeans, white, collarless t-shirt and Nikes, glaring around the deck. Hudson grinned, imagining the buzz that would build when J.D.'s guests realized one of the true geniuses of the tech boom was there. It was exciting to see Edwin on the cusp of his new fame, about to get all kinds of new attention.

"Move over Bill Gates," Hudson said. "Two gin and tonics and a Sam Light, please." He clutched the two glasses between the fingers of one hand, the beer bottle in the other, and walked back to Edwin. "Here you go."

But Edwin backed up. "I gotta go." He turned abruptly and disappeared down the internal staircase next to the elevator.

"But–" Hudson called after him. "Okay…see you…later…then. That was…unexpected." He leaned back against the railing, sipping alternately from each glass. His dark brown eyes traveled from one smooth back to another.

"About time you got here, Davenport," said J.D, extending his hand. The host wore a crisp blue and white striped shirt under a navy blazer. "Well, I hope you enjoy what we have on offer tonight."

"Who could ever choose?" Hudson said.

J.D. gestured toward the fire exit. "Was that–?"

"Edwin? Yes," Hudson said. "Briefly."

"Where'd he go? Not his scene?" J.D. grinned. "The geeks shall inherit the earth, right?"

A word flashed into Hudson's mind: "Obstreperous." But he smiled gently and said, "You should spend more time with Edwin. Nah, something important came up. Who's that girl? She's delicious." His eyes were on a blonde woman who had just turned her head. She was strikingly thin. The silky top tied around her neck and waist left her back bare. His palm tingled. She turned and smiled back at him. Caught, Hudson grinned, lazily chewing the inside of his cheek like it was gum.

"Off Davenport," J.D. said. "She belongs to a friend of mine over there. But he might make a trade. You ready to be rich tomorrow?"

Hudson had met J.D. in Nantucket over the Fourth of July, where an invitation to this roof deck party was the elusive ticket. Hudson looked at J.D.'s "friends" in the corner, and thought they must be boiling. The two burly men wore black leather jackets, belted at the waist.

"I sure hope so," said Hudson. "What do you see happening?"

"Come with me," J.D. said, guiding Hudson by the elbow. "I have a gift for you. Two actually." J.D. pulled a grey rectangle, smaller than a deck of cards, from his pocket. "A calculator. So you can watch your wealth go up with the stock price. See – 20,000 shares times $26. Or, 20,000 shares times $260. It will happen in a day. It will happen tomorrow."

Hudson laughed. "Thanks, J.D. That's cool."

"This deal is so in the bag," J.D. whispered, liquid splashing from his glass. "This is going to be the hottest IPO ever. Your twenty thousand options, my friend, are going to be worth about five million bucks tomorrow. And then a lot more."

Now he had Hudson's full attention. "Wow! You think so?"

"Totally. You are golden," J.D. paused. "No reason not to live like it now."

"But I can't sell any of my stock options," Hudson said. "Not until they vest next year."

"So? All that has to happen is the stock stays up, which it will on the D6 rocket ship. And you just keep your job for at least a year," J.D. said. "You think they'll can you when your Dad is on the board?"

"You don't know my Dad," Hudson said. The conversation forced Hudson to remember that his job at D6 had not come through his father, Sterling, but in spite of him. Sterling, the initial investor in this little idea that had come out of a lab in MIT and was about to blow the doors off the red hot technology sector of the NASDAQ stock market, had staunchly opposed Hudson joining the firm.

"I don't believe in nepotism," Sterling had told his son. "You have to earn your way up. Every step." But the CEO, Jameson Callaghan, had liked what he had seen in Hudson, out of all of the Harvard Business School interns, and had made it clear the job was his . Jameson persuaded Hudson to join D6 for the chance to change the world and make a fortune doing it.

J.D. bent over a table and scribbled something. Hudson found the blonde through the sparkling party. He winked. She tossed her straight bleached hair and then looked up at him through lowered eyes. He laughed. Hudson loved to play.

"Here," J.D. said, twisting the cap on his gold Cross pen. "Now you can buy something you like the look of. Pay me back when you vest, with a little something extra, if it makes you feel better." Hudson looked in his hand. It held a check.

Hudson gasped. "A hundred and fifty thousand dollars?"

"A dribble." J.D. said. "You'll make that in a day the way this stock will fly."

"I can't," Hudson said. "What if…you know…the company tanks or I screw up or something? I could never get that much extra cash together."

"Your dad has more money than God," J.D. said. "I know he's good for it if something happens. But you know what? This is your money. This is you making it on your own. And I'm banking on you. And D6. You're on the rocket, man, take a ride!"

"It is pretty crazy," Hudson agreed. He felt the check. He had never seen one that had his name on it with all those figures.

"Hey," J.D. put his hands up. "I thought I was doing you a favor. But if you don't think you have the stick to drive in the fast lane, by all means, wait for the bus."

Hudson folded the check and slipped it in his back pocket. J.D. was right. Edwin was right. "This is the 6th dimension. If it ever can happen, it is happening now." This was the rocket ship of a lifetime. It was time to buckle up. With the delirium of pushing an edge that gave a little more each time, Hudson doubled down.

He swallowed the rest of his drink and sauntered over to meet the pretty blonde. From the corner, J.D.'s friends watched him closely.

CHAPTER 2

EDWIN
JULY 12, 9:30 A.M., CAMBRIDGE, MA

Edwin Hoff pushed open the glass door and took a deep breath. The smell of roasted coffee beans thickened the air. Across the glass pastry cabinet, Edwin watched her. She wore her straight brown hair pulled back from her face with a tortoise shell clip. She smiled freely as she pulled the espresso levers. Her eyes were brown and lively.

"Like coffee," he said. Genius that he was with math, his poetic range was limited.

"And for you?" she finally asked.

"Oh, no thanks," Edwin said, startled.

"Seriously?"

"I mean, yes, of course. Sorry. I was…thinking about something else."

She smiled and called loudly, "Venti! Black! Right? And my name is Lula."

Edwin's sharp eyes blinked rapidly. He put four dollars on the counter and turned abruptly to the area where the coffee would emerge. He leaned against a corner cabinet with his elbow high, a blush on his round cheeks, his mouth a small, open smile.

A moment later, Lula held out a hot paper cup. Edwin took it but Lula did not let go.

"How many more cups before you ask me out?" she whispered. Edwin's face flushed, but he said nothing. After a few moments, she said, "Well, here you go."

Still grinning, Edwin found the topping table and ripped the heads off four sugars.

"Four!" called Lula. "See, I knew you were a sweetie!"

Edwin made a small clipped sound, like the firing of a tiny spastic automatic. He managed a small wave and a Cheshire cat grin in her direction as he left the coffee shop.

"That was not a giggle," he scolded under his breath. "Sort of cool? Maybe?"

It was like pressing his nose to the treat cabinet. But Edwin had to stay focused, because today the future would change for every person at his young company. They had hatched the idea off a whiteboard stained with green, red and blue, in a paint-peeling office in MIT's mathematics department. The idea had grown over folding tables above a coffee shop ....

Today Edwin's little idea was a company that would go public – offering shares on the NASDAQ for the first time under the eponymous stock ticker "D6". The company name stood for the "6th Dimension." Edwin's brainchild was software that would run on the Internet, and in every electronic appliance, to make all of these objects capable of accepting and transmitting Internet data. It was a platform for a whole new dimension of commerce, communication, energy management and community. D6.

D6's CEO, Jameson Callaghan, had spent the previous two weeks on the road show, introducing the investment opportunity to the largest funds in Europe and the U.S. The funds had liked what they had seen on PowerPoint and in the scant financial spreadsheet. With only two million dollars in sales, enough investors were interested that the book of D6 shares available for purchase was thirty times oversubscribed. Which valued D6 at $1.2 billion.

It was July 1999 and anything was possible. The hot stock market turned ideas on napkins into real money. Initial Public Offerings happened on a dream; sustaining them would require something quite else. There was serious money at stake. But to Edwin it was all just a playground. With piles of money. Which was why he took Lula's cup to MIT's courtyard and let it warm his hands as he looked over the lawn to the river.

Two men in dark charcoal suits appeared through the hedges. They hustled up the sidewalk, their briefcases banging against their legs. As if he had already run out of time, the older lawyer's eyes swept the stairs until they landed on Edwin.

"Congratulations," said the young associate. "I saw the *Globe*. After your IPO today your net worth will be like two billion dollars. From zero to two billion bucks overnight."

"Yeah," Edwin said. He looked down at his faded jeans, worn in places to thin white strings. "Might buy some new jeans."

"Or twenty million of them." The lawyer's smile hung on his teeth. His compensation would build by twenty thousand dollars each year until he made partner.

The partner set several stacks of paper on the steps. "So, Edwin, it's pretty simple. As you asked, everything you own will be left for the benefit of Oliver Kestrel, with an address of P.O. Box 1109, Cambridge, Massachusetts."

"Just a P.O box?" asked the associate. "Who is he? What if we have to find him?"

The older man frowned. "That's not our business."

"He travels a lot," Edwin said. "Always on one flight or another."

"Lucky guy," said the associate. "He gets it all."

"Only if I'm toast," Edwin said.

"Which is highly unlikely," said the partner, with a stern glance to his associate. "But you are wise to put everything in order first. However you wish."

"Thanks," said Edwin. "Where do I sign?" After a shuffling of papers and scraping of pens against paper pressed on the concrete steps, the entire estate of Edwin Hoff was bequeathed to a reclusive man named Oliver Kestrel, his only known landing spot a post office box in Cambridge, MA.

CHAPTER 3

JAMESON CALLAGHAN
JULY 12, 1:00 P.M., CAMBRIDGE, MA

When Jameson Callaghan opened the door to the conference room, he saw what the creation of billions of dollars of value looked like just before its birth.

Over 200 people stood shoulder to shoulder. The excited chatter spun up the air. A folding table – a desk borrowed from the two people who shared it – was covered with plates of crackers, cheese and fruit. People crowded up to the large monitor stacked on a television cart. The green screen was blank, but in a few minutes, it would flicker and numbers would appear, showing the first public stock trades of D6 shares, which could be bought for $22 each. Then the bids would hopefully outnumber the asks, and the prices of a share would rise. Since employees had been granted options as part of their compensation at much lower prices – pennies or a dollar or two a share – it meant that after today they could sell them for many times more. Some of them were still in college. Their first wheels were rollerblades; their second would be BMWs.

"In a few moments, everyone in this room will be rich," Jameson thought. He recognized only about half of the faces. While Jameson had been on the roadshow pitching large investors the D6 story, the company had recruited aggressively. They needed quality employees, lots of them, fast. Tomorrow the employee pool would split sharply into the haves and have nots. Those who joined pre-IPO would earn a fortune; those who came a day later, a salary.

D6 hired engineers from top computer science programs. You could hear the brain drain sucking the best talent out of India, Pakistan, China, and Israel, where countries had invested heavily in technical education and were sprouting the best technical minds in the world. Ahmed Farzi, at 49, began the second great adventure of his career by leaving his first. He had come to America from Pakistan in 1975 to study at MIT, earning degrees in mechanical and electrical engineering. Twenty years later, as a full professor, he first encountered the genius in Edwin Hoff. He was hooked. So when Edwin left MIT, teacher followed student to build D6 together.

To sell it, sales managers dialed up old, successful teams. The first investor, venture capitalist Sterling Davenport, convinced Walker Green, a bright young guy from his charity for Battered Women, to apply his good nature to Account Management. He asked Jameson to take on Maggie Rice as an administrative assistant to pay back an old debt to a friend.

These employees would have to keep their jobs and do them well to bank their potential fortunes. Options were designed as incentives: employees got nothing if they left before a year. Then, a quarter of their options would "vest", and they could sell them. After that, a little more would vest each quarter. The idea was to keep employees working hard for the next bit of worm that would appear on the hook.

The long hand of Jameson's Patek Philippe told him blast off was in twelve minutes.

"So you ready to stick it in their faces at SAC?" said Sterling Davenport, coming to stand next to Jameson. When he stopped he lifted his momentum on his toes, then rocked back on his heels, and up again. A self-conscious gesture to stand shoulder to shoulder with Jameson, although he was eight inches shorter.

"Or somewhere else," said Jameson. "Poor old economy company, tied to old stubborn metrics like profits. Good thing you got me here." After rising for twenty-five years like his suit was filled with helium, Jameson's last day as the Chief Operating Officer of the Standard Appliance Company came on a Monday, shortly after learning about the new CEO's dinner to unify his new leadership team. It had been held the previous Saturday night.

Jameson looked down at his old college roommate. Sterling even bobbed then, standing around kegs in Yale's residential college entryways, trying to best Jameson for Grace Savenor's attentions. Back then, Jameson believed one day they would be in business together. A few years later, when they were both at Harvard Business School, he was pretty sure they would not. Perhaps they had grown distant because by then Jameson was single and Sterling was married. Or because Grace Savenor was now Grace Davenport. But life had more bends in store, and around this one, Jameson and Sterling stood together to watch their net worth top hundreds of millions.

Sterling had spotted the genius in Edwin Hoff when he was a grad student, D6 was a thesis, and the investor was trawling MIT for potential new business ideas. Six months later, he asked Jameson to meet him at Rialto in the Charles Hotel, and pitched the deal over plates of Dover sole meunière and two bottles of Columbia River Valley Pinot Gris.

"I've been waiting a lifetime for this one, Jameson. It's a killer idea with a firebrand behind it. You have to meet this Edwin Hoff. He can shake it up like no one I've ever seen." Sterling leaned in. "This thing is going to go public within a year. They need a grownup to keep the wheels on the bus. You would make the difference between a burst bubble and an historic company. You're wasted on the golf course, Jameson."

Jameson had smiled thinly. He was off his pins, and did not like people seeing it. So he had signed on. Now here he stood, next to a folding table topped with cheese cubes, about to earn hundreds of millions of dollars in a single moment. SAC could...well. No need to go there.

Sterling grinned his lazy grin, and bobbed. "To think, I had to twist Edwin's arm to take this out of the lab. Now he'll have a billion reasons to thank me. Two, actually."

"These are the halcyon days," Jameson sighed.

"If the IPO goes right, we'll have hundreds of millions in the bank," said Sterling.

"Starting tomorrow, every candy bar in that free vending machine has a price and we have to tell the public what it is. It won't always be boom times," Jameson said.

"Which is why you're here," Sterling said.

"And then there's Edwin," Jameson said. Sterling nodded, chuckling. That was when the blow hit. Arms like thick belts wrapped around Jameson's belly and lifted him.

"Hey! Put me down!" Jameson bellowed. But Edwin hoisted him over his shoulder and charged through the crowd. D6 lit up. When Jameson's feet finally touched the ground beside the podium by the microphone, he was laughing hard too.

"Welcome back, Jameson!" Edwin grinned, and grabbed the microphone. "You are all about to become rich! You will make more money than you possibly dreamed of from this tech bubble. It will go on forever."

"Yeah!" D6 employees cheered and hooted.

"Now let me tell you why all that was bullshit," Edwin said, in his habitat. The room went silent. "There will be a spectacular crash. All of our customers – these dot-com paper napkin companies without revenue – will go bankrupt. Our job is to take their last dollars while we adapt. But we will keep our focus. This company will not just survive. You will not just become very, very rich - you will change the world. D6 software will be in the offices, homes and literally the hands of every person seeking digital information, making every electronic device able to accept and transmit data. PCs, TVs and cell phones will begin to do so much more – shopping, banking, downloading movies and music from their phones – and free phone calls anywhere in the world. Remote controls with our software will allow point-and-click shopping from TV ads – think what advertisers will pay for that service. You will make today's Internet work, and you will create tomorrow's. You will do this as the economy falls around you. As your customers die. You will do it by executing one task at time. Focus on your goal. Next up, world domination!"

D6 exploded. The guttural howls made even Jameson feel giddy. Edwin looked at his watch. Then he held up two fingers. His smile was gone.

"By 4:00 p.m., my shares in this company will be worth two billion dollars. Minimum. At 4:01, I will be in my office white boarding with Ahmed the next stage of our platform. So, grab a coke, pop a cheese cube, and come join us. Here we go!"

With that, the monitor flickered. Bright green text appeared on the black screen and D6 went public. For its consequences, the display was unremarkable. There were two columns of green numbers: one the price a buyer was willing to pay, and the other the price the seller was willing to accept for a certain number of shares. At precisely 2:00 p.m., the ticker appeared priced at $22 per share. For the next two hours it shot up and up, closing at $222 per share at 4:00 p.m.

As Hudson left the conference room, he pulled J.D. Sullivan's calculator out of his pocket. "$222 times 20,000 shares. That's…$4.4 million ?! Whoa."

Jameson fell into step with him. "It's all paper, my boy. Don't spend it until it vests."

Hudson laughed softly. He thought of his bank account, flush with J.D. Sullivan's one hundred and fifty thousand dollar loan. J.D.'s cash almost covered Hudson's school debt and his credit cards. But all Hudson had to do was keep his job. And, as long as D6 stayed in business, hit its quarterly revenue numbers, and the stock did not crash, repaying that $150,000, and the $170,000 he already owed, was still just a drop in the bucket.

"I think I need a better watch," Hudson decided.

At 4:30 p.m., Jameson walked the halls – using his favored "sneakernet" mode of communicating with his employees. It was amazing what one could learn about one's company by leaving the executive floor. But he saw no one.

"Kids getting rich on paper – they probably took the rest of the day off to go test-drive Beemers," he said. But at the same time, his heart fell. This was just the beginning. They had the entire business to build, and now, expectations of a public market. They would have to do better. He would have to do better. He shook his head.

Jameson took the elevator to the top floor. The grey cubicles were empty. Star Wars action figures posed on book shelves for no one. Jameson walked toward Edwin's office and its adjacent conference room.

Then he saw them. All of them. They craned their necks in the doorway, clutching notebooks. The only open carpet was the strip in front of the whiteboard where Edwin charged like a favorite professor, spun up on fresh genius.

"We build it, sell it, integrate it. Once we're out there – out there everywhere – we can build more. We will know everything people want to see and do with digital data. We will make it seamless, secure and possible. Be clear," Edwin caught the eyes of one person, then the next. "This is a non-trivial goal. You are building the sixth 01dimension."

Only one man leaned back on his hands, braked against the tight weave of the industrial carpet. Ali Hamini had come on board early, with a swarm of others from MIT's graduate Computer Science Program. His original 10,000 shares had split four times, and had fully vested, for pennies. He was one of the very lucky ones, suddenly worth over nine million dollars, Jameson guessed. Very soon he could sell his shares and pocket the proceeds. But Ali sat back, unmoved, one grain against the alert crowd ....

"And Mac – where's Big Mac?" Edwin looked for the sales leader, who was absent. "Obstreperous! We must get a deal with XTC or this dies. Who's the lead?" No one budged. "Who wants the biggest commission this company will ever pay for a single deal? Hudson – you want to get more than twenty bucks out of the ATM next time?"

"Uh…okay," said Hudson, leaning back into the wall, his cheeks flaming.

"You now own this deal," Edwin said. "Make it happen. Or you are fired."

Jameson grinned all the way back to his office. But when he clicked on his email, he saw the one name that could collapse the structure he had stacked up to stand on. Because no matter what others saw, she was the one person who knew there would always be a pit beneath him.

From: Grace Davenport
Re: Shearwater
Jamo, I have something to show you. Please call me.

CHAPTER 4

HUDSON
AUGUST 28, 2:00 P.M., CAMBRIDGE, MA

Hudson curled around his telephone receiver. "Okay, so then, you think you know someone in headquarters who would be good for us to talk to? All right, well, think about it, and I – I'll give you a call next week." He put down the phone and let out a long breath. He twirled around in his chair. Which was when he saw Edwin hanging both elbows over the edge of his cube.

"Good lord," Hudson said.

"What was that call?" Edwin said.

Hudson cleared his throat. "It was uh, my guy, at XTC."

Edwin said, "This deal is not done. This deal is not started."

"Well, it's…I've been trying," protested Hudson feebly.

Edwin held up a hand. "Stop. Come with me."

Hudson had to hustle to catch up to the intense muscled frame in white t-shirt, blue jeans and white Nikes tromping down the hall to the stairs. Edwin took them two at a time, up three flights, to the engineering floor.

"Sit," he said, closing his office door. "Get a pen and a note book from my desk. I am going to tell you how to get XTC to move. First, know this. You will save this company. XTC is the key. Whatever you need from me, you have. Nancy!" A young woman popped her head into Edwin's office. "If Hudson ever needs me – find me. He's the priority, okay? You want me on a plane, I'll get on it. If you want me on a phone call, I'll be on it. And I want to talk to you every day about where we are and what you need from me to make this happen. You will make it happen."

Hudson watched with amazement. He felt suddenly important; he believed everything Edwin said. There was simply no alternative. Even if in that split second delay before Nancy nodded slowly, Hudson got the notion that Edwin managed to make a lot of people's initiatives his absolute top priorities.

"Now, listen. And write." Edwin jumped up to the whiteboard in his office, flipped it around to the other side. Both were covered with symbols from a coding session with the engineers. Edwin found an eraser and cleared blank arcs on the board. "Who does XTC fear?"

"Us?" Hudson ventured.

"No," Edwin said. "Not at all. They could care less about us, and if we do our job right, they won't even be thinking about us as we do the deal that will let us take over the world. They fear their competition, not a little upstart with its ears wet from an IPO. So you go for both of them, at the same time. Then offer XTC the opportunity to do it first. A leg up on their competition is the enticement. The other is this – win over the engineers, and the suits will follow. If you show engineers a really cool challenge, let them build new, cool technologies, you own them. That's what we can do for XTC. With us, their remote controls will become point and click credit cards. Their TVs will become advertising exchanges. That's where we start. Screw whatever dumb marketing guy you were talking to on the phone. Get me a meeting with Ralph Major."

"Ralph Major? The CTO?" said Hudson. Chief Technology Officers were the rockstars, the standard bearer of a company's technical chops. Ralph Major topped the list of Top 10 Minds in Technology according to a certain technology magazine.

"Yes. He is a titan. I must meet with him. Go through Big Mac. He was a bigwig there, must know the CEO. Get a meeting. Ahmed and I will do the rest."

Edwin's face broke into a wide grin and he cackled. He hopped over his desk to his computer and opened his email. "Ha!" he burst with disgust. "Figby. Is he jealous or what? Listen to this email: 'Edwin, congratulations on the IPO. It seems it's always the rather mundane ideas that are the commercial successes.'"

"Who's Figby?" Hudson asked.

"Old classmate from MIT," Edwin said. "Wanted me to join his company instead of starting D6. No way. He has no idea how to lead. His team isn't inspired. 'It's always the mundane ideas' – what bigger insult can an academic give! Obstreperous!" Edwin typed. "Thanks I'm sure you will be – what's a word for 'very very'?"

"Wildly?" Hudson ventured.

"I'm sure you will be...wildly...successful," Edwin said each word aloud as he typed. He spun his chair around. "He's toast."

Hudson laughed. Edwin did not look up.

"Go make XTC happen," he said. "You're behind."

CHAPTER 1

KAH
MARCH 12, 2:00 P.M., KANDAHAR, AFGHANISTAN

Khalid al Hamzani stood outside the chicken barn, holding a box. The cackling was maddening; the stench unbearable. He set the box on the dry gravel. The cardboard had puckered from heat; its flaps scraped his arms.

First he brought out the sandwich bag and the canteen. He pinched the two white tablets that had settled in a corner of the bag, then pressed the pills through his lips. He spun the cap on the jug. Took two long swallows.

Next, he extracted the large clear thin plastic bag and a thick elastic band, the width of his thumb. Unstretched, it slipped easily around his wrist. He put a rock across the bag so it would not blow away in the stiff gusts that were scattering sand. He peered into the box. What would come next would have to happen quickly.

KAH took three deep breaths, stretching his lungs until they were full. Then he pulled the plastic bag over his head and with both hands stretched the elastic wide around his head. It made a tight seal around his neck. He coughed. The bag puffed, and then sucked back on his face.

Moving swiftly, the man withdrew a purple plastic gun. In the other hand he held a small vial full of blue fluid. He unscrewed the cap, poured two tablespoons into a shallow dish, and then dipped the gun nozzle.

This was a test vial, an advance on product he had purchased. It had been tricky: weaponized pneumonic plague is not sold on the public market, but he had found a way. Before he authorized the thirteen million dollar payment and triggered the delivery plan, he had to know it would work. This one had to work.

He had chosen pneumonic plague because it was highly contagious with a near 100% mortality rate if untreated. In its weaponized form, microscopic droplets would survive extreme conditions: heat, pressure, altitude. All a person had to do was look to the sky and breathe. Then hug someone. Within a day they would both be dead. Their end would come unpleasantly, following a high fever, raking cough and bleeding from every hole.

Sealed behind the bag, KAH's lungs were getting tight, already demanding he exhale. But he had to make it through the long barn. KAH opened the door to the coop and began his experiment. He pointed the gun at first row of chickens, and pressed the trigger. Clear blue bubbles formed from the fluid, drifting through patches of light where dust hung in the air, until they popped.

Spots flickered in his eyesight. He shook his head to clear them. Soon the vacuum in his lungs would make his chest heave, forcing him to suck air though there was nothing to inhale. His step staggered. As he pushed on through the barn, pressing the trigger and blowing blue bubbles, his sight was darkening.

The gun clattered on the cement floor. KAH fell against the door and tumbled down the steps, now clutching at the band on his neck. But he could not make his fingers follow simple commands. He scratched and clawed at the bag, losing his balance. When his face hit the ground, it felt like his cheek was on fire. All went black.

KAH had landed on a pile of debris by the back door of the chicken barn. A water pail, its seam broken and rusted to a jagged point, cut his cheek.

The thin plastic bag clung to his face like a glossy mask. But then a filament fluttered near his nose: the sharp pail had broken the seal. A breeze found it, and the plastic relaxed. After a time, KAH opened his eyes. He sat up. He peeled off the bag, and each piece of his clothes. Naked, he stumbled to the cardboard box. He brought back the can of lighter fluid, squirted it on the pile of clothes. Tossed a lit match and watched the flame grow.

Twenty four hours later, KAH returned to the chicken barn. All was now quiet. He stepped over the bloated corpse of the farmer.

KAH wound the ends of his scarf around his mouth and nose, and then opened the door.

Brown blood stains covered the hay. Chickens lay on their sides. Blood leaked from every orifice. Those few that were not dead yet would be soon. Behind the cloth, KAH smiled.

CHAPTER 2

HUDSON
MARCH 12, 2:00 P.M., CAMBRIDGE, MA

Walker Green knocked Hudson's cube with his cane. "You see the stock today?"

Hudson shook his head. "Not $432 anymore, I'm guessing. Still around $200?"

"When can you sell?" Walker asked.

"In three months," said Hudson, doing the math in his head. Two hundred dollars times five thousand shares would raise an even one million dollars and solve his problems. He exhaled a low whistle. "Or, I keep my nerve while everyone else panics and believe in the real value of the sixth dimension."

Walker looked grim. "Take a look at today's price."

Hudson brought up his stock portfolio. He saw this: *D6......$62.29.*

"What?" Hudson cried. "It's at $62.29? We've lost over $140 per share today?"

"This week. About twenty-five points a day. When's the last time you looked?" Walker said.

"I haven't been watching that closely," Hudson said. "What the hell happened?"

"Some economist wrote a book called *Irrational Exuberance*," said Walker. "It's been all over the morning shows the past couple weeks. It's about how Alan Greenspan –"

" – the Federal Reserve Chairman?" Hudson cut in.

"Yeah – how he said a few years ago that maybe tech stock prices were fueled by 'irrational exuberance' but then said probably they were not. This guy comes along and proves they are," said Walker. "The day traders got spooked. Then the institutions sold too."

"This…sucks," Hudson whistled, his fingers in his hair; his heart beating faster.

"At least we survived the last layoff," said Walker looking around at the empty cubes.

"It'll go back up," said Hudson. "It has to. This is D6, for chrissake."

PART 3
SUMMER 2001

CHAPTER 1

CAMILLE
JULY 8, 10:12 A.M., WASHINGTON, D.C.

"What on earth am I doing?" Camille Henderson thought over and over again as the train chugged north out of Union Station. It had been ten years since it ended. She had been with Yassir through all four years at Yale. Just before graduation, he had called for her. But this time, to show her he was gone. The envelope had been on the bed. Four words on folded paper.

"Uncle sent for me."

Yassir had not returned for commencement. Camille had spent the festivities stunned, the thousands of black robes swinging shrouds. She had never heard from him again.

Until last night. It was a sweltering July night, when D.C. seemed more swamp than capitol. Camille, now 32, returned home to her studio after work, around 9 p.m. But when she glanced down to unlock the door her breath ran out.

Her doormat faced the wrong way. The word "Welcome" invited the door.

Stock still, her hand on the keys, Camille remembered that warm May night in New Haven. Coming back from Sterling Library, studying late for her last finals. Smiling when she saw those backward letters. Dropping her books and slipping down the hall, through the basement steam tunnel past the snack room and pool room to the entryway – the one before Yassir's. Climbing the four flights to knock on his neighbor's door. Slipping the borrowed key into the lock. Crossing the fetid small living room where four barely adult males lived together without cleaning it for nine months. Unseen, she had passed through the fire door and into Yassir's bedroom. Eager to explore the joys that had taken four years to loosen in him, which gave at last amid warm laughter after they had awoken to find their underclothes stuck together. Only to find the envelope on the mattress , and three pairs of black socks set out in a triangle.

Yassir had insisted on signs. "Uncle cannot know about you. He would take me back." The backward welcome mat meant come to his room, where, in the bunk, he would hold her so tightly. The three black dots in a triangle? "To warn you of something very bad. Life or death."

"Yassir's secret codes," Camille sniffed. "Maybe that's why I do what I do. And here I thought I chose the Agency because they pay me to speak the language I love and study a culture I adore."

Camille eyed the upside down letters on the mat. Then she saw something she had missed. A scrap of newspaper, just an ad for the Central Park Zoo in New York. The reptile exhibit at 4:00 p.m. July 9. She picked it up.

There it was. A black felt tip pen had left slight tails on three dots that formed a triangle. The conclusion came fast. Too fast.

"Yassir needs me," Camille whispered. "Ten years ago…whatever happened…maybe he wants to explain…But he must really need me now. He still knows he can count on me. Even for…for whatever."

Camille was not good at intrigue. She was an analyst. Primarily, she considered herself a scholar. She straightened her floor mat and opened her door. Inside she locked it quickly, leaning back on the door. Her mind spun. Yassir appearing. The signs. A meeting place, left casually, so directly she could not possibly miss it.

"Something terrible is happening," Camille shuddered. Opening this note was like electrifying part of a city that had been dark for years. But here she was, all lit up.

"Who else would he call? Not his parents," Camille thought. They had died when he was very young. A gas leak from a cracked transmission, a spark, and Yassir had been left to fend for himself on the streets of Saudi Arabia, at the age of seven. Until the wealthy man he called Uncle found him, sheltered him, raised him, educated him.

"He would have called Uncle," thought Camille. "Unless maybe he's…no longer…with us?" The simplicity of the torn ad meant something. Yassir must have known she could do better. So it was more important to him that she crack it than that someone else decipher it. He did not want to risk the chance she would misinterpret it.

Camille clicked the Amtrak website. She did not drive a car, and absolutely did not fly. It was not that she did not see, or want, the advantage of the speed. It was the rising panic, the incomprehensibility of her body being at 30,000 feet above the ground. Statistics of car crashes filled her mind when she should have been watching on-coming traffic. Motorcycles were out of the question. Even mopeds. Did people realize how many organ donors came from mopeds slipping on wet leaves? Camille preferred public transportation with more than two wheels. Wheels she was not responsible for.

Wheels that churned into Grand Central Station at 2 p.m. the next afternoon. At 3:50, Camille handed eleven dollars to the clerk at the Central Park Zoo. Her cotton blouse was already plastered to her back. It was a hot July afternoon, but as she pushed through the turnstile, Camille knew she would be feeling rivulets of moisture down her spine even if it were November.

Camille coughed, adjusting to the sudden thickness of the atmosphere. The humid rain forest exhibit was empty. "Very good choice," Camille thought, as she walked along the raised planks winding through draping vines between murky ponds. The path was a constant curve. It would be difficult to be seen from many angles. The shrill gossiping of the birds would muffle any private conversation.

Camille walked past the turtles showing their bellies to the glass border of their pond. After twenty minutes she was drenched. Yassir had not appeared. Her stomach clenched on its acid. Then she laughed, a spiteful, self-punishing huff.

"The doormat reversed! Just a common prank from the teenagers down the hall. The ones who left wet marshmallows before. And the scrap of newsprint? Really, Camille? Someone else's garbage is clandestine communiqué?" she scolded.

This was the occupational hazard the Agency counseled them about in orientation. The analyst who craves the action she fears, who stays out of the field but can't stop watching. How she spirals in a breathless existence amid shadows she invents.

Beware "the madness of spies." John le Carré's warning rang in Camille's ears as the realization hit. Because all she had actually seen last night was this: she deeply wanted to see Yassir. So badly she made it all up.

Camille walked briskly through the exhibit. The path was quite narrow. It led into a dark space. The sign above said "Reptiles."

"Snakes," she spat. The sight of an armless, legless creature with baleful eyes made her shudder. How the end of the thing would contract, then propel itself forward somewhere entirely else. Finally she saw a red sign gleaming "Exit". She stepped carefully in the darkness toward the distant glow. Through the plexiglass, she caught a glimpse of a thick vine wrapped around a tree, dangling. It blinked. Then something touched her shoulder.

"Ah!" Camille yelped. She patted her chest frantically, waving her hands.

"Milly." His familiar voice was so warm. Camille's blood pounded.

"Yassir?" she whispered, her voice rising with the lilt of a question.

Even in the darkness, she could see the broad smile, the wide oval eyes that made Yassir's face such a thing of beauty to her, to most women. She never could quite believe he had chosen her. Even though he had found unmistakable ways to reassure her.

"You understood," he said. "You came."

Camille nodded. Yassir put his palm against the small of her back. The act opened a time warp: Camille was through it in a moment. It was like rediscovering a lost joint, like her ankle. She had not realized how badly she was limping.

"Hi, Yas," she said softly, feeling the longing, disappointment, confusion, hurt, acceptance, a tinge of anger. And love. They mixed; and she tasted all of it.

"I don't have much time," Yassir said, pulling Camille gently to a dark corner of the exhibit. His face broke into his wide white smile. "It's so good to see you."

"Yes," Camille said, confusion beginning to blaze. "But, god, it's been ten years! And …why…this way?"

Yassir slumped. "I know." His words were not apologetic, or guilty. They ached too. Silence hung between them.

"What are you doing now?" Camille asked, her voice softer this time.

"I'm a consultant," he said. "Pre-Columbian art, artifacts. So I go to my clients."

"Do you enjoy it?" she said with a prim smile. The small talk irritated her.

"I do," he said. "And you are…"

Camille cut him off. "What am I doing here, Yassir?"

His eyes searched hers. "I need you to – I – I know you can do something."

"I'm not sure what you mean." Camille wiped her hands on her skirt. The heat made her thighs stick together. Yassir looked at her hard.

"I know what you do." His voice cut sharply, frightening Camille. A moment ago he was the man with whom she had fallen in love. Still loved. Now he was severe, unfamiliar. Camille's brows knotted. She said nothing – the Agency's strong preference.

"That's fine," he said. "I don't expect you to tell me anything. I am here to tell you something. I put it in your capable hands now."

"What is it, Yassir?" asked Camille. She reached for his hands.

Yassir took a deep breath. He waited for two tourists to pass. "There is going to be a catastrophe. They are going to use airplanes as bombs on American cities."

"What? Who? When?" Camille shot the questions in a fluster.

"Very angry people," Yassir said.

"Why are you telling me this?" she said

"Camille. Come on. I know," Yassir said. There was a long silence between them. "Okay, fine. Then just listen. Do what you can. There is more. One of the planes will have on board a special piece of cargo – a vial with a weaponized form of pneumonic plague, timed for release twenty-four hours after impact. If there is no impact, it will go off anyway. Once inhaled, it will spread quickly. They call it, loosely translated, the Blood Boiler. Anyone exposed will be dead in a day or two."

Camille sat silently. "When?"

"Late September."

"Why?" Camille asked.

"Why?" Yassir said with surprise. "They are so angry! America plays such favorites. Goes where it wants to, puts its soldiers down anywhere, and wraps up shiny rockets for their favored son while all the others can do is throw rocks from their slums. So they are going to throw tantrums to get your attention. They are going to throw a fit."

"How do you know all this?" Camille whispered.

"Don't," Yassir held up a hand. He rose suddenly. "Just, don't."

"Why are you telling me?" Camille cried. Her fingers clung to his shirtsleeve. "Why don't you do something about it?"

"I just did," Yassir said.

"But – but…Why just one vial?" Camille asked.

"Cost," he said. "One vial costs millions. They have to make it count. Now let go, Camille. Really."

Camille looked up, her blue eyes brimming. Yassir was leaving. Again.

"I didn't want to go then," he whispered. "I still have to. Even more so. Take good care of yourself, Milly." A slice of glare blinded Camille when he pushed through the exit out into the bright summer day.

At 7:00 a.m., Camille sat nervously outside the Deputy Director Orson Lowndes' office. The train back to Washington had pulled in at 5:00 a.m., but she was too anxious to feel tired.

"You've got five minutes," said the secretary. Camille leapt up and smoothed her skirt, blinking too quickly. The chain of command was loose in the CIA – one passed information to those who needed to know it – but still she had never gone up so high.

Camille put her thumb on the fingerprint sensor next to the deputy's office door. She leaned toward a small lens that measured and confirmed the radius of her iris. By the time she reached the door, other sensors would have approved her – the scanners that measured the swing and length of her stride, the cadence of her breath. Inside, Camille shifted her weight between her one-inch square heels.

Lowndes was typing. "Henderson. Sit." Camille sat. He continued typing. Then he said, without looking up, "What do you have?"

"I…I'm not exactly sure." Camille started. She was shaking. "I have some information that is very detailed and confirms some of the noise we've been hearing." Camille breathed out deeply. She hoped it would slow the blinking, which she knew distracted people. "You know they've picked up a lot of chatter about something big happening. In the United States. With planes. And a plague. Possibly."

Lowndes considered her. There was always chatter. Analysts were among the most paranoid in the Agency. They could afford it, having been trained to interpret "the sun is shining today" to portend nefarious plans but spared cold nights clutching guns in their coat pockets. It was hard enough to get a hearing on things they knew for certain.

"So," Camille continued. "It's HUMINT...a contact from ...well, I was given more detail: the approximate date it will happen. And more."

Lowndes curled his fingers. "What else?"

"They will take airplanes and use them as bombs in American cities," said Camille, exhaling. It felt good to give it to someone else. Though her palms sweated and her face flushed like a Dutch farm girl's when she was nervous, Camille's voice became calm, slow and low. It was an arresting combination.

Orson Lowndes watched, wondering if he should listen more carefully. That thought alone made the analyst's words stick.

"One of the planes," Camille said quickly, "will have on board a live strain of a type of pneumonic plague. The explosion will release it in the smoke over the city. Once inhaled, it will spread. They call it the Blood Boiler. Within 24 hours, every man, woman and child exposed will be dead."

This made the deputydeputy laugh. "Blood Boiler? Sounds like a potboiler. You like le Carré?"

"Sir?"

"Who's the source, Henderson?"

Camille paused. "A friend. I...I mean...an old friend."

At the Agency, this was the common euphemism for tipsters. But not often uttered by internal analysts with no record of field experience. Analysts never met with intelligence officers, much less their highly protected agents – the spies who provided the intel. Deputy Lowndes began to take more interest.

"What kind of mouse is he?" he asked.

"Mouse, sir?" Camille said.

"All leakers are MICE. He's telling you for Money, Ideology, Country, or Ego."

"I...I'm not sure," she said.

"Ego...that's always the clincher," said Lowndes. "Amazing how much self-worth thirty thousand dollars can buy. People sell out their country, cost lives, just to feel important."

Camille nodded agreeably. The deputy made a face. "But not your guy."

"He goes by 'Scully'," she blurted. "He's a Saudi who's been here forever."

"And you trust him," said Lowndes. Because the question was loaded for Camille, she missed the note of mockery.

"Yes," she said finally. "Yes, I do."

"Okay," he said. "Write me a memo. Send one to CT."

"Thank you," Camille said, bringing her hands together. That she could do: sit at her desk and write. Counterterror would take it from there. Order was restored.

Watching her leave, Lowndes muttered, "Analyst with a sloppy tip from an old boyfriend, who makes no financial demand?" He heard the sound of one shoe dropping.

Twenty minutes later, a young man entered the deputy's office.

"Camille Henderson," said Lowndes, holding a thin file. "I want to know what she eats, who with, how much salt she uses. Start with our busybody in the building."

The Agency kept tabs on its recruits by putting nosy neighbors on their payroll. Often elderly women living alone, they could be quite diligent with their official peering.

By August 6, Camille had written five memos, each with increasing urgency. There had been no more contact from "Scully." Though the agency was buzzing with bits and pieces, all that emerged were requests for more memos, plans for plans of action.

Her phone rang. On every call, she leaned in to hear Yassir's caramel voice.

"Hello dear," a woman's voice crackled through the clear line.

"Hi Auntie," said Camille, swallowing guilt. "Happy birthday!"

"Come have cake with me tonight. I want to show you pictures from my trip to Saudi Arabia. We rode camels. Mine spit at the Sultan." Matilda Mace, Camille's neighbor, was an energetic woman who lived in the penthouse, and had adopted Camille when she first came to Washington five years ago. They had tea on Saturdays when Auntie was free. She knew important people and planted these facts like Easter Eggs.

Camille enjoyed Matilda immensely. Matilda took up painting in her late seventies, and now several pieces were on show at the Corcoran Gallery. She rode horses despite her physician's stern warnings. And she spent months of every year touring distant lands, often regions exploding in civil wars or hostile to westerners. Most leaders of nations, legitimate or not, had had an earful of Matilda's personal global diplomacy

At 7:30 p.m., Matilda Mace greeted Camille in a green t-shirt and black spandex shorts, a thick leather belt strapped around her lower midsection, with leather gloves and an orange headband pushing up her very short, white locks.

"Free weights, Camille!" cried Matilda. "That's the secret. See?" She lifted her right forearm and exposed her bicep. A small half plum curve appeared as she boasted with her wiggling eyebrows and flashing dark blue eyes.

"Thank goodness," muttered Amanda, Matilda's caregiver. She had been pressed into service as a spotter. "She shouldn't be doing this sort of thing at all! Now, come have some cake, dear."

Matilda rolled her eyes. Amanda hustled down the corridor, her hand pressing against her side. Matilda linked her arm in Camille's and guided her through the penthouse. In its 10,000 square feet, the home boasted six bedrooms with ensuite bathrooms, a ballroom, a sitting room, a gym, a library, a gourmet kitchen and servants' quarters.

On the sofa, Matilda eyed Camille. "Where's your mind, dear? On a fella?"

"I'm sorry, Auntie," Camille smiled. "It's hard to get someone off my mind."

Matilda slapped her thighs, bones in nylon. "Not your old – from college?"

"I saw him," Camille blurted. It was not just Yassir's disturbing appearance that was on her mind. The information that he had given her was horrific – and it had fallen into the abyss. No one at the Agency had followed up with her. She still had the hot potato.

"You saw him? I thought you didn't know where he was? Or what he was doing?" Matilda's voice rose like an avid fan catching up on a soap opera.

"He told me something very disturbing. It sounds bizarre. It is. Who knows."

"What, dear? What did he say?" Matilda touched Camille's hand.

Camille put her hand to her forehead and spilled. "He said terrorists are going to attack us with planes and unleash a plague on a major city."

Matilda covered her mouth. "Call the police."

"I did, sort of," said Camille. "They thought I was crazy."

"Well, dear, it is quite a story," Matilda said.

"You're probably right," said Camille. Too often, she could not distinguish what should be terrifying from what should not be, and she just ended up scared all the time.

"Right," Matilda concluded. "You must get over him. This is how I did it with Winston Churchill. We'll have one cigarette and you will talk. You will tell me everything you loved about him. Everything you hated. You will eulogize him. By the end of the ciggies, he will be ash too. We won't speak of him again. It's not healthy."

"Cigarettes aren't healthy," Camille retorted.

Matilda took another bite of her cake. She patted Camille on the shoulder and rose. Minutes later she returned, wrapped in a silk robe. The headband was gone. She looked quite old and small. But her face still flushed with the trace of exercise.

"Now how about that cigarette?" she said, lifting two from a cloisonné box. She pointed at the balcony doors. "This is where I sneak my puffs." Camille followed Matilda out to the railing. The cigarette burned down between her fingers. Matilda faced the Capitol and inhaled deeply.

After Camille left later that evening, Matilda retired to her rooms. She passed through the outer sitting room, the bedroom and dressing room, to her garden room. It had a balcony. This was where she wrote poetry, and painted, watching the Capitol.

It was also where she made phone calls. Matilda sat down in a comfortable chair next to a book case. She curled her fingers around the corner of her armrest until she felt the button. The spines of a row of books slid up to reveal a dark green telephone on a shelf. She punched in a string of numbers. Far away, a secure line rang.

CHAPTER 2

RAPTOR
AUGUST 6, 2:58 P.M., CAMBRIDGE, MA

At 14:58 Raptor put his hand on the revolving door. He glanced down. There it was. A crumble of white on the ground. A piece of chalk, dropped through a hole in a trouser pocket, and then crushed by a heel. Later a maintenance man would sweep it up with other unnoticed cigarette butts and dirt. But it was neon to Raptor: his orders were ready.

Raptor walked into the hotel's coffee shop and waited in line. His impatience was opportunity. When he most wanted to rush, he used that energy to slow down, like shifting an engine down a gear, then another, without jerking. That effort absorbed his excess energy so he could plan the next move.

"Venti," said the vendor, pointing. "Sugar and stuff are there." Coffee shops made for good drop locations. Cover was easy and the layouts were standard among franchisees. Three jars of sugar to the left of the napkins and waste bin. Chocolate, cinnamon and nutmeg to the right.

Raptor shook sugar into his coffee with his right hand while he felt for the sticker beneath the shelf. His index finger found a thin edge. He pinched it between his thumb and forefinger until it folded across his palm.

With his back to the wall, Raptor sat down in a chair and sipped his coffee slowly, looking every bit the tired student or worker bee in need of an afternoon jolt. He propped both of his elbows on the table and seemed to stare into his coffee. In fact he was looking just to the left of his mug at the black print on the sticker cupped in his palm.

ASP Operator: *Raptor*
Mission: *Disarm, Deliver and Extract to Deep Cover*
Unload Location: *American Airlines Flight #11 from Boston to Los Angeles, departs 07:45 a.m.*
Unload Date/Time: *Sept 11 at approximately 08:15*
Size and Type of Target: *Egg-shaped crystal containing aerosolized pneumonic plague*

"Pneumonic plague?" Raptor read. "Nasty. On a commercial jet liner. Infect the people on the jet and have them spread it. But usually they like a bigger bang – so the world will notice them for once."

Degree of Certainty: *52%. It is more likely than not that the target will be on this flight. Take possession on ground prior to flight if possible. If not, board the plane.*

"Fifty-two percent?" Raptor thought. "So the ASP does not know which plane is going to carry it."

Security Consideration: *Detonation to occur 24 hours after crash. Disarm first. Code to follow. Plane will not land.*

"Ah ha! There's the bang for you." thought Raptor. "Plane will not land. The explosion must detonate the aerosolized disease vector, which will scatter all over the disaster area while the smoke plumes carry it. The crash is just setting the table. Their real plan is to wipe out people downwind with the pneumonic plague."

And the twenty-four hour delay? Raptor's brain cranked through logic like a marble rolling down steps, hitting the next deduction at a faster clip, stopping abruptly at the conclusion: in twenty-four hours, the nation would have organized its response. Its leaders would be at the crash site, showing strength, leading the people, grieving with them.

"The President would have to be there," Raptor realized. He studied his orders bent slightly forward over his coffee cup, feet square on the floor, thighs flexed, elbows tight against his ribcage. Ready. But the next brief sentence caught him up short.

Full extraction occurs at end of this mission.

Raptor's eyebrows rose. His jaw loosened. He turned to the side as if to stretch a muscle in his neck. He looked around at the students and business people seated at the tables, reading papers, chatting. At the glass cabinets full of desserts. He listened to the spray of cappuccino makers; the drink orders coming down the line.

"So. Time to go," Raptor said. His call had come. It would end with the extraction from the cover he had worn for four years now, as comfortably as his t-shirt and jeans. He would have to let the lines go. Assure they dropped completely. After this mission there would be a new cover, a new life to learn.

Where to next? The ASP would not tell him until this mission was complete. Because it was irrelevant. If he did not complete it, there would be no need for new cover. There was to be no regret in leaving. Otherwise things went badly wrong.

Once Raptor stepped on that plane, this cover he wore would disappear forever. He would have to carry out the rest of the order without anyone, anywhere, recognizing him. Raptor took a long sip of the hot coffee. What would coffee taste like in his next post? he wondered. It was thick and delicious in the Middle East, and just about perfect in South America. Wherever he went, he would have coffee. And four sugars.

Raptor would have to get that capsule out of terrorist hands, into his own, and out of the plane. Before they boarded. If not, then before they crashed. Without anyone seeing him. And return it where? The orders were precise.

Personal Meeting Date/Time: *Wednesday, September 12, 16:00.*
General Location: *Washington D.C., Northwest, 1665 Connecticut Avenue Penthouse*
Personal Meeting Specific Location: *Service entrance, PH floor.*

Contact Procedures: Recognition Signals (Bona Fides)
Visual: *Contact will light cigarette on balcony*
Verbal: *Operator "I'm here to fix the disposal". Contact: "Is that thing on the brink again?"*
Danger Signal: *Contact says "I think I need to sit down."*
Personal Meeting Cover: *Appliance repair*
Props Required: *See Zed.*
Extraction Location: *Private airfield in Virginia, three miles south west of the Capitol.*

There was a small map showing the streets of Washington D.C. and the airfield.

Raptor held his open palm up to his Blackberry and pushed a button. In a click the order scanned into the machine, which looked like all the other portable email devices with tiny keyboards. But Raptor's Blackberry did much more, thanks to Zed. Then he dipped the paper in the cup and watched the words disappear.

From a building across the way, five floors up, the man watching the intersection saw the young man lean against the lamppost near the entrance to the hotel. When the light changed, he jogged across the street. Through the binoculars, the watcher could see it quite clearly. On the post, about waist high, was a fresh line of white chalk.

There were so many unbearable mental images from the Head's time at Auschwitz that most had to be locked in a box. But for one: the needle with the single cc of fluid, shot into the bony shoulders of men and women sitting naked on metal chairs in the hellish laboratory. The Head saw this memory every day, and created the Association to Protect with one grand mission: defend humanity against its smallest threats.

As disease vectors could pass unseen through borders, the ASP had to do so as well in pursuit of these invisible killers. ASP operators were selected from the most elite special forces without regard to flag. They were trained and willing to stop bio-attacks without approval, process or authority. ASP operators came from the U.S. Delta Force, Israel's Defense Forces *Sayeret Matkal*, Pakistan's ISI, and Britain's SAS. They were trained in every skill a deep cover operator needed to stop a bioterrorism event: hand to hand combat, munitions, breaching buildings, rooms, vehicles and planes, survival, evasion, resistance and escape, and spy tradecraft. ASP operators touched down in communities for a time – years even – remaining unnoticeable, unexceptional and unattached. This last was a stark clause of the ASP contract:

Sec. 1.2.10 No Attachments: *The Operator shall not form or maintain any significant personal relationship(s) during the Term of this Agreement other than with the assigned technical support. Any such attachments will lead to immediate termination.*

Isolation simplified the inevitable extraction. Worse, attachments could compromise an operator's loyalty and discretion, and expose the existence of the ASP. So the ASP was mortally jealous of any it discovered and turned termination into a deadly serious matter.

Upon receiving his orders, Raptor went to see Zed for the gear he would need to complete the mission. The door to the small windowless office was open. Partly assembled robots sat on shelves, staring through uncovered eyeballs, showing ghoulish, veiny red, black and yellow wires. The duffel bag sat on a pile of magazines.

"What's in your bag of tricks today, Zed?" Raptor asked, reaching for the straps.

"Ah ah," Zed scolded, snatching the bag. "This must be introduced properly. Shown respect. Like a new friend. Because you will rely on it like an old one. Tea?" Zed was just under five and a half feet tall. His hair was deep black, though he was nearly fifty. Shadows hung perpetually under his brown eyes.

"Seriously? Again?" Raptor scowled. Despite their age gap, Zed was the one solid link in Raptor's life. So he accepted the cup. He sucked at the tea, spat the hot liquid. He blew on it hard. Zed sat back in his chair, waiting for the cup to cool.

"It's nice for you to have a break, too? No? Okay. Let's see what we've got." Zed unzipped the bag and first pulled out what looked like a motorcycle jacket. Raptor shrugged into it. The body had a soft, velvety feel. It was much lighter than leather.

"This," said Zed, "is your protection."

"I'm not going on a bike," said Raptor. "It's a jump."

"Yes," Zed said. "You like speed. I can see you as a little boy, scaling the couch and announcing you could fly." Raptor blushed. "You will like this, then. You know the extreme athletes who climb the highest peaks and do reckless things with skis and swaths of nylon pinned to gliders and parachutes?"

"A Saturday," Raptor said.

Zed nodded. "Indeed. Then you may know of the wingsuit already. It's a bodysuit with nylon stretching between the torso and the arms, beyond the fingers, and between the legs. You jump into the abyss and the pockets of air in the wingsuit create enough lift that you can fly two feet laterally for every one foot you descend. You look like a flying squirrel. They are quite popular among a small and gradually shrinking group of technical climbers and extreme skiers who expend a great deal of energy to climb peaks and overcome innate human survival instincts standing on the edge of a cliff. They jump, and for a short while, they fly. Almost always."

"Two over to one down?" said Raptor. "I wouldn't want to land on that vector."

"No." Zed said. "You would be hummus. That's why I have not given you a wingsuit. It's also loud as a small jet engine. You must be unnoticeable: unheard and unseen. And under no circumstances will I send you, my friend, on this mission with your feet bound together."

"So what does this jacket do?" Edwin asked.

"Nature has all the answers," Zed said, passing his palm over the front of the jacket. "Did you know most advanced flight technology just tries to mimic what birds of prey are born doing? Feel this velvet-like material: it's like an owl's velvet torso feathers, which makes the predator soundless in flight. And the coating I've applied makes a man dust on radar."

"How do my arms and legs stay free? I need maximum flexibility before the jump."

"Absolutely," Zed said. "Dynamic stabilization. The jacket has sensors along the seams which measure propulsion, energy and inertia, and ultimately, air pressure changes. When you need them, and not before, the jacket will extend into wings and tail feathers, as it were."

"And let out a chute when its time," Edwin finished.

Zed shook his head. "Sorry. A parachute would certainly show up on radar. We've worked hard to keep you invisible. Again nature provides direction. Do you know the kestrel?"

"Another bird?"

"The smallest falcon. And the only one that can hover in midair, mid attack. It beats its wings very quickly, like a hummingbird. Your jacket mimics this. With it, you can fly, descend, rise and hover. And you'll have these...," Zed opened a small contact lens case. Two yellowish disks peered out. "These protect your eye membranes on steep dives. They have infrared vision. Anything you see scans directly into the hard drive. Now I can see whatever you see."

"How?" Raptor asked.

"So," began Zed, opening a laptop, "vision works when light bounces off an object into your eye. The light goes through the pupil to the lens, which focuses it on the back of the eye. There the retina turns light into electrical charges that tell the brain to produce the exact image you 'see'. These lenses pick up the same impulse. See? I can see, digitize, store, file and search whatever you see."

"They're yellow," said Raptor, pressing them to his eyes. The lenses blended with the bright green hue of his eye. An image formed on the screen. It was of Zed's arms, the laptop. Zed's face and eyes. The magazines, door, grey office carpet.

"There's more," Zed said, wiggling his eyebrows. "These lenses are the first known technology to make vision work in reverse. You think of something, the image forms in your brain, which sends the electronic impulse to your lenses. They pass these signals to the computer which draws a picture of what you are imagining. Try it."

Raptor tried to think of something. A random memory filled his mind. The screen showed a man holding out a trophy. "Wow. ESP," he said.

"What did you win?" asked Zed.

Raptor chuckled. "Body building competition in high school. I got entered."

The computer screen filled with the face of a skinny young boy, maybe fifteen, sitting on stone steps. A black violin case sat at his feet. Four bigger boys, laughing. "Central High Varsity Wrestling" was blazoned across their burgundy wool and leather jackets.

"Good friends," Zed said.

RT stared at the monitor. "I trained all summer. I won." The screen rolled fresh scenes: the boy with 25 more pounds, all muscle. Pinning flat each of the four bullies.

Zed continued, "And, she can type. You just visualize words and symbols. It's the new Dictaphone. Dictathought."

Raptor put his hand on Zed's shoulder. "Very cool. But the yellow isn't subtle."

"I know," Zed frowned. "It's a problem. We'll improve it. In the meantime, don't wear them near people you know. Blink hard to toggle the function. And please don't leave it on. I really don't want to see everything in that head."

Then Zed pulled a pair of laced up Nikes from the bag. "Trigger the internal magnet and these will seek the closest steel. You could hang on the edge of a window sill and just worry about the view."

"Not that I'd need to," Raptor said.

"Of course not," said Zed.

"You are a titan," Raptor said. Zed smiled, and then dipped his head.

CHAPTER 3

HUDSON
SEPTEMBER 7, 4:30 P.M., CAMBRIDGE, MA

"Not another one," Hudson said, watching the fax spit up another cancellation. The economy of the summer of 2001 was a far cry from the frenzy of 1999, where D6's IPO went over the moon. By 2001 the dot com crash had settled fully through the economy. As Edwin had warned on that heady day of the IPO – when D6 stock opened for sale at $22.00 and closed at $222.00 – the tech bubble soon would burst. In March 2000, it did. Overnight investor enthusiasm for technology companies fell away. Investors suddenly demanded that all companies collect revenue, not just "eyeballs." Technology stock prices plunged. The dot com balloon burst into shaggy threads of stretched puckered rubber.

Not a single thing had changed about the value D6 brought its customers, or the compelling vision the road show PowerPoints presented. But investors fled from D6 and all of their customers. Stock prices plunged. Debts were called in. Within a few months, old customers went out of business and new prospects shrunk from sinking ships offering solutions.

At D6, where the stock price peaked at $432, only a handful of employees had the opportunity – and prudence – to sell their shares. Hudson Davenport was not one of them.

It was September 7, 2001, the first Friday after Labor Day. Hudson stared at Yahoo! Finance. The website displayed columns of stock tickers and prices – all now short a decimal place. Or two. He clicked the ticker "D6."

"One dollar, twenty seven cents." Hudson said. His hands trembled as he opened J.D. Sullivan's calculator. "So, $1.27 times 20,000 equals….$25,400. And, I've only vested half. So…my entire portfolio is worth about twelve thousand bucks. Excellent."

This would not be such a problem if Hudson had not taken J.D. Sullivan's advice to live large over the past two years. If, when his initial shares had vested in June 2000, he had realized that the D6 price then – $42 per share – was a ceiling not a floor. Practically overnight, the market had changed from inflating D6 stock with hot hopes to burying it with grudging pessimism. Hudson was caught out cold, clutching the flashy future painted on D6's IPO PowerPoint.

He saw only one way out: close a mammoth deal with XTC and earn its commission.

Summer had slipped behind them. All eyes were on the quarter that would close in three weeks at the end of September. But the XTC deal, which everyone was relying on to reflect the aura of success through D6 at a time it badly needed to see and show traction, was nowhere.

Hudson was paralyzed. He would call XTC; someone would say they would meet in three months. He had had a few meetings but they were "all hat no cattle." Looked good. Got nowhere. Edwin was expecting him to close the deal this month. And the commission was absolutely the only way he could pay back J.D. Sullivan.

Instinctively Hudson looked at his wrist to check the time. He had not yet adjusted to it being bare. As he remembered what had happened last weekend, small bumps rose on his skin.

About this time last Friday, he had decided to call XTC again. "First, coffee courage," Hudson said. But getting coffee meant crossing Big Mac's door. So he walked briskly, though there was no need. Mac was on the phone, his back to the door. Hudson caught a few words.

"As much as you can," Mac was saying in a low voice. "Sell it all."

"Sell?" Hudson thought. "Not D6 shares, not when he knows the real numbers?"

If day traders saw the stock dive, D6 shares could go to zero. Hudson shook his head, strode to the coffee room with the air of purpose he did not feel. On his way back to his desk to dig in this time to XTC, he saw Jameson go in to Big Mac's office.

"We're looking good, Jameson," Mac said, smiling. Hudson watched Mac go to the white board with the green pen. He wrote down the deals and next to each, dollar figures. Green meant these were sales that the crew had closed. Titan Toys topped the list.

Hudson walked back to his cube. "Hey Sam, congrats on Titan Toys," A young man spun in his chair. He wore a blue polo shirt with the D6 logo and khakis – the unspoken dress code. His suit and tie hung in his cube for the unexpected customer call.

"Why?" Sam said. "Big Mac made me push it. He's doing a little sandbagging. I guess we have enough for Q3; he wanted to roll it to Q4. Could have closed it too."

Hudson craned his neck to see Big Mac's wall. "What about Linwood Paper?"

"Next quarter," Sam said. "What are you, our new manager?"

"Hell no," said Hudson. "I don't want responsibility. Where's the fun in that?"

But the hairs on Hudson's spine reversed. Big Mac was telling Jameson that deals had closed when they had not. "Mac is selling us out," Hudson thought. "We'll miss the quarter."

Missing Wall Street's expectations would tip D6 over the abyss. The hottest IPOs were in the distant past, the cash raised long ago spent. If investors did not see profits they did not want to see the stock in their portfolio.

"So why push the deals?" Hudson wondered. "Next quarter will be irrelevant if we miss this one. So why is Mac putting roses under Jameson's nose?"

Just then, Hudson's phone rang. Still distracted, he answered.

"Hudson!" boomed a familiar voice. "You coming to the rock for the weekend?"

"Hey J.D.," Hudson said cautiously. "Yeah. I'm flying out with my dad tonight."

"Great. Let's meet up for a drink. I'd like to catch up."

"Sure, great," said Hudson, relieved to hear that the banker sounded friendly.

That night, buckled into the soft leather seat, Hudson watched through the window of his father's Falcon 50 as they took off from Hanscom Airfield just west of Boston to go to their home on Nantucket for Labor Day weekend. The plane followed the arc of a stone flung into the sea. As soon as they crossed over the coastline they tipped down toward the little wing of sand and trees. He kept thinking about Mac.

"How's the quarter looking?" Hudson began. Sterling turned. The two bucket seats were separated by an aisle. The stewardess had disappeared into the small cockpit after handing Sterling a gin and tonic and Hudson a Sam Adams.

"Hasn't Mac given you all the early look?" Sterling said.

"I think he thinks it's coming in well, but," Hudson paused.

"So that's what it is then." Sterling turned back to the stack of papers on his lap.

After a moment, Hudson tried again. "You know what? I think he thinks….I saw him tell Jameson…that a couple of deals were in that were… kinda pushed to next quarter."

Sterling frowned. The parsing began. "You saw him tell Jameson," he began skeptically.

"Yes."

"You heard nothing."

"No. But I could tell."

"You weren't in the room."

"No, but I saw the white board marked up in green – means they're in."

"But he could have just picked up a green pen."

"I…it just seemed a little odd. I just thought you should…watch out for it."

"Let's stick to facts. You heard nothing and you aren't sure what you saw. That's what you are telling me to watch out for?" Sterling turned away.

Hudson clammed up. Not worth the hassle. Let it roll. He wondered who would be at the Wharf that night. He could take a taxi from the airport. Maybe catch up with J.D. tonight.

"It's better for you, son," Sterling returned softly. "If anything is wrong, it's not your monkey. You should never rat out your boss. They'll find a way to get you out if they think they can't control you. There's a reason for the reporting structure. The military would have helped you. You'd fit in more naturally to a sales hierarchy."

Hudson thought of Edwin. Should he tell him? Hudson ran a reel of the response that would come if he brought this information to Edwin. There would be no subtleties, no protocol. Informants would not be protected. Edwin would summon Mac to his office. Stare

Mac in the face, very close. He would root out anything not yet closed and call Jameson with the result, right in front of Mac. Truth and fact were the goals. Edwin looked for the redness and sensitivity of a trouble spot, and used humiliation as a tool to expose problems so they could be dealt with now, not fester and blow up later. Grey areas, like protecting vulnerable informants, obscured the truth so had no value.

"I'd have my pants around my ankles while Mac green lights the deals he's holding, makes the quarter and lives another day." Hudson thought of the Wharf. Cool beers. Pretty girls with late summer smiles. Tables in need of dancing.

"Whatever, Dad. I made my nut last month," Hudson took a long swallow.

"Good for you," Sterling said. He was pleased to bring his errant boy in line, although later as his taxi pulled away from the airport, he thought about why there was so little in Hudson that reminded him of himself.

Hudson waited at the taxi stand, breathing deeply the late summer salty air which wafted over him in the low fog. A black SUV pulled up and rolled down the window. A man in a black leather coat leaned his head out the window. He was bald but for a short grey buzz over his ears. He looked to be about fifty.

"Davenport," he called. "How you doing? J.D. asked me to pick you up."

"J.D.? Ah...I have to...my bags and stuff," Hudson fumbled. He looked down the airport exit road. His father's taxi was long gone.

The man opened the door and smiled at Hudson, "It's no trouble. I've got it." He grabbed Hudson's duffel and tossed it in the back of the SUV. "Take the front seat."

"Okay," Hudson said. As the man bent into the backseat, Hudson thought he saw the man's jacket bulge at the side of his hip. "Where does J.D. want to meet? The Wharf? The Chicken Coop?" He named two of the most popular bars on the island. Public bars.

"He's inviting you on his boat," said the driver.

"Yacht," corrected the one in the back. They chuckled. Hudson smiled, sitting stiffly as the car rattled over uneven pavement. In fifteen minutes the tires crunched the white pebble drive of the Yacht Club.

Hudson walked up the gangway to the gleaming 120 foot, triple deck powerboat. One man walked one pace in front of him; the other just behind. Hudson did not often walk between men taller than he was – or twice the girth. He noticed the one in front had a very thick neck.

"Watch your step," he warned Hudson. "The deck gets slippery with the fog. This way. " He opened the door to the deck level living quarters. Hudson stepped into a long living room appointed like a luxurious apartment in Manhattan.

J.D. leaned back on a white leather couch, his feet up on a white ottoman. The walls were covered in walnut paneling. A bar with three white stools filled the far corner.

"Hudson, thanks so much for coming over right after your flight," J.D. smiled, patting him on the shoulder. "Have a seat. Gin and tonic, right?" Hudson nodded. The driver filled a glass with ice.

"Beautiful boat," Hudson said, accepting the glass.

"She's very steady, especially out deep in the ocean swell," said J.D. "Maybe you'll come tuna fishing with us sometime."

"Yeah, sure," Hudson said, managing a smile. He felt hot in the enclosed space. The recessed lighting, soft white squares, began to form halos.

J.D. nodded to his two friends. They went out on the deck, closing the door. J.D. picked cashews, one by one, out of a bowl of nuts on the coffee table. He shook them in his hand like dice. "So...troubled times at D6. Saw the stock price."

"Yeah. We'll get through it," Hudson said. "This team knows how to execute."

"That's an important skill,' J.D. said. "Great to hear. Because I need my money back."

"Of course," Hudson said. "I'm...well...I'm sure the stock price will go back up."

"Maybe," shrugged J.D. "Regardless, I need my money. I told you to pay me back when you vested. That was like a year ago. I've been more than reasonable," said J.D.

"You didn't ask...I...," Hudson flailed.

"Surely you sold when you could? When the stock was like at eighty dollars? Forty?" J.D. stared at Hudson. "Don't tell me...."

"I thought it would ...it's the 6th dimension," Hudson said weakly. Then he felt the boat rumble. The engines were starting.

J.D. shook his head sadly. "Well, then it's true what they say," J.D. put his face very close to Hudson's. "Pigs get fat. Hogs get slaughtered. Pay me in full by the first of October."

J.D. chopped Hudson's wrist hard with the edge of his hand. The glass spun out of Hudson's grip, soaking a spot on the white rug. Hudson cried out. "Ahh!"

"I'll repossess this, for now," J.D. said, slipping the four thousand dollar watch off Hudson's wrist. "But I want payment, in full, with 15% interest – call it $175,000. Better yet, a clean $200,000. You have until the end of the month. October 1. So it's no trouble for you, my friends will pick up the check."

"Okay," Hudson said, rubbing his wrist. "You'll have it. Somehow. I guess, I think I'm going to go." J.D. buckled the watch on his wrist as Hudson stood up and strode to the door. Outside the idling engines spat water and exhaust. Hudson looked for J.D.'s friends but could not see them. Hudson pushed through the gate and forced himself to walk down the gangway. But when his feet hit the pebbled path, he ran. He burst passed the grey shingled cottages with white trim, their climbing rosebuds pinched in the night. He sprinted around dark corners on the familiar old streets. When he could see the six gables of his parents' cottage, he drew up short. Hudson, staggering, looked around in a full circle. No one was following him.

Hudson pushed through a hedge. Hidden from the street, he fell on his knees. Blood pulsed in his ears. Hudson gasped and lay back on a sandy mound. He stared up at the sky. Eventually the stars held firm.

CHAPTER 4

Ahmed Farzi placed his shoes in a cubby near the entrance to the mosque. Then he moved quietly to the basins to begin wadu alongside the other men, as he did every dawn before entering the prayer hall. He started with his right hand, washing it three times. Then the left, three times. He washed his mouth, his nose, his face, each three times. He put water over his hair, his ears, his neck.

"Shoulder to shoulder," the Imam said, nudging the men together at the basin, where strangers touched without recoil. All were equal in the eyes of their god: remembering this was one reason for the ritual. Long ago, elsewhere, it removed the sand. Today, in Cambridge, it eased them into the meditative state.

Ahmed noticed that the man next to him was Ali Hamini from D6. Three times, Ahmed and Ali washed their right arms, then their left. Three times, they washed their right feet, then their left. Then they entered the prayer hall. It was empty but for a hand-woven wool carpet, ablaze with geometric shapes of deep reds and blues. In one corner there was a black cube. Ahmed and Ali stretched forward over folded knees, until their foreheads reached the carpet. They prayed in the direction the shapes pointed, toward the black cube, a tribute to the Almighty's first messenger, Ibrahim. The barefoot men, and the cube, all pointed toward Mecca.

Women prayed in the back of the room. Early on it had been acknowledged that while equal in the eyes of the Almighty, women bent in supplication in the foreground made it difficult for some to focus all thoughts on their total submission to Allah.

This first prayer of the five he made every day was Ahmed's favorite. It was so peaceful at daybreak. Where he first thanked his god for his very existence, and for him pledged to be the model citizen, the best man he could be, to his wife, to his colleagues, to people he did not know or understand, who might cross his path, or cross him. To be sincere, to love, to forgive.

Given his professional duties, this was a deep challenge.

The Imam began quoting the prophet. "We are not permitted to kill. Killing is not right. And whoever kills somebody intentionally, his reward is hellfire."

Ahmed muttered the prayer to himself over and over again, rocking, chafing, Ali beside him. When the morning prayers finished, the Imam and other men gathered for a cup of tea. Their feet were still bare.

"Hello Ali," said Ahmed. He was startled to see his young colleague at the mosque. Traditions did not seem to hold much influence over this man who seemed to drink so deeply from America's cup. The redness around Ali's eyes told of another late night. Ahmed felt different from most of the employees at D6 most of the time. He was twenty years older. Married. He had such different goals. But Ahmed tried to stop short of judging.

"Only Allah, peace be upon him, could determine who was truly pure," he reminded himself.

"Hello, Ahmed," said Ali quietly.

"I haven't…where do you usually pray?" Ahmed regretted his judgmental tone.

"Here, yes," said Ali. They walked to the room that held the men's shoes. But the cubbies were empty. Seven stray shoes lay scattered. Yet there had been at least twenty men inside at the morning prayer. Ahmed's lips tightened.

"The fountain again?" he said sadly. Last week the vandals had stuffed all of the shoes in empty beer boxes and hung them from a tree.

Ali let loose a string of epithets, running to the fountain.

"Ali," Ahmed cautioned. It was wrong to take the name of any god in vain. Ali slapped the water hard, bringing up a sheaf of water that wet his face, his arm, his chest. Like a child he beat the water. Ahmed stood still, nostrils flaring with each deep breath.

The Imam stepped calmly into the water, mindless of his robes that were floating, white veils on the stirred water. He scooped armfuls of shoes, drenched, ruined, from the fountain.

"Here," Ahmed said. "Give them to me." He took them to a bench near the door, where the sun could shine on them. Ali was motionless, his white t-shirt soaked through.

The Imam's voice was quiet. "Allah, peace be upon him, compels us to forgive the unbelievers. To be the model citizens ourselves. Even in the most difficult moments. Everything in moderation. Even our anger." Ahmed found his shoes among the drying pairs of Nikes, loafers, brogues, and sandals. He slipped them on and turned away. He needed time alone. He could not find a path to moderation with Ali nearby pushing him into the fountain.

Later that night, after Ahmed had kissed his children and pulled the covers over their nearly grown shoulders, he told his wife about the shoes in the fountain while they ate dinner. About Ali's reaction. Jahila had a PhD in electrical engineering. Coming to America had been a shared adventure.

"I can understand the rage," he told her. "The fury at always being the outsider. Of their cries never being heard. But the methods. They are mad."

"We must give a voice to those who do not have one." Jahila sighed. "It is what we do. It is why we have free choice. To help."

Ahmed nodded. "This place — it is difficult to mix so many peoples together. Some cannot find the middle any more. They forget tolerance. Lose their way entirely."

His wife sighed, and dipped her bread. With a soft smile she said, "I suppose all that really matters is that our children, even if they wear baseball hats, know the food."

CHAPTER 5

HUDSON
SEPTEMBER 10, 8:00 A.M., CAMBRIDGE, MA

Monday's morning sales meeting was about to begin. This was where the Global President of Worldwide Sales and Service, Richard MacIntyre, met with his sales leaders to make sure deals were on track for meeting the revenue requirement for the quarter. Once D6 went public they took on the rigorous quarterly reporting requirements where the company had to tell the public how much money they made and what they spent to do it. Investors hated bad news and surprises.

Hudson was pouring a cup of coffee in the break room. He was not in that Monday morning club. Not now, maybe not ever.

"Who wants to watch this circus today, anyway," he muttered as the cup filled.

"Circus in town? I didn't know you had kids," Mac said, looming next to him. He wrapped his calloused fingers around the coffee pot handle. He saw Hudson looking at them. "I row. Every morning. They bleed but the rush is incredible." He plucked two donuts and a bagel from a tray.

"Kids? None that I know of," Hudson flashed his contagious grin. "Just a general statement about life – what a circus."

"You know what I really love about this job, my career?" Mac mused.

"Big commissions?" Hudson smiled again. Mac put his hand on Hudson's shoulder, guiding them both out of the coffee room. He laughed.

"Ah yes. The motivation of the coin. But even more – I love seeing potential in a young guy, bringing it out. That's my real job. That's why I come to work every day." Mac stopped. Looked Hudson square in the eye. "You've got something special, Hudson. I'd like you to sit in this morning."

"Okay," Hudson said, startled. Now the smile that Hudson spilled was genuine. Flattery made his pride surge and for a moment, Hudson swelled with confidence. He felt a flash of affection for Big Mac. Suddenly Hudson regretted tattling about something he had probably misinterpreted. He should really be helping Mac, he thought, as he pushed open the glass door to his first Monday sales meeting. He took a seat in a row of chairs behind the ones pushed right up to the table, and tried to look comfortable.

Jameson was at the head of the table. He liked hearing directly from the people who had their hands on the actual deals. Jameson watched their body language. They wore white or blue shirts with ties. There was always a little tension when he was around; the face-splitting smiles, stiff spines. But it was different today. They were all strangely quiet. When deals were in, salespeople were high. When numbers missed, they looked like dogs slinking off the couch.

Edwin sat against the back wall, flicking through his Blackberry and typing on his computer, when the frosted glass door swung open. Now it was Jameson's turn to go on alert. While his gut turned, he lit a smile.

"There he is! Sterling. Welcome!" Jameson said.

"Hello everyone, sorry to be late," Sterling said.

It was highly irregular for Sterling – a board member – to join an internal sales meeting unannounced. But as Jameson's boss – and one of the key financers of the business – Jameson could not refuse him. To show any discomfort would look like he was hiding something. Jameson knew he was being played. What was worse, Sterling had been invited to see it. It was clear to Jameson who had played this odd, destructive hand, but not why.

"Okay, Mac, let's go," Jameson said. It was only as Big Mac stood up with a blush on his cheeks that Jameson pinned his flat gaze on him. If Mac wanted Jameson's job, missing the quarter was not the way to get it. They would both get canned. So something else was up.

Something big. And wrong. Jameson could see the endgame. Throwing a quarter, if that was the game, would end in D6's bankruptcy. Employment lost for a thousand people. Fortunes lost. Reputations ruined.

The end of a business usually did not mean the end of a career. But this business was supposed to resuscitate Jameson. Failing at D6 would confirm SAC's predictions: that instead of accelerating in the prime of his career, Jameson Callaghan was already done.

The blue light of the projector caught. A spreadsheet appeared on the wall. Names of customers were on one side; deal sizes on the right. Closed deals were green. There were few of them. And a lot of red. Hudson shuddered. The red pen.

"So we're close on this one, and this one, and this one," Mac fumbled. "But then these guys went out of business, these guys went Chapter 11. Nothing we could do."

Edwin stopped typing. "Mac, stop. Numbers only. What do we need?"

"Twelve million," Mac said.

"What have we closed?" Jameson said. "Not what might. Tell us what is signed."

Mac shuffled his feet, smiled. The blush was back. Sterling watched from the seat to the right of Jameson, fingertips touching. He was not smiling. No one was, except for the stupid grin the sales leader wore as he sipped nervously from a paper cup.

"Seven and change," said Mac.

"You are five million dollars short, with only three weeks to go in the quarter?" Edwin said. "So we're going to miss. D6 will die." Fact. Analysis. Conclusion.

Hudson's thoughts were flailing down whitewater. J.D. Sullivan. The $150,000 check he had blithely scribbled out. Which Hudson had used to buy some treats while he calculated the rising value of his stock options. The Breitling watch. The Mercedes. The stock was down, really down, but he had never thought D6 would go under completely. If D6 disappeared, not only would Hudson's underwater stock and remaining options disappear with it, but he would not even have a commission to chase. Or a salary.

Hudson passed his fingers over his empty wrist. J.D. Sullivan was not the kind of guy to forgive a friendly debt. Let alone a six-figure one.

"Mac?" Jameson's eyes were locked on Mac. Hudson wouldn't want to be Mac right now.

"Yes sir," Mac said. But he looked at the computer's keyboard.

"What is the status of Titan Toys? Linwood Paper?" Jameson said. Hudson gulped and focused on his coffee. These were exactly the deals his colleagues had told him Mac wanted pushed. The ones Mac had lied to the CEO about closing..

"Dead," Mac said. "For now. Maybe next quarter."

Jameson was silent for a moment, his face devoid of any emotion. "You have a five million dollar problem. What's your plan for solving it?"

Mac smiled. "Here it is," he said, tapping a button. The next slide in the PowerPoint had only three letters on it. And a big number. "XTC: $5 million."

A swallow of coffee reversed in Hudson's throat. It wet his nostrils.

"Dude," whispered Sam. "How do those tire marks feel all over your back?"

"Who's on that deal?" Jameson barked.

"A young guy with a bright future," said Mac, pointing to Hudson.

Jameson said, "What's the status, Hudson? Stand up." Hudson cleared his throat. It caught as he tried to speak. He became acutely aware of the silence that fell as everyone turned to him and he just stood there. Blood rose up his face. He tried again. He could feel the water closing over his head.

"I'm working on it," he managed to say.

"Have a term sheet yet?" Edwin asked. His fingers flew across his computer, which connected to the Internet through a thick cable wrapped in blue. A nest of blue and yellow cables unwound from a slit in the middle of the table to each laptop.

"Ah, no," Hudson said.

"Met with the decision maker yet?" Edwin said.

"No," Hudson gulped.

Edwin stopped typing and looked at him. "All you do from now until September 30 is close this deal. Go to my office immediately. Stop wasting time in this one."

Hudson was never so glad to see the other side of that frosted glass. XTC was nowhere. They would miss the quarter. D6 would tank. And that would be it. J.D. would collect.

Inside the conference room, Jameson's face belied nothing but the calculations were ticking off behind the screen. Mac's positive spin did not fool him. It made Jameson seethe. But why was Mac doing this? At heart he was a sales guy. Which meant he was coin operated.

"So who's feeding him quarters?" thought Jameson.

Jameson coughed. "Mac, we've got a big problem here."

At this Sterling spoke for the first time all day. "This is news to you Jameson? I count on you to know about this kind of risk in advance."

It was a public dressing down. Jameson turned to Sterling, the man he had jockeyed with for so many years. Score one for Sterling. But what happened next is why Jameson ran companies and Sterling ran money. Men and women would follow Jameson. They liked him. Sterling had to buy his influence.

Jameson turned back to the Sales team. His voice was even and his words were stern. "Okay folks. We've got three weeks to make up five million in revenue. Pull in every favor. Sandbag nothing. You need me on a call, in a meeting, anywhere, just book it with Maggie here," he pointed his thumb toward the young woman sitting to his right, typing fast. "Because if we miss this quarter, the Street will whack our stock, the press will devour us, and none of your potential customers will sign on to what they think is a sinking ship. We will be out of business before Maggie can enroll in school for the second semester. You can do it. Now go."

Mac spun in his chair with his puckered smile. Jameson had not taken him to task. It was worse: he had passed right over him. Jameson had assumed control of Mac's team, gave them their marching orders. Fingering the key in his pocket, Mac wondered if this would be the week he got fired. This time he probably had earned it.

Jameson stood up. His meeting was over. Maggie Rice followed on his heel.

Sterling scrambled to his feet. "Jameson," he barked. "I'm on my way to D.C. I will call you from the car to discuss this."

Jameson turned and flashed his biggest smile. "Great! Maggie, get me out of whatever I'm in when Sterling calls." He could not look ruffled. So he would calmly, orderly, paste that shit-eating grin on his face, go back to his office and close the door. Then the mask would fall. Then he would find out exactly who was out for his head . And his company.

And why.

"Maggie, please ask Hudson Davenport to come see me," Jameson said quietly to his assistant as they walked back to his office.

A few minutes later, Jameson watched the lanky young man arrive on the other side of his glass office wall. Unlike most sales men, who kept shirts, shoes and shearing as crisp as ex-military, Hudson looked more like a surfer; his longish brown hair starched from the summer sun and salt. If he stood up straight he would be nearly as tall as Jameson, about six feet. Now he was leaning over Maggie's cube, shining his dark eyes on the college girl, grinning.

Jameson shook his head and chuckled. The CEO had beckoned this kid to come for a one-on-one about the public dressing down he just had in front of the whole sales force, and Hudson found time to flirt first. So Jameson hit the intercom button and roared.

"Where's Davenport?" In less than two seconds there was a knock on his door.

"You wanted to see me?" Hudson said, finding a seat, pinning his eyes on Jameson.

Jameson looked at Hudson for a long, searching minute, and said, "You know why I picked you instead of all those other super-talented Harvard Business School kids?"

"Um. Not really," said Hudson.

"Because I think you have something special in you," Jameson said.

Hudson continued the familiar refrain. "So don't let you down?"

"So you can be a hero," said Jameson. "Or you can be a goat. XTC is your opportunity. D6 needs you to close this deal or we're all looking for new jobs. I know you can do it. You went to Williams College, then Harvard Business School."

"Helps to have your father on the board," Hudson said sheepishly.

"Nobody gets a double major in Physics and Electrical Engineering without a pretty sharp set of their own tools," Jameson snapped. "So pull them out, polish them up, and put XTC together."

"How did you know about my major?" Hudson said.

"Majors," Jameson corrected. "I like to know how deep my bench is."

The door flew open. Edwin charged in as though his hair was on fire.

"Davenport. Go to my office right now. There's a way to blow the doors of XTC and I'm going to tell you how. Stop nowhere on your way." Jameson waved his hand and Hudson was on his feet. He smiled weakly at Maggie as he trotted past her cube.

Edwin shut the door behind him. "Jameson," The word shot like a bullet. Edwin was even more spun up than usual. "Someone is screwing with this company. Mac is screwing with these numbers. I closed Titan Toys and Linwood Paper myself. They were done. And we're somehow suddenly short of those deals, and 5 million more? Missing the quarter will kill D6."

"Yes," said Jameson.

"So what are you doing about it?"

"Duck on water, Edwin," Jameson said. "The world sees you gliding on the glassy surface. Underneath you paddle like mad. And with a little luck, you figure out who's spinning the wheel and how to push their buttons."

"Luck has nothing to do with it," said Edwin. "Spin the wheel yourself."

Jameson, gliding, chuckled. "So you are a philosopher too – a man of many talents."

Jameson loved how Edwin shook up the status quo. How he was immune to politics. How he bulled through anyone who used how things looked to shroud how they actually were. He made so much progress that way. He made them all make so much progress. But Jameson saw a structure that had to be climbed, maneuvered. Pacified.

"We must close XTC," Edwin said. "Can Hudson get it done? This is not a training ground. People have to execute."

"We shall see," said Jameson, peering at his email. "He's going to need your help. Let's talk more about it tomorrow morning on the flight."

"You're going to LA also?" Edwin said.

"Yes," said Jameson. "Investor conference."

"Tomorrow morning?" Edwin said. He paused briefly. "Fine." But as he was leaving the office, Edwin turned back. Generally he moved only forward, always fast. What caught Jameson's attention was how this time, Edwin moved slowly.

"It's on you, Jameson," Edwin said softly. "Hudson is a glad handing cool kid. I gave him the chance a year ago – he has gotten nowhere. He has no record of getting it done."

"Not true – ask a couple of the girls around here."

Edwin let out a sharp laugh. Then all humor drained. "I'll do what I can. But you will have twenty very hard days to close this deal or my company will be dead. You must make them make it happen."

"See you in the morning, Edwin," Jameson said, studying his screen. He did not take to being scolded. But Edwin's challenge lit a spark in him. The burn felt fresh, heat ripping through a dry field. Since Belle had died, he rarely felt much at all. There was only that one easy moment, just before he fully awoke, before the facts could assemble themselves and assault him. Belle. His soul mate. How they had looked outward at the world together, their life a volley of ideas and reflections and encouragement, particularly after they accepted they could have no children. The toxins never could take her smile. Even after her gorgeous, long red hair gave way to the burnt grey fuzz that grew between radiation sessions. The last, light scratch of it against his lips, his offer of condolence after the effort was lost.

Jameson's computer screen pinged. A new email read, "Again tonight?"

"O…K…" Jameson hunted with his index fingers. He clicked off his computer monitor, slipped its brains into its slot in his briefcase, then called, "Maggie…ready?"

Jameson's assistant was smoothing a pink lipstick across the arc of her upper lip. She put it in her bag. Clicked off her computer. "Thanks Jameson. You sure it's no hassle?"

"None. Couldn't have you walking the streets after dark, could we?"

"Okay. I am ready for you," said Maggie. "Just let me make one more call." Maggie spun her chair and dialed a series of numbers on the square pad.

Jameson found himself looking forward to the evening. He watched Maggie move between the phone, computer, and the mysterious contents of her leather satchel, that catchall for a computer, running shoes, make up and whatever else.

Youth, thought Jameson, was marvelous. He wanted to gorge on it. Youth could take any path and bounce right back. It was kinetic. It had not seen, so could not imagine, or brace itself for, the pain humans could cause each other, in broad collective assaults and in devastating individual betrayals. Youth was bouncing down the hallway next to him in size seven Reeboks. Her light perfume lifted from her hair.

As they left the corner office together chatting breezily, neither noticed that the handset of Maggie's phone did not rest quite right in the cradle. It was 6:32 p.m. on Tuesday, September 10.

One floor down, Walker Green's cane still hung from its hook on his cube. He had an important email to send. He did not like to send personal information on company time, but this he could not do at home. There would be no way a dial up connection could send all of this data. He would have to wait for hours to complete this transfer, and then it might still get interrupted and he would have to start all over again. D6's high speed connection would send it quickly. It was worth the risk. Then his special evening could begin.

CHAPTER 6

About 180 miles north of Cambridge, Massachusetts, two men ate slices at a Pizza Hut. One winced as the hot tomato sauce burned the roof of his mouth. They finished in fifteen minutes. Later, the two teens on the shift would tell friends how they remembered the men's chattiness, the Arabic words unintelligible. Then.

CHAPTER 7

When Hudson Davenport arrived in Edwin's office, he was on high alert. The alpha was at the whiteboard, scribbling, flipping it, adding more letters, numbers, arrows. Ahmed and three engineers were taking notes, nodding, buzzing. But Ali Hamini sat back against the couch, his arms crossed, his feet on the coffee table, knocking against Edwin's barrel of wrapped chocolates.

Edwin spotted Hudson at the door. "Great! Hudson!" Edwin clapped his hands on Hudson's shoulders. Hudson could see nothing but Edwin's fierce green glare. "D6 will survive because of this deal. You make it happen. They build it," he gestured to the engineers. "Or you're all fired." With the small group now focused on their collective goal, Edwin explained how they would win XTC. The nuance of the deal, the pressure points, what technical secrets to give away, what to protect. Fingers flew across keyboards.

"This is how we can get over their security objections and let them build us right in," said Edwin, underlining a string of code he had just splashed on the white board. He stepped behind the whiteboard and in the cramped space between the wall and the other side of the whiteboard, continued scribbling fast. The engineers and Hudson could only see his blue jeans, wrinkled at the knee from several days' wearing.

Then a loud snort disrupted the excitement. "So...you are...wildly optimistic," declared Ali, his hands behind his head. The scribbling stopped. The knees bent. Edwin poked his head around the whiteboard.

"Show me something better," Edwin said. There was no pique in his voice. He wanted to see something better. He waved the black marker.

"You should show more respect for other systems," Ali said.

Edwin stared at Ali. "Good – okay – how? Tell us how you'd do it."

"You don't. It simply is," said Ali. The rams collided over the coffee table. Edwin's Herculean efforts to make new things happen ran into the inertia Ali lavished in. To Edwin, hot disputes were fabulous but he could not abide lack of passion.

Ahmed looked from Edwin to Ali and back. He said nothing.

"If you are going to be in here," said Edwin, "then commit. If not, get out."

Ali picked one foot off of Edwin's coffee table, then the other. "I have one word for you. I'll spell it, so you get it right. A-R-R-O-G-A-N-T. The arrogant always fall." Then he sauntered to the door, pushed it open and walked through. Ahmed shook his head. Edwin's eyes were wide.

"Ali is now off this deal," Edwin said flatly. "But his point is brilliant. So how do we get them to see their system stays intact while incorporating ours?"

Hudson leaned forward, waiting for the quarterback to call the play. It felt good to bend over his soft belly. It was on him. The whole company. This deal. Which was the only way out of the mess with J.D.

That was when Hudson's phone vibrated. The number caught his eye. It was Maggie. Jameson's assistant. Hudson could see that Edwin's session showed no sign of letting up. But he stepped out of the room. Edwin stopped speaking and stared at the door.

"Slacker!" Edwin yelled. To the team he said, "I will hold him accountable. Your job is to build the best integration, give away nothing and make them need us."

"Hello?" Hudson whispered into the phone. Behind him, the whiteboard filled with code.

"Time for a drink tonight?" Maggie asked.

"I'm kind of in an important meeting," he said.

"Would you like to walk me home tonight?"

"You're still upstairs?"

"I meant after you meet me for a drink," she said. Hudson caught his breath.

"Yes," Hudson said, smiling. "Yes. I would definitely like that to do, to do that."

Maggie giggled. "Maritime, in the South End?"

"See you in twenty," said Hudson. He slipped his phone back in the holster on his belt. He glanced through Edwin's office window. Edwin must have been behind the whiteboard; Hudson could not see him. For that brief moment, he forgot the meeting. Put J.D. out of his mind. The XTC pressure released in a gush that floated him out of the office.

He jogged to his Mercedes S Series and tore out of the parking lot, toward the Charles River, over the salt and pepper bridge, through Beacon Hill, around the Public Garden, into the South End.

"Just one drink's okay," Hudson thought. But with this justification, part of him shrunk. He knew that group would not leave until the wee hours. XTC was "hair on fire" time.

The bar at Maritime sat eight around a curved stainless counter backed by bottles of wine racked twelve feet high to the top of the ceiling. Four stools faced a narrow window bar that fronted the restaurant. It provided intimacy, and a view of everyone waiting for a table or walking outside, and, ironically, privacy. Maggie perched on a window seat. Hudson leaned to greet her. Her fingers lingered on the back of his neck.

"What are you drinking?" Hudson asked. Maggie twirled an empty martini glass.

"Two," Hudson said to the bartender. Later, goblets of Chardonnay arrived with blue point mussels wading in broth. Heavy pours of Cabernet came with the steak frites.

"I have a secret," Maggie whispered, waggling a finger. "I live right over there."

Hudson looked at her deeply. He took in the time above the hostess desk. It was nearly eleven, much later than he intended. But he couldn't be useful to them now. He'd go back in a couple of hours. He could not go now. For a number of reasons. So he leaned in, smelling the scent trapped beneath her hair, beneath her perfume.

"You drive me crazy," he said, pleased to hear his voice thick, deeper. He knew it moved women. And he craved their response.

Maggie slid off her barstool, grabbing Hudson's hand to steady herself. Hudson dropped bills for the bartender and followed Maggie out the door. She turned down a dark street, stopping at a brownstone.

"Coming?" she asked.

"Yes please," he said, lighting the smile.

An hour and a half later, Hudson looked at the clock next to Maggie's bed. It was after midnight. He really had to get back to the office. He would hear it from Edwin. But she was worth it, he thought, feeling the grin begin. He rolled on his side to look at her. The bed was empty. Hudson grabbed the towel from the bed. It was still slightly damp from earlier, when he had wrapped it around her after their shower.

"Maggie?" he called. The lights in the living room of the one bedroom apartment were off. He could see the flickering blue of television, but the sound was off.

Hudson found Maggie staring at the television, dressed in running gear. "You're going running now?"

"Maybe," she said. The flirtation was gone. She was distant and broody.

"Don't go running out on me now," Hudson quipped. He put his hand on the doorknob. "I've got to get back to work. Time and Edwin Hoff wait for no man."

Driving back to Cambridge, Hudson felt his triumph crest. He had her, then, somehow, he lost his grip. So he would just avoid Jameson's office for a few days. He dreaded the obligatory call back. Maybe Wednesday? Not that she had asked.

"Tomorrow," Hudson said. "Probably the right thing to do. Call her tomorrow."

It was 12:20 a.m. on Tuesday, September 11, when Hudson swiped his card reader and pushed through the security doors on the fifth floor. The sales floor had been empty for hours. Not like the eighth floor, where engineers arrived around 11:00 a.m. and checked out in the wee hours. But Edwin's office was dark.

Hudson fell into his desk chair and flicked on his computer. He would do some emails, put in electronic face time with Edwin. He swiveled as the computer booted up. The window at the office building across the courtyard was dark but for a few gold squares. More dot coms breaking leases.

Hudson thought, "What Edwin wants is just not possible." Microsoft Outlook opened on his desk. The stack of emails looked fuzzy. There was nothing from Edwin.

Then Hudson's chair flew backwards. He hit the floor. Duct tape ripped with a hiss. It was over in seconds. He lay on his side, his hands and feet bound, his mouth covered. He could not move, could not scream. Someone was sitting on him.

If Hudson never had seen this happen before, he would have been absolutely terrified.

A body sat heavily on Hudson's ribs. He heard a familiar voice.

"Listen to me, slacker," Edwin said. "There are three rules of leadership. One – lead by example. Two – suffer together. And three – hold non-performers accountable. You are now being held accountable." He gave Hudson a shove as he stood up.

Edwin's footsteps faded. Hudson twisted against his bonds but could not budge. Would Edwin leave him there all night? Claustrophobia made Hudson shake.

But within ten minutes, Hudson heard fresh footsteps. He smelled something spicy. Pizza? Someone was chewing.

The tape came off Hudson's eyes and mouth first. He saw Edwin snapping the cap of a ballpoint pen.

"Davenport, you add no value here," Edwin said. "The XTC deal is your chance to do it. If you don't, D6 dies. So you will make it happen."

Edwin clicked the pen. A narrow switchblade flashed and Hudson was free. The pen blade was back in Edwin's pocket, indistinguishable from the other two pens.

"So the pen is mightier than the sword," Hudson said.

"What?" said Edwin. While he mastered logic, computers, and machines that moved fast, nuance was not his thing. Once he tried to expand his vocabulary by reading the Oxford English Dictionary. He got stuck on the o's.

"You will eat, drink and listen," Edwin said, holding a half-crushed pizza box and two cans of Mountain Dew. "You will make this deal happen. I can only download this once. Then it is all yours.

"I've tried everything. Mac was supposed to introduce me but he hasn't –"

"Shut up. Listen," Edwin ordered. "First, does XTC give a shit about puny us? No. But they give a big shit about Macrotech. Make XTC think you are about to do a deal with Macrotech then give XTC the chance to do it first with us. Oh, and the only way this really works is if you actually have a deal with Macrotech. So you have two deals to do.

"Second, why do they need D6? Because the one with us will be better, faster, stronger – even by an inch – than their competition. Always keep the focus on how we help them beat their competition. Get the engineers together in a workshop – let them sell it to each other. The suits can set up the meeting then listen to what their engineers tell them to do. From now on, your best friend is Ahmed. Who you just walked out on. So you have three deals to do." Edwin scribbled on a piece of yellow pad paper.

Do This Month:
1) Fix it with Ahmed
2) Macrotech
3) XTC

Then Edwin picked up his stapler. A mad grin spread across his face.

He cackled, approaching Hudson with his arms out, zombie like, the paper in one hand and the stapler in the other. Hudson cringed. Edwin pulled Hudson's polo shirt two inches from his chest and stapled the paper orders to it.

Hudson knew something about engineers by now. In the high tech world, they were the new kings, flush with the money and control their computer skills gave them. But it had been a hard inheritance. Most learned in school how peers handed out disrespect. Now they had the reflex, which their Pentium brains executed effortlessly. A suit who said something stupid was permanently discarded in the trash folder.

Hudson's mind felt clear. It was suddenly uncluttered by the thoughts that usually clenched his stomach, made him search for a table to dance on, a woman to respond to him.

"Everyone I'm talking to is just going about their task list," Hudson concluded. "They have no authority to think of doing anything new."

"So who does?" Edwin said.

"Maybe the top boss? Kamia Khan."

"So go see her," Edwin said.

Hudson huffed. "The CEO? You think I can get a meeting with XTC's CEO?"

"Yes." Edwin riveted Hudson with his unblinking stare. It was Edwin's rare combination of talents that made him a true leader. Some led by fear; forcing people to act while resentment built. Some led with praise, while people got away with poor performance.

Edwin could make extraordinary things happen. But his real magic was this: he made most people learn to make extraordinary things happen too. He made them commit; he spoke in plain facts; he gave people specific goals and soldered them together. He demanded total focus on that goal. Then he constantly surprised them. Many of his methods were not sanctioned by Human Resources.

So it was only when they finished, close to 3:00 a.m., that Hudson looked around Edwin's office and finally took in the empty shelves. He saw a shredder had spit up bits of paper. Large cardboard boxes were filled with books, Lucite deal trophies, and the thick volumes from the IPO with "Edwin Hoff" printed in gold on their leather spines. A Tiffany clock, engraved with the date and dollar of the IPO – the bankers' gift from the D6 IPO.

"What's with the boxes?" Hudson asked. Dramatic things happened often at D6. They lived the motto "the only constant is change." But this was Edwin's company. He was its spirit and backbone. He could not leave. Preposterous.

"Spring cleaning," said Edwin.

"It's September," said Hudson.

Edwin picked up a thick manuscript. "My thesis. I finished it after I left MIT to start D6. God, I love math." He kissed the cover and put it in a box.

Then it struck Hudson just how much Edwin put into this company. It was his consuming passion. To Hudson it was another job he was supposed to be better at than he was. But with D6, Edwin had created a world – a technology that made new things happen; real jobs for people to support their families; fortunes to fulfill their desires. He set out compelling challenges. Raised his sword and summoned the charge.

Hudson thought of Big Mac. Suddenly his manipulations – whatever his crazy reasons – were more than bad decisions. They were an affront to Edwin, to what he had made possible for all of them. Hudson had to say something. It meant crossing his father, and selling out his boss. But Edwin deserved to know someone was screwing with him.

"Edwin," Hudson began. "Something's up with the sales numbers."

"They are not up. They are down," said Edwin, shredding papers. "Way down."

"Yeah, but it's more than that," Hudson shifted his weight. "I shouldn't…."

"Speak," said Edwin.

"I don't know…maybe it's nothing…but a couple of guys told me Mac told them to push some big deals to next quarter. You have to fix this," Hudson pleaded.

Edwin's shoulders slumped. It was a pose Hudson could not recall ever having seen him in before. Later Hudson would remember the strange sound Edwin's voice made, sounding small, pleading.

"People have to step up around here. This business can't scale with me at the center of everything," Edwin stared through the dark window. In the distance the Cambridge Coffee House logo glimmered. "You take care of XTC. Get in front of the CEO. That will solve everything else. It's late. I really, really want a coffee."

There was a quiet tap at the door. Ahmed waited to be invited in. "Excuse me, Edwin," he said softly. While Edwin was always pouring gas on people to respond like their hair was on fire, Ahmed always worked in this heat without a sweat.

"Hey, Ahmed," Hudson apologized. "I feel terrible for leaving earlier."

"Yes, there is that to do," Ahmed said, offering a nod and a small smile.

"I…I want you to know I'm in," Hudson said. But Ahmed was focused on Edwin.

"Here is your new Blackberry. Fully loaded. I think you'll like it." He pushed a black square across the desk and walked out. At the door, Ahmed turned. He looked at the shredded accordions of paper, the emptied room. "Have a good trip, my friend." Edwin nodded.

The two Blackberries sat on Edwin's desk. He picked one up, fiddled with it, and tossed it to Hudson. "Take it. A prize for the deal you will make happen."

"Your Blackberry?" Hudson said.

Edwin shrugged. "Now it's just a piece of plastic made in China. Ahmed deleted all of the files and upgraded me to this one." The devices looked the same.

"Well, thanks," Hudson said. Edwin was staring out the window toward the glow of the Cambridge Coffee Shop.

"So you had a good night? Better have been worth it. Was she?" Edwin grinned.

"Yes, yes she was. One duct taping deserves another." Hudson was still smiling when the golf ball bit his shin bone. A blue welt larger than the ball rose on his leg.

"Focus," Edwin said. "You are behind." With his eyes still fixed on something outside the window, he scooped the Blackberry off the desk and strode out of the room.

Hudson scrambled for a pad of paper. He copied Edwin's scrawl on the whiteboard, below the words "Strategy for Global Domination." Then Hudson plucked his new Blackberry from Edwin's desk and left for the second time that night.

The ASP operator had watched all day through his binoculars from an empty office across a courtyard near MIT. He saw the burly young man pacing by a whiteboard, rapidly combing his fingers through his black hair. Whiteboards filled with his arrows and acronyms. Every time his cell phone rang at his hip, he would answer it briefly then return to the board. When he was not talking his thumbs drummed his Blackberry.

The operator sifted a photograph from the pile on the abandoned ping pong table. The photo showed a woman getting off Raptor's motorcycle. They were grinning, spun up on wind speed and sheer joy. Another showed them eating pizza, their ankles wrapped around a chair leg.

It was very early in the morning, but still dark, when the operator followed Raptor on his motorcycle to a low rent two family in East Cambridge. A utility bill in the mailbox was addressed to "Miss Lula Crosse." He saw the woman from the photos open the door. Raptor entered.

The operator had collected incontrovertible evidence: Raptor had an attachment, and he had violated Sec. 3.5.11 of mission preparation code:

Sec. 3.5.11: *48 hours before a Mission, all operators must withdraw to total isolation.*

The code focused an operator's mind and prevented simple mistakes: these often caused calamities. The Head of the ASP must know.

The collateral damage must be contained.

CHAPTER 1

EDWIN
5:05 A.M., CAMBRIDGE, MA

Edwin dressed quietly in the dark while Lula slept peacefully. From the duffel bag, he drew out his work uniform: jeans, t-shirt, Nikes and a leather motor cycle jacket. He stood at the door, listening to her deep breaths, matching them with his own. He checked his watch, and scrolled through his Blackberry. What he saw brought him up short: the Blackberry was blank. He turned it off and on again.

"Dammit," he said.

"What's wrong?" Lula asked, her eyes still closed. Her voice was thick.

"Nothing," Edwin said. "My Blackberry crashed. Ahmed put some new software on it. I'll fix it at the airport."

"I didn't think I'd see you last night," Lula said. Edwin sat on the bed next to her.

"I shouldn't have come," Edwin whispered, pushing a lock of her hair away from her sleepy eyes. " But I'm glad I did."

"Where to this time?"

"California," Edwin said. "Lots of customers there like to hear from the CTO."

"When's your plane?" she asked.

"Five minutes ago," Edwin said. He held her with his eyes, a pink tinge rising in his round cheeks.

"Bad," she scolded. Her thumbs locked into the belt loops on his jeans. "Coffee should be ready." Lula got slowly out of bed and stretched, her silk nightgown clinging with static. She walked two steps across the narrow hall to the kitchen where the timer had brewed a fresh pot. She poured two mugs; steam rose from their tops. She tipped a sugar bowl over Edwin's and handed it to him.

Edwin took several long swallows of the hot liquid. "Ahh."

"I never understand how you do that," she said.

"Mind over matter," he said. "I say it is not hot. Then it does not feel hot."

"That's how you only need three to four hours of sleep each night too? Say you aren't tired, so you aren't?" Lula teased.

"I have to go," Edwin said. Lula picked a small, green-striped bag off the counter, and stuffed it into his jacket pocket. "Here. Bend your mind around this. A little light reading for the flight. See you tomorrow? You're not doing another coast-to-coast trip in 24 hours?"

Edwin drained the cup. "No."

"You are a whirling dervish with his own weather system," said Lula.

Edwin wrapped his arms around her. He held her for a long moment. "You're…really great." Then he gathered his duffel bag and strode out of Lula's apartment.

Trotting down the steps to his motorcycle, Edwin was grim. If he went to Ahmed now, he would have plenty of time to get a new Blackberry.

"But I don't have time for two stops," Edwin thought. "I can reboot it myself." He pushed the helmet over his head, straddled the bike and gunned the motor. The sound split the dawn calm as Edwin headed due west to the affluent Boston suburbs. He twisted the throttle and tucked close over the handlebars. The speedometer juiced over ninety miles per hour.

Behind him, the early morning sun was a red blotch over Logan Airport. It was 6:45 a.m., Tuesday, September 11. The gate to his flight to LA would close at 7:35 a.m. He did not have enough time. But what he had to do now could not wait.

CHAPTER 2

Thousands of years earlier, indigenous people of the Afghan mountains crept along the shelf of the crumbling cliff edge and took shelter in the natural indents of the cliffs. The mountain was crumbly. Over time they dug back into the cliff, the indents becoming caves linked by narrow paths. By the end of the second millennium, the complex could hold a thousand people. Underground streams and gravity spun waterwheels that brought hydroelectric power into the cave complex.

Satellites skimmed this area in the border region of Afghanistan and Pakistan, perceiving only mountaintops and goats on trails carrying small loads. But if the satellite could follow the goat herders beneath overhangs, the picture would show a cavernous room where men gathered in dusty, earth colored robes and scarves wound around their heads to keep out flying dirt. Five oval doors, about four feet high, led off this foyer. Ducking through one, the goat herder would be able to stand straight in the hallway, climb steps up to a path that wound deeper. Electric lamps strung the length of the hallway. Smells of cumin, cinnamon, coriander wafted from the cooking chambers. Down the next long hallway were sleeping chambers. At the entrance to the next path, a guard peeled an apricot with his dagger. His AK-47 rested on the rock walls. The path fanned around the six rooms of the company headquarters.

The company's mission was to cultivate and guide a group of avid entrepreneurs.

"Good ideas can come from anywhere," the Senior Operations Chief was fond of saying. "We will make their dreams reality."

All committee heads reported to the Senior Operations Chief. The Money and Business committee brought in revenue from a string of legitimate business. Much like America's mafia, it then distributed the cash to its event planners. It obtained passports marked up to disguise time spent in nations that might concern others. The Law Committee determined whether the plans were in accord with Islamic law. Invariably, they were. These were not scholars, just zealous advocates for an unconscionable client. The Military Committee planned attacks, recruited participants, trained and armed them. The Media Committee produced the volunteers' suicide tapes.

From the office of the Senior Operations Chief, through narrow gaps in the rock, one could see the goat path, now several hundred feet below. One could see anyone approaching on the horizon, edging up the mountain or through the valley below. Although the mountaintop hid them from the sky, the Senior Operations Chief could see up. Small cameras in rocks pointed up and fed film to the cave's wall of monitors.

The Senior Operations Chief reported to the leader, a tall man with a long beard. He walked with an AK-47, picking spots between loose rocks to place the tip. Today three men came before him. Each entrepreneur was responsible for part of the Event.

"Phase 1, report status," the leader barked. The roundest man stood.

"The operation will begin in forty-five minutes," he said. "We'll know the result in seventy-five."

"How many planes?"

"You know I had wanted ten, at least. One to land myself — to claim the operation for your glory, and Allah's, peace be upon him."

"Land one?" the leader said. His gaze was flat.

"To ensure the world knew," the round man waved his hand a wide arc.

"So how many planes do we have?" the leader said.

"Four."

"And you are here," the leader said. "So you have sent others to be martyrs."

"So things go smoothly," the man pushed up his glasses. "This time and next."

The leader eyed him. This day's events would require him to seek even more remote quarters. Was this the man who would take his chair? He looked at the next man, the shortest of the three.

"And Phase 2?"

"The targets are chosen. We shall attack their centers – financial, military, and political. At once."

The leader nodded to the third man. He was older than the rest, in his mid-fifties. His grey hair spun beneath his turban. The frames on his glasses were black plastic, thick enough to contain the heavy prescription. "Now, the pricey one. Phase 3."

Khalid al Hamzami had traveled a long way to be with the leader on this historic day. The first two phases would bring surprise and fear, but it was his plan that would in fact destroy America. He had built toward this day for many decades.

"The item is with the first flight team," he said. "If Phase 1 goes as planned –"

"It will," snapped the short man. "It's not like we're using castor beans."

Al Hamzami peeled back his lips, showing yellow teeth. "Ah? That is not for us to know until Allah, peace be upon him, wills it." He bowed; the others dipped their heads. He who recalled their duty to submit to their god seized the upper hand. He continued, "The effects of Phase 3 will be felt in exactly twenty-four hours all over New York City. Impact will cause the release and accelerate the dispersion of the Blood Boiler. And if Phases 1 and 2 fail, I have designed a failsafe. The vial containing the Blood Boiler will still release within twenty-four hours. It is already in Boston – a major American city. The destruction will be massive."

The leader smiled, euphoria tingling the backs of his ears. Reaching this day had required years of toil in anonymity. But he would never again blur with the masses.

"Very good, all," he said. "Well done."

"At no small cost," mumbled the plump architect of Phase 1. His plan was the real sensation. The coordination it took – four trained teams in motion simultaneously. All for the price of a few airline tickets and flight lessons.

"You think money spent to destroy Satan is unworthy?" scoffed Khalid al Hamzami.

"No, but the ten million U.S. that has gone to your hungry project is half our annual budget. The rest of us manage to make history on pennies."

"Let me enlighten you," said al Hamzami, "as we do not enjoy the same education." The smaller man's sandals scraped the rock floor.

"Sit," the leader said. The short man eased back down to the ground and crossed his legs. The leader curled his raised fingers. "Continue."

"Phases 1 and 2 are just a flash and a bang," scoffed al Hamzami. "Decoys to draw the leaders of America to the place of impact. But the explosion also will release a huge blast of energy, which could be more useful than just theater. The cloud of ash that will consume New York City could also spread billions of tiny disease bombs."

The small man wiped a droplet of spit from his cheek. Al Hamzami laughed.

"Ever hear of pneumonic plague? With that spittle you are dead. Pneumonic plague, viral hemorrhagic fever…, is extremely contagious and invariably fatal if treatment is delayed more than one day. First you will cough, then you will get a high fever, then you will spit blood. Shitting blood will come next. It is 100% fatal without early treatment. From a drop of spit. It spreads rapidly in crowded, humid conditions."

"Like New York at the end of summer," said the leader.

"Exactly! When people are terrified, they gather," said al Hamzami. "Phases 1 and 2 will make New Yorkers grieve together, and their hugs will kill. Best, the same fate will befall their leaders, who, within twenty-four hours, will have come to help. There will be a shower of disease before the bio-attack is discovered. The sky really will be falling."

"How do you get it into the explosion?" asked the man who selected the targets. "Won't it just burn up with everything else?" He aspired to more than selecting targets. He saw in the older man one who planned layers of destruction: someone to study.

"Ah yes!" said al Hamzami, energized. "Dispersal! There is a way to aerosolize pneumonic plague – some say 'weaponize.' The virus is converted to protected droplets that high heat does not destroy. We have found a way to purchase such a substance. It is held within a sealed crystal vial until the explosion, which destroys the crystal and accelerates the droplets. A member of the team on the first flight will carry it on board."

"And if the explosion does not happen, have we wasted ten million dollars?"

Khalid al Hamzami's mouth twisted with pride. He simply could no longer diminish his genius with false modesty. "The team has a code to disarm the automatic release, before twenty-four hours pass. Then the vial can be used again."

"To the Media Room." said the leader. "It begins in fifteen minutes."

CHAPTER 3

RAPTOR
7:41 A.M., BOSTON, MA

Raptor ran through the American Airlines terminal to Gate 36 in Logan Airport. Late.

First class and business had already boarded. He followed the orders.

Take possession on ground prior to flight if possible. If not, board the plane.

The stewardesses took the boarding pass from the man of average height, with thick black hair, wearing jeans, a t-shirt, and a dark motorcycle jacket. And Nikes. She noticed his eyes were strangely yellow, and he wore a Blackberry clipped to his belt.

"Okay, cockroach, where are you?" Raptor thought, entering the plane. He swept the rows of passengers on the half empty flight. But he was not assigned their fate. He bore instead the fate of millions in another city, who were getting their breakfast, spinning turnstiles, driving to work or school. People who would never see their microscopic assassins. He was to get the vial, get it away from this plane, away from cities.

Success would have nothing to do with luck. Success would have a little to do with Raptor's training. He could fight with guns, blades, hands, feet, elbows, and common household items (like a ballpoint pen struck up the nose, or near the edges of the eyeballs, and wiggled in brain matter). He had killed a man with his bare hands – an armed man half a foot taller and fifty pounds heavier . Raptor had jumped out of planes into the ocean, and then swum a mile in the high waves. With boots on. At night. He had run for seventy-five miles straight with an eighty pound pack on his back. Twice. Three years of active duty as captain of the counterterrorism division of Delta Force, leading his team of elite combat soldiers on more than thirty missions, taught him to clear the clutter from his mind and theirs, lever his adrenaline, and cope with unforeseen interference. Then ASP training put him with the best of the world's special forces, learning the unique skills of elite soldiers from Britain's SAS, Israel's *Sayeret Matkal*, Pakistan's ISI, and more.

But mostly, the mission's success depended on total, unbroken focus on his single goal. Focus would decide which history of America would be written that day. It would be tragic, but not apocalyptic. Not the one that would tell of millions dead. Not one of total annihilation of living creatures under the wide swath spread by the breeze.

Focus. Which one had the puck? They would be in the front of the plane, close to the controls. Raptor spotted the two in the first row of first class. ASP had placed him in business class, across the aisle from the two others.

"Please take your seat sir," said a stewardess. "We need to push back."

Raptor pulled the Blackberry out of his pocket. He shut it off and pulled off the back panel to examine the security chip the ASP technology team had installed. But the chip was not there.

"Not...possible," Raptor gritted. He put it back in, turned it back on. But there was no message from the ASP. Not a single one. The inbox was blank. Raptor flicked the contacts button. Blank. The memos – blank. Software downloads. Blank. The device had not crashed.

"Idiot!" Raptor growled. "There's no chip because I took the blank!" Exactly what he trained others to avoid, he had done himself. The moment of transition from one cover to the next was the hardest. This was why the rules of extraction required complete seclusion forty-eight hours before a mission: to make sure operators separated cleanly from the invented life. Mind drift was a killer. Today it could be a catastrophe.

It happened because Raptor had not been in seclusion. Far from it. He told himself he was tying things up. He was not. He had just dived back in, to feel what it was to be king. Something that had happened, he tried to tell himself, quite by accident.

He should never have gone to see Lula. There was no way to rationalize it: he had made a massive mistake which now bore consequences. Raptor assessed new facts, drew sharp conclusions.

Fact: his Blackberry was a dummy. Consequence: he could not reach the ASP. Fact: the real Blackberry was in the hands of an innocent. Davenport. Consequence: the ASP would communicate with this innocent. This breach would require containment.

And worse, this fact: the disarming code was written in the live Blackberry. Fact: Raptor needed that code to disarm the vial. Fact: within an hour he would be dead to the world. Consequence: he would need to stay that way. While recovering the code. Or he need not have bothered with any of this at all.

Raptor pulled his ballpoint pen from his pocket. That was when he saw it: across the aisle, one row up, the small man's shirt creased over an inch-wide band around his bicep. Tape. The vial was inside of his upper arm, where it would be protected by the shoulder, ribs and arm, and cushioned in the thicket of his armpit hair.

American Airlines Flight #11 from Boston to Los Angeles lifted off the ground at Logan Airport at 7:59 a.m. on a cloudless day so bright pilots called it "severe clear." Normal ended fourteen minutes later.

CHAPTER 4

THE ASP
8:05 A.M., WASHINGTON D.C.

The Head studied the magazine cover. The Cheshire cat grin.

"He got on the plane then?" said the Head.

"Yes," said the operator.

"The girl? From the coffee shop?"

"He saw her before he left. Spent the night before with her." There was a long pause.

"How much does she know?"

The operator shrugged.

The Head added, "He'll want to come back to her."

"Likely." There was a long sigh. In the background, a woman's voice nagged.

"A moment, please!" shouted the Head, who then said this crisply into the phone: "These are your orders. One: clean up the attachments. Two: make sure nothing would compel Raptor to return to this cover. Three: commence RUPD operation."

"To clarify, the clean-up operation shall begin upon delivery of the vial, per his orders? If I may say so, he has only just boarded. He is not rogue – he is executing," said the operator.

"Begin now," said the Head of the ASP. The line went dead.

CHAPTER 5

CAMILLE
8:30 A.M., NEW YORK, NY

"Don't like elevators?" asked Niko Rhodes, Camille's counterpart in the counterterrorism office in New York. Camille shook her head. Elevators were nearly as bad as planes. "Well, breakfast is worth it at the top. Glad you came to talk to us."

"Thank you for taking it seriously," Camille said. The elevator climbed, stopped to take on more people, climbed again. "My source said it might be late September."

Just then her phone rang. The familiar voice made her freeze. "Milly."

"Yas...yes?" she said. "This is a surprise." It was just a slight correction, but Niko noticed it. That and the way she turned her shoulder to take the call.

Yassir's voice was urgent. "Stay out of the Capitol today. The Pentagon too."

"Today? But you said late September," Camille said.

"Just stay out of the Capitol," Yassir said. "I have to go."

"Well, that's not a problem," Camille said. There was a pause.

"Where are you?" Yassir said.

"In New York. In an elevator on my way to breakfast at Windows on the World."

"Camille," Yassir said. "Listen very carefully. Stop the elevator. Come down as fast as you can. When you get to the street, if you ever cared, do one thing for me."

"What?" Camille's voice shook..

"Run!" he shouted. Then the line went dead.

The elevator climbed. Camille looked at Niko and the panel of round buttons.

CHAPTER 6

HUDSON
8:40 A.M., BOSTON, MA

Hudson was in the pool when it was barely light. As his arms slapped the water and he flipped lazily at the end. His body was on autopilot, his breathing regulated by the four-stroke-one-breath pace, leaving him time to ponder things that floated to mind.

He would wander past Maggie's cube today. Just to say hi.

The deal with XTC. He had three impossible weeks to close a multi-million dollar deal or D6 was in serious trouble. He would be in worse shape. He did not even have a meeting scheduled with a decision maker. It was hopeless. This made him swim harder, beating the water. The chlorine stung his face where Edwin had torn the duct tape off his late day stubble. His shin was purple from the golf ball.

Edwin did not accept failure.

"But it's not realistic," Hudson thought, foundering. "They're never going to close a seven figure deal with us – we're a tiny bug of a company. I need to get with Edwin again."

Hudson put his palms on the pool side and pushed down. The water sucked around him as his hips pulled up out of the water. He showered quickly and toweled off.

The gym was another swanky perk J.D. Sullivan had thrown to Hudson before he had fully earned it. Hudson loved its marble countertops, gourmet coffee and couches covered in sleek blue suede, a direct entrance to the spa, and a laundry service that returned clean clothes to his locker within hours of being used.

Looking in the mirror, Hudson rubbed a towel over his hair, then shook it into place. He glanced at the watch again. 8:46 a.m. He had better hustle to get around the Public Garden and over the bridge to the office in Cambridge before he was too late. Just then his eye caught the Today Show on the flat screen, and Katie Couric pouring sunshine on everyone's morning.

"What a silly haircut," Hudson muttered. "Bangs?" Later, Hudson would think of that moment. How ridiculous to pause on such banality.

The Mercedes coupe tore out of the garage. Hudson was around the Public Garden, making his way toward Cambridge, when the radio announcer said:

"Do you see what I see? Folks, we're watching CNN – maybe the same thing you are. This is really remarkable…apparently a plane has hit the World Trade Center. There's some smoke. We can't really tell how big it was, or what's going on…."."

"Some crazy twin engine pilot taking himself out," Hudson thought.

"Oh my god, there's another one," said the announcer. "People, two planes appear to have hit the World Trade Center buildings in New York. This is no accident."

Hudson imagined the scene – someone planned to shock people, and crashed two Cessnas into the Twin Towers, breaking their wings like birds against thick windows.

Hudson clicked a friend's speed dial. "He works in the World Trade Center. Must have a good look at the action." It was busy. He hit redial twelve times. Busy, busy.

Hudson parked his car in the garage and trotted to the building. Flashed his security badge and poked the elevator button for the top floor, where Edwin worked. He dreaded looking like the loser but Edwin said to call him in whenever he needed him. And he was at a loss. He could not bring in XTC. Not by himself.

Edwin's office door was closed and dark. Nancy's computer was on. Edwin's schedule was open. Hudson glanced at the calendar to see if there was an opening in Edwin's schedule. He saw a flight number and time.

"Damn," Hudson muttered. "He's going to California today. I'll call in six hours when he lands." Hudson took the stairs down to his floor. His office line was ringing.

"Thank goodness you're answering the phone. It's Henry Senback from XTC."

"Hi Henry," Hudson said hopefully. "Ready to take a meeting with our CTOs?"

"You should call your family," Henry said.

Hudson frowned. "Why's that?"

"You've seen the news?"

"Something about a plane hitting the World Trade Center?"

"Two planes," Henry said. "They were 767s out of Boston."

"767s?" Hudson gasped. These were no sparrows breaking their necks on windows. These were long haul jets; giant planes with full tanks. The numbers "767" showed on the emergency cards in the seat pockets on so many flights Hudson had been on himself: the "nerd-birds" tech executives took back and forth between the coasts.

Hudson shuddered. "Oh, God. Someone's on that flight." A D6 sales person, an engineer, customer service rep? He doubted there was a single day that no one from their company flew to California. Just three weeks ago he and the new account manager for XTC, Walker Green, had flown out and back in less than 24 hours. On 767s.

"Glad it's not you buddy." Henry said. Hudson put down the phone.

"Hey," Walker said, holding himself up against the cube wall. His face usually broke into a broad smile, but today he looked flat, pale, spent. Like he had had a rough night.

"Hey, did you hear?" Hudson said. "767s — those are the California flights."

"I was just up on the executive floor," said Walker, his voice monotonous. "I heard some stuff....I don't know...it's not good, man."

"What?" Hudson demanded. "Who?"

"They think....Edwin. On the first one. And Jameson."

"What? Edwin? And Jameson?"? Hudson sank in his chair.

Walker opened CNN.com. "A plane hit the Pentagon too. Another crashed in the woods in Pennsylvania. We're under attack. Where's it going to end?"

They stared in silence at the screen that showed the burning towers. There were long gaps in the reporters' comments. It was nearly 10:00 a.m. when the thick cloud gave up plumes of smoke that streamed in all directions. The fire set by full tanks of jet fuel had melted the steel girders. When one floor collapsed, it displaced weight on the ones below, causing each to fail in rapid succession. Over a hundred stories of concrete, glass and plaster let go one by one, like stacked plates. Twenty-nine minutes later the North Tower fell.

"The Towers are...gone," Hudson gasped. That Edwin and Jameson had gone into one of them did not compute. "I'm going to see what's going on."

Hudson took the internal stairs up to the executive floor. Maggie would know. Hudson was struck by how much he wanted to see her. He pressed his hip to the security plaque, his wallet badge disengaging the doors. Hudson pushed through them.

The executive floor was usually a hub of activity. It was silent.

Hudson reached Maggie's cube. Empty. No purse, no running shoes. Her computer was not on. The phone looked slightly off its hook. Jameson's office was dark.

Another day, Hudson would have boasted about making a woman sleep through her alarm. Not this day. Not this terrible day.

As he rounded the corner he saw Nancy pressing into the door frame of the COO's office. She was pale. They had known since the first report.

Michael James, the COO, spotted Hudson. "You haven't heard from Edwin, have you? Get any messages on your Blackberry? Or from Jameson?"

The COO's affect was flat. He would divulge no fear or rumor to the troops until they had the facts. His own response would go into a box, pushed down until a private time. He had come to work as the diligent COO, navigating the leadership vectors of Jameson and Edwin. Now their vacuum pulled him into the center.

The General Counsel moved briskly from James's office back to his to build the list of unpleasant to-dos, such as notify the insurance company within twenty-four hours that the Loss of Key Personnel provision had been triggered and D6 was entitled to receive two million dollars. But no amount of money could do what Edwin did. No cash could drive hundreds of employees to do what was necessary to make D6 survive. This would be wind down money.

"Where is Maggie?" asked the COO. "Hudson. Find her." Young employees brought energy and enthusiasm, and their own developing concept of professionalism. Today, James found her tardiness intolerable.

Hudson nodded and turned away. He was walking down the hall back to the sales floor when his phone rang. When he saw the number, he felt a wave of comfort. Then it retreated.

"Hi Mom," he said.

"Oh, thank God," said Grace Davenport. She was crying softly, not something Hudson could remember hearing before. "Is everyone else okay? What does Jameson say?"

"I, uh," he said. "I'm not sure. There might be some bad news coming, Mom."

"Who?" she said sadly. Hudson had little air to say this.

"They think Edwin. And Jameson. They were traveling together this morning."

Silence hung on the line. "No, no," Grace whispered. "Oh, I'm so, so sorry." Hudson could hear sniffs jerking out of her as she tried to quiet the sobs.

"I know," Hudson said. "Let me call you back when we know for sure."

He hit speed dial. "Dad? Is it true?" A board member, Sterling would have been the first person Michael James called.

"Hi, son," his father said. His tone rose and fell, apologetically. "I'm afraid so. The flight manifesto just confirmed Edwin got on the plane."

"Jameson too? He was going with him," said Hudson. "And no one has seen him."

"The airlines are still confirming that," Sterling said. "But it doesn't look good. You haven't gotten any messages from Edwin or Jameson, have you?"

"No," said Hudson, feeling the Blackberry at his side. Just a "piece of plastic from China."

"I'm driving back from D.C.," Sterling said. "All flights are grounded. Rental cars were almost out. Come home tonight, Hudson. It would be good for everyone."

"Yeah, maybe, Dad. I'll call you a little later," Hudson said. It was his father who had asked. But he wanted to be with his friends. People who knew Edwin like he did. People who hadn't seen shaking trauma before, who were all dipped in the fear that the world would never right itself.

Hudson walked down the hallway, past Edwin's closed door. The light was off. Sunlight streamed in showing shafts of dust. The shelves were empty. The desk was spotless. Several cardboard boxes, flaps up, sat at awkward angles on the floor.

"What a time for spring cleaning,". thought Hudson. "It's almost like he knew." His mind went to the plane. All the people on it. Jameson.

Through a conference window, Hudson glimpsed a television. Edwin's corporate photo flashed, followed by the next victim's headshot. His eyes flooded, and he bolted to the fire escape. Edwin was not family. Edwin would not even count him as a friend. But he built things with him. Every day was bigger because Edwin stretched its edges.

The global tragedy of the day unfolded at a distance – shocking, frightening, disorienting, crushing. But the fact that someone who moved him – and everyone around him – had been cut down in it was scorching. The logic did not process.

When Hudson stepped on the stairs, he saw a small form bent over his knees on the flight below. His dark head was dipped low. Ahmed turned up at the noise. The older man's eyes were red. Hudson stepped away and retreated through the fire door. In a few minutes he returned, his hands full of cold pizza, chips and Mountain Dew. The fire door clanged as he walked down the half flight of stairs. Ahmed moved his knee. Hudson put the pizza on the platform at their feet and sat on the step with him. Then Ahmed let forth a cry, bestial, guttural. The sound bounced off the hollow cement shaft. Hudson put his head in his hands and shook.

"Suffer together." Edwin's words came back to Hudson. This could not have been how he had meant them.

"How could Edwin be gone?" Hudson said. "How could he just have been snuffed out like that? He was action; he was willpower; he was force, forward motion. Possibility."

Poof.

Ahmed drew his sleeve across his eyes, cleared his throat.

"Do you think he knew?" Hudson said softly. "On the plane, while it was happening?" He imagined Edwin momentarily confused, then calculating his response. Wondering where the hijackers would land to demand their ransom. The impact.

"All I know for certain is this," said Ahmed. "Our friend would have been absolutely the last person on this earth whom these murderers would have wanted to encounter." They sat together, the cement stairwell magnifying their rough breathing.

"I suppose I should go check in on the system," Ahmed said listlessly. "It's getting a historic load today." He gripped Hudson's shoulder, then trudged up the stairs.

Hudson sat on the step alone. It was easier to stay cocooned in the cement and metal hallway. Eventually he thought of Maggie. He had to get in touch with her before the COO saw him again. He stood up and walked down to the executive floor.

"If I call from Jameson's number, she'll have to pick up," Hudson thought. The light in her cube was still off. Hudson pushed aside her chair, grabbed the phone. It was slightly ajar and the line was dead. But after he jiggled the hook, it refreshed the dial tone. He glanced at the number stored in his mobile phone and dialed. No answer.

"Where is she?" said an irritated voice. "Haven't been able to reach her all day."

On the other side of the cube wall stood Jameson Callaghan.

"It's been a ridiculous morning. Someone slashed my tires, every single one. I missed my flight. My phone battery died. Taxi driver would not stop talking on his phone. I couldn't make out a word. Where the hell is she? I need to book another flight."

"Jameson," gasped Hudson. Then he yelled down the hall. "Michael! Jameson is here!"

The COO sprinted down the hall. "Thank God!" said Michael. "Four planes were taken...two from Boston hit the World Trade Center...your plane."

"My plane?" Jameson said. "But Edwin was supposed to be on that plane, too."

Hudson's lips drew in tight. Michael said it. "He was."

Similar experiences cluster along a neural pathway in the brain. The neurons that process a death once will do so again. Jameson was suddenly swamped by backed-up grief.

Belle's cooling cheek. Walking down the antiseptic hallway, hating the flicker of relief. Opening the door to a world where all he had was his perch near the top of SAC. Until two weeks later he broke his crown. And now Edwin, this incredibly brilliant force of nature, had been taken too. Jameson surged with survivor's adrenaline, hating himself again.

"I need a minute," he said, and closed his door on the empty cube.

CHAPTER 7

He was still sitting with her when the sky pinked. He put one of his rugs on her. She looked a little blue. The man wrapped in tattered layers had never seen a runner take such a long nap. She had not moved since the evil wizard had left her. Then, in the full light of day, the skies went quiet. The evil wizard's spell. Nothing could roar.

Officer Norton received a call shortly after 9 a.m. from HQ asking him to walk the Esplanade. The active forces were suddenly posted under bridges, in the tunnels, by the T stations, courthouses and in the foyers of large office buildings.

"It's been a bad day, Mr. Squibbs," Officer Norton said to the ragged man staring at the ground. He continued, knowing there would be no response. "Perhaps there's peace in being so lost. Can't see the real monsters." The struggling man's unwashed hair was crushed under his hat. His dark layers were crusted molds on his body. Norton guessed he was about forty-five, but the last decade had cost him double.

Then the officer heard a new sound. Mr. Squibbs' unused voice caught and skipped on the words. "The evil wizard was here. I put my rug on her after."

Officer Norton followed Squibbs' grimy finger until he saw the body of a young woman who had been dead for several hours. The policeman jumped up. "Did you see who did this?"

Mr. Squibbs leapt up too, snapping his right arm. "The evil wizard!" Then he bolted. He was gone before the dispatcher answered Officer Norton's page.

Police headquarters was in a frenzy that morning. Captain Brath assembled his officers. The group, some ex-military, sat forward, flexing to fight the war that struck from their airport that morning.

"It's fucking World War Three," one officer said.

"All I know is, one of them camel jockeys fucking crosses my path I'm going kill 'em myself," said another.

"Okay, folks, listen up," Captain Brath began. His face was pale. "We don't know what more is coming. It's going to take everyone at their best not just today, but tomorrow, and for the foreseeable future, to keep Boston safe. We're waking up in a new war today. And we still have all the old ones. Like a girl shows up dead on the Esplanade this morning," Captain Brath told his officers. "Marly and Peters – go check this out. It may not be fighting terror, but maybe there's a link – keep all options open." Brath could count on Christine Marly. He respected how she packed away the law degree for a gun. She made the rest of his guys nervous but Peters seemed to like her. "The rest of you – Boston needs all you got. Don't forget there's a whole lot of Bostonians out there, doctors in the hospitals, taking care of your sick mothers, moms taking their kids to school, who got hit three times today. Someone attacked their country, hijacked their religion, and made everyone look at them like they did it. You're here to protect their rights too. So go find the right criminals and rip their fucking throats out. You know what I mean. Okay, let's go."

Officer Norton was still sitting with the body when Marly and Peters arrived.

"I haven't touched it," he said. "A homeless man found her but he got scared and ran."

"Is he the perp?" asked Detective Marly.

Officer Norton shook his head. "Doubt it. He waited with her and showed me. Then he took off. He just doesn't want to be around people. But he saw something. Kept talking about the 'evil wizard.' I'm sorry – it was either him or the crime scene."

Marly looked at the body. She tried to see through the blue lips and grey skin to imagine the face flush with oxygen. Her hair was dark brown, tied in a ponytail. Probably what the guy used to take her down. Marly pulled on latex gloves and plucked a thin folded cell phone from the victim's jacket. She pressed a button and heard:

"Hi, you've reached Maggie Rice. Please leave me a message."

"We'll be very interested to know who did," Marly said.

Willows blew relaxed breezes across the Charles River. The green way shielded pedestrians, geese and the homeless from the unending pulse of traffic on Storrow Drive. What was strange today was the silence. Without air traffic the sky sounded like the country, clear, uncluttered.

"Why do they jog at night?" said Marly. "Pumped up on Destiny's Child, deaf to footsteps falling too close. This guy loved getting away with it but he'll hate that no one noticed, with everything else today. I bet he tries again. Soon."

CHAPTER 8

HUDSON
10:30 A.M., CAMBRIDGE, MA

Jameson cleared his throat. Shell-shocked faces gathered in the recreation area. The ping pong tables were folded and pushed back by the free vending machines. The national tragedy, the towers, the Pentagon, the plane in Pennsylvania – these losses were remote roars in ears muffled by cupped hands. He had to address the unspeakable loss of Edwin. His own brush with the same fate. But for the reckless act of some hooligan, Jameson would have been at the gate half an hour early as usual, covering three or four papers while he sipped a cup of coffee. He pictured the business class section of a 767; two aisles separating three seating sections, the fully reclining blue pleather seats. Would he like orange juice or champagne before takeoff? When would he have realized something was terribly wrong? When did Edwin?

Jameson had to start speaking. His throat felt swollen. "We have lost someone so special. He showed everyone he encountered – including me – how to make things happen: new things, hard things, things others called impossible. When others turned away, he busted through. He made each one of us find new definitions of possible."

Jameson could not stop the quiver shaking his voice. He did not care.

"Nothing could be worse for D6 than losing him. None of us can do anything about that." He blinked away tears. "But there are some losses we do not have to concede. Now, while we grieve, it is up to us – each one of us – to make our part in this company happen. We can save what he created. We can build what he envisioned. Right now Edwin's company, his dream, faces extreme challenges. Each of you is the keeper of his legacy and his lesson. Just like he showed us. Remember his focus; let it guide you. Let his passion drive you. We will recover; we will make his company survive. Every day, we will come to work and honor him with the absolute best each one of us can summon. And then do better. This starts now. We are behind." Then following Edwin's first principle of leadership, Jameson walked back to his office to work.

Many companies closed their offices to allow employees space to adjust to the horrors of September 11. But Jameson knew work was exactly where most people at D6 would want to be, as they learned how devastating and confusing it is to lose a colleague, especially Edwin. Not family or personal friends, grieving for a colleague has no recognized space. D6 employees would want to be close to Edwin as they had known him; close to others who had known him in a similar way. He thought of how startling it would feel to these young people to confront – at the loss of them – the tightness of the bond they shared with someone they worked with every day to make new things happen together. They were creative partners; they were a team. They were the wheels on a bus, the frame, the drive train. If the driver suddenly disappears, the bus careens into a ditch. Edwin left a hole that just might suck them all down it. He led so many of D6's missions. He did not just sit in the boardroom. Jameson recalled more than one time when Edwin had stood on the table. When he had wrestled board members to the grey flecked carpet. How he forced conflict to reveal underlying issues and then solved them. Jameson tried to think about how his management team would realign so D6 would survive. His job was to absorb uncertainty; his responsibilities had just exploded. But this day, in the privacy of his office, he wept.

Hudson slumped at his desk. He clicked on his inbox. The friends and family who never knew Edwin didn't really understand. But literally hundreds of emails from colleagues in other firms came in. People he and Edwin had called on together. The team of developers from XTC sent flowers. Negotiations paused; suspicions fell. It was an email memorial service.

Small groups huddled, talking in low voices about where they were, what they were doing. The hope that somehow Edwin had not been on that plane was deflating. They measured the new reality: the light in the corner office on the engineering floor would not come back on. That whiteboard would not host another meeting.

Hudson typed the words "unspeakable loss...he was an amazing person...thank you" for yet another time. He had just clicked "reply" when he felt an unfamiliar buzz on his hip. He reached for his phone in his belt holster. But that was not ringing.

Zzzzzz. Zzzzzz. The pulsing continued. Hudson's fingers felt along his belt for the other Blackberry. The one Edwin had given him. The inert piece of plastic from China, which Hudson wore like a black armband.

But something was wrong. The piece of plastic from China was buzzing.

Hudson saw a new message on it; he clicked it. A high pitched whistle screeched. Abruptly Hudson dropped the device clattering on the desk. Then he snatched it. The screen was illuminated, the time correct. September 11, 10:52 a.m.

"Edwin must have picked up the wrong Blackberry," Hudson said. "Wow, he must have been pissed." Not that it mattered now. He felt the clanging discord, trying to apply the mundane frustrations of the living to the nothingness where Edwin now existed. These were the hits that pounded unacceptable new facts into defiant, grieving minds.

Hudson flicked the inbox button. It did not feel like prying; it felt like trying to reach him. Edwin@D6.com used to bark emails late at night urging one flank or another of this little fighting company to march faster, take that mountain, leap from that edge. Edwin@D6.com said "Make it happen." Edwin@D6.com was still live on the network until someone in IT would have the task of removing it.

"Just one more message from Edwin@D6.com," Hudson whispered. "Please."

At the top of the email list, there now was a second new message in bold black letters. But the sender was identified by a string of unintelligible characters. The subject line also was garbled.

Hudson clicked it. Again, the piercing whistle stung like he had tried to leave a department store without paying. Hudson stared at the Blackberry on the desk. Then he picked it up again. He pressed his thumbs on keys. Three words, calling out in the dark.

"Where are you?" Hudson hit reply. Then he watched the inbox. But there was no response. That was what ached.

Until a moment later the Blackberry buzzed with another new message. Again the subject and sender were a mishmash of letters and numbers and symbols. There was a pause. Then a fourth message came in. Each one was scrambled, and whistled alarmingly when Hudson clicked it.

Hudson felt like he had walked in on a private, but important, conversation. The strange messages spun in his brain as if they would eventually fall into the right places.

They rested here: someone was communicating with Edwin as if they expected him to be alive. As if he were. Hudson had a flicker of hope. But then he remembered. No. It had been he, Hudson, who had answered their ping. Not Edwin. The news had just not reached everyone he knew, not yet. It was all just a sad mix up.

Hudson returned to his own emails on his computer monitor. One came from Norton Figby, Edwin's old roommate.

To: Hudson@D6.com
From: figby@figbyworld.com
That which does not kill you makes you stronger. We will all be stronger. A terrible loss. He was quite smart.

"Quite smart? He was a genius, Jackass," Hudson muttered. Even in Edwin's death, Norton Figby found a need to point out that he was the stronger one.

"What's that?" said Walker, popping his head over the cube wall.

"Weird email from a weird guy," said Hudson, pushing back his chair.

"Want company?" Walker asked, but he did not pick up his cane.

Hudson shook his head. His eyes stayed down, filling. Anything could start him off. The kind gesture of a friend. Normally crying at work would be professional suicide. Today red eyes were everywhere.

"I'll call you if anything happens," said Walker quietly. "Go take your time."

It was already 11:00 a.m. when Hudson walked out of the building to the local coffee shop. Uniformed guards and policemen marked every visible entrance to a hotel, business, and MIT research facility. There would be a black and white posted on each end of the Salt and Pepper bridge linking Cambridge to Boston.

Hudson entered the Cambridge Coffee House. It reminded him of a trip to Seattle a few months earlier with Edwin, who had ordered a very large cup of black coffee, adding four packets of sugar.

"I love sugar," Edwin had said. "I live on it."

"How many of those do you have? A day?"

"You mean in 24 hours?" asked Edwin. Hudson nodded. "About 8. But I only need 3-4 hours of sleep each night. It's all mind over matter. Your physical body can do anything your mind tells it to. I've run seventy miles without stopping, with an eighty pound pack on my back. When your feet start to bleed in your boots, you just tell your mind to push through it. Your body does what it's told."

"Seventy miles? What summer camp did you go to?" Hudson laughed.

"I did it twice," Edwin said.

Now, Hudson blew steam from his very large cup. With four sugars, the swill was much too sweet for him. He sat back in the seat and studied Edwin's Blackberry. He fiddled with the scrolling button, highlighting the inbox icon, memos, contacts. He clicked on the calendar.

What had Edwin done before he died? What would he miss? His days had been chock full in July and August.

Then Hudson began to walk. He walked down Main Street, over the bridge into Boston. He was not exactly sure what he was doing, but he needed to move. He turned right down Charles Street, barely noticing the shops. People walked by in similar dazes, the few who were out on the streets at all. Most were inside, huddling.

Hudson turned down Chestnut Street back toward the river. He found himself standing outside Edwin's apartment. Today's paper sat on the stoop. Edwin would have left for the airport just before it landed. Tomorrow's would have a picture of him.

Hudson's shoes scraped the steps. He peered through the bay window. What he saw in Edwin's apartment sucked air from him like a vacuum. There were six boxes on the floor. Taped shut. There were loose, round full trash bags leaking curls of paper that had been ground through a paper shredder. There was nothing on the walls.

"Yesterday, Edwin packed up his office," Hudson said. He had seen it. He had watched him kiss the thesis and put it in a box. "Then he packed up his house too?"

Hudson stumbled back down the steps. He ran from the quiet cobblestone street at full speed until he was safely back among the retailers and traffic of Charles Street. He took some deep breaths. His head was pounding. The CVS down the block would have Tylenol, and water to dilute the coffee and sugar in his bloodstream. What was going on?

The clerk was trying to get the attention of a homeless man shuffling in the back of the shop near the coolers.

Hudson threw an extra dollar on the counter. "For him."

"That's cool, man," said the clerk. He looked at Hudson again, pointed to his jacket. Hudson was wearing today, like every day, the corporate schwag – a blue fleece jacket with D6's white logo.

"Hey, wasn't that guy on the plane?" the clerk said. It never dawned on him that a curiosity to him was a sharp stick in another's eye.

"Yeah," said Hudson. "The founder. It's a big loss."

The clerk nodded. "Weird. He was just in here buying lot of stuff too."

Hudson turned back to the clerk. "Like what?"

"You know, like one minute he's here, the next he's not...weird."

"No – what did he buy?" Hudson gripped the counter.

"Oh," said the clerk. "Let's see...he got some alcohol gauze pads. Crazy Glue, and a whole bunch of duct tape. Maybe had a big leak? And a bunch of sugar packets."

"Thanks," said Hudson. So Edwin had bought alcohol wipes, crazy glue, duct tape. Things to repair wounds. Things to repair anything. Things to tie people up with.

Hudson needed food. He stopped at a pizza place to sit down and think this through. He had to put the paranoia back in its box. He had just bit into the hot cheese of his first slice when again he felt buzzing. But this time it was his own Blackberry. He wiped his greasy fingers on his jeans. There was a new email, from a woman he did not know.

From: Lula Crosse
To: HDavenport@D6.com
Subject: URGENT
Hang on to the POPC, slacker. At all costs.

"POPC?" muttered Hudson. "What the?" What strange code had he stumbled on? Who was Lula Crosse? Why was she calling him a slacker?

Hudson knew only one person in the world who called anyone "slacker." He did it a lot. He had done it when he gave Hudson the piece of plastic. Piece Of Plastic from China.

Hudson felt cold. He typed a message with his thumbs.

"Is it you?"

No message came back.

CHAPTER 9

KAH
7: 40 P.M., KABUL, AFGHANISTAN

Reception was best in the small chamber near the top of the mountain. But the stone walls reflected the electric pulses from the computers, television and glaring lights, reverberating white noise. It made a tense duty even more jarring.

These three men could not hear the cheering in the Media Room. They monitored the job, checking every fact against the databases, including the hack into Interpol, cell phone networks and other data sources, to make sure there had been no interference. They would know soon if the mission had succeeded.

A young man scribbled the names as he watched the scrolling headshots of smiling, unaware victims. Another took the list and typed.

"Hey," he muttered. The other man looked up. "This is strange." A database appeared showing hundreds of pairs of numbers. As he watched, more pairs of numbers appeared every five seconds. He flicked a series of keys, and the database reshaped into a graphic image. It showed a map of a city where streets met at jagged corners. A thick, dark line unwound toward the city, the ocean blotting around it.

A bright green dot flashed near the center of the city. As they watched, the dot continued moving. It passed through a green space, down a straight road, across the dark line where it turned off the road and came to a stop a few blocks from the river.

The door to the chamber opened. Khalid al Hamzami entered; a host inspecting the kitchen for a whiff of the feast. CNN would serve his dish live in less than twenty-four hours.

"So?" he said. "Are we on track?"

"We may have a problem," said the senior monitor, blinking fast, holding a paper.

Al Hamzami snatched it. His mouth tightened behind his whiskers.

The cost in time and treasure. The failure. The humiliation. This was to be his moment. It was to be his time to ascend. But now it would be none of those things.

"Someone has betrayed me," al Hamzami said through clenched jaws.

"It's unclear," offered the man. "This could just be a coincidence. A mix-up."

Al Hamzami looked again at the sheet in his hand. There was a name on it. He closed his eyes and shook his head slowly. It was the name of a businessman, one of the first casualties the news reported. But when matched to databases, the name matched an alias of a man with a much different profile. A man who certainly could interfere.

Which is why it gave Khalid al Hamzami great concern that according to the telephone company network database, the handheld email device registered to this particular businessman was not in a pile of rubble in lower Manhattan. It was instead moving steadily along a street called Charles, across a river, into a city labeled Cambridge.

"Get him!" he seethed. "Get my vial back."

Then Khalid al Hamzami picked up one of the cell phones from the tray that held a dozen of them loaded with international minutes, prepaid in cash. He dialed a long string of numbers.

A young man's voice answered, "Hello, Uncle."

CHAPTER 10

MARLY
11:50 A.M., BOSTON, MA

Marly peered over the shoulder of a Crime Scene Investigation technician. They had lifted several sets of fingerprints from Maggie's apartment. One matched a profile.

"Hudson Davenport," Marly said. "Good looking, used to taking what he wants?"

"He's got a DUI four years ago....let's see....what else....oooh. Here's something interesting," said the technician, reading from a file.

On the screen was a second offense on the record of Hudson Davenport. Two years ago, a Mandy Edwards had brought an accusation of rape against him. He pled not guilty but before the trial began the charges were dropped. But not before the DA had collected DNA samples from him that lived on in the government's database.

Just then the DNA technician appeared. "We have a semen match."

"Let me guess," said Marly. "Davenport."

The technician nodded. "Perfect match."

"Let's go," said Peters, his hand feeling for his gun. They sprinted to the car, on their way to 391 Marlborough Street in the Back Bay neighborhood of Boston. Marly was three paces ahead.

CHAPTER 11

HUDSON
12:00 P.M., BOSTON, MA

"You are nuts," Hudson said to himself. "It's not like he was the only person in the history of the world to call someone a slacker." Hudson could not go back to the office. He would not be able to keep from saying he thought Edwin had emailed him. People would think he was absolutely crazy. It would be cruel to raise their hopes with what he recognized were only his. He headed for home on Marlborough Street, lined on either side with expensive brownstones fronted by small patches of garden with thick shrubs and perfect small flower beds behind wrought iron fences.

The rhododendrons in particular made excellent lookouts. Their canopies of long oval leaves let the two men in dark hooded sweatshirts stand upright two feet from Davenport's steps. They watched the GPS beacon move toward them – it was very close now. One peered out from behind the seven foot tall shrub at 391 Marlborough St.

As he neared his apartment, Hudson was aware of a pair of footsteps jogging behind him. He did not think much of it. Then he sensed movement near his back – too close. He turned sharply. Someone grabbed his arm and twisted it behind him. Steel rings cuffed his hands, spun him around to stare into the striking blue eyes of a fierce woman with spiky black hair. And a gun.

117

"Hudson Davenport? You are under arrest for the murder of Margaret Rice," Officer Marly said. She noticed the suspect was even better looking than his mug shot.

"The what?" said Hudson, shocked. "Maggie? Is dead?"

"You have the right to remain silent. Anything you say can and will be held against you in a court of law. You are entitled to an attorney. If you cannot afford one, one will be provided for you." Peters recited the Miranda warnings, pushing his palm on the suspect's head to stuff him in the backseat of the patrol car.

For the next ten minutes, Hudson tried to block out the whip of a siren that never faded. The steel handcuffs cut into his wrists, pinching hard as the squad car jerked through gaps in the midday traffic on the uneven city streets of Boston. Then he was being processed at police headquarters. This was a place Hudson had never, ever wanted to see again, yet here he was. Mug shot. Fingerprints. His belongings in a bag, out of his control, on some open shelf behind the locked cage. Hudson shuddered. The piece of plastic from China – whatever it meant – was out of his hands.

Hours passed. Hudson sat on the bench, waiting for someone to come get him out of trouble. Somehow, it had found him again.

Eventually he was taken to an interview room. The only sound was the buzzing of the fluorescent lights. Eventually, the pretty cop with the fierce glare spoke.

"Mr. Davenport. When did you first meet Margaret...Maggie Rice?"

Just looking at him made Marly seethe. He reminded her of every privileged jerk who carried himself with the easy physicality of one who knew his body would always help him. The Alpha who used his gifts to serve his own pleasure, relishing what others offered, giving back nothing but gratitude. Never measuring the deficit. She liked seeing him shift uncomfortably on the metal chair. She liked being the one who put him there.

Hudson started to respond. He wanted to get out of there and get back his possessions. The Blackberry.

"Shouldn't...shouldn't I have a lawyer?" Hudson asked, an awkward smile passing over his lips. He couldn't help it. Smiling had always moved obstacles for him.

Marly misinterpreted it. "Is this jerk trying to flirt?" she thought. She said, "It's up to you. You want a lawyer, this whole thing stops now. You go back to the holding cell and we all wait for him. Or, you tell us what happened and maybe we let you go right now." A thin smile spread across her lips, but it did not reach her eyes.

Hudson thought, Dad'll kill me. But I have to get it back. The Blackberry. He said, "She's the CEO's assistant at D6. The daughter of a friend of my father's."

"When did you last see her?"

"Last night...this morning actually," he said, a smile escaping. "Early."

"What time?" Marly said. She forced a beat between each word.

"I was with her Monday night from about 8 p.m. until like 2 a.m. or something. We had a couple drinks, she asked me back to her apartment, and one thing led to another."

"This is the part you better be specific about," said Marly.

"Okay, if you like that kind of thing," Hudson grinned lightheartedly. Levity worked in the schoolyard, on a sales call. Not in police custody.

Marly looked like she had taken a hit. Fury built behind her eyes. "You think this is funny," Marly said. Suddenly Hudson felt embarrassed.

"No...no," Hudson said. "I'm sorry. It was a joke. I joke when I'm stressed."

"Then you're going to be a laugh riot from here on," Marly said drily.

"Okay. We went to her place, took our clothes off and had sex," he said, knowing he shouldn't grin but unable to stop. "Consensual. Well, I guess I was okay with it all."

The detective was not amused. This was one woman Hudson could not get to respond to him. Which intrigued him. He studied her spiky hair and crisp blue eyes.

Hudson loved being liked. The feedback system was so satisfying he had become an expert at getting people – particularly women – to feel good about themselves. But every now and then he would meet a woman who just detested him on the spot. Like Officer Christine Marly. It put him on edge, which fascinated him. He did not know how to deal with her, so he kept talking.

"So I left about two in the morning or something and went back to the office."

"Anyone prove that?" Marly asked.

"Yeah – I was meeting with...." He trailed off. Marly noticed his spine slump.

"With who?"

"Edwin Hoff," Hudson said softly.

"Can we speak with him?" Marly noted the way Hudson deflated.

Hudson shook his head slowly. "He...he was...he was on Flight #11."

Marly's eyebrows shot up. "I'm sorry for your loss." She watched his eyes fill with tears. Eventually she had to ask the follow up. "Did anyone else see you there?"

"No," said Hudson. The scope of his problem began to dawn on him. "But I was there until like 2:30 a.m. Or 3:00. You can check the access tags at D6."

"We will," Marly said. "So what happened to Miss Rice later that evening?"

"When I was leaving she was wearing running gear. Maybe she went for a run?"

Now he's putting her at the scene, thought Marly. She did not like Hudson Davenport. Not one bit. More than other suspects, Davenport got under her skin with his quicksilver charm and gifted looks. He stirred her up. She wanted to take him down.

Marly's phone buzzed. She answered it, and leapt quickly to her feet.

"Can I go?" asked Hudson from across the table.

"Sure, of course," said Marly, staring at him with cold eyes. "Post a million-dollar bond and you're free as a bird." Her chair scraped back and she was gone.

Hudson's fingers felt slick against the edge of the metal table.

The police evidence room held boxes of tagged items, side by side, bearing silent witness to crimes committed or the innocence of the accused. All but one. On the third shelf of the sixth row, a thick plastic bag muffled the buzzing of a small object.

Detective Peters had just chaperoned a suspicious gun from ballistics back to its temporary home on aisle six when the buzzing caught his ear. He saw the tag:

Victim: *Margaret Rice*
Personal Effects: *Suspect Hudson Davenport*

"The Esplanade girl," said Peters. "So who needs to reach Davenport so badly?"

Peters reached for a glove, then picked up the Blackberry. Pushed the button. A sharp whistle split the silence in the evidence room.

"What the?" he looked closely at the Blackberry. Just then his phone rang.

It was Marly. "Mr. Squibbs was just spotted on Charles Street, near the CVS."

Peters stuffed the Blackberry back in the bag and broke for the door.

CHAPTER 12

CAMILLE
2:00 P.M., NEW JERSEY TURNPIKE

Her finger could not hold the contact lens steady. But she had to rinse them. The ash got everywhere. Camille peered in the mirror of the gas station restroom. Her hair was dusty grey. It was like washing thin wet clay off her face.

Earlier, out on the street, Camille was feeling stupid for pushing the button. Then the belly of the plane flew over them. She pulled Niko's sleeve. They ran. They were out of range when the jet fuel fell down the elevator shaft, exploding into a fireball in the lobby. When the black clouds of smoke and paper and dust and ash bellowed up the avenues and caught them, Niko yanked off his tie to cover his mouth with his shirt collar.

The cab had appeared out of nowhere on the New Jersey side of the George Washington Bridge. They were exhausted after running for twenty blocks then walking the length of Manhattan and across the George Washington Bridge. The view was horrid. Smoke hid Lower Manhattan. It was creeping up the island.

At the gas station Niko stayed in the taxi while Camille used the restroom. He dialed a number. Most lines were jammed. Only secure ones went through.

"Safe," he said. "I was with Henderson – yes in the Tower – in the fucking elevator! Because she booked the breakfast there – with a lot of our counterterrorism officers…. She got a call at 8:36….They're….gone….But someone gave her a head start."

That night, Niko met with the deputy director of the CIA, Orson Lowndes.. "It's horrific to find it in our own," said Niko.

"We were so close!" growled Lowndes, smashing his fist on the desk. "Get her to admit it. By whatever means necessary. Then make sure this traitor never smells fresh pine again unless it's coming out of the bottle she's using to clean the johns at Supermax!"

CHAPTER 13

HUDSON
4:00 P.M., BOSTON, MA

It was the second time Sterling Davenport had stood at that desk with a cashier's check that could have been the down payment on a second mansion. But Hudson had slept with the wrong girl. Again. Sterling had begun working on mitigation measures after he received Hudson's panicked call three hours earlier. He was driving a rental car back to Boston from D.C. From New Jersey he saw the thick clouds of silent smoke drifting over the spine of a skyline he no longer recognized.

The metal bars clanged. Hudson stood flanked by guards. A man in a dark blue uniform approached. "Davenport? This your stuff?" His eyes were red around the edges, his fingers thick between the knuckles. Inside the clear bag, Hudson could see the black plastic square and his black leather wallet.

"Let me see that," said the desk clerk, taking the bag.

"It's okay...I can see it's all there," said Hudson. His eyes were on the Blackberry. "Just...please. May I have it?"

The clerk eyed him. Then she reached for the bag. One by one, she pulled out each item and placed a check mark on the sheet on her clipboard.

"Three hundred twenty, forty, sixty," she licked her thumb and made another stack. "Four hundred seventeen dollars. Lotta cash to be carrying around, Mister. What on earth is this?" she said, pinching Edwin's Blackberry.

"Nothing. It's just a thing," Hudson said quickly. Too quickly.

"Uh huh," she said dubiously. She flipped it over and saw the white tape with two words scribbled on it. "You Edwin Hoff?"

Hudson tried to stay calm. "No. He gave it to me." The clerk was unimpressed.

"Buncha cash, someone else's gizmo – we'll get you eventually," she said, reluctantly handing Hudson the bag.

He clipped the Blackberry to his belt and stuffed the wallet in his back pocket, and by 4:00 p.m., walked down the steps of police headquarters toward Sterling's rental car. The day was expiring; shadows fell long and surprisingly early in the late afternoon.

"Did they keep your watch?" Sterling asked.

"I didn't put it on this morning," was all Hudson said. "Dad, I–"

Sterling put up a hand. "Wait till the car."

Police departments are full of unfolding dramas. Like most people, the Davenports were consumed with their own. They did not notice the three agitated policemen who had surrounded two men in sweatshirts at the base of the stairs.

The men had dark hair and dark features. Both wore beards two inches longer than the close American fashion. They were pulling out wallets, producing identification.

The doors of Sterling's rental thumped shut.

Released, the two bearded men walked past the police station. They turned a corner. Out of view, the two men watched their GPS beacon begin to move. It tracked west, to the other side of the Boston Common, to Marlborough Street, to the exact spot where they had been watching, beneath the leaves, when the police snatched Edwin Hoff and his Blackberry – the one that was supposed to be in a pile of rubble 120 miles south.

Hudson stared at his father. He needed to explain. It had all gone so wrong.

"Dad, I had nothing to do with this," Hudson blurted.

"I know," said Sterling. "Poor girl. So what happened?"

"She called me. I was with Edwin…" Hudson trailed off, his throat suddenly thick.

His father reached over to pat his knee. "I know, son. It's just terrible about Edwin. An unfathomable loss. And all those poor souls." He watched his son, suddenly childlike in the safety of his father's car. But Sterling had seen upending tragedy before; he had seen how people integrate impossible facts, confronting them again and again, each collision trying to dull the stab.

"Jameson was lucky, huh," Hudson said, coughing.

Sterling nodded. "He always seems to get lucky when he needs to."

As they drove around the Boston Common, the Blackberry buzzed. Hudson glanced at it. The sender's email address was garbled. Hudson spoke like a small child.

"Dad. You don't think...is there any chance...Edwin might have...gotten out?"

"Out?" Sterling said. "No, son. Wrong place, wrong time. That's it."

"You don't think he could have been there on purpose, do you?"

"On that plane? On purpose?" Sterling looked at Hudson and shook his head, flooding with love for the little boy who once rode on his shoulders at the county fair, pointing out his favorite pigs. Softly, he said, "Now, tell me about the girl. Everything. Anything may be important."

"So she called me and wanted to meet, and I...ahh," Hudson groaned. The last thing he had done for Edwin was let him down. And Ahmed.

"I met her for drinks, and...she was really beautiful. She lived right across the street." Hudson said it as if, at that point, it was out of his hands.

"You spent the night with her," Sterling finished.

"No, a few hours. Night of my life. "

His father was grim. "Life is what we're looking at. They have your DNA."

Hudson felt stupid but he needed the levity. It was one reason Edwin though he was a light weight. He remembered Edwin's cold assessment last night. "You add no value." The words stung. To the man who created so much. Hudson amounted to zero.

"I left her place around 3 a.m. I went back to D6 to work on our XTC deal strategy with Edwin," Hudson said, remembering how Edwin had hogtied him with duct tape in under two seconds.

"Maggie got all weird when I left. Staring at the TV. I guess I don't add any value."

"What are we going to do?"

"Fix it," said Sterling. "We are going to fix this immediately."

CHAPTER 14

STERLING
5:30 P.M., CAMBRIDGE, MA

Sterling sat behind the carved walnut desk in his library. Shelves were filled with books: fiction, autobiography, American history, European history, Russian history. financial history. poetry. A well-read life was a broader life, Sterling thought. It gave one unexpected angles, nuance, opportunity to leverage in bleak times when the way through was unclear and seemed to be edging out of one's control.

Between the books were pictures. Hudson rowing for Yale, his crew collapsed over their oars after beating Harvard. Grace, Sterling's ivory princess, on their wedding day.

Sterling's gaze fluttered past the spines of books to a small picture in a cheap plastic frame. The kind a college student would buy. It was a candid shot of kids in their early twenties: Grace, Sterling and Jameson Callaghan in the cockpit of a sailboat. Behind them, the tall palms on the flat island of Anegada, just a notch above sea level.

It was the spring of their senior year at college. They had rented the boat with a fourth. But Jameson's girlfriend had not been able to tolerate the boat and had left after the second day. How different everything might have been if she had had sea legs.

Sterling kept the picture in front of him. History was important. His people were important. His family, most of all.

Sterling opened his cell phone to the call list. He began scrolling through the numbers. Periodically, he would delete one, then another. Each time, the same one:

617-555-7374: Maggie Rice.

CHAPTER 15

HUDSON
7:00 P.M., BOSTON, MA

By 7:00 p.m., 65 Acorn usually would be thick with people watching the season end for their hapless Red Sox on the screens perched above the oak bar. Today they watched rolling news coverage of smoking rubble.

A draft of lager condensed on the small oak table where Hudson sat, in the back corner, against the wall. The Blackberry buzzed. A third message, again unintelligible. Hudson had to know what they said. There was only one way to find out.

"Hey Hudson, take this one," called a familiar voice. Walker Green shuffled to the table, put down the beer. When he returned, he set his cane against the chair and studied Hudson. "How are you doing? The police came….They took your computer."

Hudson shook his head. "Yeah, I supposed they would. It's crazy. I don't think I'll be around for a little while. I'm on bail, but…probably not great press for D6."

Walker said, "First Edwin, now Maggie…unbelievable….Did you ever?"

"She called me Monday night. We had a few drinks. And then she took me home and had her way with me," Hudson flashed his lightning smile. "But then I don't know what happened. I was back at the office working."

Walker looked startled. "After six?"

130

"Ha ha," said Hudson. "A lot later…"

"Well, while you're lying low, I'll be your eyes and ears in the office," offered Walker. "If you need anything, let me know. At some point, when you're ready, we should talk about XTC. I can be your front guy, but you need to tell me what to do. We've got three weeks to close it. After today it's even more…well, just call me when you are ready."

"God," said Hudson, his gut clenched. "I really need that commission."

"No worries," Walker said, raising his palms. Pushing would only drive Hudson deeper into the pit. "I'll call you tomorrow. Hang in there, man. Be safe."

"Thanks," said Hudson, as his eyes followed Walker out of the bar. Alone, Hudson flicked through Edwin's Blackberry. "What was Edwin up to?"

When Hudson clicked on the "memos" icon, a list appeared.

-Recruits
-Music
-Movies
-Groceries

"Recruits" held several names next to universities with top math or computer science programs - MIT, Carnegie Mellon, UC Berkeley, Technion. Music listed some new songs: "Superman" by Five for Fighting and others. Hudson was about to move on when a word caught his eye.

"Groceries? I never saw Edwin eat anything but coffee, candy and pizza."

Click. The screen turned black. Bright green text ran across the page, rolling out asterisks, stars, spaces, symbols and letters linked unintelligibly to others.

"Encrypted groceries?" Hudson said. He needed help. Only one person had the skill and might not think he was stone cold crazy. Who might want to hope, too.

He put ten dollars under the salt and pepper shakers. Then he ran an errand.

"Just in case," Hudson thought. "Belt and suspenders."

He jogged across the Salt and Pepper bridge over the Charles River toward Kendall Square, where MIT students spread from labs into start-up companies. When he reached the row of storefronts Hudson slipped into one of them. Five minutes later he emerged with a plastic bag, which he tossed, empty, in a trash can.

Two blocks down, Hudson slipped his access card into the reader and hit the elevator button for the top floor, where D6 developed and kept its secrets. Security planned this layout. No one could just stumble on to that floor. Hudson raced down the hallway to the windowless office and knocked.

"Please come in," said Ahmed.

The office cube had no view to the outside. Inside, the small office was littered with partially deconstructed computer servers being "modified" and thick programming books. There were cool gadgets from MIT's Artificial Intelligence lab: a robotic dog that would sniff, wag and lick; an emotionally enabled fuzzy troll with doe eyes that would widen with surprise; a row of three-inch wide composite butterflies perched on Ahmed's metal bookshelf.

From behind his desk, Ahmed peered at Hudson through his frameless glasses.

"So. How have you been since you left us to go murder some very pretty girl while we were trying to save D6?" Ahmed said, returning to his computer.

"I didn't murder anyone," Hudson said.

"Ah, right. Then how have you been since you left us?" He typed. "Ah, perhaps this." Some people hunted and pecked for the right keys. Some used all of their fingers, one at a time. Ahmed pressed the keyboard like piano chords.

"Look, I'm sorry, I...." Hudson stuttered.

"Obvious," said Ahmed, without looking up.

"I need your help," Hudson said, moving a stack of books from the closest chair.

"Obvious too," said Ahmed. His fingers pressed and rattled the keys.

Hudson decided the best way through was with a sledgehammer.

"I found something. Edwin's Blackberry. It's been getting messages that are all garbled, and it whistles when I click them. I think he was on that plane on purpose!"

Ahmed's hands went still. His dark gaze settled on Hudson.

"I...I...I think he made it off," Hudson stuttered. "The plane."

"You have his Blackberry?" Ahmed said. "The one I wiped clean."

"That's the one he gave me," Hudson said. "But he grabbed it by accident and left me with this. A few messages came in. I tried to see them but it whistled at me. Loudly."

Ahmed stared at him.   Hudson sighed and looked away. He pressed his hands to his knees and rose. "You're right. Okay, forget it. Chalk it up to a sad suit on a very bad day."

Ahmed's palm shot out. "Please," he said.

As soon as Hudson pulled the Blackberry from the clip on his belt, Ahmed snatched it. He looked at his watch. "It's 8:37 p.m. It's been almost exactly twelve hours. This is not good."

"Someone's really trying to reach him. I guess not everyone has...heard."

"Blackberries do not whistle," Ahmed said.

"This one does," said Hudson.

Ahmed shook his head. "No. A message that is encrypted whistles when someone attempts to read it who is not authorized to do so." His thumb rolled fast over the button, scrolling through the garbled messages. "Anything else?"

"Yeah. I got a weird message from someone I don't know. Lula Crosse. But it kind of, well, it sounded like Edwin." Hudson repeated the message.

"So who is Lula Crosse?" Ahmed muttered. He spun his chair, pushed aside a loose pile of papers to open a black laptop. He clicked a few screens. A password screen opened. He filled it with asterisks; the bar turned green.

"Hey – is that my email account? How did you?"

"Please," said Ahmed, clicking keys. A picture opened from the Department of Motor Vehicles database, snapped just before the young woman's smile settled fully on her face. "Miss Crosse is 26 years old. Pretty. Harvard University Graduate School. Poetry PhD candidate. Pours coffee just down the street. Now, and probably forever."

"The Cambridge Coffee House requires a background check?" said Hudson.

"No," Ahmed said. "This is not their background check. Quite obvious. So let us deduce the facts. Fact. The message is coming from an IP address associated with an account on Jay Street in Cambridge. And Miss Crosse's address is Jay Street."

"So…why is she is sending the message to me?"

"Fact. She is not sending anything. Her email account is sending it to yours."

"But I don't know Lula Crosse," Hudson said.

"Somebody does," said Ahmed. "Somebody who knows you have this piece of plastic from China and does not want it lost. It's made in Canada, incidentally."

"Nobody knows about it except you and me. And Edwin did of course, if he had time to figure out he took the wrong one." Hudson's face creased.

"No one else?" Ahmed said.

"My father. And the clerk at the evidence desk in Police HQ."

"So," said Ahmed. "Edwin. And a fair number of others, then."

There was silence for a moment. Ahmed seemed lost in private thoughts.

Hudson gave a wry laugh. "I thought it was him. Talking to me. Sounded just like Edwin. 'Don't let that POPC out of your sight or whatever – I actually thought he was telling me not to lose the Blackberry. Nuts, right?"

Ahmed's arm snatched out and gripped Hudson's wrist with surprising strength.

"You must not," he said. Then Ahmed pushed a button on his bookshelf. A third keyboard descended on a hydraulic shelf. Ahmed spun around and typed in a code. "Mmmhmm. Someone has activated a trace for this device. You are on the grid. Everywhere you go, cell towers are triangulating your latitude and longitude. I imagine that whoever is looking for you has already located you. Within a margin of error."

"Which is what?" Hudson prickled.

"A distance of 100-200," said Ahmed.

"Miles?

"Yards," said Ahmed.

"They could be near this building?" Hudson said.

"Or in it," said Ahmed.

"Who are we talking about? The government?" Hudson said.

"That I do not know," said Ahmed. "But one thing I do know. You are going to have to get off the grid and get lost without losing that thing."

"What? I can't leave – I'm on bail!" he said, getting flustered. "What if it is – what if it is Edwin? It's the only way he can communicate!"

"If Edwin was going on some deep secret dangerous mission do you think he would have left his secret mission communications device in your custody?" Ahmed scoffed. "Some superspy he would be. And I am sorry to say I sincerely doubt Edwin has any need or desire or capability to reach you today. Things being as they are."

"I don't understand," said Hudson. "I do not understand."

They were both quiet.

"What if I just lose this thing?" said Hudson, wiping his palms. "Just chuck it."

Ahmed paused. "It's an option. But first, don't you want to see what you found? What those messages actually say?"

Hudson stared at Ahmed. "Yes," he said.

"So do I," said Ahmed. "Groceries! Ha!" He waved the device over a screen that lay flat on his desk. The scanner produced the exact image on Ahmed's monitor.

"Does it make any sense to you?" Hudson asked. Ahmed's hands covered the keys, searching for a code to unlock the encryption.

"Hmm," Ahmed said. "You have presented a challenge. How utterly surprising. Ah! Done." He turned the screen toward Hudson.

ASP Operator: *Raptor*
Mission: *Disarm, Deliver and Extract to Deep Cover*
Unload Location: *American Airlines Flight #11 Boston to LA departs 7:46 a.m.*
Unload Date/Time: *Sept 11 approximately 08:15.*
Size and Type of Target: *Egg-shaped crystal case containing aerosolized pneumonic plague.*
Execution: *Disarm automatic detonation within 24 hours of impact. 102901AK11011W850ZR011231D62M30L.*
Cover: *Business Trip to Meet Customers.*
Personal Meeting Date/Time: *Wednesday Sept 12 16:00.*
General Location: *Washington D.C., Northwest, 1665 Connecticut Avenue Penthouse.*
Personal Meeting Specific Location: *Service entrance, PH floor.*

Contact Procedures: *Recognition Signals (Bona Fides)*
Visual: *Contact will light cigarette.*
Verbal: *Operator "I'm here to fix the disposal". Contact: "Is that thing on the brink again?"*
Danger Signal: *Contact says "I think I need to sit down."*
Personal Meeting Cover: *Appliance repair.*
Props Required: *Laptop, mobile phone, Blackberry. Raptor gear.*
Extraction Location: *Private airfield outside Washington.*

"My God," Hudson said. "Aerosolized pneumonic plague?"

Ahmed said. "This device contains a coded code. Someone wanted to protect a code from anyone else finding it. A code that must be used within a day of impact."

"To stop the plague bomb?," said Hudson. What was this doing in his hands?

"Yes," Ahmed breathed. "Someone has something very nasty they want to stay on. It appears someone named Raptor was sent to turn it off. This code is the key. "

"So what does this mean?" Hudson said breathlessly.

"Two things," Ahmed said. "One, they are all going to be after it. Two, they will be after you. As I said. So, you need to disappear. This device needs to go dead. If they find you with it, they want it, not you, and you are an easy thing to dispense with."

"Edwin went on that plane on purpose," said Hudson. Ahmed shook his head. "Make the link, Ahmed! These orders have the same flight number! And "impact" – what kind of impact do we know about? This morning – the towers – the pentagon – the planes! Is this plague bomb really going to happen?"

"According to this, perhaps," said Ahmed softly. They were both quiet again.

"What on earth was Edwin doing?" Hudson said finally.

Ahmed pressed his lips together and shook his head.

"If he was on that plane...on purpose, was all this – D6 – just his day job?"

Ahmed said nothing. "If he did not get off, this bomb has yet to discharge. And if he did, it still has yet to discharge." Ahmed pressed the Blackberry into Hudson's hands. "If they think their resource has been lost, or taken, they'll fight to get it back. You have the device. And the code. They will think you are…Edwin."

"Wait," said Hudson. "The other emails! What do they say?"

"Curious cat," warned Ahmed. "Quickly then." His fingers played the keys.

One message opened. The sender address and message resolved to this:

From: Head
To: Raptor
Boots down?

"Raptor?" whispered Hudson. "What's next?"

From: Head
To: Raptor
Confirm landed safely.

"And?"

From: Head
To: RT
Make delivery as planned to prevent RUPD sequence launch. Last message.

Just then a sharp chirp from the composite butterfly made them both look up.

"Shh!" Ahmed whispered. He looked at his monitor. "Someone is out there. No badges." His computer ran facial recognition software ran against the grainy faces. "They do not match D6 employee data. Look." Two men with full beards, dark hair, and sweatshirts with hoods hunched on either side of Ahmed's door. Their appearance was not unusual. D6's programming floors were full of brilliant computer scientists like Ahmed who had grown up in Southeast Asia, Pakistan, and India where some of the best computer training was provided, where many wealthy families exported their children to the United States for better career opportunities. But these two men did not work for D6 and had no reason to be lurking outside Ahmed's office.

"You have to go," Ahmed grabbed Hudson's sleeve. The door knob turned.

"Go where?" whispered Hudson. "We're in a locked cube."

"It's an office," said Ahmed. He pushed a button. A telephone rang, then Ahmed's voice materialized. "Hello," said the voice. "Okay, but if you took a moment to think through several more steps you would quickly see that…" The audio track continued in a long rant of programmer-speak. Quietly, Ahmed pushed back his chair.

"Hurry!" whispered Ahmed. "And give me that thing." He snatched the Blackberry, then pushed his chair against the wall and squatted. With his index finger, he peeled up a square of carpet. He pulled on a ring, and an identical square of flooring pulled up.

The door was rattling. Hudson grabbed the lip of the desk and swung his body through the black square space in the floor.

"Let go!" hissed Ahmed. Hudson dropped four feet on to carpet. There was a quiet rustle beside him. Ahmed landed like a cat. He took Hudson by the wrist in the dark. Then he turned a handle, and they were out in an unfinished floor of their building.

"Why do you have an escape hatch in your…" Hudson started.

"Shush," Ahmed hushed. "There's no time for that now. You need to get out of here fast. And now you are off the grid." He tossed Hudson the inert Blackberry.

"But what if Edwin tries to reach me? What if he wants the Blackberry back?"

"That's the last thing you have to worry about. Get out of here and stay low."

From behind a brick pillar, Ahmed watched Hudson run through the alley behind D6's building toward the subway. The piece of plastic was clipped to his belt, now inert. Ahmed opened his palm and released a small object, like a magician with a handful of dust, or a dove. Or a butterfly. Off it flew, with the twinkling speed of a fairy.

"There have been complications," Ahmed said aloud. "Obvious."

CHAPTER 16

"Pull around the corner, kill the lights," Marly told Peters. "If the old guy is still around here we don't want to spook him." Peters turned off Charles Street on to River Street where Beacon Hill's CVS served newspapers, coffee and sundries to neighbors whose homes overlooked the Charles River, and to ones who lived under its bridges. Blue lights of police cruisers shone at the end of each block, where alert teams of police and national guardsman were newly posted to monitor the intersections that accessed main roads in and out of Boston.

The drugstore was selling cartons of Häagen-Dazs. Diets seemed purposeless.

"You seen a homeless guy in here tonight?" Peters asked the shaggy clerk.

"Mr. Squibbs? He was here," said the clerk. "I think he lives near the bridge."

Marly and Peters walked briskly down Charles Street. Soon they reached the Salt-and-Pepper Bridge, so named for its squat pillars that looked like condiment containers. The platforms between its stone staircases were coveted territory; a stench rose where men had marked them. The two cops walked among the cocoons of dark blankets curved into the corners. Traffic raced beside them; the Red Line clattered past above. The skies remained silent.

Marly shook the shoulder of one woolen roll. "Mr. Squibbs?" she said softly. The man grunted and rolled over. They had roused four or five more people when, under the bridge, they heard someone scrabbled down the steps.

The chase was brief. Peters pinned the terrified man against the clammy stone wall.

"Mr. Squibbs," said Marly softly. "We just want to talk to you. Would you like some of this?" She presented a chocolate bar. Cadbury's. Warily, Mr. Squibbs took the small piece from Marly's palm. His fingers were caked with dirt, dark lines at his joints. "We understand you saw something very bad last night. Would you tell us about it?"

Squibbs said nothing. He looked at Marly's candy bar. She broke off another piece. And another. They sat together quietly until there was just one piece left. Squibbs reached for it. But this time Marly pulled it back.

"You are the only one who can help us," she said, trying to catch Squibbs's wide, darting eyes. "Don't worry. No buildings, no small rooms, no bright lights. I just need to talk to you tonight. And maybe another time soon. But only out here, okay?"

Squibbs nodded slowly. Marly knew that some homeless people were veterans suffering from post-traumatic stress from being trapped, or held captive. They could not tolerate the inside of buildings. Outside they could sleep. An interview room would break Squibbs, but out here, Marly had a chance to get the information. With a little trust, and chocolate. She broke the last piece in half and gave it to Mr. Squibbs.

"Val...zard," came the garbled words from his full mouth. Marly waited as he swallowed. He eyed the last piece. "Evil wizard."

"Tell us about the evil wizard," Marly said.

Squibbs looked wild-eyed and shook his head furiously. "No...no...no."

"Is this him?" Marly pulled out Hudson Davenport's mug shot. But Mr. Squibbs would not look at it. He wept softly. "Okay, Mr. Squibbs. I'm going to bring you more chocolate soon, okay?" As they backed away, Squibbs huddled against the dank stone.

Peters said, "So what's next partner?"

Marly paused. "We bring him the evil wizard."

"How?"

"Pick up Davenport. Would you take chocolate from an evil wizard?" Marly grinned. Peters smiled back. Her techniques were unusual, but they often got them admissible evidence, and the right verdict.

"How about a drink first?" Peters said. Marly nodded. They walked past their patrol car and continued to a local pub. The sign said 65 Acorn. It was not their usual type of place. The men inside wore dark suits, pinstripes and cufflinks, or tattered polo shirts and jeans, shabby casual self-consciously styled at boarding school. Peters's shirt was kind of green, which matched one of the colors in the plaid of his poly blend jacket. He wore navy slacks and black shoes with rubber soles that could grip when he ran hard.

Peters was trying to get the bartender's eye, when he felt fingers touch his elbow. For a moment his eyes searched Marly's. But hers were sharp, turned toward the door. He had not heard her phone.

"Yeah, okay," she was saying. "We're on our way."

"What's up?" said Peters.

"Another dead girl, this time in Cambridge," Marly said.

"Why are they calling us?" said Peters. "We're Boston PD."

"The vic worked at the coffee shop near Davenport's office. And CSI said the last email from her account went to him," said Marly.

CHAPTER 17

HUDSON
9:05 P.M., BOSTON, MA

The Red Line's doors opened at the Park Street station. Hudson took the stairs two at a time up to the north side of Boston Common, then broke for the center of the park, dodging the roasted nut and ice cream vendors. He looked over his shoulder. People were walking behind him, or sitting on benches. No one kept pace.

He ran down the slight hill along a path that crisscrossed the open field, crossing Charles Street to the Public Garden. Its centerpiece was an hourglass pond belted by a small blue bridge. Fresh flowers arranged in lush beds along the paths, fragrance catching in pockets of roses.

It was shortly after 9 p.m. when Hudson reached the dark, still pond. The swan boats were docked. A middle aged woman clattered past him in her thick heels, her pace still measuring moments in billable hour increments as she pushed home, her briefcase scraping her leg with each stride. The effort drew dark crescents in the armpits of her suit.

Across the pond Hudson saw the spot. A patch of white was curled up tight on the grass near the water. Another swan glided nearby. He jogged over the bridge and around to the protected area. Two large white signs hung beside the huge oak that helped wrap the fencing and hung over the swan's nest. The front edge was open to the pond.

KEEP OUT. NESTING AREA.

"Perfect," said Hudson. No one was coming. Twenty yards off there was a pile of man spread across a bench, under a dark cover. His head was entirely covered by the blanket. The other swan drifted across the pond, occasionally dipping its long neck. Hudson guessed it would take him at least twenty seconds to get back.

"Hello, Princess," Hudson whispered, sitting down on the curb of the pond. The toe of his sneaker edged in first. The water gulped around it.

The sleeping swan did not raise her head. Hudson was in up to his knees. He moved very slowly. He pulled his legs through the water. His wet jeans and the way the sneakers sucked the mud made it slow going. It was hard not to splash.

Hudson had three strides to go when angry honks fired like an automatic rifle. He turned. Coming at him fast was a six foot, white wingspan, beating the water and hissing through open black jaws. Hudson splashed toward the nest. Just as he reached the edge of the fencing, he stuck his cupped fingers in the grass and dug fast.

A long white neck unwound itself. Her wings flared as she reared on Hudson. He had to get out of there. Hudson took one impossibly slow lunge through the water. The male swan was two wing beats away. Charging. Hudson pulled the edge of the fencing and got one foot free of the muck and mud. But the other was stuck. He reached his arms into the water and found a lace. His foot came free of the sneaker. That was when the first sharp blow fell hard across his back. Something hard stabbed at his back.

Hudson scrambled out of the pond. The swan was out of the water, beating his wings. He raked his neck, hissing and honking until the intruder was gone.

Hudson raced past the statue of George Washington on the rearing horse and ran home on one shoe. Animals, when frightened, exhibit one of two responses: flight or fight. Hudson had a glimpse of his true nature. Running like hell from a bird.

What he did not notice was the dark green truck that pulled up to the nesting area, yellow lights flashing in slow, gentle circles as it drove on the pedestrian pathway. A man in green overalls got out.

"Geez, ladies," he said to the swans. "What has you in such a state?"

Three minutes later, Hudson gripped the banister of his brownstone and swung up the stairs. His shirt was soaked. His jeans were dirty and wet below the knee. One sock was black from mud. When he closed the door tightly behind him, he was breathing hard. So Hudson did not notice the small moth like creature fly in silently, just behind his head. Or how it rested in a shadow where the moldings met in the corner of his high ceiling.

Hudson pulled his black roller board from the closet. All the travel for D6 had left scrapes of paint and dust marks and the occasional loose string. The zipper ripped as he opened the suitcase, throwing in boxer shorts, a couple pairs of jeans and a stack of shirts and a blue sweater into the suitcase. He grabbed a fistful of socks and two dress shirts still folded in their dry-cleaning package. He pulled his dopp kit off the bathroom counter, tossed in his toothbrush. He tapped his right hip, where two objects were clipped. His phone, the size of an extra thick candy bar. And a Blackberry.

Hudson was draining a glass of cold water when a hard knock rapped his door.

Marly and Peters stood outside Davenport's apartment door, guns drawn. Peters rapped hard. They heard shuffling inside.

"Boston PD, Davenport, open up!" barked Peters.

A chain drew back, the bolt chunked. Hudson Davenport opened the door wide.

Marly noted this with some surprise. People with something to hide show it in their body language. They hide part of themselves behind doors, or cross their arms. At conference tables they rest their chins in their hands. But when Davenport saw the police at his door, Marly thought she saw....relief? Then she noticed his jeans were wet with mud from the knee down.

"Is everything okay?" Hudson asked.

"We'd like to talk to you about something else," said Marly, waving a warrant.

"Okay," said Hudson, locking the door quickly. "What do you need?"

Marly noticed he was acting more host than hostile. She thought, "So he is a sociopath. Capable of murder, showing no guilt." Or, a little voice registered, he is innocent. And scared.

"Mind if we take a look around?" asked Peters, his eyes already at work.

"Suit yourself," said Hudson.

"Going somewhere?" Peters asked, spotting the open suitcase on the bed.

"Uh, coming back," said Hudson quickly.

"That's good," said Marly. "Because your bail doesn't allow trips."

"No, of course not," Hudson said. "I-I...."

But Marly was after something else and did not want him to clam up. "Do you know Lula Crosse?"

"This question didn't go very well the last time you asked me," Hudson smiled, inviting her to a lighter place. But the name "Lula Cross" sent a bolt through him.

"It won't now," Marly clipped.

"OK," said Hudson warily. "I do not know her."

"This your computer?" Peters said from the bedroom. Hudson nodded. His remote log in process over dial up was taking its usual slow time. Broadband was only in office buildings. For now, Hudson had to plug a normal telephone cord into the laptop jack. It would dial up with the hum and ping of a fax machine searching for an open line.

"She might have been a friend of a friend of mine," Hudson added.

"What do you mean 'she might have been,'" said Marly.

Hudson sighed. "I think Edwin knew her. He was on the first plane today." His eyes were moist. The sad, helpless words were fresh. He would say them many more times for the rest of his life. Long after these strangest of words became rote.

Marly blinked. She was expecting Hudson to correct his verb tense, to persuade her it was a slip and charm her into almost believing it. She was not prepared to see his wounds. Or to feel the frisson of someone's personal horror in this public tragedy. She was regrouping when Peters put a print out in her hand.

"So Mr. Davenport," said Marly, cool again. "If you did not know Lula Crosse, why is it that the last email she sent was to you?"

"To me? I don't know. Have you asked her?"

"I can't. She's dead," Marly said, thinking Hudson's shocked expression deserved an Academy Award. "She was strangled on her bed. Rapist got distracted before he could complete the job, though." Sociopaths had trouble faking the range of emotion she had seen from him this evening. "You go running in your jeans tonight? Or do some gardening?"

Hudson looked at his muddy clothes. "Sometimes I walk home from work."

"Just down the street from where Miss Crosse worked," said Peters.

Marly looked at the sheet of paper, then showed it to Hudson.

"What does this mean to you?" she asked. Hudson took the piece of paper.

From: Lula Crosse
To: HDavenport@D6.com
Subject: URGENT
Hang on to the POPC, slacker. At all costs.

"I wish I knew," Hudson So the last email sent from a dead woman's account was sent from a dead man. What on earth was going on? Hudson felt for the Blackberry without thinking.

Hudson was not at all sure he wanted to know what was dawning on him. He just wanted Edwin to be alive. He wanted reprieve from the tragedy. But now he was forced to deal with more, much more, than he felt he could handle. And murders?

The dropped hand, the unconscious graze of fingertips on plastic, caught Marly's attention. "Mind if I take a look at your Blackberry?"

Hesitantly, Hudson unclipped the device. She dropped it into a Ziploc bag.

"I'll get this back to you," said Marly.

"When?" asked Hudson. Too quickly.

"As soon as possible. A week or so. Thanks for your help. For now, stick around," said Marly, adding wryly, "But of course, you need to do that anyway."

"Am I a suspect in this thing too?" Hudson asked.

Marly shot him a grin that would have appeared flirtatious if not for the edgy thinning of her upper lip. "Should you be? You know, I could actually use your help."

Marly was well aware of how hard Hudson was trying around her. That her reserve had a strong pull on him. She did not know why. But she was glad. Because Hudson's handsome smile, his constant invitation to play, could take her out like a wall of water. No doubt it was how he got away with so much.

"Don't reward him too soon," she thought. "He won't buy it." She needed to lure him tonight. Before they lost Squibbs again. She said, "I'm sorry I've been so rude. Occupational hazard. We're paid to find the guilty; that's how we start to look at everyone."

"Very smart," joked Hudson. "Guilty until proven innocent."

She nodded and smiled again. "So, assuming the opposite, we came over tonight wondering if you would be willing to help us with the case." Peters was frowning.

"Sure," said Hudson, surprised. "I really liked Maggie."

Hudson was astoundingly open. Surely he knew better, thought Marly. But if he was willing, she would take all she could. All the evidence was hovering around Hudson Davenport.

Hudson knew his father would not approve. He knew his father's lawyer would not approve. But he also knew if he could make someone laugh, they might like him. This was how he engineered a life warmed by people who were enjoying his company. He needed to make Marly like him too. And, he needed his Blackberry back.

Shortly, Marly, Peters and Hudson were outside the CVS on Charles Street.

"Wait here," said Marly. Peters shifted his weight uncomfortably. The last time he was with Hudson he was slapping cuffs on him. Now Marly had invited him to help, and he had agreed? He did not like this one bit.

"Unmentionables?" Hudson said, flicking his eyebrows at Peters. Suspect or not, Hudson felt safer with a police escort.

Peters chuckled. The guy was a regular guy too. Maybe he hadn't done it.

When Marly emerged with an opaque plastic bag, the three retraced the officers' steps. The tunnel beneath the bridge was empty.

"He's gone," said Peters.

"Can't be far," said Marly. "You go north, toward the Museum of Science. If you see him, shout. We'll go back toward the Hatch Shell."

Peters did not like leaving his partner with Hudson Davenport. Marly was trying to demonstrate she trusted Hudson, break him down. The guy would not try anything with Peters in earshot. He would just jog down a bit then turn back to follow them.

Marly shot a glance at Hudson as they walked along the river. The moonlight fell across his face. He was focused on private thoughts.

"Come this way," she said. "Move slowly." She wove between the trees.

There sat Mr. Squibbs, on the same bench, his grey military blanket around his shoulders. Staring at the night.

"Hi Mr. Squibbs," said Marly. "Do you remember me? I have something for you." She reached into the plastic bag and pulled out a Cadbury's bar. She unwrapped it slowly. The dim light from the lampposts along the pathways lit up the tinfoil.

Marly gave the chocolate to Hudson. Puzzled, he took it. Squibbs followed the bar. Marly studied him. Listened for Hudson to shift, or make a reason to leave the site.

"What do you want me to do?" Hudson whispered. He stood naturally. If he recognized the spot, he was showing no sign of it.

"Give him some," said Marly. "He looks hungry."

"OK, sure," said Hudson, crouching down. He broke off half the bar, held it out.

To Marly's surprise, Squibbs looked Hudson in the eyes and took the chocolate. But she needed to be sure. "Mr. Squibbs, do you see the Evil Wizard?"

"Where?" he cried, lurching to his feet, toppling over.

"Hey buddy," said Hudson, catching Mr. Squibbs by the shoulders. He shot a confused look at Marly. "What are you doing?"

Marly kept watching. Footsteps clattered down the pavement. Someone was running toward them. Squibbs slipped behind Hudson. Peters appeared.

"False alarm, Peters," said Marly. "Okay, okay, Mr. Squibbs. I'm sorry to worry you again. Here, take these." She produced another bar and a pint of milk. Squibbs huddled back on the bench, his eyes darting. But he did not shrink from Hudson.

So Marly knew. Hudson was not the man Squibbs saw in the wee hours of Tuesday, murdering Maggie Rice on that spot.

"I don't understand what just happened," said Hudson.

"It's not important," Marly said. "Let's leave him be."

Hudson lingered for a moment, studying Mr. Squibbs. "Here you go, buddy," he said, peeling off his thick polar fleece jacket. "Put it on. It will keep you warmer than your blanket." Hudson held out the coat, feeling the chill on his arms as he stood in just a D6 polo shirt.

The gesture startled Marly. Easing Squibbs' suffering had not even occurred to her. Quite the opposite. She had used him to find a clue, scaring a very lost man.

Squibbs snatched the jacket and stuffed his arms into it. He looked up as if to say thank you. Then he shrieked.

"The Evil Wizard! The Evil Wizard! The Evil Wizard!" Squibbs jumped to his feet, pointing at Hudson and screaming at the top of his lungs. Then he ran off into the night. The jacket, still unzipped, flapped as Squibbs disappeared into the darkness.

Marly ran after him but he was gone. "What just happened?" She turned back to Hudson, who stood with his mouth agape.

"I don't know!" said Hudson. "One minute he was taking my coat and the next he started pointing at me and screaming about some evil wizard. What's going on?"

"Do you know this place?" Marly said.

"Yeah, I mean, I go running around here all the time."

"No, this exact spot," said Marly.

"No, nothing particular," he said.

"This is the spot where Maggie Rice was found murdered. Squibbs saw who did it. And all he can talk about is the Evil Wizard."

Hudson took it all in, did the math. Hurt shone in his eyes. "So you just wanted to see if he recognized me."

"No," Marly said sharply. "I wanted to see if he was afraid of you."

She had used both of them that night. Used? Marly caught on the word. Since when did doing her job become using someone? Somewhere between Hudson's apartment and the Esplanade, something had changed. After Squibbs's reaction, she did not know what to think.

"Why the chocolate?" Hudson said.

"When he took it from you, he didn't seem to think you were the Evil Wizard."

"No," said Hudson. "And I'm not. Though some say I do have magic fingers."

Marly smiled thinly, troubled more by her own behavior than his joke. "But something spun him up after you gave him that coat."

"It wasn't the coat," added Peters. "He ran off in it."

"I don't know how much logic you can attribute to a schizophrenic. But I was counting on some, at least." Marly said, studying Hudson. If Squibbs had seen him the night of the murder he would have reacted well before Hudson gave him the jacket. So what made him so wild? A guy in short sleeves, a dark t-shirt with a white logo. Jeans. She eyed the logo and name. D6.

"What's 'D6'?" she asked distractedly.

"D6? The company I work for," Hudson said.

There was only one thing about Hudson that was different from when he was wearing his jacket. The D6 logo. Marly was not at all comfortable with where that left them. Had Squibbs made the logo? Had he made Hudson less of a suspect, or more? She was more than a little troubled to feel herself rooting for the guy who would take the jacket off his back to give it to a homeless man. Usually she only had a scent for blood.

From his condo, Hudson watched the police cars pull away. It was just after 11:00 p.m. Detective Marly still had the Blackberry.

Hang on to it at all costs, Slacker. Edwin – could it really be Edwin? If it was, Hudson knew Edwin would be coming for him – for it. And he was not the only one. Those guys outside of Ahmed's office had found him once; they could find him again.

Maybe Hudson's plan had not been such a good one after all. But it was the only one he had. And so far, Part 1 had worked. Now for Part 2.

Hudson left his lights burning, his computer on, music blaring, and cracked a window. He hoped anyone watching his apartment would think he was still there. The stairs to the roof deck were steep and narrow, really more like a permanent ladder. They had served him well, requiring that he hold a hand out for more than one lady in heels coming up to see the view with her glass of wine.

Hudson stepped out onto the roof. Then he began to run. He scrambled over the brick walls and cedar flower beds that separated the roof decks. In his effort to be as quiet as possible, he did not notice his companion. A small butterfly, with a wingspan of about three inches, flitted from a flower pot to alight on the deck railing, haphazardly following Hudson's journey across the rooftops of the brownstones on Marlborough St.

At the last deck at the end of the block, Hudson reached for the fire escape that led down to the dark alley below. But the rust gave way. His hands slipped. He pressed hard against the wall. The rest of the rungs held. In a moment, he dropped to the ground and cut through to Beacon Street. Hudson sprinted down the sidewalk, against the stream of white lights.

What he had to do now, he needed to do quickly, and on foot. The stoplight at Berkeley Street turned red. Westbound traffic poured toward Storrow Drive. Hudson leaned on his knees. Caught his breath. The last car in the traffic was a large black SUV. Hudson jogged in place, trying to see the break to get across. But the SUV stopped. So Hudson stepped off the curb behind it.

That was when the back double doors opened. Two men jumped out. Before Hudson could react his hands were bound under his knees with plastic cinches. They picked him up. Banged his head against the seats. The doors shut. The van moved off. Hudson never saw his attackers before they pulled the tape across his eyes.

CHAPTER 18

MARLY
11:10 P.M., BOSTON, MA

The sharpshooter on the roof deck buzzed Marly, who sat in the patrol car. After dropping off Davenport, they had pulled around the corner and paused out of sight.

"Good call, Detective," whispered the lookout. "He's on the roof, heading South."

"Let me out right here," Marly said to Peters.

"I'll come," he said.

"No," said Marly. "I don't want him to see us. Me, on foot, by myself, I can talk my way through that. Off duty, meeting a friend."

"Not a good idea," Peters frowned as she sprung the door.

"I'll be fine," Marly said. She rapped on the window. Peters rolled it down. "Keep this. It means something." Peters closed his fingers around Hudson's Blackberry.

The radio crackled. "He's going down the fire escape into the alley. Fast."

Marly trotted up the short flight of the nearest stairs, pretending to study the names on the door buzzer. She had a clear view of Hudson. He was running out of the alley, then turned abruptly right. Then he turned right again on Beacon Street. She hurried down the stairs and broke into a run. She needed to keep him in sight. What was he up to? She saw him pause at the light on Berkeley. Bright lights and honking horns jockeyed for position. Hudson must have been running hard; he bent over to catch his breath at the corner behind a stalled SUV.

If she hadn't been watching so closely, she would have lost him entirely. She had just reached the corner, steps from the SUV, when it happened. It took only seconds. The SUV doors flung open, two men jumped out, bound Hudson and pushed him into the back.

"Hey! Stop! Police!" Marly banged her gun against the window of the SUV.

The driver looked at her. Later, she would think how the expressionless eyes reminded her of a snake, or a shark. Unblinking killers.

The breath left her body when someone knocked her to the ground, hard. She dropped her gun; it skittered across the sidewalk. Everything went dark.

The first thing Marly felt was pain in her wrists. A sharp edge bound them tightly, straining the tendons in her shoulders Carpet fibers scratched her cheek. She could smell someone close by. A man. She had never noticed the scent before, but it was not unfamiliar to her. Or unpleasant.

Tinny voices came through a small speaker. A television, she guessed, its volume low. She heard a door open, then shut quickly. The television snapped off; someone shuffled to their feet; springs creaked. A sofa? Or a bed? The confusion of senses made Marly want to shake her head as if that would clear her eyesight. It was a terrible itch. But she stayed still, on the floor, on her side.

A man spoke. The words rolled up in his tongue to the roof of his mouth. They made no more sense to her now than when she heard taxi drivers talking on cell phones. But this man's tone was very different: it was harsh. Another man responded softly, apologetically, she thought. Their exchange was terse. The door opened again, more footsteps came in; it shut.

Someone scraped the carpet near her. Marly stayed very still.

"You!" said the first man, this time in English. She heard the grip of hands pulling on cotton. "Get up." Marly remained inert. They were not talking to her.

"What...what do you want?" the voice sounded very frightened. "Are you...did J.D. send you? I'm trying to get his hundred and fifty thousand...I'll have it."

Marly recognized its tenor immediately, though she had not heard the fear before. She guessed Hudson Davenport was in the same condition as she was.

"Shut up," said the man. There was tapping, a dial tone. Distant ringing. Then more Arabic, with the discordant sound of English words inserted into the stream of the other language. Marly distinctly heard the man say "Edwin Hoff."

"Right," Marly thought. "Hudson's boss. On the first plane. His alibi."

The speaker moved again. "Tell me your name."

"Hudson Davenport," choked Hudson.

"No!" barked the interrogator. Marly heard a hard crack of palm on flesh.

Hudson swallowed hard. He said again, "My name is Hudson ...Hudson Davenport. You can check. Look at my...."

"Shut up!" said the man. "Where is it?"

"Where is what?"

"Where is the device? Where is the vial?"

"I...I..." Hudson stammered. "I don't know what you are talking about."

The blow came hard, a stinging slap. Marly shuddered. Hudson cried out.

"Don't be stupid," said the man. Then in a sadistic, slow cadence, he purred, "We searched you thoroughly. Where is the mobile device, Edwin Hoff? And what have you done with our prize? It is quite costly. We want it back, still ripe, and very soon."

There was a hard rap on the door. The room went quiet. Marly heard more shuffling. Tape ripped off its spool. Hudson groaned. The door opened. The captors exchanged a brief greeting. Marly heard quick steps move backwards from the door, lilting, explanatory cadences. Sounds of supplication. Marly sensed someone quite different had entered the room.

Again, the words "Edwin Hoff" caught Marly's ear. They were said with pride this time. One set of footsteps strode to where Marly thought Hudson was sitting quietly.

The man paused in front of Hudson. Then he laughed, a short, demeaning burst.

"No. Idiots! This is most definitely not Edwin Hoff." He stopped next to Marly. Then he let out a long thread of what sounded like condemnation. "You will let them go." There were sounds of protest; he shut them down in a phrase. "They don't have it. You've been chasing a false lead."

"Maybe all went as planned then," said one voice.

"We will know that by 9 a.m." Then the door opened and shut. Whoever the man in charge was, he was gone.

There was bickering back and forth. The interrogator who had rocked Hudson had the loudest voice. Marly heard the safety of a handgun pull back.

"Good lord," she thought. They had been fighting, apparently about whether to obey the man who had shown some reason, some mercy. She braced.

There was a loud bang and a white flash so brilliant it made her wince even through her tape. She felt a sharp pinch on the back of her neck. All went black.

PART 5
SEPTEMBER 12, 2001

CHAPTER 1

MARLY
3:24 A.M., NORTH OF BOSTON, MA

When Marly awoke again she had a stunning headache. The light hurt her eyes; the tape was gone. Her hands were free. She was in a dingy motel room on a bed covered in a brown polyester quilt with cigarette burns on it. The light was on. The alarm clock read 3:24 a.m.

She saw and heard no one. Hudson was gone. The drapes were closed, but they ruffled and sucked back with the relentless pulse of traffic, even at that hour. Louder than it should be. Marly stood up and approached the window. When she pulled back the drapes, she saw it.

One large pane of the window was ajar. The vacuum pulled the drapes to the wash of traffic, blew back in again. Had someone gone out the window? Or come in?

Marly recognized the dingy roadside of Route 1, north of Boston, the unholy couplings of strip clubs and motels. Fear pricked. She was suddenly alert and broke for the door.

Marly had her hand on the doorknob when she noticed a strange shape on the other side of the bed. Dark clothes. Four tangled legs. Arms jutted in unnatural angles. There were two bullet holes in each of their throats. One on top of the other. Exactly one inch apart. The attackers would not be coming back for her. Not these, anyway.

"So where's Davenport?" Marly said. Her last memory of Hudson, wincing from a crack across the jaw, did not give her the impression that he had the upper hand. "Who is this 'J.D.' person? Why does Hudson owe him so much money?" She remembered that flash and the bang. Someone had touched her neck, knocked her out.

Marly pulled the door open and ran down the hall, toward a glowing exit light.. The door crashed as she pushed through it. There would be cabs at the all night restaurant a few buildings further along the strip.

Thirty minutes later, Marly double bolted her apartment door. A healthy pour of Maker's Mark melted four ice cubes. Bourbon worked fast to blunt her shaved nerves. By the third swig, she could think about the next step clearly enough.

She picked up her phone and dialed. "Peters," she said, when he answered.

"What happened to you? I called like a dozen times," her partner said.

"This is big, Peters." Her words came fast, a little blurred. "I don't know what it's about, but there is some terrorist thing underway here. They were definitely speaking Arabic. They thought Davenport was Edwin Hoff – yeah, that's right – yet these guys seemed to think he was alive and in control of some 'prize' – something they said was expensive and dangerous, and they said they wanted it 'ripe.'." It was supposed to go off by 9 a.m. And, they were after Davenport for his 'device.'." Which he didn't have. You have it. It's the Blackberry we took from him – on the floor of your car. He didn't have neither. Either."

"Okay, slow down," said Peters. "Do you need to go to the hospital?"

"No," she said, feeling her head. "You have the Blackberry, right?"

"It's being analyzed. You go catch a few hours. Can you be at HQ by seven?"

"Yes, thanks, Peters," she said. "You're the best."

"Just tell the big boss that," he said.

Marly was smiling as she sunk into her couch with the remains of her drink. It was good to have a partner like Peters. She did not have someone at home to be on her side, which made their bond all the more important. Not romantic, but charged with the intimacy of teamwork, danger, survival. They would figure this out together.

CHAPTER 2

HUDSON
12:10 A.M., NORTH OF BOSTON, MA

Hudson could not see through his blindfold during the half hour ride over pavement that pushed the SUV's shocks past their limits. He could hear a woman groaning. Another person had been pulled into the van —a hapless passerby who saw something she shouldn't have.

Were these J.D. Sullivan's thugs? Hudson thought. His blood pressure was pounding. Or had the people from Ahmed's office somehow found him again? Sightlessness disoriented him; fear made him panicky. He struggled to make sense of what was happening to him.

The vehicle jerked abruptly and swung in a tight semicircle until it stopped. The back doors opened and two men, black stockings over their heads, pulled Hudson out of the van. They dragged him, stumbling, into a building. Someone opened a door and pushed him through it. He lurched a few steps and fell on carpet. Hudson heard low, foreign sounds, rounded trills that could have been Arabic or Hebrew. Or Gaelic. He could make no sense of it. He thought someone came into the room, and voices rose. Then sharp English words cleared the rough.

"No. Idiots!" the voice said. "This is most definitely not Edwin Hoff. You will let them go."

The muddling of other sounds and senses sharpened Hudson's hearing. He thought he recognized the voice, but he could not place it. Then a door opened and closed. Hudson did not hear the English speaker again. When the foreign speech began again, there was clearly some new dispute. Hudson heard a gun cock.

A terrifying bang shook the thin plaster walls. The room filled with brilliant white light that blasted his eyes at the edges of the blindfold. There was a rattle of gun shots – four of them. Bodies collapsed heavily. Then there was silence. Hudson felt a hand on his shoulder, pushing him down on to the bed. Then, in a short second, his hands and feet were free.

Hudson opened his eyes first. He listened but heard nothing.

He lay at the edge of a ratty motel bedspread. The two men who had grabbed him off the street lay motionless on the floor. Dark lines of blood squirted in pulses from perfect pairs of bullet holes, exactly an inch apart, colons stamped in the center of each of their necks. Beside him on the bed, a woman lay unconscious on her back. Her hands and feet were free. A small pillow from the couch was under her head.

"Marly?" Hudson gasped. Then he heard someone moving behind him. Slowly, without making a sound, he tucked his chin down to his chest and peeked out.

A man stood by the dresser opposite the bed. He had his back to Hudson while his right arm moved in quick strokes, as if he were writing something. There was a small tapping and scratching noise, like plastic pushing plastic over a hard surface.

The man's head was bent low. From Hudson's angle, the man's shoulders looked broad, his torso solid beneath a dark motorcycle jacket. The jacket was unusual: the leather did not smooth across his shoulders but seemed to have elaborate vertical rows of stitching that spread slightly when he moved. He was not particularly tall or short. He wore faded blue jeans that fit comfortably over his slightly bowed legs.

"Get up. Now!" said the man.

Hudson pushed himself up slowly with his elbows, drawing his knees toward his belly in a subconscious protective motion. He looked up. The man stood no more than two yards away from him. He turned, and glared at Hudson through sharp eyes with a yellow cast. It took a few moments before Hudson could speak.

"Edwin?"

The pleasant features frozen in the photograph that had been scrolling across television sets all day were there in front of him. Vivid and wound up tight.

Edwin Hoff put his face close to Hudson's. "Listen!" he ordered. His commands were sharp. "One. You do not see me. Two. No one ever will. Three. I am dead." Edwin raised a finger with each command, never blinking. They hammered into Hudson's brain. "Now – I need my Blackberry."

Hudson locked up. The shock of Edwin's loss in a brutal mass murder hammered at him, digging out a place to settle. Yet here he was. But something was very wrong.

"Edwin, what happened?" Hudson said. "We all thought – you're okay! You need to call them! You need to – "

Edwin clapped his hands together so close to Hudson's nose that he could feel the air push out between them. One finger snapped up. The second. The third.

"I need that Blackberry," said Edwin, waving his ballpoint pen. He had been using it to sift through the items on the desk. "The one I gave you, not that bullshit copy on the dresser over there. Where is it?"

It was the same voice that had walked Hudson through the deal negotiations, narrowing distractions and providing focus. Hudson could see now that Edwin's fluency in leadership had come from some other set of experiences. Now he put those skills to their proper use. Edwin was at war.

"I don't have it," Hudson said. "Not on me. But I know where it is. I can get it."

Edwin's shoulders dropped an inch. His eyes blazed as he recalculated. "Okay. Then do what I say. We don't have much time."

"But what happened? They said you were on the plane," Hudson said hoarsely.

"You don't need to know that," said Edwin. "We have one goal right now. Get that Blackberry. Come." His fingers folded tightly, a crisp wave. He moved quickly toward the flowing drapes.

"What about Marly?" said Hudson.

"She is not your concern," said Edwin.

"How did you find me?"

"Little bird told me," Edwin said. Then he gripped Hudson's shirt, hard. His fierce eyes commanded Hudson's complete attention. "It is 3:12 a.m. We have five hours, thirty-four minutes to put that

Blackberry to use, or life is over for everyone you know. You will find it. Think of nothing else."

Edwin scooted through the window, a tight gymnast's dismount. Hudson clambered behind him. Edwin was astride a motorcycle in seconds. Hudson lifted his leg awkwardly over the backseat. Edwin snapped the visor shut on his helmet. He handed Hudson a second one.

"Wear this. And stop worrying. She'll be fine," Edwin's voice was muffled. "Now where is my Blackberry?"

CHAPTER 3

MARLY
7:00 A.M., BOSTON, MA

Captain Brath was leaning on his desk talking with Peter when Marly walked in.

"Ah! Marly. Peters has filled me in but I'd like to hear it from you," he said.

Marly explained the full story of the night. How Davenport had made a rooftop escape only to be kidnapped. Then she was too. The Arabic, the demands for "Edwin Hoff," the "device" and "the ripe prize." The mysterious leader who spoke English and demanded they be saved. The touch on her neck. Coming to. The broken window. The precise bullet holes.

"There's a terrorist link here, sir. I'm sure of it," she said finally.

Captain Brath studied her. Then Peters. Then Marly again. Brath saw what was happening. He had seen it all before. Peters just saw the open shot and took it. Brath didn't like it much, but he understood.

"How are you feeling, Marly?" said Captain Brath.

"I'm all right, sir," she said.

"You sure?"

"Yes. So what do you think about all this?" Marly asked.

"I think this is an extraordinary time. I think people have different...capacities for it," said the captain. "And murder investigations are difficult, particularly ones that can't be solved despite all the chocolate bribes out there."

Marly stared at Peters. Peters would not look at her. But a smile hung on his face holding a confidence with Captain Brath. She felt the captain's arm around her shoulder. It took every bit of self-control not to shake it off.

"Hey, I would have tipped back more than a few myself," he said. "Totally understandable. So Peters got forensics out to your location last night."

Marly took a deep, deep breath. "So do we have IDs on the vics?" she said.

"See, that was the thing, Marly," said Captain Brath. "There were none. They searched the room. No dead bodies. No blood."

"They found nothing?" she said, incredulous. She knew she had identified the motel and the room number when she gave Peters the instructions. "And the Blackberry?" Marly said. Her throat was dry.

"Nothing," said Peters. "It was brand new. Not a thing on it."

Strange, thought Marly. Then why was Hudson so protective of it? Why were the kidnappers so interested? Unless Hudson Davenport wasn't just the happy stooge he wanted to appear. How deep was he in?

"So Detective Marly," Captain Brath was saying. "It's a time of scarce resources around here. We're all strapped responding to these horrific events of Tuesday morning. You've got your hands full with the Esplanade murder, and now this Davenport link to the Cambridge one. I want you to follow the Davenport links, but Peters is going to left-seat the terrorist angle."

People in the left seat drive ; everyone else is a passenger. Peters was hijacking her terrorist case.

"But sir," she said.

Now Brath spoke sharply. "Focus on your job, Marly. There's more than enough there even for an ambitious woman like you. Find me that Esplanade killer."

This was why Marly always focused on quantitative results. Why she built her career on numbers: crimes solved, criminals put away, number of days open, fewest casualties. Quantitative results were hard not to reward. Because eventually, there it came. The death knell accusation for a very competent woman. The "a" word.

"Sir," Marly said quietly. "They kept saying something would happen by 9 a.m. Today. Something is going to happen to their prize – in less than two hours."

"Okay then, Peters, you get on it." Brath waved them out. His eyes were red. He had been up most of the night girding Boston's defense.

Outside the captain's office, Peters turned to Marly,

"Gosh Marly," he said. "I don't quite know what happened in there."

"No?" she said. The chocolate crack gave it all away. He had dropped crumbs for the chief to pick up, with practiced apology. Just enough to sow doubt in Brath's confidence in Marly but not so much to appear the blatant schemer. How often people rose in the ranks through the coincidental demise of their partners, or immediate superiors, while they positioned themselves as trusted supporters. Their negative comments, placed sporadically and with such reluctance, seemed dense with truth. For that they were rewarded.

"Look Peters," Marly said. "You've got to find these people – immediately – if we have any chance of tracking down this prize. Something very, very bad is going to happen by 9 a.m. if you don't. I heard them talking. It could be worse than Tuesday. And it sounds like it will happen here because Boston is where they are looking for it."

Peters put on a smile. "You free to help, partner?"

"Sorry," said Marly. "Gotta find the Esplanade killer - with or without chocolate."

In the hallway the overhead fluorescents spread harsh light. Red tinged the tips of Peters's ears above his high and tight haircut.

CHAPTER 4

On the ride back into Boston, Hudson's questions piled up. He tried to shout over the motorcycle's roar. "You missed the plane? Thank God!"

Edwin hunched low over the handlebars, racing toward the tall buildings.

"How did you find me?"

"Why is the Blackberry so important?"

"Why does it whistle?"

"What's going to happen? Don't you have to respond to those emails?"

Edwin drove. Said nothing.

"Why are you dead?" Hudson's voice was barely audible. "Don't you know what you're putting everyone through?" He shivered.

He had never ridden double on a motorcycle before, not on the back. It was very odd to have his arms around a man, hanging on to his torso so he would not fall off as they hurtled, unprotected, through air. The ride was surprisingly stable, but if they hit the ground, the friction would rip the skin off them, pull apart their bones and muscle and arteries and veins.

His helmet knocked against Edwin's with every gear change, and speed shift.

"Thanks for saving my ass, by the way," Hudson added to his monologue. "I was kind of in a bind back there."

"You're welcome," Edwin shouted.

"So what happened to you?" Hudson shouted again. Edwin put up a hand as he steered with the other.

"Focus!" he shouted. "Anything else is a distraction. Find that Blackberry!"

Within twenty minutes, the Boston skyline came into view.

"Turn here. Fastest way to the Garden," Hudson pulled on Edwin's jacket pocket as they came over the bridge into the city. They spun down the ramp that wound around a cement and gravel company. When Edwin turned his head to steer the bike around the tight angle, what Hudson saw made him gasp.

A piece of grey tape, torn loose by the wind, fluttered against Edwin's neck. It exposed the gash, a three inch jagged line, swollen, stained purple, shellacked with a clear sheen. The gauze was stained dark brown where blood had gathered and dried.

At 4:50 a.m., Edwin idled the bike by the edge of the Public Garden.

"You left the Blackberry out here? God, you are blonde," he said.

"It...I...I thought it would be safer away from me," said Hudson. He blushed, remembering his fantasy that Edwin would be proud of his foresight. "I carried two backups just in case. The cops already took the blank one. You saw the other in the hotel."

Edwin paused. "That was good thinking." Hudson smiled.

Behind the dark visor, Edwin ran a series of logical deductions at lightning speed. He had assigned Hudson one mission and demanded his total focus. Edwin also had to maintain that same level of focus – but on multiple goals.

On the ride, Edwin had formed a plan. He knew what had to be done, but could not do it himself: he could not be seen. Because Hudson already had seen him, he would become Edwin's tool. Later Edwin would deal with the consequences of that breach.

So at the exact moment Edwin heard Hudson's voice falter, felt his weight shift back, slightly, and fall into a deeper crouch, he administered the shot. This positive comment – "good thinking" – was genuine praise, and particularly effective when given at the moment he could sense Hudson flagging.

"Go get it," Edwin said. "I'll keep the bike moving. I'll pick you up at the light on Arlington and Commonwealth Ave. Traffic stops naturally there. Keep an eye out for me and don't hang around. Do not linger."

"Why is it so important?" Hudson said. "Is it about what Ahmed and I found...RUPD?" Edwin twisted fast. His hand gripped Hudson's neck. "Hey! Ow!"

"Speak."

"It was on your Blackberry. It whistled. I took it to Ahmed and he decrypted it."

"Ahmed," Edwin said slowly. "Anyone else?"

"No. Just him. The guy is amazing. I don't know how he does what he does."

"Tell me exactly what you saw. Every single key stroke."

Hudson took a deep breath, "We saw orders. For someone called 'Raptor' about something that was on the plane – a plague bomb – supposed to go off in 24 hours."

"Not in 24 hours. 24 hours after impact. Which was yesterday morning at 8:46. What else?" Edwin stared intensely.

"And there was a long string of numbers and letters."

"The disarming code," said Edwin. "And?"

"Three messages," said Hudson. "From someone called the Head. The first was something like 'boots down', the second said 'confirm boots down' and the third said 'deliver as ordered or the RUPD sequence will begin.' What is RUPD?"

"Not good," Edwin said.

"So where is the bomb?" Hudson asked. "How are you going to get to it?"

Edwin waved him off. "You. Get the Blackberry."

Hudson slipped off the back of the motorcycle and ran through the Garden. He neared the southern bulge of the hourglass pond that formed the center of the Public Garden. Just across from the small island was the spit of land sheltered by a large willow tree. This was the spot the pair of swans of the public garden had chosen for their nest.

Hudson strained his eyes in the pre-dawn darkness to see the chain link fence. But he could not make it out. He slowed to a trot. When he reached what he thought was the willow, his gaze swung up toward the bridge, and back the length of the pond. But there was no mistake. The enclosure was gone. The nest was gone.

Hudson ran toward the water. Where the nest had been there was now a stake in the ground with a laminated note pressed to it. It contained a press article that had been issued that morning by the Park Service explaining why they took it down.

"Long Wait for Nesting Swans, Both Found to be Female"

The displaced swans were skimming the other side of the pond for breakfast. Hudson searched on his hands and knees, hoping the Blackberry would be somewhere. But it was gone. The Blackberry was gone.

"This is not good!" Hudson cried. "God, I can't even do this one thing right!"

The night before last, he had been carving another notch in his belt with an intern at D6. In a day the world had changed; his world too. America was under attack; he was wanted in the girl's murder, pursued by unknown people who looked a lot like America's new enemy, and had lost a colleague. Then found him in altered and confusing circumstances. And he failed him. Again.

Hudson bolted. It was just a reaction. He ran hard. Away from the cops, away from D6, away from J.D., away from Edwin. He ran toward the pathway that would lead to the formal entrance to the Garden, where George Washington raised his sword on his rearing horse.

Just as he came even with the statue, Hudson heard footsteps. Just two paces. Right behind him. Too close. He tried to spin, but the muzzle of a gun knocked his temple.

Both arms twisted tight behind him. "Do not speak," said a man, in a clipped accent. He was tugging him back into the shadows of the park.

The full throttle of an engine split the serene pre-dawn. Agitated ducks beat the water. The motorcycle crashed in from the street. It rode up over the curb, and spun around the statue. Its headlight blinded Hudson. The man holding Hudson released his grip. A pinpoint of blood appeared on the side of his neck, then spurted in bursts, long arcs of red, sticky spray. The man crumpled.

The biker clicked the top of what looked like a ballpoint pen. It was not. The blade had gone straight through the man's neck, through the jugular and major arteries.

"Get on!" growled Edwin. With one arm he swung Hudson up on the bike.

They roared over the little bridge and out on to Charles Street.

"This is suboptimal. They came sooner than they should have. Hold on!" Edwin crouched over the handlebars. He swung the bike up Beacon Street. They tore to the left, then he powered the bike down Chestnut Street. They sped through Beacon Hill, past the Episcopal church, its spires looming amid the brick brownstones. Edwin bent the bike on to Storrow Drive, then crossed over the bridge into Cambridge.

"We lost them, for now," said Edwin. "Give me the Blackberry."

Hudson did not move.

"Give it to me," Edwin repeated.

"It's gone," said Hudson softly. He stared at the pavement. There was no response. "I lost it!" He did not know whether Edwin had heard him.

"I lo–" Hudson's voice was shrill again. Edwin held up a hand.

"I heard." They were now at the entrance to a movie theater parking lot two blocks from D6 headquarters. Edwin drove up the eight stories to the roof level, pulled off to an inconspicuous spot far from the staircase. He pulled off his helmet.

"Okay," he said. "I didn't want to be here. But we are. Now give me your shoes."

"What's going on?" said Hudson. "Who was that guy? Was that the terrorist?"

Edwin studied Hudson. What they would do next would require complete synchronization. And what came after that, everything that came after that, would demand total and utter trust. Edwin had to build it. So he paid up front with candor, and borrowed with a promise. Edwin locked his yellow eyes on Hudson.

"That guy is a colleague."

"At D6?" Hudson gasped.

"No," Edwin chuffed. "Not D6. That's a playground. This guy is from my job."

"I don't understand," Hudson said. "Why is he after you?"

"Because they think I've left." Edwin said. "And I have."

Hudson opened his mouth and closed it. He did not know where to start. So Edwin showed him. "Here's what we are going to do. First, we need to get something I left in the building. You meet me in my office. Then we retreat. Then, I will tell you everything. But first I need your help. You can do this. And give me your shoes."

"My shoes?"

"Yes. We're about the same size. You need better traction."

Hudson kicked off his boat shoes, and pulled Edwin's Nikes over his bare feet. They were warm, moist. It was a bit gross at first, like using someone else's toothbrush, but then body temperatures and textures blended and became indistinguishable.

"Why?"

"Simple," said Edwin. "People who don't want to be seen change their hair, their clothes, sometimes their face. But they keep their shoes because it's harder to find a fit at short notice. So people who want to find people watch the shoes."

"I don't think I want anyone else who wants to find you to find me," said Hudson.

"No," said Edwin, strapping on the helmet. "You don't. So don't wear a helmet. They'll look at your pretty face and ignore your shoes entirely. Now go to my office."

Then Edwin flicked down the visor and sprinted for the edge of the parking lot. On this strange day nothing should have surprised Hudson. But what happened next did.

While Hudson stood flat footed in another man's warm shoes, Edwin ran toward the edge of the parking lot roof. He leapt onto the lip of the roof. And was gone.

Hudson ran to the edge. He looked down expecting to see some special forces ninja wire belaying Edwin down the edge of the garage. Or an alternate possibility, Edwin's arms and legs tangled in a pile below, an unexplainable finale.

But Hudson saw only the cement frame of the car park, the grass and walkway. Then he looked up. Just in time to see the wings fully extend. The odd leather jacket had spread nearly six feet across, two feet deep.

There was no other way to put it. Edwin was flying. Silently, he dipped from the garage over the streetlights. The sun heated pockets of air along the façade of D6. These thermals caught under the jacket fabric and lifted Edwin, like a falcon in the city, through the air up the side of the building. He planted securely on a window ledge on the eighth floor. In a silent shuffle, the wings bent sharply and folded back inside his jacket.

Hudson looked down at Edwin's Nikes. He stepped gingerly toward the red exit sign where the steps led one by one to the street.

The eighth floor was empty. No engineer would show up before 10:00 a.m.

"What will the world look like by then?" Hudson thought, jogging down the hallway along a bank of multi-colored cubicles. During the dot com boom, the rainbow promised the pot of gold at the end of the IPO. But with each round of layoffs, the colors seemed frivolous.

White paper blocked any view through the window alongside Edwin's office door. The light was off. He twisted the knob. With a push, the door swung in. What hit him first was the smell.

It was human; it was Edwin. It was a living, personal scent, a mix of the hours he spent there, pizza in boxes left sitting too long, old clothes. The door had been closed since the news of his death. Nothing had gotten out. Not even the scent of him. It would evaporate. Eventually. One day, someone, probably his secretary, would have the numbing job of sorting through everything he left there. Though most of it was in boxes.

Hudson felt a cool breeze begin to stir the stale room. Then he saw the window. The salty scent of the Atlantic Ocean was slipping through a twenty-four inch wide hole in the window where someone had carved a perfect circle.

"Close the door," said a voice in the dark. Edwin.

Hudson obeyed. A small dot of light appeared in the room, bouncing off the floors and walls. A dark shape moved. The light caught, just for a moment, words on the whiteboard. They were the last Edwin had written at D6 – code and strategy for his developers and Hudson on the XTC deal. The last precious gift of his unique brilliance, his passion, his ability to spin up the team at hand, was running across that board, in black and red and blue and green.

Even if D6 went defunct, the six foot wide, five foot tall whiteboard would take up an honored residence in someone's office. No one could wipe away his last marks.

Hudson saw the glow bounce as Edwin moved silently behind the whiteboard. Then Hudson heard a snap. The light clicked off.

"Got it," Edwin said.

"Got what?" Hudson whispered.

"The disarming code. I left a hard copy here. In case," Edwin said, carrying a chair in one hand. He put it under the window sill directly beneath the hole. He tapped the wall. "Okay. You first."

"Meet you downstairs," Hudson turned toward the door.

"No time," said Edwin. "It's 6:22. People will be coming in. We need to get out now. And I have exactly two hours and twenty-four minutes to shut this bomb down."

"You – you have it? On you?" Hudson's voice was shrill.

"This way," Edwin motioned at the window. "You'll be fine." Hudson fixed his eyes on Edwin as he slowly did as he was told.

"Out the window?" Hudson said. "We're on the eighth floor."

"Yes," Edwin said. "First tie your shoes."

"You go first," Hudson said, backing away.

"No. You won't go unless I'm here. Now go. You're wasting time."

Then it dawned on Hudson. Edwin now had the disarming code. What he had needed from the Blackberry. So he no longer needed it. Or him.

Hudson stepped backward. "Edwin, man, I promise. I won't tell anybody. Whatever is going on–"

"You think I'm going to push you out the window on the eighth floor?" Edwin's eyes popped. He let out a high pitched laugh. Then his face fell. "I need you. I don't want to, but I do. So this is what we are going to do. We are going to go out of this building as quickly as possible before anyone sees us. Some eager beaver sales guy is going to be in here by 6:30 a.m. So before that we are going to get on the bike. We are going to get as far east of the population as we can. Then we are going to take this code and use it to disarm this."

Edwin pulled up his shirt. Hudson saw a stubbly patch where a large square area had been shaved into Edwin's chest hair centered on his belly button. A strap of grey duct tape wrinkled and clung to his flesh. In the center it held something the size and shape of a ping pong ball.

"What's that?" Hudson whispered, shrinking back toward the window. He must have nearly touched the bomb when he was clutching Edwin on the motorcycle. Maybe he did.

"Carry-on luggage," said Edwin. "It's a nasty piece. Now I have to shut it down and deliver it to a safe place."

Hudson's mind whirred. He felt very cold. So Edwin had been on that plane. This thing had been on the plane. Now they were both off of it. But all that was left of that plane was a photograph of its jagged silhouette tilting into the North Tower.

"Is that the prize?" Hudson finally said.

"What prize?" Edwin said.

"The guys who grabbed me thought I was you. Is this what they wanted?"

Edwin nodded. "This is what they wanted. It must have cost them a pretty penny. Probably all the cash they had. And someone watching the clock right now in some cave is going to be very disappointed. Unless we don't get where we need to go and disarm it in the next... two hours and eighteen minutes. So move."

"Disarm? What do you mean?" Hudson said. Edwin sighed. He did not like to reveal any more information than was absolutely necessary to help one person to achieve his specific goal. Extraneous information, related to other goals, was a distraction. Distraction was a liability. But Edwin knew candor could work like a catalyst.

"This sphere is highly pressurized manufactured carbon – it's diamond. It holds inside a vial of weaponized pneumonic plague – a particularly nasty strain that would survive the heat. The nice guy who brought it aboard Flight 11 yesterday morning intended it, like him, to blast into a million zillion particles, released over Manhattan and its surrounding areas.

The idea was that terrified New Yorkers grieving the losses and attack on the Towers, Pentagon and planes would be holding each other. Crying. Breathing on each other in small enclosed spaces. Within twenty-four hours they would be coughing, spitting blood, shitting blood, then dying en masse. All of them."

"Good thing you have it, then," Hudson said.

"You may not think so."

"Why not?"

"Whoever taped this nice little gizmo to the armpit of their suicidal friend liked belts and suspenders," Edwin said.

"The twenty-four hour thing – from the message on your Blackberry?"

Edwin nodded. "They weren't sure the mule would actually get on the plane. So it's set to go off anyway. In two hours and fifteen minutes, give or take."

Hudson shrank again. He did not want to be near that thing. "So...won't I just slow you down?" The blow came fast. Edwin's forearm rose so quickly Hudson did not see it. Edwin cracked Hudson across the cheek. Hudson's eyes watered, rage boiled. And he focused.

Edwin was right in his face. "Look. I don't like this. Not one bit. But I can't do it without you. So you are going to help me get as far east as we can to take care of this thing. Then you are going to find that Blackberry." This last was an order.

"But why do you need it? You have the code now, don't you?"

"Its loss is not trivial," said Edwin. "You will find it."

"Okay, okay," said Hudson.

"Don't jump. Just roll forward. Like you're doing a somersault. I'll hold your feet until you are ready. Just do it."

Edwin must have felt the slight flinch in Hudson's ankles as he tried to resist. Because that was when he pulled both of Hudson's feet off the chair, held them straight and pushed them out the window.

CHAPTER 5

HUDSON
7:20 A.M., CAMBRIDGE, MA

Hudson fell headfirst, his legs flipping fast over his head in a perfect somersault. In that first moment, Hudson felt abject terror. The ground rushed at him. But he was upside down for only a fraction of a second. His feet spun faster than the rest of him. Then they hit the wall and stuck. His body snapped forward; his hands slapped bricks.

"Now walk down," Edwin called. "Hands first."

Hudson's head was growing heavy with blood as he clung improbably to the side of a building like a chipmunk. He looked up to the Nikes which somehow anchored him to the wall at the second floor. Above, Hudson could see Edwin perch on the windowsill.

Edwin's helmet concealed his face as he shook his sleeves gently. Then he dove. His arms extended and bent back, his jacket filled. He caught the wind and carved an arc in the air, swooping like a silent bird of prey. In a few short seconds he was on top of the garage and out of view. Then Hudson heard a motorcycle engine catch.

A minute later, a motorcycle rolled down the alleyway. It stopped directly below Hudson. The rider looked up and beckoned, a short, sharp wave. Hudson pulled with his hands, then pushed with his feet, until his hands found the cement sidewalk.

"Nice kicks," Hudson said with short breaths when he reached Edwin.

"Limited edition," said Edwin. "Give them back." Shoes swapped, they raced east as the dawn splashed pink and pale yellow streaks over the Harbor Islands.

"Where are we going?" Hudson shouted through his helmet.

"Fishing," Edwin said. "The Coast Guard, cops, National Guard – will be everywhere today. And for the first time ever, and only if we must, you do the talking. No one sees me. I say nothing. Ever."

It was 7:25 a.m. They drove on as the spit of land stretched out into the Atlantic and curled south to give a look at the wide open ocean to the east, and Logan airport to the south. They drove east, and further east, until they came upon a small wooden structure near a short pier. Old blue paint peeled off in large flakes. A stack of metal fishing boats rested on a trailer in the dry weeds. It stank of stale fish.

Edwin idled the bike, pressing cash into Hudson's hands. "Get a good outboard. And poles. Meet me down the beach 200 yards." Then he was gone.

A few moments later, a middle-aged guy with a worn green t-shirt hiked up his khaki shorts and took one end of small skiff off the racks while Hudson held the other. They carried it to the end of the dock and lowered it into the sea.

"Does the motor work?" Hudson asked as the man cast him off.

"These do too," he nodded, offering Hudson two wooden oars. The polyurethane finish was blistered and cracked. Dings spread short splinters along their edges.

Hudson held his breath as he pulled the throttle on the outboard motor. Nothing. He was drifting away from the dock. The waves slapped the side of the boat.

"Give it a couple," the boat man called over the growing breeze. Hudson pulled again. This time it caught. The man at the dock waved and turned away. Hudson turned the gear lever and twisted the handle to pull out in reverse to clear the docks. Then he slowed, pushed the lever to FWD and powered over the chop. Hudson left a small wake as he rounded the pier, then headed down the shoreline to find Edwin. First he saw a small restaurant and a few beach explorers with their morning coffee and muffins. Then he spotted Edwin. He was standing on the beach holding a box.

Hudson turned in toward the shore. When he was two yards away, he revved the engine once. The boat burst toward the beach. He quickly tilted the engine and lifted it out of the water. The metal bottom of the boat scraped the sand.

Edwin caught the bow and handed Hudson a cardboard container. It held four paper cups that let steam through small holes in their plastic tops. There were two thick discs wrapped in foil and a cardboard box.

"Eat when you can," Edwin said, sitting in the bow. It was only then Hudson realized how hungry he was. And tired. Edwin pointed toward the island that was the furthest east. "There. Outer Brewster Island. Fast as you can. We have 52 minutes."

"Is that enough time?" Hudson said.

"It's all we got." Edwin said.

Hudson kept the helm. He stole a glance at Edwin, perched on the prow of the boat, his head turned ninety degrees, looking over the ocean. His shoulders seemed to slump, just a little. Edwin unpeeled one of the wrappers and stuffed the sausage, egg and buttermilk biscuit sandwich into his mouth. In three bites it was gone. He reached for the container, pulling out a glazed coil of pastry larger than his hand.

"Mmmmm," he said. "Cinnamon rolls. This I will really miss."

He was licking the glaze from his fingers and sipping from the second cup of coffee when they reached a point two miles from shore, the rock face of Outer Brewster rising before them. Logan airport was framed in their wake.

"It's 7:59," Edwin said. "We took off exactly 24 hours ago."

Hudson looked at Edwin.

"Eat," Edwin said, shoving the cardboard box towards Hudson. So Hudson reached for the tinfoil while keeping his hand steady on the tiller, pointing the boat toward Outer Brewster Island. They could see its steep cliffs of granite and the opening of the bunker built in World War II. Unnaturally straight lines made a cement box near the water's edge, behind craggy rocks, a place to disembark briefly without slamming the rock.

"Put some speed into it," Edwin said. "We have work to do when we get there."

But when Hudson twisted the throttle, the engine coughed. Hudson revved it again. It sputtered and went dead. Their momentum carried them forward, but without the forward torque, the three foot swells made the boat rock and sway from rail to rail.

"Oh, come on!" Hudson cried. "I don't know what's wrong!"

Edwin's eyes went wide. "Get it started. We need to reach that bunker, Hudson. We have twenty-nine minutes. It's further away than it looks."

"I know!" said Hudson. He eyed Edwin's belly. The small dent in his shirt.

Five minutes later, the engine had stalled completely. The tide was pushing the boat away from the island, south and east. The wind was offshore.

"Oh God," said Hudson. "Gas! He sent us out without a full tank."

Edwin shook his head.

"I...thought I...okay. I did not check the gas. Stupid!" shouted Hudson.

Edwin held the gunnels of the small boat steady. He did not hurl epithets at Hudson. He did not make plain how useless Hudson was in all respects. Edwin just moved to the center of the boat. He held out an oar.

"Pull," was all he said. "Hard! We will make it."

There was no roadblock of blame or accusation. Edwin had swept through it and was fully focused on the solution. Insisting Hudson do the same. So Hudson sat down on the rickety seat in the center of the boat beside Edwin. He pulled on that oar with all the fuel he would have spent burning himself up.

They rowed. Hard. Yet they seemed to be going nowhere. It was 8:24 a.m. Each time Hudson checked, the island seemed to be exactly where he saw it before. Maybe even further away. So he stopped looking and just pulled. 8:31.

"Harder!" barked Edwin. They pulled together. 8:34.

This time when Hudson looked up, the twenty foot cliff of Outer Brewster Island was fifty yards off. The currents were strong, trying to push them past the island.

"We're going to miss it!" Hudson cried.

"No!" shouted Edwin. "Row! Go! Go! Go!" Edwin barked a stroke time. He put everything into each stroke. Hudson pulled as hard as he could. His arms were burning.

"I'm...I don't know...if I can," he said.

"No!" shouted Edwin fiercely. "Do not...be the one....to say...you are done.   We'll take it in three's. One! Two! Three! Good!" Edwin braced his feet against the transom seat. With each stroke his arms and back and legs strained together. His thick neck bulged with the effort of forcing each dip of the oar through water against the tide and wind. A trickle of blood seeped below the patch on his neck. It mixed with sweat and traced down his collarbone.

So Hudson pulled too. His arms were heavy as anchors. His fingers were numb, blistered clips hooked over the splintered oars. He was exhausted and in pain. But he could count to three. One. Two. Three. One. Two. Three. From somewhere came growls that matched Edwin's. Somehow, his oar stayed even. They pulled in a straight line. He fixed his mind where Edwin told him to put it and he reached. And reached. And reached.

"Good!" gasped Edwin between strokes. "You...are...a...titan!" The praise felt like caffeine. Hudson found another bolus of juice. One. Two. Three. 8:44 a.m.

The boat cracked against rock. Edwin scrambled for the line and threw it around a metal post that jutted out of the bunker.

"Two minutes, Edwin!" Hudson shouted.

"Get out fast," Edwin said. "The wind is from the northwest. So get as far north and west on this island. Do not be downwind of this cave. I'll find you. Go!"

8:45:22. Edwin disappeared into the bunker.

Hudson scrambled for a natural staircase edged into the cliff near the bunker. It must have been an old lookout path. Hudson was a few steps up when he stopped. He looked back at the bunker. Then he crept down the path and quietly peered around the cement edge. His clock read 8:45:42.

"Down! Now!" Edwin knocked Hudson behind the knees. Hudson crumpled to the ground. Edwin heaved the boat up and over Hudson, sealing him in.

CHAPTER 6

HUDSON
8:46 A.M., OUTER BREWSTER ISLAND, MA

Hudson lay in the blackness. His back ached on the hard pebbles. He beat and kicked the roof of his sudden tomb, but could not move it. He gasped, but there was no need. There was plenty of air. Just no light. As Hudson's eyes adjusted to the blackness, he saw a crack of light near his shoulder. There was a small rock just under the edge. He could get just his fingertips around it. He spun its edge, and wiggled it until it came out. What he saw through the peephole was this.

Edwin knelt on the ground. He had placed a small crystal orb into a black holster. He was totally calm. 8:45:58. He tapped a long series of numbers. His fingers flew. Hudson could see Edwin brace. The tendons in his short neck were taut. He crouched low, covering his mouth and nose. There was a loud click. The cube popped open.

Edwin fell back on the sand, flat, his arms outstretched. He looked at the sky and pumped both arms. He breathed a long, full breath like it was the first in days.

Hudson rapped on the boat. "Anybody home? Pizza man!"

"Okay," said Edwin. "Keep your shirt on." Hudson could hear Edwin's sneakers crunch the pebbles against the granite as he walked away. Five minutes later the footsteps settled next to the boat. When Hudson's eyes adjusted to the brightness he saw Edwin grinning, holding a rusty can of gas. He tossed him a fishing pole.

"Provisions," he said. "Let's catch lunch. Then I need a nap."

The breeze caught the surface of the ocean in patches. Dark blue lines filled in the glassy surface. The outboard engine revived with the stale fuel Edwin had found in the bunker, and they puttered to an inlet on the southeast side of the island, where the waves deposited fish in pools behind the protective rocks. Occasionally, one of them would spin his reel, hoping to draw in something they could put on a fire. It was warm and comfortable in the sun.

Without anything to do, anywhere to go, the question could no longer wait.

"Edwin," Hudson said. "What happened to you?"

Edwin was quiet. He stared out over the ocean. "So," he began as an engineer would explain a software integration. "D6 is my day job. Obvious."

So began the story of what had happened to Edwin Hoff the morning of September 11. At least as much of it as he wanted Hudson to know.

CHAPTER 1

EDWIN
7:41 A.M., LOGAN AIRPORT, BOSTON, MA

Edwin's tongue still felt thick from Lula's hot scald of coffee when he pulled the motorcycle to the curb of the American Airlines terminal at Logan Airport. He grasped his backpack and ran into the terminal, pausing like a base runner just long enough to catch the departure gate number. He pushed to the front of the security line and through. He ran full throttle down the wide blue carpet to the gate.

"Don't close it!" Edwin called to the agent, who had kicked up the doorjamb and was about to close the gates. He flashed her the ticket and slipped through. American Airlines Flight #11 from Boston to Los Angeles would have one more passenger. Tragically, it would make no difference to any of them. But to millions of others who were not catching planes that morning, it would mean everything.

The two men seated in the front row did not notice the harried executive finding his seat in business class. But Edwin saw them. And the two others in business class.

Edwin counted the rows between the door and his seat. Dimensions were critical. They translated into strides. Fractions of seconds. This was a 767. The layout opened like a PDF in his mind's eye. The front exit was in the galley between the flight attendants' jump seats and the small closet. The aisle began there. It was four feet from the galley to the back of the first row in first class. Four more feet to the back of the second row in first class. Three feet from the divider between first and business. Five rows, three columns of seats.

Edwin sat in 10C, the second to last row of business class. He assessed the scene. The good – he had a full view of the business class cabin and a glimpse at first if they left the curtain open. The bad – he had twenty feet and six inches to cover to get to the exit alley. He either would have to go through a narrow aisle that would certainly be blocked in parts, or over six rows of seats filled with innocents. The terrain required different strategy, immense leg strength and agility. Fast eyes, because it was impossible to watch two moving targets simultaneously. He would have to predict the correct sequence. This was why their toughest training was for the airplane hostage situation.

"Still a go?" Edwin looked at his Blackberry. "Not possible!" he groaned, realizing his colossal error. But this was no time to dwell on the consequences. Edwin had made one mistake; he would not make another.

At 7:59 a.m., American Airlines Flight 11 rose through the sharp early fall air, so clear the visibility hurt the eye. The hydraulics wheezed, chucking the wheels into the plane.

Edwin sat very still. He breathed deeply, quietly filling his blood with as much oxygen as possible. And he watched. He had passed two of the five in the first row of first class seats. Two were a row in front of him, across the aisle. The one on the aisle bent his head; the one by the window bounced his knee. That was the one. Through his polyester shirtsleeve, Edwin could see horizontal seams where tape wound around his arm. The fifth sat directly behind him. Edwin would take him out first.

The Tuesday morning flight to Los Angeles was not full. There were only a few other men in business class, catching up on sleep or flipping through a copy of Red Herring magazine or SkyMall. Edwin knew the five would be watching everyone closely, so he was careful not to appear alert. He closed his eyes, or nearly. He watched their breathing. When their chests barely rose, barely fell, he could tell the time was near.

The small sound of his seatbelt releasing was lost in the white noise of the cabin.

The scream that came from first class was high and brief. The one across from Edwin bolted forward toward the cockpit. Edwin remained still. For one second more. Then he was on his feet, on his seat.

Edwin expected the one with the vial to be armed and ready to fight. From this position, Edwin kept the advantage of sight and, more importantly, height. The three rules of hand to hand combat training barked familiar orders to Edwin's muscles.

1) Your goal is to kill.
2) Everything you can reach is a tool.
3) Nothing is off limits.

The one behind him stood on the floor, a sharp triangle of steel flashing at the end of his fingertip. He lunged up toward Edwin, who dodged easily, using the movement to catch the attacker at the end of his swing. There would be a single moment when he was vulnerable: where his arms were extended, he was out of momentum, and off balance.

Edwin watched it come. As the swing missed, Edwin came behind his head, drawing him to his chest. His arms and chest hardened to the vise that had closed death on an enemy more than once. Edwin gave the head a sharp twist. That one fell. Now Edwin sprang to the aisle. He had to get the vial without catching a blade. Had to do it quickly, before the three in front realized something had gone very wrong behind them.

Suddenly the plane dove. It dipped one wing, then overcorrected and swung the other. Everything not tied down hit the ceiling. Plates and cups shattered. Edwin hit his right shoulder hard and came down on his side. The plane was making an abrupt and uncoordinated turn from due west to southeast, veering dizzyingly back and forth, attempting to regain its balance. It was no longer in steady hands.

Edwin could not breathe. He coughed. For a moment, the wind was out of his lungs. Thinking fast. "Southeast. Descending. So the target is…New York."

The second hijacker, the one with the special cargo, was belted into his seat. He had his bearings when he saw this unexpected challenger rise in his seat, snap the neck of his partner and go sprawling on the aisle. Before Edwin could fill his lungs, the attacker had straddled him, his right arm drawn and ready to open Edwin's neck with the box cutter in his hand.

But a career of counterterrorism training builds a lot of muscle memory. The muscle memory of martial arts and anaerobic training were designed to train one to respond when flat on the floor, out of position, out of weapons and out of air.

Waving the weapon with one arm, the attacker could only hold Edwin with the other. He crouched over Edwin like a jockey when Edwin bucked. Flush with adrenalin and power, Edwin grabbed the attacker's arm as he flew over his head. Broke it backwards at the elbow. In seconds the terrorist was on his back, shrieking. Shards of jagged bone in his forearm poked through his shirt. His knife skittered under the rows of seats.

Edwin saw the sharp bone splinters. "Everything is a tool. Nothing is off limits."

He gripped a piece of wet bone. Snapped it off. Then he stabbed it through the underside of the terrorist's arm into the floor. The hijacker shrieked, then lay still. The small package was exposed.

"Now you're disarmed," Edwin said. He crouched by the whimpering man, and pulled a ballpoint pen from his back pocket. He clicked it, slicing through the shirtsleeve. Another stroke left a stream of blood on the man's arm, severing thick layers of duct tape. Skin and hair ripped when Edwin tore the vial from the limp arm.

The rest would have to happen very quickly.

Edwin pulled a roll of duct tape from his pack and lifted his shirt. There was a wide strip where he had shaved his stomach. Knowing humans instinctively protect their gut first, Edwin wound the tape around his waist, securing the vial against his belly button. He threw the backpack over his shoulders, and bolted for the exit door near the cockpit.

The cockpit door was shut. Two stewardesses lay bleeding in the galley. One was breathing with great difficulty. But Edwin's orders were explicit. He was not to stop to save these people. This was exactly why orders were precise, and there was zero tolerance for variation from the goal. If he were distracted, he would fail. Then casualties would not just come from the plane, the building it hit, or some pedestrians. The vial would wipe out all of New York City, a good portion of the populated Northeast.

"Get it done," Edwin gritted. "Remove the puck." But the stewardess's eyes were on him. It was her shriek that had come first, after she reprimanded the man unbuckling his seatbelt before the pilot had turned off the seat belt sign.

Edwin kneeled over the blood-spattered woman. "It's okay," he said.

"Thank you," she whispered. Edwin pulled the duct tape out of the side pocket of his backpack. Tearing a piece with his teeth, he bandaged the bleeding woman where the stab wound pumped rivulets of blood, now too weakly. He took another long piece of tape and wrapped it around her chest, then the leg of the refrigerator. When the door opened, the unpressurized air would suck out everything not bolted down. That at least, was one horror he could spare her.

"Now focus," Edwin growled. In a stride, he was at the door to the airplane.

The cockpit door flung open behind him. Edwin heard shouting. The unauthorized seconds spent on the condemned stewardess had a serious cost. He could have been gone already. He was not. Edwin put both hands on the cabin door. Instinctively, they fell precisely on the handle. He pulled the lever hard.

Two hands grabbed his shoulders. A sharp blade stung his neck. Edwin strained against the door as the man shouted spurts of fury in ululating trills.

The cabin door gave way with a huge suck of air. Inside, oxygen masks fell. The wind whipped across Edwin's face. He blinked. Thick, viscous tears released from Zed's lenses. His eyes did not dry despite the blowing air. He could see objects on the ground in focused detail even though they rushed above it at 500 miles per hour.

The man behind him pulled hard against him. He must have had his foot wedged against the door. Edwin just needed a little more angle. So he dipped his chin. That was all. The pressure sucked him out of the plane. He grabbed his knees, now free of the plane and the roar the engines made as they resisted gravity.

Falling was quiet. Windless. Edwin watched the massive wings of the 767 pass above his Nikes. Once Edwin could no longer hear the terrified shriek of the man who had fallen with him, the jump was like every other one he had made.

Except this time he did not have a parachute.

This was a HALO jump. High Altitude, Low Opening. Edwin left the plane at about 15,000 feet. In the first six seconds, his body accelerated to 120 miles per hour: terminal velocity. The speed at which the force of gravity on a human body meets the opposite force of the object's air resistance. The terrorist who left the plane with Edwin would have found martyrdom a little earlier than planned, meeting ground at that speed. Edwin counted a third kill.

The mission was on course. The vial was taped securely to his belly. These were facts. Edwin did not allow pride to distract him. He could no longer see the plane as he held his arms and legs out, back arched, like a starfish. From here he got his bearings. Without goggles, a normal skydiver would be blind with tears and wind. But with the special lenses Zed had produced, Edwin could fix his gaze below, and images of the ground stabilized even though he was moving fast toward it. Infrared images scanned across his view, showing him where warm bodies took up space, and where he could land unnoticed. At night it would provide him with vision as clear as daylight. The acuity was uncanny – three times sharper than normal. He could focus on an object and magnify it. He could see like an eagle, a kestrel, an owl.

A thick black ribbon below him stretched south and east to the horizon. The sight made Edwin review the plane's flight path. The abrupt turn south after about twenty-five minutes, its meandering southeast path. Rapid, purposeful, descent. At twenty-five minutes into that cross-country flight he knew so well, the pilots usually announced they were over Albany, at cruising altitude of 30,000 feet, and were turning off the fasten seat belt sign. Today, inexperienced pilots flew west until they saw the Hudson River below, paving the way to the Manhattan skyline.

That river rushed toward Edwin. He could see a highway crossing it, and crossing forests and fields. He located a space in the field with only small pulses of infrared light – rabbits and mice, likely. After six seconds, his watch read 5500 feet. Then he snapped his elbows sharply. For this flight where he would have to soar like an eagle and land like an owl, the jacket spread connected layers of fabric from Edwin's torso to his elbows and out beyond his fingertips. Behind him, fabric extended in a wide swath the length of his legs. Comb-like filaments lined the edges, and velvet tufts covered his torso. This let the air pass: he flew silently. As he pulled his elbows close, he made a concave pocket that caught the air within it and let the air pressure slip easily over the top edge. It lifted him abruptly. He shook his fingertips, then widened the fabric extending over his feet. Each gesture fed the dynamic stabilization sensors and brought the physics of flight under his control, providing forward and backward motion, lift, and descent. To remain unseen, Edwin must miss the bridge and the river. It would not help to hang up in a seventy-five foot white pine.

He was somewhere upstate. Less populous than Manhattan if anything went wrong with his landing, or his cargo, but still largely settled. And the easterly breezes would carry the problem to the densely populated coastal areas very quickly; within a day. The mission was on course, but not complete. And there were non-trivial complications. He had caused them; he would fix them. Edwin had the vial, although he still had to disarm it and deliver it as his orders instructed. Then extract.

The fields came at him, lines and lines of ripe crops. In September, it was high as the elephant's eye, brimming for harvest.

"Uh oh," Edwin thought. "Corn!" He came in fast, holding his billowing jacket above him. With the slightest movements from his arms, the material made lightning fast adjustments on its own as he kicked both legs forward. He was not falling anymore, but he was not on the ground yet, either. He was twenty feet above the stalks, hovering.

Thick woods lined the edge of the field, oaks and maples that wore a few of the yellow leaves that would soon take over completely. The thicket was impenetrable. Whatever went on beneath that canopy was hidden.

Edwin turned his yellow lenses toward the sturdy branches that overhung the field. The focus adjusted, locked. His arms swept the air, turning the hover into a swoop. Fingertip fringe and multiple articulations in the jacket buckled and billowed, sending him from the air above the corn field toward the tree line at high speed, passing him through the craggy maze of branches without touching one. Ten yards inside the canopy, he stretched out his feet while his jacket puffed. He reached his feet forward toward a thick branch. The Nikes grabbed it and held.

Edwin stopped. He stood on the branch and shook his arms. The jacket retracted to a normal appearance. He sat down against the tree trunk. Touched his belly. The tape was secure; the bump where the vial nestled in the crease of his belly button was there. He ripped off the tape, and for the first time, examined his quarry. It was an almost perfect, clear sphere of some hard crystal. The sphere was the luggage; embedded inside was a small, round vial with a blue liquid. He turned it over. On the outside of the vial, magnified by the thickness of the diamond was a timer. Red numbers blinked. 23:55:12. 23:55:11. 23:55:10.

Edwin thought, "So it was set to begin twenty-four hours after the plane hit its target. In case it did not hit. Belts and suspenders." It had hit. The plane. Somewhere. Just under five minutes ago. As he sat, gathering energy, on the branch, Edwin thought of the people he had seen on the plane that morning. The business people. The families. The stewardesses. The faces preoccupied with whatever business took them from one coast to another. Anticipating six pleasant hours of peace, where they had brief reprieve from the world that expected constant communication except where it was forbidden, on a plane. A smooth flight in good weather, offering a beautiful view of the vastness of the country, patchwork fields laid out in crisp surveyor's squares, each seed planted precisely within them. Service in business class. Rich coffee with creamers. A menu offering smoked salmon and a surprisingly appetizing omelet. A glass of wine at noon and warm nuts. Time to improve a presentation, read a paper, a trade journal, or watch a movie. On a normal flight, Edwin would have slept, mining the hours to add to the handful he generally snatched each night. Then someone had screamed.

"But the plane is just the warm-up act," Edwin said, looking at the countdown. He had less than twenty-four hours to disarm this device and return it to the location specified in his orders: a penthouse apartment in Washington D.C. Drop and Load Orders always specified delivery times and places so the Head would know as early as possible if the mission had gone off course. If the Operator had.

So to complete his mission, Edwin had to recover the code. Which was on his new Blackberry. Which was out of his hands. He hoped it was just where he had mistakenly left it.

"With Davenport," Edwin shuddered. "Of all the goons." He had to get to Boston quickly. And stay dead. Edwin took stock. Limbs bent where they should, bore weight as they should. Face, intact. But he felt fluid sticky against his neck. Instinctively, he touched it. His fingers were covered in red.

The cap of his ballpoint pen, which survived the departure in the side pocket of his pack, reflected his face, making it look absurdly oval. But it was clear enough to see where blood pulsed from a very thin, two-inch-long slice against his neck. The hijacker must have caught him with the blade. It fortunately missed his jugular, but Edwin knew from the speed of the blood that it was deep enough. It had to be closed soon, and treated. An open wound in the open air and dirt and dust was a bad combination. He had to stop the bleeding and prevent infection.

Edwin's dark jacket would hide the dried blood. He pulled a CVS bag out of the side pocket, extracting a gauze pad and duct tape. He strapped the bandage to his neck. He buckled his jacket around his neck and got to his feet. What he needed now was a roadside pizza joint. Preferably one just off a major roadway.

The bridge he had seen during his descent appeared to have at least four lanes; two on each side. A feeder for the traffic straight to New York via Route 9S. Drivers headed north would hit I-90, which could take them east to Boston. Edwin estimated that the bridge was about a mile north of where he landed.

Edwin hopped down from the branch. His jacket billowed: the jump was from two stories. He crept to the edge of the forest. The corn field came right to the trees, an odd juxtaposition of nature and machine. Acres of stalks grew exactly eighteen inches from one another, in rows exactly three feet apart. One could look through them like orderly aisles of a supermarket.

That one mile through the thick brush took him an hour to cover. He kicked through the last of the scrub and fell in a crouch at the edge of a highway. He would have to move faster. He could not waste time in the woods, slogging through wetland and pressing through shrubbery. The highway was elevated; the grassy drainage area fell away sharply. It would give him some protection from drivers' sight. He pulled the ice cube, as he now thought of it, from the taped nest in his belly button.

The numbers shone in a baleful red display: 22:20:19. Edwin set his watch to it. Then he looked down the drainage valley for as far as he could see. After a few miles, it disappeared around a curve. No exits, no signs for food.

Edwin breathed deeply. He could feel throbbing at his neck. What he was about to do would not lessen the pressure at the wound, now slicking up the inside of the duct tape. But he had done much more than this before. He set off at a stable clip, seven miles per hour. He needed to keep moving, steady, unhurt, unseen.

Edwin had spent a week in SERE training: seven days in the desert and woods of a desert country, outside the United States, with only a knife, a flint and a bottle for trapping what water he could find. Edwin not only survived and evaded capture but managed to incapacitate three of the four Hunters, deciding to leave the fourth terrified at having turned prey, and free to report the story.

His body heat rose, trapped under the jacket. He felt the fabric adjust, and a breeze ruffled through the fabric. His jeans chafed. At least this time he had sneakers. And these were not just any Nikes. But the jeans were rough. If he were spotted, a man running along the highway in a motorcycle jacket would not raise another look — just a guy out of gas. A man running along the highway in a blood stained t-shirt would be another story. 911 would ring off the hook.

An hour passed. Edwin chugged along, dipping seven times into the woods. But no one slowed. A police cruiser passed him at the speed limit. Not trawling. Two hours. He must have run close to twenty-five miles before he saw the familiar symbols: a fork and knife.

Edwin crept back into the woods and skirted the exit route. Near the connecting road, he could see a brown building with a sign. Three motorcycles were parked outside.

"Rhinebeck's World Famous House of Pizza," Edwin said. "Outstanding."

In all of two minutes, traffic disappeared outside the World Famous House of Pizza. Edwin stepped out of the woods and slowly, casually, crossed the street. Then he walked past the entrance to the back parking lot. Where the garbage would be.

In the bright sunshine, the dumpster reeked of sour milk and cheese, rancid tomato sauce, rotten spiced meat, stale beer, and their stew. The rusted edges were caked with it where the late night waiters had casually tossed dark bags that split when they hit.

"There you are," Edwin said. Behind the dumpster, nearly three feet tall, were the grooved stalks sprouting brown burrs. Reddish purple flowers bloomed like thistles. Edwin grabbed the stalks, ripping fistfuls of the flowers and stuffing them in his pack.

Next, he peered into the dumpster. Suppressing an urge to gag, he pulled up a black trash bag and sliced through it. He grabbed two plastic bottles, both nearly full of water, stuffing them in his pack.

There was a half-eaten piece of pepperoni pizza lying in a bent piece of tinfoil. He folded that in his hand.

Through the window, Edwin saw the television in the kitchen. Smoke and fire high on one of the Twin Towers. A second jet barely hitting the corner of the other, as if the pilot had flinched. Fire, smoke. Stick figures falling. Implosion.

Edwin shook his head hard to scatter the thoughts that were pricking his brain.

"I could have taken the cockpit. I could have landed the jet."

But the training barked, "Not your mission."

Both were true. Landing the jet safely was distinctly not his mission. He was to take control of the vial of plague, keep it away from people – on the plane, or near the plane, and disarm it. But because orders were open as to the method by which operators accomplished them, the only issue was this:

"Did I choose the best way?" Edwin thought. His brain clicked, seeking the clear conclusion that never came. He felt the orb, still armed. This mission was on track, but not over. He surveyed the parking lot. Trees grew thickly in front of the three parked motorcycles. He stood up, stepped across the lot, and crouched to examine the bikes from behind. He patted the exhaust pipes. As he rose to his feet, he ran his hands along the soft leather with the touch of a man who loved fast machines.

He had about ten minutes. He went thirty feet back into the woods, peeling off his jacket. Sweat made the leather clingy. He pulled the purple leaves out of his pocket and rubbed them between his palms. They wept reddish purple moisture.

Edwin poured the contents of one filthy water bottle over the exterior of the other, until it was passably clean. He twisted off the cap and poured a capful of water on the crumpled flowers in his hand. He mixed it with his fingers until the crushed petals became a reddish purple paste.

Trash was full of treasure. Edwin knew what to look for in each region of every country he set foot in. He set the crumpled tinfoil down. He rolled his pen across the thin sheet, soon producing a very smooth, somewhat pocked, reflective surface. Enough to see the wound pulsing blood. He crushed the Great Burdock poultice in his hands, sterilizing them. He pulled a small tube from his bag – his second favorite drugstore survival item. Crazy Glue. He remained stone silent as he tore the duct tape from his neck. Hairs ripped and a layer of ectoderm came up on the tape. Fresh blood dripped on his t-shirt. He peered into the reflective piece of tin foil like a person shaving carefully. He squeezed the purple-stained skin together and lay a line of the super adhesive glue along the cut. Better than stitches, it sealed in the antibiotic flower as well as bound the cut. Over that he pressed a clean gauze pad, securing it with tape. He used another to wipe the blood off of his jacket collar. All of the materials he used – the torn duct tape, the bloody gauze, even the plastic bottles – went back into his pack. No trace.

Edwin chewed someone else's cold pepperoni pizza. The acid in his gut was tough enough to neutralize any bacteria that had settled on the pizza. He needed fuel. Edwin slugged what was left in the water bottle and stored it. It was time to move. Edwin crouched beside a row of motorcycles. He added five silver strips to the license plate of one. NY4L761 became NY HE78L. He slipped his hand over the back of the bike and grabbed the helmet. He pulled it over his head, flicked the visor and drove slowly out of the parking lot.

"Two hundred miles to Boston," Edwin thought. "Two hours, tops. More than enough time to get the Blackberry back from that useless suit." He just had to do it without being seen by Hudson or anyone else. If he failed, in 19 hours and 28 minutes the world would suffer its largest single act of mass murder. And Edwin needed the Blackberry back. Without it he saw three problems: Civilian Breach; False Perception of Failed Mission; and Urban Center Annihilation.

There was enough data on that Blackberry to expose the mission to whomever could crack the encryption code. Any messages coming through would just sound like a whistle and look garbled to anyone who did not know how to unlock it. Davenport would never be able to do it. But in the wrong hands, someone might. The ASP would not wait. Fiddling with the Blackberry carried mortal risk.

Second, if Edwin did not respond to any communications, he would be expected at the Personal Meeting place specified in his orders – the penthouse in Washington D.C. If he did not appear there at the appointed time, the Head would label the mission "Code Black: Failed." Edwin would be listed as "RUPD." Rogue Until Proven Dead. The ASP never accepted mere disappearance of an operator as a death. Operators were too good at it – their trade was deep cover. So the ASP required physical proof of critical body parts or enough of what was left of them. Always, the rogues were proven dead. One way or the other. The ASP did not rehabilitate lost Operators.

Edwin had once been sent on an RUPD mission, searching for Lennox Alida. The legend who had blocked a poisoning of the London Water Supply had gone missing. Edwin tracked him. Found him. Delivered three toes and bags of sand soaked in his blood. The case was closed. But that did not keep Edwin from thinking about him.

Edwin had made some mistakes on this mission. Non-trivial mistakes. But he had the puck. And belts and suspenders, too. If he had presumed correctly that his last days on earth would be enshrined.

Edwin did not tell Hudson some things. How the skyline of Boston rose into his view as he flew along the turnpike. How his mind went instantly to the memory of that view at night, from the tallest building in Boston. How he had sat for hours one night early that summer, with Lula, at the restaurant at the top of the Prudential Center. Sipping a rare second beer, giddy with making that choice.

"What are all these people doing out?" Edwin had said. "It's a Thursday night!"

Lula laughed gently. "Thursday is kind of a big night out…for some people."

Edwin flushed, realizing he had exposed something of himself, something that showed where he was not as experienced as his peers, where he was vulnerable.

"This is a naughty place," he accused. "These people have no responsibilities to anyone – not even to themselves." Lula put her hand on his. He healed instantly.

"Look at the planes," she said. "Orderly shooting stars."

Edwin watched Lula watching the dozens of planes ring the sky around them. He wanted very badly to kiss her.

That June night was a lifetime ago. For Edwin, this cover had been beyond fun. Rising to the top of the technology world in the boom. Becoming a kind of celebrity. He had not expected to see the Boston skyline again. Coming back was startling. It was different this time. From every other mission, he had extracted so easily. It had not been hard to disappear from the firefighter team in Atlanta. From the temp worker office pool in Austin. The ski-bum winter in Colorado had been fun, and good practice, but he was ready for action when the call had come.

This time he was supposed to be a grad student studying obscure mathematics, but he had become a technology wizard with global celebrity status. He had become wealthy. Distractingly wealthy. And he had developed an attachment.

But things did not just happen to Edwin Hoff. He made them happen. From a boy who loved math and orchestra, but not the teasing it attracted, he sought weights, muscles, guns. In the military he learned to master everything that a man's brains and physical force could control, and the men who could master both. But he had encountered something new in this last assignment. He tasted the thrill of personal recognition, public and private. He had become the popular kid. Women liked him. He had mastered "cool." And he liked it. Which was a problem.

"But Edwin Hoff is dead now," Edwin said to himself. "He had no real responsibilities. I do. And I almost screwed up. It's obstreperous." He pulled off the highway on the Cambridge exit. Idled the engine.

Edwin should have continued to Hudson's address. He should have tucked the bike in an alley and snuck into Hudson's apartment. He should have found the Blackberry on the kitchen table and slipped out a window, taken care of business with the prize, and been on his way with an inert vial to the Personal Meeting in his orders.

But he did not. Faces flashed through his mind. Ahmed. Sterling. Jack. Michael James. Nancy. Even Hudson Davenport's silly grin. And Lula. He felt slack lines grow taut.

"But did Edwin Hoff matter to them?" he said. He checked his watch. Sixteen hours. There was no time even for a brief detour. So he would have to be quick.

By 11:55 a.m., Edwin was crouching on the roof of the garage opposite D6's office building, behind a ledge that afforded him a view of the building. He did not need binoculars to see through the windows: Michael James, moving crisply from office to office. Then he closed his door. Ahmed, in the window, his stare unbroken. Jameson holding his head. Edwin's engineers bent at their desks. They would be quite busy. D6's Interface products and the software system would underlie communications on the Internet. That day the Internet would be the primary means of communication as telephone lines choked on the volume. This contribution was trivial compared to his current mission, but Edwin flushed with pride.

It was time to go. There was just one more stop he could not resist.

Lula lived in a small studio apartment in East Cambridge, near an area of promised redevelopment. He cut the engine when he was a hundred yards away.

"Be quick," Edwin said. "You're a blip to her. Get your damn focus back."

But when he peered above the bay window into Lula's apartment, he lost it completely. Lula slumped at her computer, typing slowly. Doing email. In the distance, he could see a small television set. It filtered through photographs. He saw his own picture from D6 website – all smiles, confidence, joy. This cover was so much easier than his real job; so much more fun. Irresponsible – very nearly. But it let him be productive and creative. And for the first time in his life, close to someone. Close to a lot of people, actually, Edwin realized.

When she saw Edwin's photograph flash by again, Lula broke down. Her hands covered her face. Edwin could hear her cries through the window, which was open a few inches. She shook with sobs. She wept.

Edwin's hands were on the window sill when he noticed the door to Lula's apartment. A slice of light came from the hallway. This was new. It was habit for Edwin to notice all entrances and exits in every room. And any changes in them.

Someone else was there. Edwin stepped silently back into the shadows, watching. If Lula had a friend over, she did not act like it. In her private grieving, her legs gave way and she lay face down on her bed. Edwin did not like that she was so upset. He did not like how she cried in her pillow. It would give someone opportunity, and purchase.

It happened very quickly. A figure in black clothes came from behind her open closet door. Silently he pulled the edges of the pillow up around her ears. She thrashed silently. In a few moments she lay limp.

Edwin raged. His hands were on the window sill, paint stripping under his gloves. He was about to blow through the window when the attacker turned toward the window, and opened it about five inches. Then the killer turned back to Lula's body. He tugged her pants down to mid-thigh. Then he left.

What Edwin saw made him stagger back into the shadows. It changed everything. He knew who killed Lula. Edwin had trained him. For several minutes Edwin stayed very still, calculating.

"So," Edwin said. "There is no next cover for me. I was not supposed to make it. They are cleaning up what's left of Edwin Hoff, and the RUPD hunt for me has already started." Then he swung through the window. With a gloved hand, he held Lula's limp body. Beneath a thick film, his yellow lenses blinked back to focus.

This was clear. If the ASP knew about Lula, there would be others they would consider close enough to Edwin to require maintenance. Edwin thought about Sterling, who he let convince him to start the business, who gave him the ticket to the biggest ride in the amusement park. Jameson, the only one who never got too spun up, never showed doubt. The one person Edwin would let give him advice; the one person who had it to give. Nancy, Edwin's assistant. She was in charge of his calendar, knew where he was and when he wasn't where he was supposed to be. This would be more than cause. Ahmed. They were such a team. But where would his allegiance be in all this, now? And Hudson. The RUPD team already would have triangulated the device to Hudson's address. They would be tracing his every move. This was exactly why deep cover was supposed to be solitary. Explainable, believable, but dull enough to inspire dread in small talk.

"I should have stayed in school," Edwin said. "There's only one way to protect them. Appease the lion." Only one person could change the cleanup order: the Head of the ASP. Then Edwin's people would live. "Easy. Just complete the mission. Deliver the vial. Show them all just how much better I am than the ASP ever guessed. They can't bleach me."

That is what he would make them believe. But their betrayal took root. Edwin was, at his heart, an entrepreneur. Now he was on to the biggest start-up experience of his life, against the most hostile competitors. Fortunately, he had the financial resources to do whatever he wanted to do.

Edwin pressed his lips to the top of Lula's head, and it became very clear what he owed Nancy, Hudson, Jameson and Sterling and anyone else he had endangered by playing loose with the ASP's rules under this cover. For the first time in his life of duty, Edwin knew the names of the people to whom he owed it. He went to Lula's computer. In a few simple strokes, it appeared that Lula Crosse had sent a brief but vital message to HDavenport@D6.com.

PART 7
SEPTEMBER 12, 2001 RESUMED

CHAPTER 1

EDWIN AND HUDSON
9:45 A.M., OUTER BREWSTER ISLAND, MA

"So now you know," Edwin told Hudson. Some of it, he added privately. His hand raked the beach, sifting the pebbles, while he watched Hudson process the facts. It had been a huge risk to tell him. But Edwin knew that to keep his team of two tight he had to build the bond. He would let it set before testing it. It would take a few minutes.

Meanwhile, Edwin took out the vial and held it carefully between his thumb and forefinger. Neutralized, Edwin could now study it.

"Man," Hudson said. "You're like a superhero." And a killer, he thought. Edwin's familiar face warped as Hudson imagined it in new contexts. Those same hands clutching a dry erase marker, waving at a whiteboard. Then breaking off a human bone to tack flesh. The same fingers spread wide, catching air at 120 miles per hour. "And I lost the Blackberry in a bird's nest. So what now?"

Edwin shrugged. "I disappear. I'm dead, remember?"

"But what about the ASP people who want you...? What about them?"

"I have to disappear convincingly. And immediately."

"But what about...what...," Hudson muttered. He did not want Edwin to go. Alone he never matched expectations. But in Edwin's presence, something happened. Hudson borrowed. Edwin offered. He insisted anyone with him play by the same rules he did. Focus on the assignment regardless of distraction. Make it happen. Get your job done. Done right. With Edwin, Hudson got airborne too.

"It was supposed to be a quiet cover, just a place to hang until the next call came. But then I met your dad at a conference and he was so gung ho to start this company. The least noticeable path, I thought, was to go along. Plus it was…." Edwin hesitated.

"Fun?" Hudson drew out the word, his smile leaking to his whole face.

"Yeah," Edwin laughed. "It was fun. You – you go out at night, come back and there's one less cranky woman in the world."

"Maybe two," Hudson grinned.

"When I come home, there's one less bad guy," Edwin said. "Sometimes three. Everything I have ever done since high school has been serious. Life and death serious. Regimes rising and falling serious. Living one cover, taking on a mission, going to another life that isn't mine and leaving that for another before too long. But D6 – turning an idea into action – this was not duty. It was play. And it was mine."

They were both quiet for a while.

"So is the ASP…are you in, like, the Army?" Hudson said.

"Like the Army?" Edwin threw back his head. Something was funny. "No. Nothing like the Army. After high school I was in the Rangers for a while. I was the best. The best they ever had. So I got picked." This was not a boast. Just fact.

"For what? Delta Force?" Hudson had turned a knee, fascinated.

"After Delta Force. You have to be strong but not the strongest, brilliant not smart, strategic and tactical. Fused to your goal. And…."

"What?"

"Alone," Edwin said. "You can't have…."

"Friends?"

"Anyone. You have to be able to disappear anytime, forever, and unnoticed."

"Good job with that one," Hudson said.

"Yeah," Edwin said, looking down with a small smile. Grains of sand rolled on the tips of his fingers. "This cover got a little out of hand."

There were three effects to revealing confidences they both knew Edwin should keep. First, Hudson believed what Edwin said.

Second, he felt trusted and respected, which built a solid bond. And this: trusted to be candid, Edwin could choose to be opaque.

"Delta Force is the U.S. Military," Edwin explained. "What it does, the government is accountable for. All governments are ultimately accountable for their own special forces. So there has to be something else. Something above nations. Something above party and policy. An organization that does what is right, when it is needed, without waiting for the constitution or politics. Particularly about bio threats. The Head started the ASP after World War II, when the Nazis experimented with precursors to these weapons on their captives. Rumor is the Head was one. But you'll never find a reference to the ASP. Only the best are tapped. Even operators rarely know who else is involved. Orders come from the Head. We get technical support, occasionally work in teams, but usually you're on your own. You live some kind of quiet life until the call comes and then you respond to the duty. Sometimes you come back to the life you have. Sometimes you are extracted to another mission, a new life. Then you can never return to the old one. Ever. So it's not only best not to get involved with anyone, it's crucial. For everyone."

Edwin considered telling Hudson the cold fact that he was now in the sights of the ASP because of his dabbling on their Blackberry. But Hudson was bent forward holding his knees, as if the breeze was colder than the soft warmth coming in off the warm September ocean. No, Edwin concluded. Too much truth could paralyze. Edwin needed Hudson high, confident, and able to complete the mission he was about to give him. Alone. He could not go running to Mommy because monsters were after him. Then the monsters would get Mommy too.

Hudson was staring at Edwin's hands. The thick fingers, not particularly big hands, wrapped gently around the fishing pole. The ones that scrawled genius trails of strategy with a pen on a whiteboard, or clicked. out clever code. Hudson tried to imagine those fingers pulling triggers on a semiautomatic. That warm grin bent flat. He just could not put it together.

"What if you want to – come back," Hudson said. "Sometime?"

Edwin shook his head. "Can't. ASP operators do what the Head wants. If you don't do it, you get RUPD."

"What's that?"

"Not good."

"Reported Up to Police Department?" Hudson ventured.

"You're like a dog with a bone," Edwin said. "No police. RUPD means Rogue Until Proven Dead. You are designated a rogue by the ASP, and a task force is sent out to get evidence of your death."

"What if you aren't dead?"

"They still get it."

It took Hudson a minute. "Oh."

"I was on a RUPD recovery mission once. The guy was a legend. Lennox Alida. British guy. Had personally stopped two presidential assassins and a terrorist group from poisoning the London water supply. That was just in the year before he had trouble."

"Did you find him?"

"I delivered the proof," Edwin said. "Toes. Three of them from the right foot. Carried them back to the Head in a Ziploc sandwich bag with three pounds of sand saturated with his blood. No one could lose that much blood and live."

What Edwin left out no one needed to know. How he had traced the target to the Maldive Islands. How he had watched him for five days. Forty-eight hours from a sniper hole, through sea grass and moss dangling over his forehead. How the target had dressed in white trousers and a white t-shirt and loaded a cushioned folding table in the back of his jeep. How he had driven out to a thatched hut at the end of a long pier, to provide massage services.

How on the third day Edwin had followed him back to the windsurfing bay. Had a Coke at the bar and smeared lotion on the back of his neck, red from the equatorial sun. Watched the target's bright yellow sail rise out of the sea, streak across the bay, snap in the wind, steal back. Wondering what it felt like to hit the wave and flip the small board in a back circle, floating on the sail like a wing until the board at his feet came down to the water again.

There was one thing Edwin would never repeat: what he saw at night through the gold light square of Lennox Alida's hut. The masseur's hands working on the woman's calves as she rested back on the stack of pillows she would sleep upright on, her hands on the sides of her bulging abdomen.

Edwin had asked a concierge to book the appointment. As the first of the morning light filtered into the water, he had waited twenty feet below, between the pilings of the piers, coated in barnacles, surrounded by the feeding throngs of puffer fish, parrot fish, an sweetlips with their black body stripes a polka dot tail fins. The masseur arrived early for his day's schedule. The sound of his flip flops slapping on the wood, a hollow echo in the air below bouncing back on the water. The smart snap of the table as the hinges opened and held.

Edwin had crept silently beneath the edge of the deck. Climbed up. He had swung his leg sideways, chopping the target's knees. Used the falling man's weight to flip his shoulder. They had splashed into the sea, Edwin's hands on the other man's throat. They wrestled until they came up under the pier. Lennox Alida held up a five inch blade. And his open palm.

"My duty is done," he said in sparse English. He plunged the knife straight down. Red clouds bloomed in the water around them. He closed Edwin's fingers over a handful of stones. Edwin opened his fist. The three severed toes ran blood into the water.

Lennox swung down the pier slats like monkey bars toward a piling near the beach. He slashed three plastic bags, heavy with dark fluid, spilling into the sand, thickening it. Solids that could be picked up and produced for the Head. When Edwin looked up, Lennox was gone.

Edwin was searching the beach with his eyes when something like sandpaper scraped against his leg. Large dark bodies were suddenly there, snapping through the blind clouds of sand and blood toward the scent. The bump came hard, knocking the air regulator from Edwin's mouth. The toes, slick with blood, fell out of his hand into the sand below. Edwin had to get out of the water. Instead, he kicked hard, reaching down. Grabbing at the ocean floor. All that came up was sand. His flipper ripped off. It was just a matter of two or three whips of tail. But then Edwin spied a glint of light on a flake in the sand. Maybe a shell. But maybe a toenail.

He pulled and kicked his way through the three yards of water below him. Grabbed the two toes lying next to each other. And the third. In a suck of water, Edwin reached for the splintery dock. Clung there as fins turned just a few feet below.

Later, Edwin had packaged the toes and bloody sand. And part of him felt lifted. It was like letting a bird out of a hole in the ground.

Edwin turned to Hudson, a hard glint in his eyes. "I do my duty. Always. There are bad things out there. Trust me. You need me to keep the wheels on the bus."

"SuperEdwin," Hudson joked, deflecting his nerves. Even though no one would believe Hudson if he ever repeated this outlandish tale – something Edwin had factored in – it mattered to Hudson to know it. To know why Edwin had been on that plane. To know he had survived. That he had saved millions. That for all the tragedy and fear and horror of the day, the terrorists had failed. It mattered.

Edwin smiled. He traced a big "E" across his chest. Then he held the vial to the light and his brow tightened. He recoiled like a street fighter. "This is suboptimal."

"What?" asked Hudson. He absorbed Edwin's response, tightening, as he looked at the small vial in Edwin's hands. "What did you see?"

"Yes," said Edwin. He was on his feet. "Yes of course."

"What is it?" said Hudson.

"Look. There's a number etched into the vial."

"It looks like...'AL11491.002'. So?"

"So," said Edwin. "If this is .002, then where is .001?"

Hudson felt suddenly cold. "There's another vial?"

Edwin studied Hudson. It could work. It had to. "Yes. There is another vial. And when the people who bought the first one realize they failed, the price will go up."

"The people who grabbed me," said Hudson. "They were looking for you, and they were talking about their prize, how expensive it was."

Edwin nodded. "Them or, more likely, the people they work for. Someone has to bankroll the buy. We need to know where it comes from and who's doing the selling. And get to them first." Hudson nodded crisply, punctuating each of Edwin's sentences.

"Okay," Edwin said. "I will be gone for a few hours. Here is what you will do."

"Where are you going?" Hudson said. "I have this court date, and–"

"No," Edwin said. "You have one mission, which I will tell you. Nothing else concerns you. Focus on nothing else."

"Okay," said Hudson. There was purity in receiving one of Edwin's commands. It was simple and reassuring to be told what one's job was not. It lifted clutter that bogged the mind and spun the compass, so the needle could settle firmly on its point.

"You will find my Blackberry," said Edwin. "In the next 24 hours."

"But it's gone…" said Hudson.

"Make it happen," Edwin said. The words were an assignment, not a threat. These three words opened the green fields. They restored – relied on – his independence of thought and action and inspiration. His capacity. It was a potent shot.

"You will meet me with the Blackberry – my Blackberry – tomorrow at 2:00 p.m."

"Where?"

"Starbucks. Corner of Charles and Beacon."

"Okay," said Hudson. "But what about Marly – the police officer? I need to find out if she's okay. And I'm…a murder suspect. Maggie Rice. I hooked up with her Monday night. You don't know – Jameson's assistant was killed on the Esplanade. "

The lamb was straying. Edwin brought his elbow up sharp against Hudson's cheek. The pain stung. Hudson blazed at Edwin. Now Edwin could focus him.

"Know this. You used my Blackberry. You sent a message. The ASP knows about the breach. They know exactly where that device has been. In your apartment. In your pocket. They will kill you for it if I don't convince them not to. And if you tell anyone anything about this, them, or me, they will seal those leaks also. They will seal leaks they don't even have to, just in case. So don't tell anyone anything. And for the love of Lincoln do not go to the police. Even to find out if the pretty cop is all right."

Hudson went pale. "Okay."

"Find the Blackberry. Deliver it to me tomorrow at two. Make it happen. You will save a lot of people. Including me. You will be a hero. I will take care of the ASP."

Hudson felt the surge again. He had no idea yet how he would get the Blackberry back, but he was suddenly very sure he would. It was simple: this was his assignment. He would apply everything he had to completing it. He would complete it. The prospect of failure became, for the first time, irrelevant.

"Find the Blackberry," Hudson repeated. "Make it happen."

"You understand why we have to get that Blackberry," Edwin said.

"Yes," Hudson said. "Ah, no, actually…."

"It's how the ASP reaches me. If I don't answer, they will begin RUPD."

"A Blackberry? That's your only link? I lose mine all the time," said Hudson.

"I don't," Edwin said. "There's also a backup plan. I have to deliver the vial to the Head by 4:00 p.m. today."

"It's only 10 a.m.," said Edwin. "You have plenty of time."

"Not here. In Washington, D.C." Edwin and Hudson looked at each other.

Within three minutes, Edwin pulled the engine cord and it chucked to life. They sped toward the beach shack where he had tucked the motorcycle behind a dumpster.

"What about the vial? What's going to happen to it?" said Hudson, grasping.

"It comes with me. I complete my mission," Edwin said. He studied it again. What would really happen next, Edwin thought, Hudson did not need to know. No one did, except for one other person in the world. Whom he trusted with his life.

Twenty minutes later, the poles were stowed and they were humming back toward the boat rental dock in Charlestown over the blue chop of Boston Harbor. Edwin was at the helm. Hudson leaned evenly on the rails at the bow, flattening their trajectory to speed and smooth their ride. He took the spray in his face. His plan was taking shape.

CHAPTER 2

YASSIR
10:00 A.M., CAMBRIDGE, MA

The phone had been on automatic redial for hours. On September 12, telephone calls between Pakistan and the United States were rarely going through. When they did, a strange metallic sound echoed on the line.

The ring broke the reporting that rambled from the exhausted anchors. The television had been on constantly all night in the corner of Yassir's apartment. The computer browser opened to www.cnn.com. Latest reports included stories of anti-Muslim hate crimes, even in the first twenty-four hours. So he had tucked away at home. Others would assume he was afraid. And he was. For the first time he felt like a foreigner on the streets of America, the streets that seemed to welcome anyone from anywhere.

The sudden excise surprised him. Because it hurt. Friends from the mosque and work had invited him to spend the evening together. They were Americans who were suffering twice – first from the attack on their country and second from the way strangers started looking at them. But Yassir could not be with them, either. He was neither American nor the victim of false prejudice.

He had a second monitor. It was open to the home page of the Center for Disease Control. But he was barely watching now. It was Wednesday September 12, 10:00 a.m. sharp. By now there would have been at least some reports. There were none, just the fatigued rambling of the same news, more details on the people behind the numbers lost, their families, the uprising of people on Flight 93.

Yassir had been sitting on his small, neat bed since 6:00 a.m. He was transfixed, giddy with hope, hearing his heartbeat rise each time the broadcaster touched his earpiece and broke a new angle of the story, each time it did not breathe a word about a mysterious illness befalling the terrified New Yorkers.

"Good girl," Yassir said. Then the phone rang. He answered. "Yes?"

"Pigfucker," said the caller in rigid Arabic.

"Uncle," said Yassir, answering in Arabic. A frisson of fear rose through him.

"You have shamed me, Yassir. You have brought shame on me, on you, on the memory of your poor dead parents!" With each word, the older man's cadence rose and quivered.

"I-I-I don't understand, uncle. Your project has been a success, no?"

"No, pigfucker. No it has not. The others' projects have succeeded but the star of the show, the one all eyes were on – never lit! And why do you think that has happened?" He seethed. The sentences slithered through the telephone line.

"Why, Uncle, please?" Yassir curled on his bed with the phone as if protecting himself from blows. "Was there a problem here? Boarding?"

"Oh no," he said. "It boarded."

"Then...I don't understand. Perhaps the release is just delayed?" Yassir said.

"No no," said the man. "It was removed before it reached its destination."

"I don't understand," said Yassir. Truly he did not.

"There was a complication. There was someone quite special on board that plane. Or do you think it a complete coincidence that one of the most elite commandos the world has produced happened to fancy a trip to California, happened to be sitting just across the row from our carrier pigeon?"

"How?"

"Because someone put him there! Someone knew." Then Uncle swung the bat. "Which means someone told."

"But still," Yassir said, "Where would he be able to go but down with the plane?"

"Let's think," said Uncle. "Where would a paratrooper go on a doomed airplane?"

Yassir could not speak.

"That prize was expensive," said Uncle. "You of all people should know that. I do not know exactly what you did to set these events in motion but I know your heart has not been fully engaged. That woman from your university, Camille, she turned your head but it is more than time to turn it back. This was my moment – you destroyed it. You have a debt. Now you must repay me. Or I will find this Camille, and kill her with my bare hands while she sleeps. I may do that anyway."

"No, Uncle," Yassir pleaded. "I…I….Please…what can I do?"

"How the lowest crawl back on their bellies. It is good to finally have your attention. We will try a second time. And this time we will succeed. You will purchase a second package from our source. You will do it as soon as possible before anyone can look closely at the first and shut it down. Today. Tomorrow. But not next week."

"Yes, Uncle" said Yassir. "And Camille…."

"You get this done, she lives. You fail, well, there are so many casualties this week. One more won't be noticed." He paused. "I am surprised at you, Yassir. You once knew your loyalties. I hope you rediscover them. Today."

A flood of shame rose through Yassir. "Forgive me," he whispered.

"And you will do one more thing for me," said the terrible voice.

CHAPTER 3

Marly watched Peters dial his phone again. Like every other call, he soon slammed it down. He had made her feel foolish for trusting him. Which also made her feel small. She was grateful that she had another focus: find the Esplanade killer. What was the connection – was there a connection? – between Maggie Rice and the terrorists? If so, it would be found near Hudson Davenport. He worked with Maggie. Slept with Maggie. And was the target of bad guys looking for his boss, who had perished on the first plane. But as Captain Brath had commanded her to drop the terrorist beat, she would keep these theories to herself. For now.

"Yuck," said Chuck Young, another detective on the force. "Check this out. I knew San Francisco was a dark and disturbing place, despite all that sunshine."

He spun the monitor around. The photograph showed a young woman, her face angled to the side and framed by blades of grass. Her eyes and mouth were open, staring, but taking nothing in. Blue tinged her cheeks, her lips, her nose.

"A rape and murder at the SF Marina in August," said Young.

Marly looked over. Something about the girl looked familiar. The victim's shirt was missing; all she wore was a tight tank-shaped bra with a swoosh logo on one side. She appeared to be in her mid-twenties. Out jogging by the Bay.

All too familiar. She leaned over Young. Municipalities posted the details of unsolved crimes on a secure website. Sometimes it helped solve crimes if people saw similar things, or if a perp drove across state lines. But San Francisco and Boston were unusual collaborators. The distance was too great. Why would a killer do his work in San Francisco, then pick up shop in Boston?

Marly dialed the number on the website.

"The vic was in her late twenties," said the detective in San Francisco. "Jogging at night, at the Marina. The park goes from the Golden Gate Bridge to the Fort along the Bay. During the day there's lots of folks out there running, playing Frisbee and soccer, flying kites. A lot of people just sit and watch the boats."

"Not at night, though," Marly said.

"Nope. Just homeless people. And stupid people. He strangled her with her work-out gear and raped her."

"We've got something like that here, actually. Same thing. Let me know if you find anything unusual," said Marly. As soon as she put her phone down, it rang.

"Officer Marly," said Helen Otteroy, the CSI technician. "Come see me."

This CSI lab bore no resemblance to the glinty ones on television. It was more like a chemistry lab at a high school that had neglected its capital improvements. Helen Otteroy leaned forward from her perch on a four-legged metallic stool, her elbows on the chipped, black examining table, surrounding the magnifying glass. White lines showed through where the black vinyl cushion had split. Marly knocked on the open wooden door.

Helen spun back. "Take a look."

When Marly's eyes focused, she saw a thicket of dark blue fiber.

"Looks like blue fuzz to me," she said.

"It should," said Helen. "It's lint. Or, as you might know it, belly fluff."

"The stuff from guys' belly buttons?" Marly said.

"Yes. It's an identity treasure trove," said the scientist. "And we found it on your vic. But it didn't come from her."

"How do you know?" asked Marly. "Where does it come from?"

"First of all, Maggie Rice had a belly button ring."

"So?"

"So it's highly unlikely that she produced this fluff. Belly button rings seem to break the magnetic vortex that sucks fluff into the belly button."

"Whoa," said Marly. "Belly button rings? Back up. Where does it come from?"

"So, people with hairy chests – men, generally – have more belly fluff than other people," Helen explained. "Their hair scrapes little fibers of cotton or whatever they're wearing against their skin, and gravity pulls it down, and it collects in the belly button."

"And belly button rings?"

"Seem to break the magnetic pull. People with belly rings don't get belly fluff. We also found fibers that don't match anything she was wearing, so, it had to come from someone who got close enough to inadvertently transfer his belly button fluff. During the rape."

"So we're looking for someone with what, a dark blue shirt?" Marly said.

Helen slipped another slide under the microscope. "You have to look for the silver lining in this kind of work. This time we found it."

Now Marly peered through and saw a thick, straight fiber. It was metallic silver.

"It's silver stitching thread." Helen spun back and forth on her chair. "You are looking for a guy with a blue shirt and a silver logo. Who's got some hair on his chest."

Marly's mind snapped to the previous night on the Esplanade. Hudson had taken off his jacket to give to Squibbs. Squibbs freaked at the sight of what? The shirt he had been wearing? Or the bright logo?

Back at her desk, Marly flicked the keyboard and the corporate website for D6 appeared in front of her. The website ran a deep blue banner across the top fifth of the screen. On the upper right corner was an elongated oval, bright white. The front page bore a full-screen tribute to their fallen leader, Edwin Hoff. She flicked through a few screens. Pictures of employees in happier days, playing softball. They wore dark blue polo shirts with the D6 logo. White stitching. Not silver.

She called Helen. "Any chance that fluff could have come from someone other than the rapist? Like the person she slept with earlier in the night?"

"Doubt it," said the technician. "That fluff would have had to survive the shower she took after the sex, the sweat from her five mile jog, and the spandex, the struggle and the rape. I'm pretty sure this came from the last physical contact she had. The attacker was either wearing it, or had worn it since his last shower."

"Do me a favor," said Marly. "You have the Cambridge girl too, right? Check her for the fluff too. Or anything that matches the Esplanade girl."

Next, Marly called the D.A. and secured the second search warrant for Davenport's apartment. This time she knew what she was looking for. Then Marly pulled tight latex gloves over her hands. She pressed record on the tape player that rested on her desk next to the thick plastic evidence bag.

She cleared her throat. "This is the message recorded on the mobile phone found in the possession of the victim, Maggie Rice." She pressed play and held the thick, candy-bar sized brick face down over the recording device.

6:46 a.m. Tuesday September 11. A man's voice. Professional. Holding back irritation, not wanting to unload it on an innocent but having trouble containing it.

"Aghh, Maggie. It's Jameson. Would you call me? I was planning to drive to the airport this morning but some idiot slashed my tires. Actually, don't call me. Call the driver and have him pick me up, then call me. I'm afraid I'm going to miss my flight. Probably have to get the next one."

7:12 a.m. Same voice. "Not sure where you are, sorry to bother you so early in the morning. Would you call me as soon as you get this message?"

7:40 a.m. Now the speaker was jamming levity into his voice. "Hi Maggie. I hope everything is okay. You're probably at your spin class or hot yoga or whatever. Ha. Ah, I'll just get a cab on my own...somehow...out here in the burbs and come in to the office. You can book me on the afternoon flight. Okay, see you soon."

"You have no more messages," said the electronic voice. Marly hit save and zipped the phone back in the bag.

"So let's see about you, Jameson," Marly said, clicking the D6 management team web page. Jameson Callaghan's picture showed dark brown eyes paired with a confident grin. Grey heathered his wavy chestnut hair.

"Three calls? Certainly makes the point that he expected her to be available. Creative alibi, Jameson," Marly muttered. Just then her phone rang again. It was the cop from SFPD.

"CSI did find something. Some fibers…fluff from a–" he said.

"Belly button?" she guessed.

"Yeah," he chuckled. "CSI found skin, oil, and dark blue fibers from a shirt. And, there was a little of something else in it. Something tougher. Like thread."

Marly's grip tightened. "What color?"

"Silver," he said.

This was more than a copycat. This was the same rapist. The same killer. Who, for some reason chose two cities on opposite coasts to leave his mark. Who frequently wore a blue shirt with silver stitching.

No one answered the door at Hudson Davenport's apartment. Christine Marly stood on his welcome mat with the warrant shielding her chest. What would his eyes show when he opened the door? Surprise? Guilt? Betrayal?

Marly could not shake the look he had given her on the Esplanade. How sensitive he was to what Mr. Squibbs needed. How he saw how numb she was. That was no killer. Marly knew it though her cynical, honed survivor's skills, her analytics and her better judgment told her to resist. Her confusion boiled out in anger.

"Knock down the damn door," she told the uniformed officers.

The apartment was dark. The air felt stale. Windows and doors had been closed while the atmosphere baked in the late summer sun. A coffee maker on the kitchen counter was about a fifth full. She poured it into a cup and tasted it. Then spat.

"Ugh," she said. "Yesterday's."

"You think he's flown?" said an officer. Marly shrugged her shoulders. She put the warrant down on the kitchen table. Where the hell was he at 10:30 on a Wednesday morning? Marly had told him yesterday to stick around. This was not good. The D6 link to the Cambridge murder made her very nervous. What Helen Otteroy would find there would help sharpen her frazzled instinct.

"In here," called the other cop. "The mother lode."

In Hudson's closet were a stack of navy blue golf shirts. There must have been ten of them. Navy blue. Just like the belly fluff. She could see the logo on the top one.

Marly grabbed the top one and shook out its fold, holding it by the shoulders in the bright light of Hudson's bedroom. The logo was stitched into the upper left chest. Exactly like the one Squibbs had reacted to. She looked closely at the stitching.

"This logo is white," she said. "CSI found silver. Any silver logos back there?"

The cops tore through the blue shirts like they were in a discount shop looking for the right size from a sale bin.

"They're all white," said the cop. "Not a stitch of silver."

"Bizarre," said Marly. But she breathed a deeper sigh of relief. "I'll take one down to be analyzed anyway. Clean this place up."

"Clean it up?" asked a surprised cop.

"We don't need bad press for ransacking citizens' homes," Marly said.

"Citizen? I thought he was a suspect."

"He's both," shot Marly. "That's the whole point, Officer."

By 11:30 a.m., the day after the world had changed, the television in the Boston Police Department bullpen broadcast footage of the World Trade Center wreckage continually. The once familiar lattice design of the skyscrapers had reduced to splinters askew in clouds of smoke and ash. Broken masts in fog. Captain Brath's brain tried to organize the strange elements. Was that a thirty foot ladder tossed aside? Or a chunk of wall, ten stories tall, windows where the eye saw rungs. It leaned over a pile of rubble as high as some older buildings in lower Manhattan, floors pancaked over hallways, offices, desks, chairs, carpets. Filing cabinets. People. Fires that would burn for weeks, feeding on trapped oxygen, releasing eerie billows of smoke.

"What do you have, Peters?" Captain Brath frowned, pausing at the officer's desk.

"Nothing sir. So much for the dreaded 9 a.m. deadline," said Peters, casting blame like a fly. "Need me at the airport? Somewhere closer to the 9-11 leads?"

Captain Brath watched Marly only two desks away. The mail cart squeaked down the row. She pulled several photographs from a large manila folder.

"Don't get comfortable," Brath told Peters. "No one saw yesterday coming either. Take a team back to the hotel. Make sure they looked at the right goddam room." He tapped the desk, then walked down the row. "How are you, Officer Marly?"

"Fine, Captain, thank you," she said, a stiff salute. Marly's voice was tight and polite. Any sign of displeasure would be condemned as a pout. Her best option was to just get her job done. Closed cases, convicted felons, justice for victims – this was her job. "Getting somewhere. There's a physical link with a marina murder in San Francisco. We're looking into the Cambridge strangulation, also."

"What's in the mail?" he asked.

"Someone sent pictures. Of our Esplanade girl earlier the night she was killed."

There were three 8 x 10 color photographs, with white stamps in the lower right corner confirming the date and time they were taken. **9/10/01. 18:36.**

The first showed the top of Maggie Rice's head and her back as she walked toward a waiting car. The shot came from several stories above. The picture showed the brake lights on as the car waited at the curb of a busy street just before train tracks and an intersection.

"This is D6's site," said Marly. "Someone took these photos from inside. This is the last time Maggie Rice left the office."

The second shot showed Maggie's face as she turned to open the car door. The third was magnified. It showed the license plate of the car into which Maggie Rice stepped hours before she met up with Hudson. Hours before she was killed.

Marly picked up her phone. "Hi Helen. Could you run the plate – Massachusetts 655TRE2. No. I'll wait." As she held the receiver she pushed the photos toward the captain.

"Anything catch your eye?" she said.

"Besides the car?" he said. The Maserati was sleek and curvy, the powerful engine roiling the steel mold. "Someone likes speed. Likes to pick and choose the limits that apply to him, doesn't count the cost of breaking them."

"Or," Marly ventured, "it belongs to someone who always goes the speed limit but likes to do it holding back immense power." The voice on the line spoke then. Marly looked up. "The car is registered to Jameson Callaghan. D6 CEO. Maggie Rice was his assistant. And Callaghan made real sure it looked like he expected to talk to her in the morning."

Captain Brath frowned. "Follow me." At the end of the hall, he closed the door of his office behind Marly. "The FBI was in touch with me today with some information that may have a connection to the Esplanade murder. I don't know if means anything or not, but I wanted to make sure you knew."

Marly understood why Brath told her in person. The agencies were so tight with their information. The Feds rarely shared it with each other, and were not going to give the local authorities any more power than they already had over police interests. But sometimes friends had pull, offered favors.

"Apparently the Securities Exchange Commission began a serious investigation of Jameson Callaghan for suspicious trading of D6 shares a couple of weeks ago. D6 stock was at fifteen dollars a share two weeks ago, when the suspicious trading began. Now it's barely a buck. After an all-time high of $480 about a year and a half ago. That's a lot of sugar to spill out of your sack."

"D6 is where Davenport works," said Marly. "And the coffee shop where the Cambridge victim worked is a couple blocks away. Must be their local java hut."

What Marly saw no reason to share with the captain, as she could not make sense of it herself, was that the kidnappers thought Davenport was Edwin Hoff. That the one who spoke English knew he was not. With no sign of the dead men, or the dire consequences that she said they predicted by 8:46 a.m., it would not help the captain's confidence in her to mention that these imaginary terrorists also seemed to presume that a passenger from Flight 11 was very much alive on September 12.

"My friend thinks maybe Callaghan saw their quarterly numbers coming in short and decided to squeeze some cash out," said the Chief. "Maybe his assistant knew too much about his trading. Maybe she called it in to the broker for him."

"That's motive," said Marly. "And he trumped up an alibi. He left three messages on her phone yesterday. Like he wanted anyone looking to know that at 7 a.m. he thought she should be able to answer her phone."

"The pictures show he starts the night with her," said the captain.

"But," Marly added, "she ends up with another guy. She sleeps with Hudson Davenport, a young sales guy from D6. He comes back to work. She ends up dead."

"The tragedy of King Lear," said the captain. "Old buck unwilling to relinquish the crown. Young buck takes old buck's catch. Old buck takes her back. Punishes her."

Marly enjoyed talking about strategy with the captain. The puzzle part of her job. Who dunnit and why? He understood the nuance of human behavior, pressures, weaknesses and pathologies. He should have appreciated the chocolate ploy.

"Or she's the only witness to his unlawful trades," Marly said.

"Call this guy at the SEC," the captain said. He scribbled a name and number on a piece of paper and pressed it into her hand. "Then go see Jameson Callaghan."

As Marly left Captain Brath's office, something occurred to her. Despite the flap with Peters, Brath was helping her. He had exposed a confidence for her benefit. Marly felt the warm inkling of relief that comes in the presence of a friend. Though she habitually walked with her shoulders high and tense, she felt them release just a bit.

Marly crossed from Beacon Hill over the Charles River to Kendall Square in Cambridge. The mid-day sun washed MIT's dome. A Red Line train swooshed past her, blocking her view for a moment. It was time to pay a visit to D6 and Jameson Callaghan.

Her phone rang. "Marly here," she said. There was a pause.

"Officer Marly?" said a man's voice. "Are you okay?"

"Who is this?" she snapped. She did not like being approached by a man she could not identify, even over the phone.

"I just wanted to make sure you were okay. After the hotel," said the man.

"Davenport? Where are you?"

"I'm here. Just like I'm supposed to be," he said.

Marly shot questions in a flurry. "Who were those people? How did you get away? What happened to them?"

"I...I don't know much," he said.

"It'll take me about five minutes to get a court order," she said.

"Please," Hudson said. "Just...I just wanted to make sure you were okay."

It surprised Marly how good it felt to hear Hudson's sympathetic voice. "I'm okay. Thanks. Of course everyone thinks I'm so bent on getting a promotion that I've made up a terrorist case – kidnapped by three nasty terrorists who mysteriously disappear from the hotel they abducted me to and let me make my way out on my own. Just happens to be cleaned out by the time they got there. It did happen, didn't it?"

"Yes," Hudson said. "You are not crazy."

Marly grimaced. Never, never let a suspect know your mind. Your doubts. She kept having to remind herself that Hudson was a murder suspect. He was not her friend even though he kept treating her like one. But maybe a friendly suspect was just what she needed. A friend with access to the D6 email system. A friend who might be able to get info about Jameson's phone calls, his meetings.

"Keep your friends close, your enemies closer," she thought, refreshing the Machiavellian mantra. She felt better with a reason to justify being drawn in by this man.

"Hudson," Marly said. "I need your help."

On the other end of the line, Hudson grazed his cheek with his fingertips. It was still tender from where Edwin had cracked him with his forearm. He focused again. He had one mission. Find Edwin's Blackberry or he and Edwin and others would be targets of assassins that did not miss. Maybe even Marly.

"Please," she said.

Hudson had a problem. When a woman needed him he responded without thinking of any consequences. His reaction was so automatic, so compelling, it bore consideration. But Hudson was always too caught up trying to help.

Hudson thought about Edwin; how he was focused, always, but he did so with more than one thing. He focused exclusively, but in parallel silos. Couldn't Hudson do the same? Couldn't he be better? Couldn't he be great? Greater?

"Okay, Marly," said Hudson. "I will meet you at 8 p.m. tonight at 65 Acorn."

In the meantime, Hudson would complete his first mission. Find that Blackberry.

At 2:00 p.m., Detective Marly sat in D6's reception area, which looked to her like NASA's Mission Control. She sat in a triangular chair covered with blue felt. Behind a glass wall flickered hundreds of monitors. A spinning globe flashed starbursts of all different sizes. These were the Interfaces, populating the world, an ever-expanding net. Another wide screen showed a map of the earth, half of it in a dark shadow, the other brightly lit. What looked like airplane routes dashed across the map in bright green and yellow arcs. Some blinked red.

A small table stood against a pillar. It held a large photograph of a smiling young man with beaming green eyes and a shock of black hair. The light in his face gave the impression that posing for it was a lark. A printed framed card on the table showed a smaller version of the same picture.

"Edwin Hoff, 1970-2001," Marly read.

Fresh lilies with green stems and soft ivory petals were at rest on the table.

"Officer?"

Marly looked up to see a young girl with long brown hair extend her hand.

"Hello. I'm Nadia. Mr. Francis asked me to bring you up to his office. He is in charge of…well…a lot of things. I think he used to work with your office," she added.

"Yes. I've heard of him," Marly said. D6 had directed her to this ex-cop who was in charge of all security and interface with local authorities, be it for permits to illuminate the sign on the outside of the building, prevention planning for disgruntled former employees, or any other possible infraction. Brath said good things.

But, Marly thought, now he has a client to protect. Perhaps an indirect strategy would work better. Particularly as her guide wore something of great interest.

"Nice jacket," she said to Nadia.

"Oh thanks. Every new employee gets the latest schwag. People wear it, like, every day."

"Excuse me?"

"Sorry – schwag. It's the term for all the corporate id stuff we get. They used to spend a lot more on it but now there's going to be some cutting back. They've even started to charge for the vending machines!"

"Hard times," said Marly.

"I was eating way too many Twix bars," said Nadia. "D6 – hah – more like D15."

"Love the logo," said Marly. "It has beautiful colors."

"Thanks. It took us a while to choose Azure Blue and Snowdrop White but now they won't change it. I was a Brand Management Marketing major. It's really important to stick with your brand so people recognize it. One hymn, many hymnbooks, they say."

"Makes sense," said Marly.

"You have to show someone a message 17 times before they absorb it," Nadia said, escorting Marly off the elevator. She turned toward the closed glass doors that framed the elevator bank. She pulled her id card from an extension cord on her hip and passed it over a black square. The red light turned to green and the door opened. They turned down the hallway alongside rows of office cubes.

"Usually there's a lot more life – I mean – chatter on this hall," Nadia said softly. "Sales guys sit here. But, you know, with everything…yesterday… I didn't know Edwin well but people are kind of a mess." Nadia's voice fell to a whisper. "I really hope we make it. Finding another job these days would be rough." Nadia stopped at a non-descript door on the interior wall. "It looks like Mr. Francis is still busy. You want a cup of coffee?"

"No thanks," said Marly.

Nadia looked unsure of what to do. Should she have brought her directly up from reception? She did not want Mr. Francis see her making a mistake.

"You want to see something?" she said with a small smile.

"Sure," said Marly.

"I'll show you the schwag closet. You can see all the stuff we brand. Only I have the key. And Mr. Francis, of course."

Marly could taste gold on her shovel. Nadia subtly took off the key that hung on a lanyard around her neck, eyeing the group of salesmen who were leaning over a cube wall, another tossing a football up and down.

"Dude, beware my magic wand," said a voice behind the cube wall. Marly saw a cane twirl in a circle.

"I heard you have an extra-long wand," said another one.

"Yeah. I put a spell on your sister once," said the first one.

The sophomoric joking was half-hearted. Marly guessed they needed the release. As Nadia pulled her quickly through the door, Marly heard a sharp cry from the gang. The man with the cane had cracked it across the fingers of his taunter. Then Marly watched him shuffle out of the cube, leaning heavily on his stick.

"Abracadabra!" he said. "I command your fingers to break." The other men laughed now at the tormentor's expense.

"Go guy with the cane," Marly chuckled, following Nadia into the trove.

"We have to close the door quickly. You wouldn't believe how many people use the five finger discount around here." Nadia said, wiggling her fingers.

"What – it's free if you get your five fingers on it?" Marly asked. Nadia giggled. Both sides of the small storage room were stacked to the ceiling with just about anything that could be painted, dyed or stitched dark blue with light blue ovals on them, and the slogan "D6." There were boxes of coffee mugs, small footballs, magnetic pens, ballpoints and markers and stationery, exercise bags, small toy parachutes, golf balls and golf umbrellas. And hats, hats, hats . Fleece jackets and windbreakers, and windbreakers with fleece in them. Boxes of golf shirts.

"So has the logo always been light blue?" Marly fished.

"Azure Blue? No," said Nadia. "It started out as white, so some of the old timers still have that stuff. It's kind of legend now. There's a real split you know, between the people who were here before the IPO, and those who came after. It's like, the lucky ones and then the worker bees. Kinda sucks to be us, you know."

"Why's that?"

"I started a few months ago, when the stock was still pretty high, and now it's way, way under water so our options aren't worth anything," she said. "So we basically get our salaries, which are all blood, sweat and tears – the stock is where the upside is supposed to be – while the old timers are all sitting around getting rich just as time passes. Resting and vesting," she added.

"But doesn't the stock go down for them too?" asked Marly. This was a foreign language to her. She put in for overtime when she worked it – time and a half – and was thrilled to see the bulge in her paychecks. But remembering Davenport's apartment – the $6,000 stainless steel range that belonged in a restaurant, the swanky leather sofas and flat screen television, and the closet full of Zegna and Armani shirts and sweaters – she could tell what side he was on. So why did he owe $150,000 to a guy named J.D.?

"You can still make a pretty penny on fifty multiples of penny stock," said Nadia.

"Lucky for them," said Marly.

"Yeah. But some people borrowed against it, taking cash and betting the shares would go up forever. That's when people really lose their shirts. When they bet on shares that go down. Because they have to pay taxes and stuff anyway."

Marly thought, "So, who made the wrong bet around here? Hudson? Jameson?"

Aloud she said, "This is impressive. Thanks for the tour. You have quite an eye for this. I hope you get your chance to call the shots on the next schwag."

Marly saw her beam shyly at the carpet. "Thanks, Detective."

"Ever think of silver stitching instead of white or the light blue?" Marly fished.

"I don't know," said Nadia. "We're committed now. But it's a good thought."

Half an hour later, Marly left D6. The meeting with Mr. Francis had been perfunctory. Nadia and her closet, on the other hand, were a find. But Marly found no silver thread: only light blue, and a tale of white. The white Hudson had in his closet.

Marly's instincts said that somehow D6 was involved. There were too many coincidences. But were they supported by fact? Or was she forcing them to fit? It was time to dig. Hard work led to hard facts. Her foot pressed the gas pedal and the powerful shocks bounced the cruiser like a carnival ride as she shot over the potholes back towards Boston.

Captain Brath set up a meeting for 3:00 p.m. that afternoon between Marly and the SEC's local investigator, Tom Davis. They carried their paper coffee cups across the street to the generous steps that framed City Hall Plaza. They sat down, out of ear shot of anyone else on the steps. The cement was warm under their legs.

"It's the SEC's general practice not to talk about ongoing investigations," said Tom.

Marly nodded. "Sure. Still, you might know some non-material information that – you never know – could be helpful to our investigation. And maybe we have something useful to you. Like a tape from a security camera that shows our victim getting out of Jameson Callaghan's car, going into the building, and returning to the car."

"What night?" asked Tom.

"September 10 at 6:37 p.m. Mean anything to you?"

Tom frowned. "Callaghan went in with her? September 10 at 6:37 p.m.?"

"No," said Marly. "His car stayed idling outside – she went back in."

Tom was flipping through a notebook that he pulled from his jacket pocket. "I don't get it," said Tom. "We've got different information."

"You want to let me in on it? Maybe it's nothing," she offered. "You ask me, we all ought to be sharing more information with each other. Maybe that would have kept us out of Tuesday's mess. Some say CIA knew something was coming but didn't say anything to the FBI or FAA or anyone. What a tragedy. Could have been heroes."

It was an unfair trick to escalate her murder investigation to the level of global terrorism, and to lump Tom Davis in with the people who may have had some power to prevent it. But sometimes Marly used tricks to get what she needed. Even if sometimes it pricked her conscience.

Tom finally spoke. "You did not hear this from me. We're investigating Callaghan about an unusual trade his broker made on his behalf on Monday September 10. D6's records show a call from Callaghan's extension to the broker that night. At 6:41 p.m."

"But he was in his car," said Marly.

Tom shrugged. "His office lock is keyed to his access card. No one can get in it but him. Maybe someone else was at the wheel?"

"Or maybe Callaghan has his assistant make the call for him. Then offs her."

"Wow, I don't know about that," said Tom. "Insider traders aren't usually violent people. They try to get away with stuff. Because they think they can, and they create a logic that persuades them they deserve it."

"Sounds like we both need a chat with Mr. Callaghan," said Marly.

An hour later, Marly snatched a page off the fax. Despite the chaos, a contact at American Airlines reservations had been able to do her a small favor. Marly's hunch circled around D6, the dead girl, and the silver fiber. When SFPD found the same silver fiber, Marly made this connection: the roller board suitcases propped against cubes during her visit to D6 all had AA tags. The founder was on one of their fated planes. D6 probably had a deal with the airline. Which meant the airline would know when they took D6 employees anywhere. To and from the West Coast, for instance.

But still, the pieces did not quite fit. The silver thread dangled like a hangnail. Her visit to the schwag closet and its gate mistress had shown her every iteration of D6's brand marketing evolution. There was no sign of a silver logo.

Marly scanned the report of D6 bookings for August and September. The last entry was for a September 11, 7:45 a.m. flight to LAX. Two passengers were booked. Jameson Callaghan, Edwin Hoff. One person boarded. The printout looked so benign.

Marly's eyes flicked back over the earlier dates. "Okay, so who was still in San Francisco the night of August 8? And back in Boston by Monday, September 10?" She parsed the list by individual, matching dates of their comings and goings. Certain people flew to California every week. Edwin Hoff held the record with three red-eyes in a week. Marly marveled at his pace. She suddenly wished she had met him.

Ultimately, Marly deduced that American Airlines had deposited three people from D6 in Northern California on August 8 in the morning, and returned two of them to Boston on a red-eye that night. None took flights that would have removed them from Boston the night of September 10, when Maggie Rice was murdered. It was a step, but not a lock. Marly looked at the names she had written.

Hudson Davenport, Walker Green, Jameson Callaghan

"Hudson and Walker flew back together on the red-eye August 8," Marly said. "But Jameson flew back on August 9. So he was in San Francisco the night of August 8."

Hudson was traveling with a companion, on a tight schedule – difficult conditions to commit murder. Marly was surprised to feel a wave of relief. But Jameson Callaghan's itinerary left him quite a lot of unaccounted time. Time to get a late run in after dinner. Something to make sure he slept well.

The stairs outside D6's curved edifice pleased the eye. But they could not be a welcome sight to the young man Marly was watching at 4:30 p.m. He had a routine. He flicked his wrist, and what looked like a sturdy black cane collapsed, bending awkwardly in four places like a trick golf club. He folded it deftly and stuck it in his back pocket. Then he put both arms on the railing and skipped the first step, taking his weight on his arms. Marly watched his face stay animated and engaged with the person who walked beside him, at least for the first three steps. The last four seemed to take more effort. He waved off the friend who clipped down the stairs beside him. At the bottom, Walker Green leaned his back against the railing, and set his cane back up.

"Can I buy you a cup of coffee?" Marly asked. She liked to approach friendly witnesses with an offer before she opened her badge. "Boston P.D."

He leaned on his cane, and his face broke into an easy smile. "Oh sure," he said, and with a wink added, "Donut too?"

"Of course," she added. "Why do you think I didn't suggest tea?"

Walker Green was playful without being offensive. He was the kind of person who could see a lot and say nothing, putting himself in a position to see more. He would be as important a source at D6 as Nadia, the logo maven; more, if he could tell her details about the trip he took to California with Hudson and Jameson.

"Light and sweet?" she asked. "Jelly or glazed?"

Walker nodded. "You're trying to sweeten me up, obviously."

Marly smiled again. Walker's joking was purposeful. It put her at ease, for which she felt grateful. What passed between them in those first exchanges were her apology for noticing his disability, her guilt for having none herself, and his forgiveness. It was a dance he did every day, with everyone, until they both got past it. But it always started this way. Walker led, and they were soon gliding.

"I'm investigating a murder," Marly began. Walker's smile dropped away. He looked at her seriously. "Maggie Rice; she was killed Monday night on the Esplanade. Did you know her? Jameson Callaghan's assistant?"

"Yes, of course," said Walker. "There's been a lot of terrible news around here. Shocking. At least Jameson missed the flight. At least there's that."

The papers were filled with stories of the 9-11 victims, and those who would be forever grateful for the alarm clock that did not go off, or the traffic that made them miss the fated flight. Or for vandalism.

"There was another murder that had some striking similarities," Marly continued.

"Oh really? Where?" he asked.

"Not around here. In San Francisco. A few weeks ago."

"Wow," said Walker, looking concerned.

"You go to California a lot?" she asked.

"Some," said Walker. "We have some big partners there, big customers. I only started a couple of months ago but, yeah, it looks like air travel will be a part of my job. Once they get back to normal. Not sure how psyched I am about that, to be honest. I have MS – multiple sclerosis. Maybe we'll do more by video conference."

"You go there with anyone on your last trip?" she asked.

He nodded. "Hudson Davenport, my sales executive. Really, really great guy."

Marly logged the nuance. Walker clearly wanted her to know he backed his guy.

"What did you do?"

"Oh, it was one of those crazy trips," he said. "We went out there that morning, had a meeting in San Mateo with XTC, and then grabbed some dinner up in the city at a place Hudson knew about in the Triangle before our flight home."

"The Triangle?"

Walker grinned. "They call it the Bermuda Triangle – three bars on a corner of Union Street. There are lots of disappearances there…at least for the night."

Marly grinned back. She hoped flirting would encourage him to keep talking.

"In fact I thought I lost Hudson to a leggy blonde, but sure enough he showed up at the gate at SFO with a few minutes to spare before we red-eyed it back."

"He abandoned you?" Marly said.

Walker shrugged. "A good wingman knows when to peel off."

Marly smiled again. This was interesting. In the braggadocio, Walker placed Hudson within blocks of the scene of the crime, and left him there without a witness, or an alibi. She had seen pictures of the Marina neighborhoods. The stucco two- and three-story apartments of the Union Street neighborhood fell gently towards the ocean. These bars were close to the scene of the murder. Close enough.

Marly pushed a photograph across the table. "This her?"

Walker held the photo against the palm of one hand, straightening it with the other. He studied it for a long time.

"I can't be sure," he said finally. He looked at the picture again, and then put it down. About a beat and a half later than Marly expected him to. The disruption in rhythm caught her ear.

"They found her dead. Coincidentally, the same night you guys flew back."

Walker blanched. "Wow. That's just…really weird to think…."

"I know," said Marly. While he was chewing over the fate of someone he passed in a crowded bar, she asked, "Anyone else go with you that day?"

"Just Jameson Callaghan, our CEO," Walker said. "It's how we got the call with the decision makers. They all knew each other from the training program decades ago at SAC. Sometimes the only way you get a deal done is by getting the honchos to see eye to eye. Everyone else down the chain is executing orders; you need someone to give one to get something new done. Or so I'm told."

"Did he brave the Triangle too?" Marly asked, smiling.

Now it was Walker's turn to blush. "No, he declined. He drove up to the city with us, but said he had dinner with some bankers, then more calls – customer visits – the next day. I think he came back the next day or the one after that. I'm not sure. You could check with his assistant. She'd have his whole schedule."

"Is that Maggie Rice?"

"Yeah, Maggie. Oh. Right," Walker trailed off, shaking his head. He pushed the empty donut wrapper.

"Another glazed for the road?" she asked.

"Glazing and roads aren't my best mix," he said, reaching a hand up for help getting out of his chair. "I better keep my grip firm from here on out."

"Thanks for your help," she said, pressing a business card into his free hand. "If you remember anything, give me a buzz. And I'm sorry about your colleagues."

"Okay, yeah," Walker smiled. "And thanks. I didn't really get a chance to work with Edwin yet, but he was like no other, they say. And Maggie, well, she was a real beautiful girl. One day would have been someone's mom. Such a shame."

Back at headquarters, Marly began to dig. She was on the phone with a sales rep from a printing company. "I'm looking for someone to make up a bunch of shirts for our company. Our logo is blue and silver – can you do that?"

"Can I do it? Only every day, dear, by the thousands." The woman on the other end of the line let out a raspy, asthmatic laugh.

"I don't want thousands," said Marly.

"No, I mean, it's pretty popular branding. You aren't a tech company are you?"

"Uh, yeah," said Marly.

"Oh gawd," said the woman. "It's not my place, but you really ought to think of something else. You want your brand to stick out. How about blue and fuschia?"

Having learned something about branding from Nadia the closet maven at D6, Marly was not about to have her fake brand tinkered with.

"Thanks, but the powers that be have decided. Blue and silver. Unless one of our competitors has it. You got a list of all the companies that use blue and silver?"

"Yeah, I got one. But I can't give it to you."

"Is D6 one of them?"

"No. They're blue and white. But I can't tell you that either."

"Okay, so ballpark. How many in Boston, and in San Francisco?"

"I guess I could do that for you. Hold on." Marly clicked the button on her pen. Several minutes passed, during which she was privy to the woman's breathy counting. "So, you ready?"

"Mmm-hmm," said Marly.

"In Boston, you have forty-seven companies using blue and silver corporate id. In San Francisco, you have eighty-three. And that's just the ones that use our company. I'm telling you. Fuschia. Its time has come."

"Thanks," said Marly. "I'll pass that along."

There was only one piece of physical evidence that connected the two murders, but at least 130 companies had the shirts that could produce it. But not D6.

This was a goose chase, Marly thought. So she would check Callaghan's alibi, rule him out. She would check Walker's story if she could, and rule out Hudson. And then she would be, well, nowhere. But at least she would be working with facts.

CHAPTER 4

CAMILLE
10:00 A.M., MCLEAN, VA

Camille Henderson was generally an anxious person. But in the past twenty-five hours the needle had gone red and stayed there. Yassir had saved her life with a phone call. Camille had pushed the button, but had been too unsure to call the ones waiting for her at the top.

"I got Niko, at least," she thought, remembering his face tipping up to the underside of the giant wings.

What Yassir had predicted two months earlier had happened. The planes were hijacked. They blew up buildings. Thousands died. But there was still another shoe to drop. The pneumonic plague rain cloud, twenty-four hours later. Designed to infect everyone who lived there and everyone who came to help. The leaders who came to plant the flag and rally the nation would be right under the cloud. Appearing strong, but beginning to die. The President. It would have started by now.

"Why did he leave me with this?" Camille moaned. She was an analyst, not an intelligence officer. In the cafeteria, she watched those men who appeared from time to time, often very fit, not noticeably tall or short, pleasant looking but not movie stars, in the Barbour coats with square, deep pockets, casual suits and brown laced up office shoes with Vibram rubber soles. She knew the pockets made a good place for cold fingers to close around a gun; that laced shoes stayed on better than loafers when one started to run.

231

Camille looked down at her clothes. The cotton dress with brown and blue flower print had enough material to cover her substantial shape and still let air circulate. September was still summer in D.C. She had once seen a similar fabric on curtains at Laura Ashley.

"I wrote memos. I tried. I did everything I could," Camille muttered miserably. This refrain had been with Camille since she was very young. The first time she said it came after she took a break from the sanctuary during a long service to get a drink from the water fountain. She liked pressing it soft, and then hard, making the arc of water jump. She was playing with it when Timothy, her best friend in the third grade, crashed through the doors from the sanctuary to the foyer.

His father was a short, thick man with fat red cheeks. He grabbed the boy's jacket. Opened his palm. Swung his arm like baseball bat, smacking Timothy full across the cheek. Reloaded. The blows beat the child around the foyer. Timothy wept. His father noticed the water splashing on to the floor. Hit the boy again.

"The boy's out of control," he shouted. Then taking a few breaths. "I'm sorry, Tim. Come here. Come on. Aw. Why won't you come give me a hug?"

A couple of weeks later, Camille saw a fresh cut across the boy's nose.

"I think Timothy is maybe getting in trouble at home a lot," she told her parents. "I think he gets hit sometimes." Her parents looked concerned. But they did not do anything. Camille stopped playing with Timothy. Just seeing him made her mad.

A couple of years later, listening to the grief counselors at school, Camille told herself again. "I did everything I could. I did everything I could."

Today, thousands of people were dead. At the Pentagon. In Pennsylvania. In New York. Some of Camille's own colleagues died waiting for her to join them for breakfast. At her request.

Camille sat at her desk, watching CNN's news feed. Her hands were twisting clumps of her dress into moist wrinkled towers. Then Camille picked up her phone.

"I need to speak with the deputy director, please," she said. "I know he is. This is critical...Henderson. Camille Henderson. I'll come right now."

She put down the phone. Then she stood up, took a deep breath, and pushed her swollen feet back into the tight leather flats. They squeaked air pockets beneath her arches as she passed the other analyst desks and pushed open the glass door. Then Camille followed the black line in the center of the marble floor past closed, unmarked doors. Hallways turned often. It was impossible to tell where anyone was headed.

Camille came to a door that looked no different than any other. She turned the handle and a thick double door opened to a reception area. Grey carpet, brown desk.

"I need to see the deputy," she said, flashing a badge.

"I heard you on the phone," said the gatekeeper. "He's still busy. You are aware of what happened yesterday."

"Of course, of course," Camille said, flustered. "I have more information, there's something he has to do. It's about the President!"

Just then Deputy Lowndes opened the door. A younger man walked out. For a moment they looked at her with surprise. Then the young man tucked his head away from her and passed quickly. This was code in the Agency. One knew what one was supposed to know. Snooping was not acceptable. Camille looked down too. Which was when she noticed his shoes. Brown leather with laces: they were unremarkable and stayed on in a sudden sprint. Relief washed over her. They were on it. An operator was on a mission.

"Sir, I tried to stop her," the assistant said. Lowndes held up a hand.

"Come in," he said, smiling. "You had a narrow escape yesterday, I understand."

"Yes," she said. "Scully called me."

"Again?"

"Yes – no. He got in touch with me before with a sign. This was a call."

"How did he get your number?"

"I don't know, sir," Camille stammered.

"So what's this about the President?" Lowndes asked.

"You're probably way ahead of it, I'm sure," said Camille, sitting down quickly. She was sure he had read her memos. Knew about the big plan. "You know, from my memos this summer. The HUMINT warning of the attack, with the planes, then the third phase."

"Be specific."

"Well, you know. The trigger – twenty-four hours after the bomb – pneumonic plague spreading over a city after the crash. Manhattan! So I'm sure you've stopped the President from going there," Camille said.

The deputy stared at her. He said nothing, which compelled Camille to fill the void using words she had not thought out well.

"So he won't be rained on. Affected. If it happens like the source – Scully – said it would," Camille trailed off. "Like the other things did."

Then Deputy Lowndes smiled and rose from his chair. He helped Camille from hers. "You've done very well, Henderson. This is no longer your concern."

"That," she said, inhaling deeply and letting it all go at once, "is a great relief."

Camille put her hand on the edge of the open steel door. The walls were so thick around the deputy's room that the entire face of her palm could lay flat on the edge of the open door and only the tips of her thumb and pinky could curl around the edges.

"One can only do so much, right?" she said. The deputy nodded.

After the heavy door locked behind her, he walked to his desk. He dialed a long series of numbers. When the green light came on, he dialed more.

"Pick her up," said Lowndes. "Yes, ourselves. I don't care. I will not give the FBI this ammunition. It cannot leak that we have an enemy combatant in our own shop." Then he hung up the phone and clicked on the news. It was twenty-five hours after the worst terrorist attack on American soil. An attack someone on his staff had warned him about two months ago. Then she set up a meeting with the counter terror experts at a target site. Then she walks out, just in time.

Deputy Director Lowndes had exactly what he needed. Camille Henderson was now the top domestic priority. Her name pushed up the list of persons of interest to be held by the government in time of war for interrogation for an undetermined time without probable cause or counsel to assist her.

When Camille returned to her desk, a reporter was speaking on the television monitor that hung high on the wall.

"At noon, the President will address the nation from the site of the World Trade Center collapse, or what is now being referred to as Ground Zero."

Camille's external phone rang. Her mouth felt dry when she answered.

"Oh I'm so glad to hear your voice!" said Matilda Mace. Her voice quivered. "With the planes, the Pentagon, I was worried about you."

"Thank you, Matilda," said Camille. "I'm okay."

"Oh it's so tragic!" cried Matilda. "What is afoot in this world?"

Camille's internal phone rang. "Could you hold on for a moment, Matilda?" She pushed the other line.

"This is Deputy Director Lowndes. Come to Room FF23. Bring every file you have on Scully. CT wants to talk with you."

"Room FF23, okay," said Camille. Counterterror wanted to hear what she knew. What she was supposed to have told some of them yesterday at breakfast.

"Matilda," said Camille into the other line.

"Still here. What's room FF23?"

"Just an office," said Camille. "I have to go. My boss's boss's boss wants to talk to me about something I heard. Can I bring you dinner tonight?"

"Thank you, dear. You are such a comfort. In times like these we need to be with each other," said Matilda. "And try to remember, this shall pass. I have seen much worse."

Camille was gathering up her files when Joel Andruski on the Egypt desk pushed back his chair and whispered, "Did you say Room FF23?"

Camille nodded. "Deputy Director Lowndes wants me to talk with some people from the Counterterrorism Division."

Joel shook his head. "Don't you know that room?"

"No," Camille said slowly. There were no nameplates on rooms in the CIA headquarters. Just letters and numbers. What went on behind the doors was only relevant to you if you were told to go in. As she was now.

"FF23 is OSS. Office of Special Security. That's where they took Aldrich Ames. At first. They're not looking into what you know. They're looking into you."

Camille blanched. "No, couldn't be."

The Agency had its own protective services. The SPOs – Security Protective Officers – were obvious cops. They wore dark trousers and white shirts and state trooper hats. They wore pistols and badges on their belts. They were responsible for physical security duties around facility and the gates and were called in to assist at certain times.

But SPOs were not Office of Special Security. That entity operated in the dark corners of the CIA and filled the shadows in agency employees' minds. This much was known: the OSS defended the agency from any and all threats. They controlled all security clearances of all employees, regardless of rank. They gave the polygraphs. They protected senior officers, stations and classified material abroad. Their office was on duty 24/7 against all threats to the agency from any source. Including spies within.

Analysts shared nightmarish rumors of what went on when one of their own was suspected. How OSS intimidated even directors of the CIA. How they reported only to themselves. How they alone determined if an internal employee was committing espionage. How they got their information. Some said it was like being captured by the North Koreans. The surprise, two-day polygraph test. Simulated drowning. Lights burning for days on end. Fingernails torn out. Electricity and genitals.

How it would end. Even if one was cleared, the shadow of doubt over one would never shift. One would have trouble boarding planes for the rest of one's life.

"Be careful," he said. "Give them what they want. It's not worth the battle. If they even suspect a thing you are out of here. You lose your job, your benefits, your pension. Remember, this is accepted service, not civil service. The director can fire anyone for any reason or no reason at any time. Start your life over somewhere else. But don't lie to them. Do not lie. Then it will be over for you, Camille. Good luck."

Camille watched Joel roll back into his cube like a hermit crab. Proximity meant Camille often had lunch with Joel. On a good day, Joel was sure the people seated at the nearby table were actually intelligence officers from the secure side, meeting with someone without clearance. At the end of one long day, he told her not to look directly at the truck in the parking garage with its lights on. Yes, the one that just turned them off. He told Camille how he parked his own car somewhere different every day, sometimes blocks from his own house, then walked a different SDR – Surveillance Detection Route – each day of the week to draw out anyone who might be watching him. Every day he wore Corefams to work. Military dress shoes. Standard issue. He told Camille why.

"For them," he nodded. "They think I'm military – they're already off the scent."

Camille had nodded, doing her best to keep the corners of her mouth flat. But today, Joel's hysteria seemed reasonable.

Camille frowned. She had information that might help and she was glad they wanted to hear it. Finally someone would listen and do something about it. She hurried down the hall, her leather flats digging into her heels where, by the end of the summer, calluses had hardened thickly over the blisters that formed early in the spring.

FF23 looked like every other door. Grey. Beside it was a square plate with black numbers on it indicating the floor, the hallway and the room number. She knocked tentatively. The door opened quickly.

"Come in," said one man. He wore dark trousers, a white shirt, and a trooper hat. She saw a gun at his belt, and the flash of a badge on his hip.

"Just a SPO," thought Camille. Then she looked around the room. She saw no one she knew. Her boss was not there. The director was not there. Another SPO in the corner slung an automatic rifle over his shoulder. Two men in regular clothes stood beside a metal table. One was very large.

Camille's thoughts shot to Joel. The truck in the garage with its lights on. Fear shot through her. This was the Office of Special Security.

"Sit down," growled the large man. To Camille, he looked like he ate what he killed. His eyes were bloodshot; his nose showed hundreds of veins at the surface. His meaty frame held plenty of muscle and fat.

Camille's flower dress caught under her as she sat down on the metal chair. There was no cushion. Fluorescent light blazed and hummed.

"We know what you've done," he said, glaring at her.

"I haven't done anything," Camille whispered.

"What?" he bellowed, pounding the table with his closed fist. Camille flinched. She felt tears prick her eyes. Surprise, unfairness, humiliation. Fear. "There are thousands of people who kissed their kids and went to work this morning who are now dead. Because of you and your friends!"

"No," Camille said. "No, no."

"You will tell us everything you know or you will never work again. We will follow you everywhere. Every town you move to, every job you apply for, we'll be there first. Your credit report will stink. No one will hire you. No one will give you a mortgage. No one will help you. What will a fat single girl do without a job or a home?"

Camille was shaking. She had never been spoken to like this. There was no one in the room who knew her. No one she could turn to for help.

"What do you want to know?" Camille finally said. Then they strapped her to the machine. Placed electrodes on her head. Her palms gripped the sensors.

Hours passed. Camille had no idea how many. There were no windows in the room. Periodically the interrogators would change. She sweated through the billowy fabric of her dress. Her hair was a humid mess, getting in her eyes. The air conditioner was off in the room. She was getting very thirsty and hungry. Hungry. Matilda!

"I have to bring someone dinner," she said weakly.

"Sorry," said the big man. "We have more questions. They will bring in a cot and you can sleep here. By tomorrow perhaps you'll be more willing to talk."

"But I had plans to –" Camille started.

"Sorry national security has interfered with your social life," growled the man. "You can expect that trend to continue."

"Could I at least call the woman I was supposed to bring dinner so she doesn't worry? She's very old and she'll think the worst, " said Camille.

"She should," he said. "So how long have you and Scully been planning this?"

The hours passed. Camille could barely see. The light was becoming blurry. Sweat seeped into her eyes and drew moisture out of her contact lenses, which now scraped across her corneas. Fear drained her. Joel's words came back with no trace of the silliness she initially had heard: "Give them what they want."

The door opened. An OSS officer held a long narrow board, about twenty inches wide. He put a block under one end. In his other hand he held a bucket. Then Camille heard the squeak of a spigot.

CHAPTER 5

EDWIN
10:00 A.M., I-95 SOUTH

The ride from Boston to D.C. is just under 450 miles. Without stops, obeying speed limits, it would take eight hours. Edwin had five. He was expected at 4:00 p.m. By whom, he did not exactly know. Completing the mission was the first step to finding the Head - to convincing him to reverse the RUPD cleanup orders.

Edwin blinked. The lenses that cast a golden hue across his green irises slipped on the viscous layer, adjusting. An image floated before Edwin at a focal point he could see without taking his eyes off the road which he covered at 100 miles per hour.

The image contained these words:

Purpose: *Hand Deliver the Prize and Extract Deep.*
Personal Meeting Date/Time: *Wednesday September 12 16:00.*
General Location: *Washington, D.C., Northwest, 2933 Connecticut Ave.*
Personal Meeting Specific Location: *Service Entrance to Penthouse Floor.*

Contact Procedures:
Recognition Signals (Bona Fides)

Visual: *Contact will light cigarette on balcony.*
Verbal: *Operator "Disposal busted?" Contact: "That's not my domain but come take a look."*
Danger Signal: *Contact says "I think I need to sit down."*
Personal Meeting Cover: *Appliance Repair.*
Props Required: *Overalls, Toolbox.*
Extraction Location: *Private airfield in VA, four miles south west of Capitol.*

Five hours of uninterrupted time was a pleasure Edwin had not enjoyed since his last flight to the West Coast. Complete flight. It was these chunks of time when, as a graduate student, he solved mathematics puzzles. Like all deep cover operators, he had a real day job. The difference here was this: he loved it. Loved solving the complex problems of distribution, producing the rocket science that powered D6's surprisingly important commercial solutions.

It was effective "cover for status" – what people believed he was doing, who he was. Operators conduct meetings in hotel lobbies. So do business people. Customers could be anywhere in the world. So could Edwin.

Edwin was proud of the solutions. D6's underlying technology was a very clever use of "consistent hashing," matching objects to buckets, where information was imperfect and incomplete. One could pinpoint an exact match by using logic about approximations. If you knew one point, near enough, and another, near enough, and so on and so on, eventually you had enough precision to find a target.

D6 was a lark against the backdrop of world politics. Where anger and fury at America crept to its shores. Sleeper cells of terrorists, lying dormant for years, planning, waiting, anticipating their call to destroy the world – while Edwin waited for his call to come protect it. These people were bent on destruction, while Edwin put every ounce of energy into making new things happen. To scaling that effort by making others make new things happen. The criminals would extract to their vision of seventy-two virgins and honey, which would surely disappoint. Edwin would extract to another cover, another new community where he could form no attachments, so he could leave when new orders called.

Tearing over the highway, Edwin saw the link. If one could locate mathematical targets, one could substitute human targets into the same equation. If his algorithms could find the best path through the maze of the Internet to connect the right digital impulses with the right eyes at the end of a D6 interface, couldn't they also find the best path through the maze of people and business and residences in the United States – even the world – to locate dormant terrorist cells?

Edwin spoke softly as he drove along the Garden State Parkway, trees making lush green walls along the winding, empty highway. His voice was just loud enough for the tiny microphone to pick up. And as he spoke, computer code printed line after line after line in the floating screen blinking before him.

It was 3:42 p.m. when Edwin idled at a stoplight just across from Washington, D.C.'s National Zoo. 3:42 p.m. Not bad. But he had more work to do before 4:00 p.m.

There were things he did not like about these orders. First, the penthouse. It was a terrible choice for a personal meeting. Operators met in public places like hotel lobbies where one could fit in just by reading a paper. Where there were multiple obvious exits.

Why a penthouse? Maybe they did not want to risk his face being seen in public – it was on TVs whenever the news scrolled through the victims. Or the contact could not be seen. Or the ASP had something else planned for him. Not delivery. Not extraction.

Edwin had something else planned too.

He drove around the target building on a small road. It circled behind, reconnecting to the main road, with alleys in between. The zoo and Rock Creek Park stretched behind the small road. These were all possible exit routes. The indented service door on the location building was a good place to duck and take cover. The motorcycle could make it through the alleys if necessary.

The only part Edwin did not like was the penthouse. Once inside, exits would be limited to the roof, stairs, and windows. But fortunately he had a few extra options.

"Thanks Zed," Edwin said, shrugging in his jacket, kicking his Nikes on the motorcycle pedal.

At 3:57 Edwin was sucking long draughts of iced coffee through a straw at the outdoor café across from the zoo. The sugar came up crunchy. Half a dozen sugar packets were twisted into tiny white cigars on the metal braids of the table when Edwin saw someone open the door to the balcony on the top floor of the building, catty-corner from the café. Hands cupped, two fingers crossed and tipped up. The other hand shook something and tossed it. The fingers came to the person's mouth and away. Then again.

Edwin dropped bills on the table, enough to cover the coffee and a tip fair enough to be forgotten. Then he walked across the street. He pushed the intercom at the service elevator for the penthouse.

A woman's voice came over the line. "Yes?" she said, her weak voice lilting.

Edwin paused. He blinked, reviewed the order. This was the right building. Unless something had gone haywire in the visual transcription technology that scanned impulses in his brain from the images he saw through the Raptor lenses, and then sent the data to a particular databank of secure computers far away from Edwin.

"Ah," Edwin paused. "Disposal busted?"

"I don't know dear," said the elderly woman. "Let me check."

Edwin's gut clutched. The Contact's verbal Bona Fide was "That's not my domain but come take a look." Not "I don't know dear." Bona Fides were specific signals Operators gave to and received from contacts. Bona Fides had to be executed precisely, so no Operator could, for example, leave a capsule of weoponized pneumonic plague in the hands of somebody's granny.

"This is a trap...," he thought. Edwin spun his back to the wall. He swept the small service foyer, the glass entrance and the steel door on the other side of the elevator.

The old woman's voice crackled, "It's not really my department, dear, but you can come check." It was not perfect. Edwin hesitated. But when the empty elevator opened, Edwin backed in, keeping his eyes on the foyer. He pressed PH, and the elevator carried him up eight floors.

The doors opened to the blue eyes, so dark they were nearly purple, of a very old woman. She looked about a hundred years old. A smile spread lines across her cheeks like a stone dropped in water. She crushed her cigarette and took Edwin's hands in hers, kissing him on one cheek, then the other.

"It is a joy to finally meet you," she said. "I have watched you closely since you joined my little organization. I am so glad you made it here. This was the hardest challenge I have ever given. The loss of life on the planes, in the buildings...oh, it is horrific. But without you, there would have been millions more. Millions. You have done well. I knew I had chosen well. Who better for this flight than Raptor!" The old woman shook her small fist high.

Edwin stared, riveted by this tiny, ancient woman. Now he understood why the penthouse was the meeting place. It had nothing to do with him. It was chosen to protect her.

"Thank you, Head," he said, clasping his hands behind his waist tightly, chin high, his feet square to face his superior officer. The Head bustled down the hall.

"In here," she said. "We have work to do before that old biddy gets back. I told her I needed saffron. Should keep her busy for a bit. Let me make you some tea. You really must cut back on coffee. It's not good for you."

The reference brought Edwin up short. There was never a spare word. He thought of Lula, from whom he had drunk much too much.

Matilda Mace shuffled to the end of the pantry where an electronic kettle had reached boiling. She plucked two cups from a low shelf by reaching carefully up on her toes, and plopped a teabag into each one. She held one out.

"Now, report," said Matilda, fixing him with the chill, pointed gaze of the highest ranking general to whom he could report mission results. They stayed in the kitchen, where the disposal provided his cover and the service stair offered a fast exit.

"I took possession of the vial in flight then evacuated," said Edwin. "It had a twenty-four hour timer that has been disarmed."

"Disarmed or destroyed?" said Matilda.

Edwin paused slightly. "Disarmed. I have it."

Matilda put forward her small palm, soft, warm and fleshy. Edwin unzipped his overalls, reached through his jacket and shirt and ripped the duct tape from his belly. He gingerly placed the vial, still encased in its protective crystal, in her open hand.

"Task well done," said the Head. "Now this can be disposed of properly." The Head shuffled to the counters and pulled a jar of flour. She stuck the vial deep inside. "Don't worry. She only bakes on my birthday. It will do for the moment. And now…"

"Head," Edwin said. "A question."

"Yes."

"I exited with the puck," he began.

"Yes. Exactly," she said.

"I can fly a jet, ma'am," Edwin said, still at attention. "I did not."

"No," said the Head. "You did not fly the jet because that was not your mission. You were to possess this vial, exit and deliver it to me. Without variance. You have succeeded. Because you did, this little prize is in our hands, not theirs, not lost. You have performed very well. Better than anyone could have expected. And now,"

"Extraction?" Edwin said. The Head squinted at him.

"This part of the plan has been very well planned. Belts and suspenders. First, the vial itself placed on the jet. For insurance, the twenty-four hour explosive device," she said.

"But that is not all," Edwin said. "There is another vial. There is a mark on this one. .002. Which means there is a .001 somewhere."

"That fits," the Head said. "Our intelligence is that there is much at stake for these terrorists. The passing of the crown from the leader to the successor hinges on which of the three phases of this attack is deemed most destructive of Americans, most heinous. Thus the backup plans. The authors of the planes phase and the targets phase must feel quite confident. But the third is back on his heels. So this second vial's price just went up. On the order of tens of millions of dollars. And cash is not unlimited. Each of these attacks is something of a bootstrap undertaking. The leader provides infrastructure – cash for living expenses, wiped passports, and travel; but the planning, the finances and strategy, often depend on the operation leader – the terrorist entrepreneur. I'm quite sure Phase 3 could happen independently of the planes. They hinged it together to the others simply to overshadow the competition in the successor battle. A plane hijacking doesn't sound as terrible as landmarks – the Towers, the Pentagon – brought crumbling down. And neither of those makes quite the same impression as wiping out the entire eastern seaboard with a contagious plague. So your success, Raptor, has also ensured there will be a second buy, and soon."

"When? Where? Who?" Edwin asked.

"By tomorrow night," the Head said. "You must stop it. I can give you one source. There is a resource who has a strong connection, historically, to someone quite close to Phase 3. Someone who has leaked about it already. Someone who could leak again. You must use this resource as bait to lure the leak. Your new mission is this:

"One – find out when and where the second buy will happen.

"Two – find out who has been chosen to succeed the Leader. Then, Raptor, you will extract to a new deep cover until you are called upon to serve humanity again as you have done so honorably here."

THE FIRST SECRET OF EDWIN HOFF

"Who is the contact? Where do I find him?"

The Head twisted her bony wrist to look at her watch. "Her. I imagine you can find her at work. In a bit of a tight spot."

"Where, ma'am?" Edwin asked.

"Langley. She's an analyst. Her name is Camille Henderson."

"Okay," he said.

Matilda sipped slowly, blowing the steam from her cup. "And so we must discuss your complication."

Edwin stiffened. The Head set the rules of engagement for ASP operators. He had broken them. He put everyone at too much risk. Lula was a case in point.

"There is no complication," he said evenly. "I will get you the second vial."

Matilda exhaled a long sigh. Then she said quietly, "Edwin, I fear this is the first and last time we shall ever see each other. As I am such an old lady."

Whatever the original plan, Edwin knew the Head wanted the other vial more. And only he could get it for her in time.

"Camille is special to this leak," said the Head, gripping Edwin's forearm. "She is also quite special to me. You must get her to want to help you. Fortunately, she needs quite a bit of help right now. She's being looked at quite hard right now."

"Why?"

"OSS has her. She's being polygraphed in Room FF23. I assume it has become unpleasant. The way they do things there – some things don't change. Though I understand they have gone green and no longer incinerate their trash. Now they mulch."

"Day 1 or 2?" Edwin asked.

"The hard one. Day 1," said Matilda. "She's not the type to last. She's really not up to this level of stress. But you need her with you to lure the leak out of his hole."

"Done," Edwin said, as they heard a key turned in a heavy lock down the hallway.

"And Raptor, one more thing?" the Head put her hand on his wrist, twisting the skin painfully. She smiled the sweetest smile. "Can you give up coffee?"

Edwin looked straight at the Head. No emotion tightened his eyelids. Despite what the ASP had taken from him. He said, "I can do anything. Anything you ask of me." Their eyes locked with the same intensity. Edwin wanted the Head to feel that he was on board, so she would stop wiping up his world.

Then they heard soft shoes shuffling down the hallway.

Moments later, Matilda's carer, Amanda, plopped a seeping brown paper bag on the pantry table.

"Peach saffron melba…There you are! Oh! You haven't! Matilda Mace! Smoking in the pantry! It's as if you are sixteen years old, not 96," she said.

Matilda had a spoon in her hand. "I need fresh air," she said, snatching the paper bag from the table. "And thank you."

Amanda huffed and bustled. "Then I'll get you a blanket. We can't afford another chill. The last one had us in for more than a few belts of oxygen you may recall."

When the nurse left, Edwin Hoff slipped out of the broom closet. He disappeared down the servant's staircase, the Head's cool grip still bruising his wrist.

Later, wrapped in a cotton quilt, the Head made a call from her private quarters. "He delivered. Hold RUPD for twenty-four hours."

At 5:20 p.m., across the river in Virginia, the interrogator said again, "You're going to tell us now. Everyone talks after this."

The door opened. A different SPO walked in. His hat was dipped over his eyes and he held thick canvas straps. "Camille Henderson?" he said.

"Yes," she whispered.

"Get on the board," he said. But before anyone took another step, there was a shuddering bang. Blinding light flashed. Thick black smoke filled the room. Camille heard the large man cry out, then a heavy thud. She heard something rip. Overhead sprinklers shot wide sprays of water that turned the smoke into choking steam. She tucked her face into her dress and pulled the edges of the cardigan over her stinging eyes.

In the clear hallway, Camille could see nothing. She had no idea what force spun her chair around and sent her flying fast on its slick wheels over wet linoleum until she crashed into the wall. Someone pushed her through the door. It closed behind them.

Camille could see again. Two SPOs sprawled motionless on the hallway floor. Then someone grabbed her arm. Camille jumped, turning to find fierce, oddly yellow eyes focused on her. The intense muscled man spoke in low, urgent tones.

"If you stand here for three more seconds you won't see daylight for years. You will flat out disappear. So come with me. You have the chance to be a hero. Again." Edwin Hoff turned Camille by the shoulders, pushing her through an unmarked office door. He closed it tightly.

In the small office, Edwin moved to the wall and dropped to his knees, scrabbling at a square panel. In a moment, it fell away, exposing a large tubular vent.

"Go! Now!" he said. The door jamb rattled.

"Wait a minute," Camille cried. "Who are you? What are you doing with me?"

"These are burn chutes," Edwin said. "Where the trash goes to be incinerated."

Camille's eyes flared. "What?"

"Don't worry," Edwin said. "The CIA doesn't burn its trash anymore. They mulch it. So get out quickly when you hit the bottom. Now hush."

Edwin stretched a piece of duct tape across her mouth. Her eyes looked wild, but the sounds she tried to make were muffled, overcome by the wailing alarm. He scooped her up, rocked her back and funneled her feet first through the opening in the wall. Then he swung both of his feet through and pulled the panel closed behind him with the makeshift handle of duct tape which was, for once, used in a duct.

Twenty minutes later the men in the hallway revived to the muffled grunts of their beefy boss kicking furiously at the blocked door.

"We had her!" he shouted. "She was going to crack. We were that close to getting the confession out of her. Get her back here! There is no way out of this building."

They had lost twenty minutes. But it was impossible to get out of the building without passing through one of the ten guarded exits. A team of agents would be at her apartment in twenty-two minutes; others at every train station and highway checkpoint. A red-headed peach-cheeked woman would stand out from the growing deck of suspect photos, all of whom had dark skin, black hair and Muslim names.

A long road led into the sprawling woodsy campus of the CIA headquarters in McLean, Virginia. The campus was designed to keep people out. The building itself was designed to keep people in. No one could exit without going through the physical barrier guarded by the entry level SPOs. Guards checked bags and badges coming and going. This was how the CIA monitored secrets people carried. Controlling secrets on physical items, like trashed paper, was another matter. They burned it all until politics turned the CIA green. Then they mulched it, soaking it in blue dye so the pulp was illegible.

But the building had not changed. Old incineration vents still ran from the top of the building down stagger steps through each floor to the basement sub level. Loads were now pulverized in the same room. The openings in the offices were just covered over. Nothing passed through the vents anymore. Not usually.

Edwin and Camille slid and banged through a vent, tumbling into a dark room. Camille was squealing behind the tape.

"Okay. Be quiet," Edwin said. She nodded. With a quick swipe he released her mouth. She gasped for air. "Sorry. We were making too much noise as it was."

"Who are you?" Camille hissed. "What are you going to do to me?"

"I'm the guy who's saving your butt. And then you're going to save mine. But I haven't done it yet. Come with me." Edwin grabbed her elbow and opened the door.

They stood in a small, well-lit garage on a loading dock. A shipping container at their feet was ready for pick up. It was piled to the top with mounds of blue goo.

At 5:26 p.m., exactly when the fourth truck of the day was scheduled to leave the garage, the doors opened and the uniformed driver showed the guard his license. The truck hauled its blue load away from the loading dock at CIA headquarters and lumbered down the long road. It stopped per its usual course at Langley House, the CIA Visitors' Center, pulling behind a dumpster near the old farmhouse.

Edwin put his arm across the truck seat. Appraised his new recruit. He saw white all the way around her irises as she crouched behind the seat. Her hands crossed her chest. She held tightly to her plump freckled forearms.

"Who are you?" Camille said. Her lips would not stop moving.

"I'm Edwin," he said.   Keeping this one productive would require a softer touch.

"Why…what are you doing here? With me?" she whispered.

Edwin knew offering trust was the fastest way to gain it. That, and the offer of a higher purpose, would seal and motivate a new recruit. Even an improbable one.

"I need you," Edwin said. "You have an asset that no one else does. You can save millions of people. Again." He let that sink in.

"Me?" she said. Now he had her.

"Yes," Edwin said. "There is another vial – at least one more."

"Vial!" Camille said. "So there is one!"

"Two, actually," Edwin said.

"How do you know about it?" Camille whispered.

"Irrelevant," Edwin said. "This is what we know. Three things: someone is making it; someone is selling it, and whoever bought it the first time is sure as hell going to go after the backup now. We need to find the source and destroy it before they do."

"W…w…we?" Camille said. "Why me? You can't need me."

"You are the most important person in this mission," Edwin said, holding her attention with his unblinking eyes. "You know who leaked about the first vial. He will know about the second – or he can find out where it came from, and where the next one is coming from. We need to find him, and convince him to tell us."

Camille shook her head. "I don't know how to reach him. I hadn't talked to him in ten years. He found me." She stopped, wary she had revealed too much. What side was this man on? Edwin's eyes felt like drill bits boring into her.

"There's always a way," Edwin said. "Tell me what you know about him. Anything at all. No matter how insignificant it may seem."

"His uncle took him in. After his parents died in a car accident."

"You were in love. Maybe still are. This can work for us," Edwin said.

"I don't even know who you are," Camille stumbled.

"You don't need to," Edwin said. "Let me be clear. Your life here is over. You think you were going to go back to your little analyst cube tomorrow? After your little chat with OSS? You were not. They were fifteen seconds from taking you away to a place where you would not see the light of day or speak to a lawyer for six, seven years. If that. You are being hunted – not sought – hunted –

with guns and dogs – as an accessory to the biggest act of war on American soil. Treason. They will kill you for it."

"But why? I tried to help!" she cried.

"Exactly," said Edwin. "You told someone about the tip; he did nothing about it; so now he's sold you up the river to cover his own butt. You have one chance to save yours. Now put this on." Edwin threw Camille a jumpsuit, and then a helmet.

"No way," Camille balked. "A motorcycle? That's where they get organ donors."

"Yours aren't going to be much use anyway, with the bullets they put through them if they catch us sitting in this garbage truck in the Visitor Center parking lot in the next twenty seconds. Fifteen. Now move!" When Edwin barked, Camille began floundering with the jumpsuit.

"What's your address?" Edwin said. "I need a picture of him. You have one."

"Yes," said Camille.

"Also," Edwin said, "that's where the cops are going."

"We are going to meet the cops?" Camille gasped.

Edwin shook his head. "Beat them. It's the only way to send them off in the direction we want them to go. We can just make it."

It was very hard for Camille to see anything but the spot Edwin Hoff shined on. Five minutes later, two tourists boarded a motorcycle in the Visitor Center parking lot and drove slowly past an idling garbage truck. They cruised to the street, past the cacophony of howling sirens, squawking radios and swirling red white and blue lights of the police and emergency vehicles which now swarmed the main building.

The motorcycle's throttle opened wide when Edwin found the highway and pointed them toward the northwest quadrant of Washington D.C. Camille tucked her head down against Edwin's back, gripping his Kevlar jacket. She clung on for dear life.

As the miles passed, Camille was surprised at the stability of the ride. She imagined it would feel like balancing on a wobbly fence rail, but the bike's bulk and speed made it feel like sitting on a sturdy chair. She sat up straighter. Eventually she looked around. The lights of the Capitol were on. The Washington Monument. The Jefferson, lighting up its pool. Such a peaceful place on a late summer evening.

Twelve minutes later, Camille closed the door to her apartment and threw the bolt. She ran to the living room and grabbed a photo in a frame.

"Here," she thrust it at Edwin.

"Camille, slow down," Edwin said. He sat on her couch, clasped his hands behind his head. "First rule of evasion – make haste slowly. Frenzy scatters you – you make mistakes, attract attention. We have time to do what we need to. Do what I say."

Camille noticed Edwin never said "you will be fine." The false promise would have made her doubt everything else he said. Instead, she felt her blood pressure begin to settle. She caught her reflection in the picture frame. Even in that dusty image she could see that her cheeks, which flushed easily, were steaming.

Edwin took the picture out of the frame. He scanned Camille sitting at a piano in the arms of a young man. She was fifteen pounds lighter then, but showing the beginnings of the battle with twenty. Her red hair was shorter. Her face beamed. She was young. In love. She was once quite beautiful. Edwin looked up at the woman who stood in front of him now. Strain had set layers on her face. She looked less and less interested in the pursuit of fitness or fashion. She was fading from the picture.

This was his recruit? Edwin thought. No, this was his team. To win, you play your team's strengths. You bolster their weaknesses. You do not doubt them. So this person standing in a flowery dress that covered her ankles, fear mincing her words and capillaries expanding near her skin, was his clay.

Different motivations worked with different people. Edwin had never worked with a woman before. Weak men, frightened men, silly men, he could shape with a combination of animal dominance, a sharp sting, the fear of humiliation and, more powerful, the opportunity to be a hero. But at their core, he believed humans responded to similar cues. Camille would be an experiment. One that had to succeed, because he needed her help. Right now she looked like a pillar shaking to ash.

Edwin returned to the photograph. It was a bad shot of the guy. His arms circled Camille as she sat on his lap, the piano behind them. But his chin was tucked behind Camille's neck. The picture only revealed that his hair was black and spiky short, his skin a warm light brown. He held Camille with one arm, the fingers of the other around a green bottle. His faded blue jeans were visible under

Camille's dress, and the slight curve of his gut rolling over the side of his jeans looked like the Freshman Fifteen had ballooned to twenty-five or thirty. Edwin saw the frame of a young man filling up. But not his face.

Edwin squinted; his lenses shifted, focused and scanned the picture from the impulses on Edwin's optic nerve. "Clever," he thought. "Vision in reverse."

Edwin could think a command, or look at an object, and the technology would seize the electronic impulses the optic nerve captured. This image uploaded to the computer that was safely stored in a very remote location. Thanks to some clever coding, it was accessible by only Edwin, and one other person.

"A lot depends on him," Edwin thought. "For what I do next, even more will."

Aloud Edwin asked Camille, "Is this the leak?" Camille nodded. "Name?"

"Yassir Mettah."

"You have any other pictures? One with his face." He stuffed the picture in his pocket.

Camille shook her head. "After he left…I was pretty mad. This is all I have left. None of them were very good anyway. He always seemed to be looking away from the camera."

"So, Yassir Mettah of Saudi Arabia called you ten minutes before the first plane hit the Tower, and told you to get out?" Edwin said. "Oh yeah. You're in a heap of it."

Camille swallowed.

Edwin spoke calmly. "They are on their way here. We will now do what we need to do. Then we will go. First, where do your parents live?"

Camille whispered, "Florida.".

"Get the phone book. Dial Amtrak. Buy a train ticket to Naples, Florida for this evening. Use your credit card. Print the ticket here," Edwin said.

Camille's sweaty thumbs made the yellow pages cling.

"One leaves at 7:15 p.m.," said Camille. "We're going to Florida?"

"Buy it," said Edwin. "It's almost six now. You could make it."

Camille bought the ticket. An email pinged her computer. Her printer hummed.

"Now, take this pad of paper and a ballpoint pen. No, not a felt tip. Press hard. You want it to leave an impression on the pages below the one you write on. So they have to work to find it, but they find it."

Camille pulled a notepad with her name embossed in rainbow colors.

"Go online. Find hotels in Naples, Florida. Good. Now call four of them and make reservations. Write them all down on this pad of paper. Press hard."

Edwin checked his watch. Time was getting close. The CIA could not pursue a suspect on USA soil – local police or the FBI had to do it. Legally, the CIA could only operate outside the U.S. On September 12, 2001, however, Edwin knew better than to count on procedure. Lines would blur. Protocol breaches would be covered up in the hot pursuit of one responsible for the heinous attacks. Edwin and Camille needed to move.

"Now rip off the sheet you wrote on and leave the rest here," he said.

"Won't they find it?" asked Camille.

"Yes! They'll look for you on the train. In each hotel. While we go elsewhere."

Camille left the seemingly blank pad of paper on the desk next to her computer and phone. She clicked to her home page but left the computer on so every previous page she searched would be stored in the computer's cache, showing what she had browsed.

"Where are we going?" Camille asked.

"What's your favorite wild animal?" Edwin asked. "Mine's the panda."

Four minutes later, the lock to Camille's door shook slightly. The knob turned. The door opened. The apartment was empty. But the fine grains of the dusty powder spread across the piece of paper with "*Camille*" printed in flowing brightly colored script above fell into the ridges in the paper made by a shaky hand:

7:15 - Naples.

A few blocks away, Edwin pushed Camille through the turnstiles. The evening tourists were milling about, arriving to watch feeding time at the zoo.

"I have really had enough of zoos," Camille whispered. "What are we doing here? Shouldn't we be at the train station, or going somewhere?"

"First we need to know where your friend Yassir is," Edwin said.

"I told you – I don't know!" Camille snapped. The adrenaline was burning off.

"We will find out," Edwin said, "Because you are going to tell us things. Random things. Anything. Things that may not seem so helpful but are. Where in the world a certain person may be is a distributed problem – a non-trivial one. But I know how to solve distributed problems. We need a few minutes on our own to walk and talk."

"Won't they follow us?" Camille said.

"You think they expect you to take in a tourist site this evening? America's most wanted?" Edwin said. "Just avoid the panda cam. You like chocolate or vanilla?"

Shortly, Edwin leaned on a railing, licking a chocolate swirl. From the crest above, a nervous grey wolf trotted back and forth between the walls of his confines.

"So where did he go to school?" Edwin asked.

"Yale," said Camille. "Via England. He went to Rugby School."

"Excellent," Edwin said. "Where did you meet him?"

"Art History. He's a genius. He only had to look a picture of a work and he had it memorized. I spent hours flipping flash cards over and over. He'd just laugh and make up ditties on the piano. He was good at that too."

As Edwin listened, his thoughts fired the inputs to his program. The screen before his eyes populated. "When did you last see him?"

Camille gulped. "Before this summer? It had been ten years."

"How did he get in touch with you?"

"He left me a sign. A distress sign he made me learn at school. I always thought it was strange he wanted me to know that stuff."

"What was the sign?"

"Three dots – like a triangle – on my door. And a code for the rainforest exhibit at the Central Park Zoo. He was there," Camille said.

"Where do you think he lives?" Edwin said.

"I have no idea. East Coast? He came to D.C., then told me to go to New York."

"Traveling north," Edwin said, adding inputs to the program. Two of the planes originated from Boston. One had the vial. "So why did he tell you about the attack?"

"Me? I don't know," she said. "I think he wanted it to be stopped but could not do it himself. I tried, but no one wanted to listen. He should have asked someone else."

Camille lived constantly on the precipice of action. All of her effort went to holding back, to keeping herself from plunging over. Winning that battle fed her a constant rush of survivor's adrenaline, simply staying on the sidelines despite the pulls and missteps that beckoned from the brink. The lost opportunity – experience – was the price she happily paid to save herself from sure destruction. But when inaction cost others, her brinksmanship revealed cowardice that set its tentacles and sucked.

Edwin cut in. "He asked you. You responded. Now there is more to do. You will answer again. I will help you." A guilty hand wringer was not a productive fighter.

They ambled around the zoo, Edwin asking questions, Camille's answers flowing into his ears. He visualized his thoughts; they became data that fed directly into the program Edwin had composed driving toward Washington, D.C. at 100 miles per hour.

Far, far away, a small group of computer servers crunched the data. The data that could be crunched from the photograph – hair color, forearm length, approximate height as compared with the measurement of Camille's upper body – flashed against databases of passports, visas, criminals and motor vehicles departments. It was crossed with location – images picked up by ATM security cameras, street security cameras. Corporate security cameras. And more.

A yellow light blinked in the corner of Edwin's left lens. "Interesting," Edwin said.

"You found Yassir?" Camille gasped. Edwin shook his head.

"I found nothing, which is interesting because at least something should have shown up." "So how are we going to find him?" Desperation tinged Camille's voice.

"My program isn't the phone book," Edwin said. "It uses known fact and logic to assign a bucket – a location – to an unknown quantity. It would probably make me another billion if I commercialized it. I'd call it "CrossPathz." But what is more interesting, is that CrossPathz is telling me there is no record of Yassir Mettah, Yale Class of '91. No person with his background even shows up."

"That's not possible," Camille insisted. "He existed. Yassir is real."

"Yes," Edwin said, keen as a hound. "And very, very smart. Yassir Mettah has the skill to live on the East Coast of the United States under a new identity for the last ten years, and wipe his history completely off the grid – digital and analog." Edwin eyed Camille. "And he's had the discipline to maintain it. Until recently."

"So how are we going to find him?" Camille said.

"More data," Edwin said. "What do you think he is doing now?"

"He said he's an art consultant," Camille said. "He must be using that incredible brain. I loved that brain. In our art history class he could just look at pictures of paintings once and they were stored in his memory. And he could play the violin like a maestro."

Brilliant. English boarding school. Distress signals. Advising wealthy patrons. Snakes. The code ran.

"Lots of music," said Edwin. "Interesting." Half of his best engineers were musicians. The logic of musical language appealed to brains the way the logic of computer languages did – the rules and the limitless possibilities for reconfiguring them to create feeling and change it, or to make new things happen and change them.

Edwin set a variable for this in the program, which drew on remote facts, linked them to logical associations, crunched assumptions about what was near enough to fact, then found true fact where these near enough assumptions crossed. It derived certainty from vagaries.

They paused near the birds of prey exhibit. The snowy owl had rolled its eyes open for the evening and was scrolling his territory for the limp white mice the keepers would soon drape over sticks.

"I don't like zoos either," Edwin said. "This one wants to fly away."

Then a green light flashed in his lens. There was an equals sign followed by a street address. "Ah! Excellent. Now we can go."

"Where?" asked Camille.

"Union Station," Edwin said. "Don't you have a train to catch?"

"But I thought that was just to throw them off? They'll be waiting for me!"

"Yes," said Edwin. "And if they don't see you there, they'll know it was a ruse. And they'll get back on our tail. So do exactly as I say. And Camille…"

"What?"

"I'll be there too," Edwin said.

Ten minutes before 7:00 p.m., Camille paid the taxi driver twelve dollars and trotted up the alabaster stairs of Union Station's grand entrance. She carried a small overnight bag over her shoulder, a bright floral, quilted print. The cameras would pick her up easily, right when she emerged from the cab. From there, it was a matter of timing.

Blinking rapidly, Camille hustled to the large list of arriving and departing trains and tracks. She cast a glance over her shoulder. No one yet. Not obviously. She checked her watch. At exactly 6:52 p.m., she popped into the ladies room.

The agents tracked the woman with the floral bag from the taxi stand. One spoke into his cupped fist, "Ladies room, south corner first level."

A voice piped in his ear piece. "Send the agents in. Watch out for ambush."

Two female agents walked into the bathroom. The janitor pushed open the door, pressing ahead with the steady slow shuffle of an old woman. The agents could just see the bright overnight bag sitting on the floor of the third stall. The toilet flushed. No one else was in the restroom.

"Go on, go on," one agent whispered to the lazy janitor, bolting the door after her. Her partner counted silently, holding her fingers up in quick succession. One, two, three. Then one officer kicked in the door to the stall.

"Hey! Occupied!" A small woman with white hair piled on her head sat on the toilet clutching her skirts. Her face twisted with anger. "I'm calling the union!"

"Excuse me," said one officer, backing away. "So sorry."

Down the service hall, a woman in a grey smock shuffled behind a janitorial cart. Eventually she reached the service doors and went through them to the where trucks unloaded goods for the shops and restaurants. No one noticed her tuck the cart next to a line of others. She walked slowly through the open loading dock to a white van. The front passenger door opened.

"Well done," Edwin said as he pulled the banged up white van away from the parking lot full of a dozen other vans that looked just like it.

"Where did this come from?" Camille asked, pulling off the janitor's bib.

"Had to get a new ride," Edwin said. "CIA would have made the motorcycle by now. Watch behind us." He hit the gas hard.

"Whoa, Nelly!" Camille said. Edwin grinned. It was an odd expression from an odd girl who looked like her horse had taken off from under her. He liked it.

"One more stop, then we go. I'm guessing you were never in the Navy."

"Navy? I can barely swim," she said. "The only water I like is in my tub. If God meant me to swim he would have given me flippers."

"So," said Edwin. "We're going by boat."

"Good lord. Where?"

"Boston," Edwin said. "That's where your buddy is."

"How do you know?"

"Logic," he said.

"I can't – a boat? All the way to Boston?"

"Look," Edwin said. "We have to get there as soon as we possibly can. Before they buy the other vial of this nasty stuff. We can't drive – they'll be watching the highways in and out of D.C. We can't take the train – they're already after you there. I'm pretty sure a private plane would be noticed today, since all flights are grounded in the entire country. Trust me, I would leave you here if I could. But I don't think you'd last very long with the brunt of a nation's frustrated intelligence agencies targeting you."

Camille made a small sound – a huff of exasperation.

"Plus, I need bait," Edwin said. He pulled the van into one of a thousand spaces in a large shopping plaza. Camille sat with her hands folded in her lap.

"Come," said Edwin. "We have shopping to do."

Edwin grabbed a cart and headed toward the clothing aisle. They passed throngs of people filing in and out of the Wal-Mart. Their carriages were full; the shelves showed bare patches. In the aftermath of the tragedy, people were hoarding, preparing for the unknown, which apparently required a lot of extra toilet paper, matches, bags of chips, many cans of stewed tomatoes.

"Try these," Edwin said, tossing Camille a pair of white canvas shoes with rubber soles and laces. "Make sure they fit. Then go to the women's section. In exactly two minutes, return with a white shirt and khakis. You have to ditch that dress."

"I made this dress," Camille said, clutching the brown floral cloth. There were grease streaks in its folds and large dusty patches from their trip down the vent.

"Yeah? So can the FBI," Edwin said. "I need you to be able to run. And kick."

Camille flushed. "I don't know how to – I can't fight!"

"Not yet," Edwin said. "Go! Meet me at the checkout line twelve. Two minutes."

A few minutes later, Camille stood in line, holding a pair of khaki trousers and a white polo shirt. Then she saw Edwin pushing the contents of a very full cart toward her. He must have known exactly what to get and where to find it in the behemoth store. Edwin paid the clerk $124.63 from a stack of crisp twenties.

"Do you need some cash?" Camille asked.

"No." Edwin picked up a rubber duck. "I could buy 3 billion of these. Let's go."

At the van, Edwin said, "Put these on." He tossed Camille a dark blue windbreaker lined with fleece. He flicked a floppy wide brimmed hat toward her like a Frisbee. Plastic sunglasses came next.

While Edwin stashed the bags, Camille turned her back. Within the partial privacy of the back of the van she dressed quickly. This guy did not seem the type to waste a moment for modesty's sake. She pulled the khakis on under her skirts, then dropped the dress. Camille was used to wearing a lot more fabric. These clothes felt close, but not tight.

Edwin hopped in the back just as she straightened the shirt over the top of her new trousers. In two swift moves, his t-shirt came off and the polo shirt was over his head. It was then that Camille saw the bandage on Edwin's neck.

"Are you okay?" she asked. "What happened?"

"Turbulence," he said, driving out of the parking lot and down the multi-lane street, stopping nearly every two hundred yards for stoplights that fed drivers into the shopping malls on their way to and from the Maryland shores.

Fifteen minutes later, Camille's feet were plonking down a wooden dock. In a slip at the end was a beautiful wooden picnic boat. Edwin rolled a cart behind her. They looked like any other couple heading to the water for an evening cruise.

"Slowly," Edwin said. "Slowly. Just a few minutes more." Camille forced herself to slow her pace and her breathing. But walking on a bridge with water on both sides and at the end of it was not calming. The boat was straining on its lines, pulled by the tide a foot and a half from the end of the dock. Edwin hopped over the gap with two large shopping bags. Camille handed him the others. He extended a hand to her. She looked down at the black water.

"Now," he said. His clear eyes held hers. They were like a magnet, pulling her scattered nerves to a functioning cluster. She stepped over the gap. "Now hide."

Edwin turned the key. The engines sputtered unevenly, pushing water and air through the system while they warmed up in neutral. Camille went forward down a small ladder to the cabin. There was a small kerosene stove and a lidded table that held a nautical chart showing the Chesapeake Bay out to the Atlantic Ocean. She lifted it and felt a blast of cool air; the chart table was also the refrigerator. A table with folded sides followed the middle line of the boat. Cushioned seats hugged the sides, long enough to be cots.

"Whose boat is this?" Camille asked.

"Mine," said Edwin. "What would I do with three billion ducks?"

Camille giggled, her frayed nerves releasing just a bit through the high pitched titter. She sorted through the bags. This was what they held:

A large white Styrofoam cooler with ice;
Binoculars;
Two beach towels;
Swimsuits, male and female.
Four small rubber ducks;
Three rolls of duct tape;
Charts;
A bottle of bleach;
A bottle of champagne;
Six apples;
Sticks of Mozzarella cheese;
A package of sliced turkey;
Six gallons of water;
A loaf of wheat bread;
Peanut butter;
Instant coffee;
A sack of sugar;
A box of small nails;
Candles.

The engines caught, the boat started to move. Camille grabbed the table to steady herself. Now she felt the swell of the sea. It was nauseating her. She needed air. She pulled herself toward the ladder

"What are the ducks for?" she called over the engines. Edwin appeared not to hear her. He pushed the throttle forward. Now they were pounding over the waves, spreading wings of white water behind them. Spray splashed up over the bow. Camille zipped her jacket up to the top and put her hood on. The evening was quite cool.

As they spun out into the Bay, Edwin looked at his recruit. She sat in the corner of the cockpit, tightly gripping a cleat that was bolted on the deck. Her face had lost its ruddy complexion ; she had gone very white.

Edwin saw a small cove, its white beach standing out against the twilight. They did not have time for this. But it needed to be done. He slowed the boat and took it in to very shallow water where he idled the engine, then ran up to the bow and tossed the anchor. He came back to the cockpit and pushed the throttle in reverse gear. The boat backed down on the anchor.

"I know one thing, Camille," Edwin said, glaring at Camille. "Before this is over, you are going to get caught. You are going to get tied up. Maybe by the good guys. Maybe by the bad guys. But it will happen."

"What?" she wailed. "What's going to happen to me?"

Good, thought Edwin. The fear is right at the surface. Survival skills drilled into her now will bind to the fear, and come out instinctively when she feels it again.

Aloud he said, "So treat it as fact. And prepare. To the beach!"

Edwin dropped his jeans, and pulled on the swim trunks over the boat shoes. In a swift swing of his arms, Camille was over his shoulders like a yoke. He jumped into the water. Camille shrieked. But she did not get wet. The water came up to Edwin's waist. He trudged through it fifteen yards to the beach where he deposited Camille on her feet.

For the next thirty minutes, Edwin taught Camille three skills of hand to hand combat. How to place one's feet for best balance. How to compromise an opponent's weight and force to use it against them. And one more.

Camille was covered with sand. Edwin wrinkled his lips. He pushed his tongue to the side of his cheek and rolled it forward. A small nail stuck through his teeth.

"You keep these on you. Always. Very useful tools. Keep one in the tips of your shoelaces. One in your cheek, but don't swallow it. Let me see your palms." Edwin flipped over her hand. He smoothed his thumb across it. "No. Too soft. If you had calluses, like mine, you could keep one right there in the hard skin."

"How about my heel?" said Camille. "Walking around in flats all summer turned all those blisters into rocks. My pedicure lady tries to go after them with a razor."

"Excellent!" said Edwin, squatting back on his heels. "That's even better than a hand or a shoe. They check the palms; they take off the shoes. But they don't expect the backs of your heels to be packing." He watched Camille kick off her boat shoe and produce the advertised callus. "Whoa, Nelly!" They laughed.

"Gross, I know."

"No," Edwin said. "Fabulous."

"So, like this?" Camille said. She took the thin nail and slipped it slowly into the back of her heel. Not even a wince. She beamed.

"Your shoes must really suck," Edwin said. He was pleased. The terrified rag he had carried to the beach, paralyzed by the many possibilities she could conjure for being caught and restrained, now sat upright on his shoulders as he waded back to the boat. She had a creative survival idea. The fight instinct just might have a chance.

They pulled out of the harbor in darkness. It was nearly 8:30 p.m. Before they reached the channel, Edwin saw another motorboat approach them. A blue light swirled. "Stop there," squawked a voice through a bullhorn. "We're going to board you."

"Coast Guard," Edwin said to Camille. "Go below. Now."

In the last moment that Edwin still controlled, he struck a match. So when the police pressed a bumper between the two hulls, they saw six small candles burning in the cockpit.

"How ya doing?" Edwin said with a smile. His cap was pulled low.

"You alone?" the captain asked.

"No," said Edwin. "My fiancée...well, hopefully, is below. It's a special night."

"Yeah?" He eyed him suspiciously.

"Yeah." Edwin pushed his hand into his pocket.

"Whoa there buddy. Let's see the hands," said the other officer.

Edwin brought his hand slowly out of his pocket. He flipped it over. In his palm was a small square box. He popped it open with his fingers, hoping the light from the candles would catch the plastic facets and make it look more special than the gumball trinket he had picked up at Wal-Mart. This was where the plan would succeed or fail.

Cover for action. The authorities would leave alone a couple out for a romantic evening – if they bought it. If they did not see Camille. Or recognize cubic zirconium.

"Times like these – life is short, right?" Edwin smiled.

"So why you signing up for a life sentence?" chuckled the officer. "Okay, man. Where you headed? We'll clear you through; otherwise, you'll get stopped over and over again. No need to waste our time on you." The two officers laughed.

"I don't know," Edwin said, scanning the dark horizon. "North-ish."

The captain spoke in his radio, then gave a half wave and sped off. Edwin edged the boat along the finger of the bay to where it opened wide and spilled into the Atlantic. The swells deepened. To stay above them, Edwin pushed the throttle forward. They needed to stay flat and fast. But the needle pointed in the right direction now. In seven hours they would be rounding Cape Cod. They would have some space on the ocean.

Edwin saw Camille's eyes grow wide again. Her fingers were white from gripping so tightly to the parts of the boat that were bolted down. So she needed a job. A big one.

"Here," he said. "Stand in front of me."

Camille moved gingerly across the cockpit as it pounded hard over each wave. Her legs felt like Jell-O. He reached for her and she was soon standing between his arms facing the wheel. Another wave hit and she grabbed for it.

"Good," said Edwin. His hands dropped away. "You take the wheel. Turn to the left, boat goes left. Turn to the right, it goes right. Keep it pointed at 110 degrees. And if you see any big waves coming at our side, point into them."

"Are you crazy?" Camille hissed. "I don't know how to drive this. We'll sink!"

"It's suboptimal, I agree," said Edwin. "But you slept last night. I did not."

"But," Camille protested.

"Three rules," Edwin said. "One. Point to 110 degrees. Two. We cannot stop. Three. If you need me for anything, tap my right shoulder. Once."

"But," Camille protested, as Edwin took his place in the corner. A dodger stretched up and over the cockpit like an umbrella, keeping the spray off them. He folded his arms and closed his eyes. In less than one minute he was sound asleep.

Camille looked ahead. She could see only black swells. Her hands wobbled the wheel. She looked down at the compass and gasped. They were fifteen degrees off their mark. She turned the wheel hard to the left and the boat banged sloppily off a large wave. Then they were twenty degrees off in the other direction. Camille swore, turning the wheel back to the right, this time more gently. The boat kicked sloppily, slow out of the trough. A heavy wave splashed over the deck. The boat shuddered.

"Oh!" cried Camille. "Hey! Umm…guy?"

Edwin slept. Camille watched the needle ease toward the right number. Soon she learned how to ease it back before she overshot the mark. She felt the link between the turn of the wheel and the momentum of the boat, how it carried her onto the right point. Still Edwin slept. Right where he was, despite the roar of the engines, the chop and the cool ocean spray.

Camille steered on into the night. For one hour. Two. Three. She saw a few other boats, more Coast Guard lights near the shore. None came near them.

The black ocean stretched before her. The stars seemed to have fallen out of the sky just above her head. Between her hands was the ship. It went where she moved her hands, like an extension. She had never been so big before.

The white froth of a large wave caught Camille's attention. She looked at Edwin. One tap would wake him. But she gripped the wheel and eased the bow of the boat slightly off course, just taking the wave up at an angle such that the wall of water slipped beneath them. Deftly, Camille turned the wheel. They were on course again.

It was nearly midnight when Edwin opened his eyes.

"Look at that," he said. "We're still afloat." Camille smiled sheepishly. She kept her eyes on the needle, the waves and the horizon. "I'll take her from here. Good job."

Camille stepped surely when she handed off the wheel. She put both hands on the gangway and stepped down to the cabin where she stretched out on the cushion and put a towel beneath her head. The boat rocked and engines hummed as she fell asleep.

CHAPTER 6

HUDSON
10:00 A.M., BOSTON, MA

Hudson watched the biker round the corner of the Public Garden from Beacon Street on to Arlington, square his knee to the road and accelerate into the morning traffic.

"In a few blocks he'll be at the Mass Pike," Hudson's thoughts began to follow Edwin's bike, but then the bruise on his cheek pulsed. Hudson shook his head and blinked hard. He had his own goal and not much time to accomplish it. By 2 p.m. tomorrow, he had to be on the very same corner with Edwin's Blackberry. Even though he had no clue where it was. Before then, at 8 p.m. tonight, he would meet Officer Marly.

Hudson jogged across Beacon Street through the wrought iron entrance gates to the Public Garden. He loped around the west bulb of the central pond. The Public Garden was a place for quiet contemplation of nature where the paths wound through weeping willows and circled large rose gardens. Elaborate floral plantings were tended daily and exhibits changed frequently. Wooden slat benches offered occasional places to sit. A small, light blue bridge cinched the waist of the hourglass pond. Tourists glided on rafts propelled by men peddling waterwheels between two swan-shaped facades.

This morning an elderly woman was practicing her Tai Chi exercises in her usual shaded patch. Hudson dropped his pace when he was yards from the tree where the swans were nesting. Hudson's shirt stuck to him as he sucked in the humid air.

His thoughts were coming fast, rushing through without the resistance they usually met. "Get the Blackberry," Hudson said under his breath. He did not doubt that he would do it. What consumed him was how.

A man in dark green pants and a matching shirt kneeled at one of the flower beds.

"Excuse me," said Hudson. "When did they take down the swan's nest here?"

"Last night," the gardener said. He eyed Hudson. "Late. Vet report came back they were both girls and we took the thing down ASAP. Why you so interested?"

"I lost something around here. Before they took down the fence," Hudson said. "You didn't happen to be here when they took it down?"

"Lost something like what?" he said.

"A Blackberry," said Hudson.

"A berry? You think a berry would survive with all these birds and...forget about the birds...how about the squirrels?" The man scoffed.

"No, no," said Hudson. "It's a Blackb...it's a little thing, shaped like a flat square, like this, see, with a keyboard and little buttons with letters all over it. For sending email."

"What would a squirrel want with buttons?"

Hudson chuckled. "I don't know, man," he said. And as always, Hudson's genuine smile and kind laugh put another at ease and made him a new friend. The gardener was so pleased with his joke he thought it worth another run.

"Yeah, like what would a squirrel want with buttons?" He laughed hard now. "Fish and Wildlife put the swans back in the water. One got pretty pelted by that wingspan. Then I came in and took the nest away."

"But there was nothing plastic in it? No squirrel-button thingy?" Hudson asked.

"Nope. Sorry man," he said, pushing new plants into the holes he had dug.

Hudson felt a twinge of disappointment as he walked off. "No. Never be the one...to say...you are done," he repeated. "Find the Blackberry. Make it happen. So. What do I know?" Pointed at one goal, it was amazing how clearly Hudson began to think. The logic stair in Hudson's mind rolled out new steps.

"First, I put the device there after I saw Ahmed," Hudson muttered. "After about 8 p.m. But the device was gone when the fence came down at midnight. So if the Blackberry disappeared from the nest before Fish and Wildlife freed the swans, then someone took it. Who would be stumbling around in a swan's nest after dark?"

Hudson kept talking in low tones, working through the problem. "Someone who knew it was there. Who would have known it was there? Someone who saw me put it there. Who was watching me? I didn't see anyone. Who was there who I wouldn't have seen?"

Hudson looked around. The shapes on benches, under dark blankets. They were part of the landscape. He had never talked to any of them. Except one. Tuesday night.

"You know any of the regulars around here?" Hudson said to the gardener.

"Regulars?" The gardener looked around. "Oh, you mean them," he waved his trowel in the direction of a lumpy dark grey military blanket stretched the length of a park bench, black trash bags tucked neatly underneath the bench. "Yeah I know most of them by now. They don't hurt anyone. Just mixed up themselves. Don't know why."

"Yeah. Any of them around last night?"

The gardener thought for a moment. "Yeah, I think so. The older fellow. They call him Nibs, or Squirrel or something. Hey, maybe a squirrel did take your berry after all." He grinned through lips flecked with wet dirt.

"Squibbs?" asked Hudson.

"Yeah, that's it," the gardener said. "That guy was around, kinda close. I watch them. Don't want anyone to eat one of my little friends here or nothing."

Hudson whistled. "No. That would be so wrong."

"Not right," said the gardener, pushing down soil so water would pool around the new plant. "This is a magical place. There's no room for evil magic here."

Hudson put a hand on the gardener's shoulder. "Thanks, buddy." He took a few steps, and then sprinted for the west side of the Garden and the brick red cement bridge that spanned Storrow Drive to the Esplanade. To the spot Detective Marly had showed him.

It was 10:45 a.m. Hudson had to find Mr. Squibbs. He tried to think of what he looked like. It occurred to him he had never really looked at the man's face. He could not count on him wearing the blue fleece flying Hudson's company flag.

What if the confused man had taken an unhealthy interest in him? The thought was not comforting. But Hudson did not know any other way. If he made himself available, maybe Squibbs would find him.

Hudson did not usually act on strategy. He took the easy route; he made friends; sometimes friends in high places, like Jameson Callaghan, who greased wheels, got him a job in a high-flying tech company with the opportunity to make a bunch of money. Friends liked him and put him on the roster. So he dressed to play. But how good he was, he never really knew. Hudson had never had to find the field himself. But today he had one goal, and the logic led there. And he saw it as the best way to get his answers, and his Blackberry, before two o'clock in the afternoon the next day.

Hudson walked slowly down the length of the esplanade. The Charles River reeked of mud in the warm windless day. He found the concession stand and bought two large bottles of water, and a couple of chocolate bars. Cadbury's. He found the bench near the willows. The police tape was gone. It occurred to him that while under suspicion for a murder it might not be the best thing to spend an afternoon sitting at the scene of the crime. But he knew no other way. This was where Squibbs hung out.

But after a few hours in the sweaty midday sun, Hudson drank the water and ate one of the Cadbury's. Then he stretched out on the bench. He awoke to a dark cloud blocking the sun. He blinked and sat up. A grizzled man stood in front of him. His beard was long and matted.

"Move!" he growled. Hudson stood up. The old man settled down on the bench.

Hudson looked at him again. "Mr. Squibbs?" he ventured. The man did not respond. He muttered and pressed at his coat, making himself at home. For the moment.

"Did I meet you with the lady with the chocolate? Give you my jacket?"

The agitated man showed no awareness that Hudson was still standing there. He was buzzing in his own world, a place of some certain discontent.

Hudson turned his empty wrist. Then looked at his own Blackberry. It was 5:13 p.m. He had slept the whole day away. Maybe Squibbs had come and gone while he was there. Maybe he had missed him entirely. He felt a crevasse of self-doubt crack open. He plunged. But then Edwin's words cut through. "Make it happen."

The Cadbury's bar had suffered from its long afternoon in the sun. The tinfoil barely held its liquid mass. It hung like a dead rabbit over the edges of Hudson's palm as he kneeled before the old man fussing on the bench.

"Hey," he said softly, tapping the man's knee with the limp bar of chocolate. "I need to find Mr. Squibbs. Do you know him? It's really, really important."

Hudson did his best to absorb his own anxiety. If the man sensed Hudson's fear he would shut down. But the man shook his head. His eyes never left the oozing candy.

Hudson sighed and stood up. "Okay. Thanks anyway, buddy. Have a good one." He put the candy bar on the seat next to the old man. As Hudson turned away, he saw the man tuck the bar into his ripped grey blazer, the layer visible now that his overcoat was spread out on the bench, a mattress.

"Saving it. Definitely not Squibbs." Hudson said.

He was walking back toward the bridge when a stone hit his back. Stung, Hudson spun. A man in rags shuffled away. Hudson scanned the ground for the rock. He wanted to throw it hard. Even at space.

The projectile lay a yard from his feet. But it was not a rock. It was flat, about the size of a deck of cards. Hudson picked it up, and gently scraped the grit that clung to the plastic, settling between the small rectangular buttons with grey and black painted letters. The setting sun was bright in his eyes. He shielded them, squinting at the man moving away down the path.

Despite its rough condition, Hudson hoped the Blackberry would work. But he did not test it. Not then. Because to turn it on would be to reappear on the grid, where enemies were still hot on the hunt for Edwin Hoff.

CHAPTER 7

The fluorescent lighting glared on the metal desk and bounced up to the faces in the small interview room. Tom Davis of the SEC watched closely behind the mirror.

"How can I help you?" Jameson Callaghan asked the police officer.

"I don't know if you can," said Marly, studying him. This Callaghan character was cool. Confident? Or careless? What was going on behind the screen? Marly would press him to see. "We're looking into the death of a young woman."

Jameson nodded sadly. "Maggie Rice was highly thought of – smart as a whip, a hard worker. Very pretty, too. We need more people like her. Not less. Definitely not less." His brown eyes filled with a film. Marly felt the emotion coming out of him but could not quite understand it. She could not read the tears. Everything was out there: was it truth or cover? He reminded her of someone, but she could not place it.

Marly pulled a picture from the manila file folder on the desk. Maggie Rice, in better days. Her hair was long, straight and dark. Her eyes were green, with light irises with an unexpectedly dark grey-green edge. The unusual color caught one's eye. She smiled openly at the camera. She wore a scooped collar that exposed her neck and the parallel bones of her clavicle. Everything about her was inviting.

271

Marly pushed the photo toward Jameson. He pulled up sharply, pain creasing his face.

"There she is," Jameson said, shaking his head. "Maggie May."

Marly prodded. She wanted to bait him, see if he bit on the easy fall guy. She would give him his out. Her guilt gauge would register how quickly he leapt for it.

"Maggie Rice. She was your assistant," she said.

"Yes," said Jameson. Marly pushed several more photographs toward him.

"You have a Maserati, right?" she said. "This your plate?"

"You already know that," he said.

"Maggie gets into your car Monday night. Then someone kills her."

Jameson said nothing. He was focused on the photographs. The views from D6.

"Were you driving your car September 10, around 6:30 p.m?" Marly asked. When Jameson did not answer, she added, "Did you know Maggie Rice was quite close with one of your employees? Very close, later that night?"

"Who?" Jameson asked.

"Hudson Davenport," Marly said.

"Hudson was with her?" Jameson made a strange face.

"Right after you. But maybe you already knew that," Marly said.

Jameson looked down at the picture for a long time. Then he bobbed his head once, sharply, a punctuation. He sat back in his chair and raised his eyes to Marly's.

"I did not know that," he said, leaning back in his chair.

"No?" said Marly. "She called Hudson later in the evening. Which makes me wonder…."

"What?"

"Why she needed to. That make you mad?"

Jameson stared at the table. His brown eyes were dry now. Focused inward.

Marly tossed a pebble. "What's Shearwater?" she said.

Jameson faced her. "Shearwater?"

"Ever heard of the Shearwater Company?" Marly saw Jameson hesitate.

"No," Jameson said. "I've never heard of the Shearwater Company. Why?"

"The SEC says the Shearwater Company has been shorting your company stock for two months now. They do very well if you miss your numbers at the end of September. Funny thing is there's no website for the Shearwater Company. Seems to be just a private operation. And we can't find a single thing that it does, other than short your stock."

Jameson's jaw rippled.

"Or," Marly said, the word rising high, before she plunged for the kill, "after you found out D6 would blow its quarter, you made Maggie Rice make an illegal trade for you from her desk right before you drove off with her. Is that why you had to kill her?"

"Okay," said Jameson. "I want my lawyer. Now." He would say no more.

"Of course," Marly said, pushing a phone toward the suspect. Her guilt meter went red.

Across the table, for Jameson, the pieces were beginning to fall into place. So now he would take control. First, he abruptly changed his demeanor. The officer would remember how he pulled up short at the mention of an illegal trade. That moment would magnetize their flecks of evidence. Which was exactly what Jameson wanted. Even though he knew what would happen next. There would be whispers. A journalist would get wind that he was a main suspect. That was worth a front page article. Which the D6 Board would not tolerate.

"The guys at old SACSEC will probably laminate it," Jameson said. His gut clenched. So it was surprising how his next thought came with such conviction that he felt almost giddy.: "Screw the damn newspapers."

As she closed the door to the interview room, Marly's phone rang.

"So we got lucky." It was Marly's San Francisco Police Department contact.

"Did we?" Marly said. "Good. I could use some luck."

"I found the gate list for August. Just talked to the stewardesses who covered the red-eye. One of them did remember a guy racing down the ramp to get on at the last minute. They couldn't ID him, but the description was young, maybe thirty, male, sweating and sprinting for the gate. And, he caught the plane," he added.

"Is there a security video?" Marly asked.

"Working on that," he said.

Whoever killed those girls would be a good runner, Marly thought. She remembered Hudson's physique. Lanky, broad shoulders, long legs. No doubt he could cover a lot of airport carpet when he needed to.

"So Walker's story checks," Marly said. "At least that part of it. But Walker didn't take the bait and throw Hudson under the bus. So why did Jameson Callaghan go quiet and lawyer up?"

Jameson Callaghan had something to hide. What it was, Marly did not know.

CHAPTER 8

STERLING
5:30 P.M., CAMBRIDGE, MA

Sterling Davenport thought it was said far too often that a picture is worth a thousand words. Far more interesting are its stories. One photograph tells so many different stories to different people looking at it. To the different people who are in it.

To anyone entering Sterling's study for the first time, the photograph looked like a memory of a favorite vacation where steady breezes filled the white sails and scattered worries. The Caribbean blues framing the three young people grinning, sunburned, through dark glasses. The boat heeled beneath them; they braced themselves on an angle. Their fourth, Jameson's girlfriend, unseen behind the camera on a good moment.

To her, the picture would no doubt remind her of deep nausea, her constant vigil along the leeward rail. She had left the boat at the next dock. Sterling, his fiancée, and their now unattached friend Jameson would continue on the trip, and for the rest of their lives, without seeing her again. Though perhaps, thought Sterling, she would remember a different source of her unbearable nausea than the sloppy waves.

To Grace, Sterling knew the photograph meant something much else. She was his fiancée then; they were finishing college and she was planning a summer wedding. This was their break from the stress; a last fling with frivolity before they finished school, her graduating in

Yale's first class with women, in 1970, him facing the call of the draft for Vietnam which thankfully never came.

Each time Grace came into his office, she would certainly see within that picture frame her husband's tattoo, indelible stains left by the sharp needles she drove there.

For Sterling it marked the beginning. A photograph snapped at just the moment when everything changed. There would be before; there would be after. Much would pivot on that moment they sat in the sun when the photograph flashed. Sterling at the helm, ironically. Jameson's girl, invisible, bravely gripping the camera between bouts of nausea. Jameson and Grace bracing on the windward bench, feet locked into the center console, four parallel legs, two thick with roping muscle, sun lightened curls of hair over bronzed skin, two fine, curved and long. Jameson's arms stretched out on either side, behind them, each hand gripping a cleat. Grace, hiding from a splash in the curve of his shoulder.

Sterling looked at the picture often. And so, decades later, when the opportunity came to find just the right person to take the helm of a shaky young start-up company where the stakes were high – a lot of investors' money had gone into it and they all wanted a return, when the market was showing signs of overheating – he knew whom to recommend. Jameson Callaghan was available and primed for risk.

He stepped right into it.

What Sterling had not counted on, though, was what Jameson did next. He recruited a flank of Harvard Business School graduates to work at D6, including Hudson Davenport. And Hudson had done well enough. There was nothing Sterling could do about it, not publicly. He proposed the board discuss anti-nepotism policy, but they just took it as his good politics, had a polite debate and rejected it. But he knew it was bad for everyone. And had not happened by accident.

This was why Sterling had had to expand his initial plan.

CHAPTER 9

HUDSON
7:55 P.M., BOSTON, MA

Hudson walked past the broad bay window of 65 Acorn. Through the small panes and mottled glass he made out blurry figures gathered around high bar tables. He pushed open the door to his familiar haunt, struck immediately by how nothing felt familiar anymore. There was no late season Sox game on the television at the end of the long oak bar. Sports venues halted games until they could secure the large crowds.

Drinks in short glasses wet napkins on tables. People were choosing hard liquor.

Hudson checked the time. It was 7:56 p.m.. Four minutes early for Marly. With Edwin's special Blackberry device now duct taped securely to his thigh beneath his loose blue jeans, Hudson was spun up with his success and ready for more. Goal one, find the Blackberry, was complete. Now he could focus on goal two – help Marly.

"Davenport!" A voice called from the bar. Hudson turned to see a member of his old tribe – the clutch of single professional men and women friends in their thirties who provided one another community. Friends would rent ski and beach houses together, sleep on floors and pile into bunk beds, cook together family style. The tribe filled all free time when they weren't working, jetting across country, or dropping off dry cleaning after brunch and a hot yoga class, so its members did not have to spend too much time alone, wondering why they had not moved on to the next stage of life. But it expelled members once they paired off for good and could no longer provide constant companionship or hope of a dating opportunity for the other members.

Hudson Davenport was a tribal stalwart. Chris Evans had been expelled years ago. "Chris! How's married life?" Hudson said, smiling.

"Great! Ella is walking now and we're expecting another in January," he said, beaming. "A boy this time. My heir. Kids are the greatest man, you should try it."

"Yeah," said Hudson. The word hung like a two day old balloon.

"It's the meaning of life," said Chris. "Kids. Not work. You're over at D6? Quite a ride. So sorry to hear about ...."

It was the first time this reference did not suck the wind out of Hudson. Because Edwin Hoff had not died on that plane. Far from it. He was still spinning him up, wherever he was. They were fighting back.

"Thanks," Hudson said. "Yeah. Such a terrible tragedy. Did you know anyone?"

Chris nodded. "Two friends from b–school. They worked at Cantor Fitzgerald."

"Above?"

"Yeah," Chris took a long sip of his scotch, spun his phone on the table. "I tried to reach them about fifty times yesterday. They weren't the type to take that crap, though. I bet that dive was the best rush of their lives." He raised his glass to the space in front of him.

"Sorry man," Hudson said.

"How's D6 taking it? I know a guy over there. Ricky MacIntyre? In sales?"

"Ricky? Oh, you mean Richard MacIntyre?" said Hudson. "Big Mac."

Chris laughed. "Big Mac. I like that. I used to work with him at XTC."

"Oh yeah," said Hudson. "Wasn't he President of the Americas or something before he was thirty? Maggie showed me his resume once. Pretty impressive for a young guy. No wonder D6 hired him for the big job."

"President of the Americas?" Chris laughed. "Ha! He was on the inside sales team, making calls at his desk. Once in a while. We played a lot of football with those little paper folded triangles."

"What?" Hudson was stunned. "He didn't run the sales force?" For months he had been waiting for Big Mac to introduce him to the top brass at XTC.

"No way," Chris laughed. "He left because he missed his numbers too often."

"Wow. Well, he's got the big job now – Global President of Sales and Service."

"Helluva jump," said Chris. "Well, however it happened, good for him. Ah man. It's good to get out of the house for a little while."

"I thought kids and family are the meaning of life?" Hudson smiled.

"They are. And it's relentless. I don't know how my wife does it all day long. You'll probably see her in here later ordering a double," Chris slipped off the bar stool. He put his hand on Hudson's shoulder. "Good to see you, Davenport. Stay safe."

Watching the windows for a head of spiky black hair, Hudson felt cold. Big Mac had falsified his resume. Big time. Beside the management committee, probably only Maggie Rice knew what was on his resume. Now she was dead.

"So you are here," said a crisp voice. Officer Marly stood across the table.

"I said I would be," Hudson said. Marly edged into a seat. "What are you drinking, Madame?" Hudson raised a finger for the bartender.

"Club soda and lime, I guess," she said. "This is all a little unorthodox."

"Deputizing a suspect, you mean?" Hudson beamed. "Where's your partner?"

"Busy," Marly said. "I'm in a tight spot. I think you might be able to help. We've learned a few things since yesterday."

"It's been quite a day," Hudson said. "Glad you made it out of there okay."

"Yeah," Marly said with a curious frown. "I took a taxi. What did you see?"

"I'm not sure, really," Hudson said.

Marly paused. She could tell he had more. In the meantime she would get what she could from him about the murder of Maggie

Rice. She studied Hudson. Tall, broad shouldered, long legs. Very appealing with his wavy chocolate hair, deep brown eyes. Always ready to share the sugar, making everyone feel happy and relaxed.

"Delicious," she thought. "Like a chocolate rabbit. You want to nibble on him." But her thoughts sobered. "He's athletic. A guy who could sprint through an airport to catch his plane."

Aloud Marly said, "There's been some strange activity with your company. There's an entity called the Shearwater Company. All it does is short D6 stock. Ever hear of it?"

"Shearwater?" said Hudson. "No."

"You guys about to miss your quarter?" Marly said.

Hudson thought of XTC. The deal that Edwin said would save D6. The deal that he had not even secured a phone call commitment for a meeting with a decision maker.

"Don't know," he said, sipping from his bottle. "That's above my pay grade."

"Well, it looks like the rats are leaving the ship all over the place. Jameson Callaghan sold a large amount of stock on the tenth, through an order traced from his assistant's phone. Maggie's phone. Or maybe she placed it."

"Doesn't he sell on a planned schedule?" Hudson said. Most key management people traded shares of D6 on disclosed schedules so they avoided the appearance or effect of trading on information not available to the public.

"This one wasn't. And it was 100,000 shares."

"That's a chunk of change," said Hudson.

"At $15 per share, it certainly is," she said. "But if you miss your numbers this quarter, plus the uh…loss of key personnel…."

"It'll be over," said Hudson. "Could go to zero. It's…already fallen like a rock."

"That's the Shearwater effect. Someone's shorting and pushing down the price," Marly said. "And, the SEC also just picked up another big sale from last week. A guy named Richard MacIntyre sold his entire holdings."

Hudson whistled. "That's weird." Then Hudson told Marly the rumor about Big Mac falsifying his resume.

"And only Maggie knew? And you?" Marly said. This was interesting.

Hudson shrugged. "I just heard about it a few minutes ago. I don't know if Maggie knew it was false. She just saw what he wrote on it. But sure, Mac would have known she saw it because he would have sent it to her to get it to Jameson. Maybe she found out like I did and asked him about it. Wow. Miss a quarter, never work again because he made up his resumé – that's a bad month for squirrel just trying to get a nut."

Marly frowned. "So MacIntyre has motive. And a couple of big problems."

"Why are you looking at Jameson?" Hudson asked. "He's a great guy. Lonely since his wife died but he's as solid as they come. Loves D6. Lives and breathes for it."

Marly pushed a manila folder toward Hudson. "Or he wants it to look that way. Someone sent these to my office. They were taken Monday night."

Hudson looked at the photographs. "That's Jameson's car. That's Maggie getting in it. Whoa. Weird. She was with him and then called me?"

"Jameson had motive. If Maggie isn't around, she can't testify that he told her to issue the sale order." Marly said. She let the information sit, watching Hudson closely.

"Who's taking these pictures?" Hudson picked up a photo. "Looks like the view from the window near my cube."

"Another mystery," said Marly. "I don't know what end is up. We have at least two solid suspects. MacIntyre with motive that she was going to blow the whistle on his trumped up cv, and Jameson with motive that she knew he was trading illegally in the stock."

And, she thought, one athletic suspect with opportunity for bicoastal violence? A love interest gone wrong? Jealousy? It did not feel right. Hudson just did not arouse her suspicions. Quite the opposite. He put her immediately at ease. He was warm and funny. With him, she felt a current of happiness. Marly thought how psychopaths mimic highly social behavior, then sate their furies.

"What do you need from me?" Hudson asked.

Marly studied the warm eyes looking at her from under his tangled hair. She risked it. "I think this killer is going to strike again. Soon. I need access to the suspects' emails. I can subpoena them, and will, but time is of the essence here and I want to see if there's anything there between Maggie Rice and either Jameson or MacIntyre."

Hudson frowned. "I'm no hacker. And I'm not supposed to be in the office. I'm on temporary leave pending this case." He thought for a moment. "But, I do know someone who has access to all the management communications. I might be able to follow some email trains there. Plus, I know his password."

Officer Marly dialed a number on her cell phone. The one on Hudson's belt rang.

"Now you have my number. Call if you find anything. Any time," she said.

It was a few minutes before 9:30 p.m. when Grace Davenport answered the deep chime reaching back through the large rooms of her elegant Cambridge home. Her sweep of graying hair was short and parted on the side. She viewed each strand as proof of the weave of life's complexities. Her light blue cashmere sweater set off the color of her eyes. She wore grey tailored trousers with expensive soft leather loafers that had little rubber grips on the sole. Her earrings were sapphire drops in a diamond setting, with a matching necklace. On her fingers she wore several rings, one with a large emerald next to a simple gold band. She wore several more bands studded in diamonds.

"Hudson!" she said. "Dad said you might come by. How are you? Hungry?"

"Hello Mum," Hudson said. He folded his arms around his mother. Even though he was now much bigger than she, he hung on her like a small boy.

"I'm so terribly sorry about Edwin," Grace said. "Come in. I'll get Dad." Hudson's arm dropped last. As Grace turned into the house, Hudson followed her as if a vacuum sucked out all other matter and fused him to her. He felt the familiar pang, and he looked at his phone. Marly's number was there. He smiled. She was coming toward him. And he liked that.

Grace Davenport had graduated from Yale College in its first class of women. Then she celebrated the women's movement by getting pregnant, married and never entering the official workforce. So she compensated by applying her significant intellect to building the Davenport's now well respected collection of art, arranging brief tours of particular pieces through various museums, and managing the design, construction or remodeling of their homes. Of all the rooms in their three homes, in Boston, North East Harbor, and St. John, the Red Room was her favorite. It was a long rectangular room with a relatively low ceiling that opened off the foyer. There were two windows with cushioned seats on the far end; three on the long end. The interior wall held one of the home's four fireplaces as a focal point. Bookcases, full of hard covers that had been read at least once, covered the walls. But rather than a cozy couch and wing chairs, Grace had designed the room with four pairs of upright wooden armchairs covered with thick cushions, each pair surrounding a table with a light. Hudson loved this room.

"Hey, there you are," Sterling strode through the door, embracing his boy in a bear hug until Hudson laughed and shrugged himself free. "Staying out of trouble?"

"So far, so good," Hudson said. "Did you tell….?"

"Mom? No. No need yet," Sterling said. "I'll join you for a drink. Scotch?"

"Just a Coke, if you have it," Hudson said.

"A Coke? I don't think you've asked me for a Coke for twenty years!" Sterling laughed.

As soon as he was gone, Hudson slipped out of the Red Room. He crossed the foyer and ran through the large living room without noticing the Chagall, Miró and Picassos that were the common trappings of his childhood. Sterling's office was tucked in the back wing, behind the formal living room. It caught the eastern sun and had a full view of the limestone swimming pool through the large glass paned bay window.

The computer was still on. Hudson clicked the mail icon and typed the password.

M-y b-o-y

Sterling's email opened. Hudson sat down and flicked through the inbox looking for anything that related Maggie Rice and Jameson Callaghan or Richard MacIntyre. Nothing stood out. Just hundreds of condolences coming in. Frustrated, he spun the chair.

That was when he saw the photograph.

"Easier days," Hudson muttered, looking at the young faces of Jameson, Sterling and Grace splashing over the waves, his father at the helm.

But then something caught his eye. He looked closer. The camera picked up his father at the wheel, and just behind him, part of the boat's white life ring. Hudson had seen this picture a thousand times but he had never noticed the letters printed on the life ring. The name of the boat. Sterling's body blocked three letters.

"S—RWATER," it read.

"Hudson?" Sterling called from the other side of the house. "Where'd you go?"

Hudson leapt up. Clicked off the email. Straightened the desk chair.

A file caught his eye. It was just under the keyboard drawer. He did not want to look. This was not what he had come to find. He put his fingers on it.

A label across the edge read "The Shearwater Company." Hudson opened it. A moment later Sterling stood at the door.

"Hudson? What are you doing?"

"Just looking at pictures," Hudson said, now standing near the bookshelf.

"Come on. Let's go sit by the pool and have a drink."

Hudson pushed past his father. "I have to go. Sorry Dad."

Condensation made the cold coke bottle slip in his grip as Sterling watched Hudson leave. Then he walked around to his desk. Everything looked how he had left it. The manila file was still under the keyboard. So he shut off the lights and walked out.

Sterling had not noticed the way Hudson pressed his left arm to his side as he squeezed through the door. Or that the manila folder, though in place, was now empty.

It was nearly 10:00 p.m. when Hudson waited in the darkness behind one of the brick pillars near the back entrance to D6's building. Prime time for the engineers' lunch break.

Soon the door pushed open and two men in t-shirts, shorts and Birkenstock sandals walked through. They were debating something intensely. Neither noticed Hudson slip into the wake of their footsteps and through the door before it swung shut.

In the foyer, Hudson grabbed a glossy brochure. Then he slipped up the staircase to his old floor. The fire entrance would open directly onto the floor. But it was locked from the stairwell. Which was why he had the brochure. Hudson pulled the heavy staple off the binding of the shiny paper. Flattened one end with his teeth. He wedged it into the lock. Nudged it under the lever. The lock clicked. Hudson was on his floor. He ran to the window near his cube. Looking down to the street, he could tell this was the exact angle from which Marly's photographer had taken his shots. So who had ready access to this spot? There was his desk and Walker's. Big Mac's corner office.

"So, any of the sales guys could have taken this shot. Even Big Mac." Hudson concluded. Then he looked at Walker's desk. The space was clean and orderly, as usual. The janitor had not come yet that night. Hudson peered into the trash can tucked deep under Walker's desk. Paper cups, weakened by stale water and coffee, melted their remnants over the papers and an empty white envelope.

Something about that envelope caught his eye. Small green print in the corner. Hudson plucked the envelope out with his fingers. It was misshapen, as if it had held something the shape of a thin brick. It bore the words: "The Shearwater Company." Hudson pressed the last incoming number on his phone.

"Marly, it's Hudson. I've found something. But I'm not exactly sure what."

CHAPTER 10

MARLY
9:45 P.M., BOSTON, MA

Richard MacIntyre could not stop bobbing his knee under the table. He leaned backward, forward, raked his long fingers through his thinning blond hair. Tried to look calm and serious. The officer had spiky black hair. She had green bullets for eyes.

"How can I help?" MacIntyre said with a weak smile.

Marly let the silence suck at his nerves. "What do you drive?"

"Hummer," he said.

"Ooh. Pricey," she said. "How much?"

"Mine was close to seventy grand, all in," he said.

"Hmm," she said. "How much does seventy thousand dollars weigh, do you think? Like, a book?"

"More than you think," he laughed. "Like an encyclopedia."

"I thought you'd know, considering you just dropped that much cash at the dealer the other day. You must know a very generous ATM. Mine cuts me off at $300," said Marly. Big Mac's fingertips slid across his temple. He said nothing.

"I hear you once worked at XTC?" Marly said.

"Yes," he said. "It was my b-big break. Just before I went to business school."

"You were President of the Americas?" Marly led. MacIntyre nodded, a half dip. "Really? I heard your only big break there was for cigarettes. That you just made telephone sales calls there. Someone find out about that? Someone like Maggie Rice?"

Marly saw Mac was suddenly pale. He said, "Hey. I didn't have anything to do with Maggie."

"No?" said Marly.

"No," Mac said. Then he let out a long breath. "But maybe I know something else."

CHAPTER 11

MARLY
11:00 P.M., BOSTON, MA

"You look like the bad guys have the better of you, Officer," said the woman in slim grey trousers and dark blue turtleneck. She had left the white lab coat and stethoscope in her locker at the hospital.

"And what does the neurologist prescribe?" Marly asked her former roommate.

"Take orally one glass of Chardonnay, possibly two," said Vanessa Bennet.

After college, their careers had branched. Vanessa had pursued medical school, specializing in neurology. After law school, Marly worked briefly at a firm, then hopped to law enforcement. But when they met the women were eighteen years old again, giggling, goading and telling tales about boys. These had a new twist now that Vanessa could provide details about the growths, rashes, and grotesque swellings of anonymous patients.

Marly held the table while Vanessa attracted attention at the bar, returning with two round-stemmed glasses.

"Wow," said a man's voice. "Boston is a small town." Marly turned to see Walker Green leaning on his cane, grinning at both women.

"Hello," said Vanessa warmly. Marly noticed she did not say Walker's name, though her eyes and voice indicated she knew him.

"Hi Walker," said Marly. "How are you?"

"Can't complain. Doesn't help anyway," he lifted the cane briefly. "I better go find my friends. They're here somewhere. See you next week, Doc," he said to Vanessa.

Marly turned to Vanessa. "He's one of yours?"

Vanessa smiled and shrugged. Marly continued her side of the conversation to let her friend chime in without compromising her obligation to protect patient confidentiality.

"Blind date?" Marly asked. Vanessa giggled and shook her head. So Marly continued, "He works with a guy who is involved in one of my cases. Walker seems like a great guy. Such a shame…he has MS or something like that. Can't even be thirty yet, and he has to walk with a cane and put up with all that guy bullshit. Though he seems to handle that pretty well."

"Does he?" said Vanessa. "I'm not surprised. Maybe he'll be lucky."

"Lucky? Isn't MS like a death sentence?" Marly was surprised.

Vanessa shook her head. "It really varies. Even within one person, its effects come and go. So the lucky ones don't have it as bad, as soon, or as often."

"He can barely walk," said Marly. "I hate to see where he'll be in five years."

Right then Marly's phone rang. She answered crisply. A woman responded.

"This is Grace Davenport. I think you are the person with whom I should speak."

CHAPTER 1

EDWIN AND CAMILLE
6:00 A.M, BOSTON HARBOR, MA

The sun broke the eastern sky of Boston Harbor as Edwin held the wheel.

"What else can you tell me about the leak?" he said. Camille sat comfortably now, her body finding balance in synch with the constant movement of the boat on the water. She looked at the skyline.

"He saved my life," she eventually said.

"Your leak is a killer. He is a mass murderer responsible for three thousand deaths," said Edwin. He never smoothed pointed words. Bare facts were sharp. Sharp sticks made people move. It was precisely the lack of pretense, the lack of politesse, which worked. Discomfort brought out problems. Aired, they could be solved.

"No," said Camille. "He tried to help. He heard something, that's all. And he tried to help by telling me. He got me out of the Towers. He did help."

"So he had a pang – maybe. But if he knew anything at all, he is in up to his eyeballs," Edwin said. "He must be eliminated like all of these killers. They are plague-ridden vermin who will kill any American they can. They do not change."

"No," said Camille. "You've got this wrong. He told me months before it happened. We screwed it up. No one listened to me. I-I – didn't make them ."

This was not a debate. "He knew," Edwin said. "He did not stop it. Three thousand people died. He put those people to death."

Camille felt tears push over her eyes. Stifled sobs overrode her normal breathing, jerking in and heaving out. "I just don't understand. That's not the man I knew. In college he was my best friend."

"Ever meet his parents?"

"They're dead."

"Ever go to his home?"

"Saudi Arabia isn't usually in the undergrad's travel budget," she said.

"Saudi orphan goes to elite American university after a stop off at an English boarding school?" summarized Edwin. He spun the wheel as they rounded the inner harbor making their way to the locks by the Museum of Science that provided entry to the Charles River. A picture was forming for him. "Who paid?"

"His uncle," sighed Camille. "He believed in education. When his parents died, his uncle took him in to the church school he started, then sent him to England to one of the top boarding schools. From there he went to Yale. He could have gone to Cambridge or Oxford but wanted to come to America."

"His uncle is a religious man?" Edwin asked.

"Yes. An imam. And a doctor."

"Bet he didn't go for the Camille story," said Edwin. To this she said nothing. The memories of Yassir's uncle's bias against her still stung. He had interfered and forced on her a life she did not expect. Did not want.

"He just had so much influence over Yassir," she said finally. "I was an intruder in their world. An American. But Yassir wasn't like that. He was a devout Muslim, expected women to be as smart as he was. He didn't believe –"

"He left you," Edwin said.

"Yes," Camille admitted. She began to recite the same worn explanation, wondering if it persuaded either of them. "He owed his uncle everything. He picked him up off the streets, gave him an education."

Edwin paused. "You weren't intruding. You were risking Uncle's long term plan."

Camille felt cold. She saw one image. Then, without adding any new elements or taking any away, her perception simply shifted and put the same elements together to produce a very different picture.

"They plan for decades," Edwin said. "Saved orphans are angry at their loss and fiercely loyal to their saviors. Easy to mold because they have no alternative. They can be made into chameleons, to live like us and look like us. And because they are human, they have weaknesses. They're men – they can't resist what is deeply deprived to them in the Middle East – they can't hold back from what is on offer in America. Exposed elbows are more than some of them ever see. Freedom. A smart one gets to go to college. Screws a pretty girl. Who knows? Maybe even falls in love. So the managers have to watch their charges closely. Particularly once they are deployed to America. Like this Yassir and you. So you had to be eliminated. You are actually very lucky."

"Lucky?" Camille thought. "Why?"

"He's saved your life more than once," Edwin said. "He must have been able to convince them he broke contact with you. Maybe he did love you, after all."

"But he says he's an art expert now," Camille protested. "He works with all sorts of wealthy people, helping them buy for their collections."

"So he's in finance," said Edwin.

"No, art," Camille said.

"Finance," Edwin insisted. "How would you raise the tens of millions necessary to fund this type of project? Say this one, where the cost of buying breached information is in the hundreds of thousands? And the vial itself? Tens of millions. You think they raise it with straight donations from the oil kings? That would be tracked, too obvious. This amount of cash has to come out of nowhere so it won't be missed."

"I don't know what they do. But I can't imagine how an expert in pre-Columbian painting, sculpture and artifacts could be at all useful."

"No? Even if he knew exactly the value of priceless pieces of art, the locations, who bought them, where they would be in transit, and where they would be installed in an unsuspecting buyer's estate? Close enough to the owners to know on occasion when they might be out of town?"

Camille was dumbfounded. She had read news stories of art disappearing but it felt more like a heist movie, going to some unprincipled collector with an overactive need to keep works to himself that should rightly be circulated and enjoyed by the public. She had never considered that a black market in art could provide rich inflows of cash to terrorist organizations with good information and skilled thieves.

But as they entered the lock, and the water rose to float them up to the level of the river, Camille had to admit what Edwin said made sense. She remembered Yassir's words as she rode the elevator up the North Tower , "Get out now!" How had he known?

Edwin knew he was making Camille think. So he eased back, enabling her to make conclusions on her own. Even if what he said next was a bluff. That is what a habit of true candor bought him – the occasional fib swallowed whole. Which was sometimes necessary to get the right result.

"Your contact is not my main concern," said Edwin. "What I want, what I need, is what he knows. Where did the vial come from? Who sold it? Most importantly, when is the next transaction? My mission is to put them out of business. The others are irrelevant. You can't crush every cockroach. Why start trying?"

"You want to talk to him," said Camille. "I don't exactly have his number."

"Don't worry about that," said Edwin. "I know where to find him."

"You do?"

"We're on our way right now," Edwin said.

"How?" Camille said, as they passed underneath the salt and pepper bridge that linked MIT's neighborhood to downtown Boston.

"I scanned your photograph into the algorithm."

"Scanned it? With what?" Camille asked. Edwin smiled at her and blinked twice. The yellow irises of his lenses expanded.

"Let's just say the facial proportions have been registered and scanned through INS databases, international phone call patterns, passport records, drivers' licenses, tax forms. Security feeds from ATMs. And the other details you provided about his intelligence, art interest, music – this data has all been included in the algorithm."

"But you don't know any of the exact inputs," she said.

"No," he said. "But the program I wrote makes assumptions of what is more than likely, or very likely, or nearly sure, about each of them. Then it crunches the statistical likelihood of the whole and produces a refined result that, if not exact, is within an insignificant delta. That's the beauty of it."

"So what does it tell us?" Camille asked.

"A lot of things that are associated with his attributes. This produces a geo-location of his residence that is nearly exact. Within twenty feet," Edwin grinned.

"Wow," she said. "How did you do that?"

"Rocket science," he said. "And some very cool toys." They drove slowly up the river, passing the boathouses where early risers were stepping gingerly into their sculls.

"He needs to *want* to talk to us, Camille," Edwin continued. "He's not the front man on this stuff. That's your job – you need to make him want to. What can you say that will make him want to talk to you? It's important, Camille. We stop them from getting the second vial, then they're out of cash and a source and we buy more time to take down their whole organization. We miss it? Then pneumonic plague gets loose in a big American city. Boston first. They'll do it fast so they don't screw it up again. Someone has a lot of ego and pride invested here, possibly more."

"More? Like what?" said Camille.

"The future. The past. Legacy. Succession," said Edwin.

Camille thought for a long moment. Something unusual was taking hold of her. The plain facts, stated plainly, blew the fog of Yassir away. She never wanted to admit it, but she always had known this: Yassir had done what he wanted to do. He left. He had free will, and used it to leave her. No matter what he said his uncle wanted.

Camille always believed that Yassir had left because she did not matter enough. That pain was so blinding she could not see any other reason. No matter how many different ways she reviewed how she had acted, she could not unearth that mysterious thing that she should have done to make him want to stay. Why his debt to his Uncle mattered so much more. A debt called in on three thousand innocent people.

All of this flowed like sand down curved glass. When the last grains piled on top, Camille was ready. She was an analyst. The facts compelled this conclusion at least: in July, Yassir had known more than he admitted. Maybe he knew enough to help again.

Suddenly, Camille did not feel anxious, not bound by those old belts of regret, sorrow, and hurt that usually wrapped around her. Instead she was angry. Fueled.

"Okay," she said as adrenaline shot to the ends of her nerves. "Let's do it."

"Good," Edwin said. The word popped like a starting gun. "We need to know two things. One, when and where will the buy of the second vial go down. Two, who will be named as the successor to the Leader. You find out those things, you will be a true hero. And one hell of an intelligence officer."

"I'm an analyst," Camille said.

"Not anymore," Edwin said, pulling the boat beside an unused dock on the Cambridge side of the river.

Ten minutes earlier, on the other side of the river, FBI dispatch picked up a ship-to-shore transmission. It was the Coast Guard.

"Suspect just entered the Charles River by the Museum of Science in a Hinckley Picnic Boat. She is wearing a blue windbreaker. So is her accomplice."

"Get a tail on her now!" barked the FBI. "Assume she is armed and dangerous. This one slipped the CIA during an interrogation. We are dealing with a whole new breed. Be careful but get her. Now!"

By 8:00 a.m. Edwin had tied off the boat to a dock in Cambridge up the river from MIT.

"You look good dark," Edwin said, sipping coffee on the deck. "Ugh. Instant."

Camille was peering at herself in the small mirror over the boat's tiny sink. It was not a bad dye job. Her raven hair contrasted with her pale cream skin and blue eyes. She no longer looked like the native offering directions to tourists in Amsterdam.

"Now I'm an international woman of mystery," Camille mused. "A khaki-wearing, boat-driving action figure." She struck a pose before the mirror as if rolling cameras caught her mid leap, in hot pursuit, mouth agape. "Sha-zaa!" she giggled, taking a last look at the mirror. There was a bright blush on her cheeks.

It was nearly 8:00 a.m. The roads buzzed, though the skies were still silent.

"Stay on my six," Edwin said. "Directly behind me. Four paces. Keep up."

They left the boat at the small marina and walked up to the busy crush of traffic on Memorial Drive. They crossed at the light, passing a dingy pizza and beer parlor, nail salons, liquor store and grocery nooks. Edwin turned sharply on a residential side street.

"Now come up here with me," he said to her once they were moving down the sidewalk of modest wood framed row houses to the next corner. She walked beside Edwin when he abruptly turned again.

"Where are we going?" Camille said.

"First, to the address the program spit out," Edwin said. "But we need to run an SDR – Surveillance Detection Route – see if anyone is following us. We follow a path; find a place to duck and cover, burn anyone on our six – tailing us."

"Burn?"

"Identify," Edwin said. "We burn the person they send to follow us under cover, then they have to send another we don't recognize. Delay for them while we go on." They walked on at a pace that was much more relaxed than Camille felt.

"There must be a bug in the program," Edwin said. "I don't get how your guy is a big money art dealer living in East Cambridge. He should be on the other side of the river, Back Bay, or Beacon Hill, near the estates, or in a South End loft. I reran it three times – still gives me this address in East Cambridge with only .005% margin of error."

"Maybe all of his cash is going to the buy," Camille said.

"Mmm. Good thought. You have good instincts." Edwin sensed Camille begin to gain confidence and momentum. Just the time to shovel on the coal. Fire her up. "And you're a solid skipper. You did great back there by the way."

Camille smiled so happily it tickled .

"So he's putting all his hard-earned art dealer entrepreneurial cash into the mission, you think," Edwin said. "That could explain it. Then he's in deeper than you thought. He's using his own cash to fund the purchase – that makes him a mission leader, not just a loyal doobie overhearing plans with one eye closed."

"I don't know," said Camille.

"See facts as they are," Edwin said. "Not as you wish they were. Cut in here!" He pulled Camille into a driveway, behind a tall hedge. They waited thirty seconds. No one walked by. A minute. Two more.

"Clear," he said. Then his fingertips gripped her elbow. "Back!" he hissed.

A dark Lincoln Town Car rolled slowly down the street.

"Feds," Edwin said. "Must have grabbed your face off a security camera. Stay low. It's not just the Feds we have to avoid." They were within a mile of D6. Smack between Harvard, MIT and the start-up corridor, East Cambridge was a popular neighborhood for students and recent graduates. Some of whom would recognize Edwin. Because they worked for him.

"86 Hay Street." Edwin whispered. "There it is." He pointed out a yellow house across the street. Tall trees grew over to the peaked two-story roof. Rickety wooden steps led to the front door. The house next door had no roof; its walls were charred.

"Now what do we do?" Camille said.

"We meet the neighbors," Edwin said. He motioned for Camille to follow. They crept to the back door of the burned house. "Give me your hand. Bite your nails much?" Edwin held a ball point pen in his right hand and gripped hers with his left.

"Okay, yes, but I've been doing better lately," Camille said. "With my left hand." She spread her palm and waggled her fingers. The nails were carefully curved, nurtured like garden seedlings peeking over the fleshy fingertips. The pinky one was the longest.

"This might work," he said. With a flick, he drew a line with the pen across the top of her nail. The crescent fell into his palm.

"Hey! That one was really working!" Camille said.

"It has a new job," Edwin said. "Grow another." The screen door squeaked. Edwin held the edge of the clipped nail to the door frame, near the lock, and slipped it through the crack. He maneuvered it slightly. When he twisted the knob, it opened. They stepped into the condemned building.

"Stay back from the windows. No one's expecting to see anything move in here. Don't give them reason to take a second look." From inside the hallway, they could peer through what was once a dining room, into the kitchen of the neighboring house. At 8:10 a.m. Thursday morning, across the garbage cans, at 86 Hay Street, a kettle screamed in the kitchen. Edwin squinted. His special lenses focused an image of infrared clouds on Edwin's cornea where the heat from the kettle steam billowed. An outline of a human being, about six feet tall, moved from room to room upstairs.

"He's upstairs," Edwin said. "In the bathroom. Getting ready for work."

"How can you tell that?" Camille said. She saw sunlight glare on white curtains.

"Watch the window. Tell me if it's your guy." Edwin whispered. The heat shape descended in steps to the first floor. "Stay here."

Edwin crept down the charred hall. He needed to get a look inside the house at the things this person kept with him. More inputs would help with the program. More specific personal detail would confirm the result, or amend it, explaining why it thought a highbrow art dealer was slumming it in East Cambridge. They could not risk a mistake.

Edwin looked hard at problems. Like the chance his sleeper cell algorithm fingered the wrong person. He needed proof that it had, and why. So he could fix it.

He went up the rickety stairs, looking through the window to the target's bedroom, which also was a study. This man lived alone. There was a computer on the desk. The bookshelf was lined with books that looked familiar to Edwin. They were thick books with words on the spines. "JAVA Programming," "C++", "PERL."

Something was wrong with Edwin's program. This was not the home of an art dealer. An innocent MIT student was about to get mixed up in a nasty problem.

"Dammit," he said, heading down stairs. "On!" His lenses produced the screen, hovering in the air at a comfortable distance. He must find the bug in the code and fix it.

"Here he comes," Edwin said, appearing behind Camille.

She leapt and patted her chest frantically. "I do not know how you do that."

"Watch the window. He's going to get close to it when he pours the tea."

"Tea?" Camille peered through the drapes. For just a moment, a man's face filled the crack between them. His head tipped down, spilling thick, glossy black hair. Like Yassir's. But the man turned away before she could see his face.

"I can't tell. I can't get a good enough look. I think it...could be."

"There's nothing art related in this guy's house," Edwin said. "Just computer books. We've got the wrong house, wrong guy."

"What do we do now?" Camille asked. Edwin sat on the floor, his back against the wall. What had he missed? The result from the debugged program appeared in view.

Residence: *86 Hay Street, Cambridge, MA.*
Margin of error: *+/- .0001 percent.*

"CrossPathz says this is the place," Edwin said. "Effectively no question. But there's no art here. Just computers. He's got all the same books my programmers have."

If this was the leak, he was a student, probably at MIT. Or graduated and now probably working at a local dot com. Possibly even D6.

"Maybe Yassir's not involved in the money part," Camille said. "Maybe he's just trying to help us, like I said in the beginning."

"Maybe," Edwin said. He put his hands on her shoulders. "Okay. Now. You must remember absolutely everything I have told you. You're going in. I'll be out of your sight but you won't be out of mine."

A few minutes later, Camille walked up the stairs to 86 Hay Street, carrying a newspaper still wrapped in its blue plastic. She was muttering under her breath the words she would try to make believable to the resident who would find a strange woman on their doorstep bearing an unfortunate likeness to the picture of a fugitive on TV.

"Hi, I hope I'm not bothering you," Camille rehearsed. "I just moved in here. Do you know how I get to the nearest T station? I think they delivered your paper to me, and I just thought I'd introduce myself." She knocked on the door. No one answered. Behind the house, a large crow flew from one perch to another.

The door creaked open.

"Hi, I hope I'm not – " she began.

But Camille never saw the person's face. She just saw the hand reach around the door, grip her forearm and pull her off balance into the house. The door slammed shut.

CHAPTER 2

CAMILLE
8:22 A.M., CAMBRIDGE, MA

Camille tripped over her feet when one caught on the carpet. A man held her up.

"Come with me," he said. "Quickly." The voice was unmistakable.

"Yassir!" whispered Camille. He hustled her up the stairs into a small study with a window. Camille could see a rickety fire escape, rusted by harsh winters.

"How did you find me?" Yassir said.

"It's a long story," Camille said. "You helped, and you need to help us again."

"Us? You haven't told anyone about me. Camille. You haven't have you?"

"I don't understand," Camille cried. "How are you involved with this terrible thing? How did you know about the Towers? Ahead of time?!"

Yassir was pacing around the room, raking his fingers through his hair. "This is not good, Camille. This is very bad. For me. And for you."

"Have you watched the news, Yassir? See anyone you recognize in it? I've been labeled an enemy combatant or aider and abettor to terrorism or something. I've been polygraphed, fired I'm sure – and they're after me right now. Can you imagine that? Me, the subject of hot pursuit?" Camille laughed wryly. "Because they think I'm in cahoots with you. And you are somehow responsible for all of this. Or know who is."

Yassir's eyes were cold. "It is not imaginable. You could not evade a bike cop."

Camille smiled reflexively, expecting to meet his where they always did – a joke about her clumsiness, her blundering, the senseless obstacles she put in her own way that would trip up her considerable talents. Instead she saw him seethe. He gripped her arm.

"Ow – that hurts!" she squealed.

"Who did you tell about me? What did you tell them?" Yassir raged.

"I told them the truth," Camille spat. "You ever been strapped to a lie detector for forty-eight hours with a meathead bully who tells you you'll never work again or get a mortgage and are too fat to do anything but die an old spinster in a rental unit?"

"Breathe, Milly," Yassir said.

"I told them someone who used to be very important to me, but who I hadn't seen in a decade because he up and left a month before graduation without so much as a word, barges into my life and drops in my lap that the United States is about to be attacked with its own planes, and, oh yes, they'll also be sprinkling a little pneumonic plague to go with it. Who happens to find my phone number for the first time in ten years ten minutes before I get blown to bits with everyone else in the Twin Towers? And guess what? They are very, very interested in what I know, who I know. They want to know who the hell you are. And so the hell do I." Camille sat on the bed, her chest heaving.

Yassir shook his head. "When?"

"When what?"

"When did you first tell anyone about what I said?"

"When? When you told me to," said Camille. "Earlier this summer."

"So they did stop it," Yassir said. "I made a huge mistake. Why are you here?"

"Because," Camille said. "They think there's another vial of the plague stuff somewhere. They think you know when and where the sale is going to happen. They think you can be a hero again."

"Some hero," Yassir scoffed. Now he was sitting on the bed next to Camille. He held her hand. Kissed the back of it. "I'm so sorry I got you into this."

The gesture swamped Camille. Tears came. She blinked them rapidly away. The last twenty four hours overwhelmed her. But what she found unbearable was sitting on a bed hearing Yassir disconnect words from their meaning.

"Stop. Don't jerk me around," she whispered, drawing her windbreaker across her eyes. She cleared her throat. "So how's the art business?"

Yassir huffed a short laugh. "Slow."

"That was cover," Camille said.

"Well, it's not my day job, really," he trailed off. "I don't know how you got here but you must go. Don't come back, Milly. It's not safe. Say you didn't find me."

Camille bit her lip as she stood, moved to the door. Holding the brass knob, she would not cry again. She would not slink out, accept whatever line he drew, erased, redrew. Perhaps what she did next came from the memory of ten years earlier. Or perhaps it was something that had taken root more recently.

She turned. "Tell me when the next buy will be, and I'll go. Happily."

"Go now," Yassir said.

"No." Their eyes met coldly. "How did you know about the vial?" she pressed.

"I knew because of people near me," said Yassir. "Very near me."

"Your uncle," said Camille. Yassir did not contradict her. "So it's true then. You are part of this. You always have been." Yassir shook his head, slowly, then insistently.

"No!" Yassir yelled. "I am not part of this. It is…around me. I take my faith seriously. Killing is not part of it. I don't believe in what they do. But sometimes I understand, part of it anyway. America puts its soldiers down like the whole world is their game board. How else are they supposed to fight back? They don't have the shiny toys. They have to use brains. They've been at war for a long time – America only just heard. I tried to help. I tried. Telling you was such a betrayal. You can't imagine."

"Nearly three thousand people died!" she said.

"It would have been so many more," he whispered.

"But you could have stopped it all," Camille said. She put it to him, and to herself, in words for the first time. "You chose not to."

Yassir shook his head again. "No, I couldn't. It was unstoppable. It *is* unstoppable, what is around us. You think that was the last of it? The American blood they want to pour? That was a pinprick."

"I need to know more about the vial," Camille said. "Who sold it? Where?"

"Why?" said Yassir.

"Because there is more than one of them." Camille said. "Which you also know. And you are going to stop it this time. For good."

Yassir was quiet for a long time. Camille felt a flick of fear. And fury. Was he always a stranger? Or had he just become one?

Outside, near the roof, there was a small perch between the eaves and the fire escape. Edwin thought about the algorithm again. It really should not have taken him this long at all. There was only one way a computer science student in this neighborhood got his hands on obscene amounts of money – the same way Edwin had. The leak – Yassir – must work at a tech company. One that had been successful. Very successful. Such that even engineers made millions off the small amounts of stock they were issued.

There was only one company like that nearby. Edwin leapt to his feet.

From the doorway, Camille noticed a shadow cloud the window. Yassir glared at Camille with his back to the window. He did not see it. Shattering glass made him spin. But the fight was brief. Edwin shoved Yassir to the ground face first and held his wrists together behind him. He ripped a piece of duct tape with his teeth and bound him.

"Tell us the source," Edwin said. "Or your life will end here, with a lot of pain."

Yassir said nothing.

Edwin pounded his kidneys. "Speak!"

Then Yassir cried out, "Edwin stop, please!"

Edwin kept his hands on the man on the ground in a tight grip. The voice made him recoil. He knew it well. It carried brilliant opinions, but more often than not, disagreeable ones. Edwin flipped the man over.

"Ali," Edwin said. His disgust was plain.

"Ali? This is Yassir," said Camille.

303

"Maybe. Now he calls himself Ali. He is an engineer at my company," Edwin said. "Was. You're fired."

Ali – Yassir – the man with his hands bound – glared at Edwin. "I tried to help."

"You failed. Three thousand people are dead because of you," Edwin snarled.

"Not you, though," Ali/Yassir spat. "Smartest one in the room again, Edwin?"

Camille watched the energy between the two men. They had a history. It was not good. What was unfolding here would not improve it. Edwin opened his palm and smacked Ali/Yassir's jaw with the thick padded muscle at the base of his open hand. Ali/Yassir shook his stinging head.

"So you're the leak. Tell us when and how the second vial is going down or you are dead. I won't have to kill you. If they know you are the leak, and believe me they will if you don't get useful real quick, they'll do it for me."

There was silence.

"It comes from a lab," Yassir finally said.

"Where?"

"Here, in Cambridge. At Blagler Labs. I don't know the seller," coughed Yassir.

"When is the transaction? Where?"

"It's this afternoon. Four. At the Cambridge Coffee House."

Then the obvious struck Camille. "You...are you the one making the trade? You have that kind of cash?" Just like Edwin knew. Yassir – Ali – was in finance. Whatever his mixed feelings may be, if any were even genuine, Camille saw that Yassir was in up to his eyeballs. He was making it up to his uncle for blowing the first deal.

"Stupid use of a windfall," Edwin shook Yassir. "How will you know the seller?"

"Blue shoes," he said finally. "The seller will be wearing blue shoes."

"How will they know you?"

"My order. A skinny quad cappuccino. Not much risk of multiple orders of four shots of espresso with skim milk at exactly 4:00 p.m. When they hear it called, they are to follow me to my table, which will be as close to the back corner as I can get."

"Won't the bag of cash stir up some interest?" asked Hudson.

"Payment is not in cash. It's gem stones," Yassir said. He reached into his pocket and pulled out a suede pouch. He shook it into his palm. "Transportable, unparalleled quality," he said admirably.

"One more thing," Camille said. "Who is the successor? To the Leader."

Ali shrugged. "No one I know."

Edwin looked at his watch. "Camille, come with me. We need to go."

Camille looked at Yassir, this Ali, this new man unfolding in front of her. Suddenly her entire history with him was upended. None of it was true. Nothing she had loved so deeply, or mourned so desperately, had ever been there at all. Her own history – her own life – was fiction. The new facts melted ice patches of her sense of self.

"No," said Camille. "I'm staying here. I need to know a few things."

"Don't do it," Edwin said. "This guy is a killer. He will kill you."

"Always so dramatic, Edwin," said Ali. "Death has made you creepy. Camille, stay. It will be good to talk. Finally. I will tell you everything."

"No," Edwin said. "He is alive only because we need to see if he told the truth."

"Edwin," said Camille. "It's…it's complicated."

"This man is trained to kill – me, you, anyone who gets in his way," said Edwin. "To him, everything in this room is a deadly weapon. He's thinking right now how to use them on you. He stays bound."

Yassir caught Camille's eye and nodded to the floor next to where he lay.

"I'm sorry," he whispered. For everything you wanted that I couldn't give you."

This was the Yassir she remembered. Not the enraged extremist Edwin saw, who was connected somehow to this horror. Who Camille just met. The two masks, and the facility with which Yassir swapped them, chilled her.

Edwin looked at his watch. He had twelve minutes before he was supposed to meet Hudson to reclaim his Blackberry. He would need to deploy Hudson on one more mission. Then he could disappear. This was Edwin's mission. It demanded his total focus. If Camille insisted on putting herself in danger, he could no longer help her.

"If there is ever even the slightest rumor that I am not dead," Edwin said to Ali/Yassir, "I will hold you responsible for it. Seriously, Camille. Don't stay here."

"I have to," she said, her eyes fixed on Ali/Yassir. She had to integrate new facts into reality. She had to do it now, or wondering would trap her for another ten years.

Edwin growled. "Fine. You do what you will. You are on your own now." He sprang to the window. "And Camille,"

"What?"

"You are outstanding. Next decide where you want to go. Then make it happen."

"Edwin," she said. "Thanks for showing me…everything."

Edwin smiled. Then he reached into his jacket and pulled out one of the toy rubber ducks. He tossed it to Camille. She bobbled it but she kept hold of it, and put it in the pocket of her blue windbreaker.

"Thanks," she said. Edwin lifted his arms. The sun warmed the air against the house. His wings caught the light thermal lift and raised him over the roof tops.

"Untie me, Camille," Yassir said. "Please."

Camille looked at him. Edwin's warning began to register. "Let's just talk first."

"There's not much trust here," he said.

Camille flared. "There's exactly as much as you've earned. Maybe you can add to zero with what you say now." Yassir sighed. He scooted a few inches across the floor to lean more comfortably against the bed.

"Uncle saved me from who-knows-what when my parents died. He had big plans for me. He gave me an education. Sent me to America. Then I met you," Yassir smiled.

"Not in his plan," Camille said.

"No," said Yassir.

"So why does he care now? You're an adult. You've made a lot of money at this company. You aren't committed to a daughter of Satan's nation for the rest of your life."

"This wasn't the career he wanted for me. There are other things than money," he said. "Although money is central to everything."

"Like what? Fame? Glory?"

"That's part of it. Legacy."

"He wanted you to be a suicide bomber?" Camille scoffed.

"No," said Yassir. Then he heaved a huge sigh. "This is not my country. I don't know who my family is, where my home is. Except my uncle. And you." This was an old refrain, a yawning pull that always had made Camille feel like she had to fill him up.

"So why tell me about the attack?" she asked.

"Because of the kids. Maybe one with a blue eye and a brown one." Yassir held her hand as they mourned a lost hope. "I want to hold you again."

"Come here," Camille reached out her arms. A few moments later, Camille used a knife from the kitchen to cut through Yassir's tape. He reached for her.

"You should not have let me go," Yassir murmured, his face buried deep in Camille's warm neck. Behind them, the closet door opened.

"No, she should not have," came a clipped voice in heavily accented English. "She would have had something to bargain with." Camille saw Yassir's face go white.

"Uncle!" he gasped. Then for the first time Camille saw evil wrapped in skin. He was a man with long grey hair and dark glasses, pointing a gun at Yassir.

"You betrayed me," seethed Khalid al Hamzami. "You, who I took off the streets and fed and bathed and groomed and raised with pure Islam, you disrespect me, you shame me, and you humiliate me! You caused my mission to fail. So you must pay now. You will do it. You will shoot her. You will take the body to the tub. You will dispose of the pieces. It is the only way you can prove your loyalty to me. The only way to protect our future. She knows now exactly who you are. Who I am. You played loose with the rules and now she must die. You will kill her to restore your honor, to do your duty to me."

Yassir's hand shook when he pointed the gun at Camille.

CHAPTER 3

HUDSON AND EDWIN
2:00 P.M, CAMBRIDGE, MA

At precisely 2:00 p.m., as agreed, Hudson stood outside the Starbucks on Beacon Street across from the Public Garden, just about where Edwin had dropped him off the previous morning. Hudson watched the traffic, a Venti with four sugars in one hand. Edwin's Blackberry was in the other.

Suddenly both hands were empty. Edwin settled next to him, draining the cup through the open visor on his helmet. He checked the Blackberry. Pressed a button. The familiar whistle screeched. Edwin typed a series of letters and clicked. The whistle changed to a pleasing ping. He clicked it off.

"Good job finding this," Edwin said.

"Thanks," Hudson said. "It was crazy. I –"

"Now you have a new mission," Edwin said. "There's going to be a second buy. Today. You are going to stop it. The transaction will go down at 4:00 p.m. at the coffee shop by the office. You figure out what you need to do, who to involve, to make sure that deal does not go through and the good guys get the vial again. The seller will wear blue shoes. The buyer – you – order a quad latte. Here. Hold this for a second." Edwin handed Hudson the Blackberry to reach into his pocket for a small zip lock baggie. At first Hudson thought it contained jellybeans – their colors were so intense – red, green, blue, yellow and lots of clear ones. "Pay with these," he said.

"Done," said Hudson. He now returned Edwin's orders with the same force, same energy, same confidence. It was not just modeling a form of speech. Hudson's thoughts were crisp and orderly. He saw facts. He cleared out the curtains of doubt that once hung between him and his goal. He focused all of his ability on how to make it happen. It was as if Edwin had replicated his methods through another person. This was how his personal genius could scale.

"Then you have a second mission," Edwin said. "Save D6. Please. I can't…I have to go now. You know someone is trying to tank the numbers. It doesn't matter who or why. There's only one way to beat it. You must make the number this quarter. So you will close the XTC deal by the end of September. You have two weeks."

Hudson nodded. He felt no urge to slide away beneath a slick smile. He felt no frisson of fear. Instead he bore down. He would apply all of his brain, all of his style. He took a sip of his coffee. When he looked up, Edwin was gone.

"Wait!" Hudson cried. "Your Blackberry!"

The purpose of their meeting was so Hudson could return Edwin's Blackberry. But he had forgotten it. It was so unlike Edwin to forget something. Things did not slip his mind. But things slip everyone's mind, no matter how sharp the trap. Hudson thought about how memory lapses slide out silently, yet make affirmative statements. Edwin left the Blackberry with him exactly when his real calling forced him to disconnect, extract to new and dangerous duties. To isolation. So he kept a link with his world of joys, where pleasures were sated, ego nurtured and fame built. Of friends. And now, at the point of extraction again, he left the device - his main means of contact with the ASP. As if he did not want any, Hudson mused.

CHAPTER 4

EDWIN
3:00 P.M, CAMBRIDGE, MA

Edwin landed in a soft rush of air, his Nikes scraping the rooftop garden. It was dark now.   Crouching low he could see the sharpshooters on the roofs of the buildings closest to the coffee shop. He could see the lines of cop cars, lights out, waiting for the call to the take down. The acute problems – the vials – were being addressed.

"But this is just the beginning," Edwin said. There would be many more attacks. Many terrorist entrepreneurs trying to destroy what free people could create. There were some odd parallels to Edwin's entrepreneurial experience. The terrorists would also need brilliant, inspirational leadership to make the most of the willing. But unlike the people he molded, innovators of destruction would be ego-driven, money driven criminals, with half-hatched plans bent on new ways to make nothing out of something. To make a big, bright boom and leave the world with less. They needed leadership to organize, fund, inspire and coordinate. They needed investment. Their current leader had proven his effectiveness, but now he would be on the run from the woken fury of America's military. If he survived, he could not lead operations.

Edwin saw it plainly. Winning this new war would depend on defeating the leader's successor. But who would it be?

"No one I know," Ali's words rang in Edwin's ears as he watched the men dressed head to toe in white hazmat suits march out of the coffee shop. It was a muddled, strange expression. He should have said "I don't know." But that is not what he said. In fact he said "I know." And "No one." None. I know none other.

Edwin ran full speed across the roof garden and leapt up off the rail. He soared.

There were only two things compromising proof of the successor's pure loyalty to the leader: a supposed victim of 9-11, and a plump CIA analyst. They knew the successor's identity. What he had done to compromise the planned third prong of the 9-11 attack, which in their inner circle would be considered a massive failure. That presented a non-trivial problem for his career trajectory.

A few miles away, in a two bedroom house in East Cambridge, Camille sat on a wood chair, her hands locked in steel handcuffs to her feet. They had taken her shoes.

"Yassir, don't," Camille whispered softly. "Put the gun down."

Tears wet Yassir's eyes. The gun barrel waved in his shaky hand. Uncle – Khalid al Hamzami – started laughing. It was a giddy, bitter crow. He tossed his head back, taking in the pleasure of smashing people into each other. Then he screamed in pain. His hands dug frantically at his eyes. He crashed around the room.

Because as al Hamzami had gorged on Yassir's weakness and Camille's fear, he did not notice her small fingers. How they pressed gently against her heel. He did not hear the handcuff gears release.

In that split second when al Hamzami took his focus off Camille, she was on her feet. The rubber duck toy was in her tight fist. She squeezed with all her might, sending a sharp spray into his eyes. The bleach blinded him. He could not see Camille heave her whole body weight at his knees, cutting him down. The duct tape she had cut off held firmly as she wound it around al Hamzami.

"Wow," said Yassir. "Camille!" He wiped his eyes with the back of his left hand. His right held the gun, still pointed at her.

"What are you doing?" she said.

"It's time for all of us to move on," he said.

"So go," she said. "You haven't done anything wrong yet. You can be free."

"I can't. You see, Uncle has bigger plans for me. So my weaknesses here in America can never be told. It's over for me here anyway, now."

"Yassir, what are you saying? I'm not going to tell anyone," Camille pleaded.

"Oh, you will. You are an American first. You all are. I am an outsider; I look like the worst of them. I'm related to one of them. Maybe I am one! They are my people. Not you. Not the arrogant Edwin Hoff," Yassir flared. "I will never ever suffer the likes of him again. No. Uncle is right. It's time to become who I really am."

"And who is that?" Camille asked.

To which Yassir said nothing. His eyes were dry as he pulled back the safety and his forefinger curled around the trigger. Only Camille saw the shape move in the hallway.

Suddenly, a sharp blade pressed against Yassir's jugular vein.

"Stop," said Edwin. The word shot like a bullet.

"I don't care if I die," Yassir said.

"You do," said Edwin, his bicep bulging around Yassir's neck. "You're no blind moron tricked into doing the dirty work to die for someone else's glory, money, ego. You want to give up the chance to be king? Right when the moment you have waited for your entire life has come? The old leader is done, and on the run now. They need you – the westernized man with a pure soul! And millions in valuable stock options! Who else would be better? You know you want it. You are no suicide. You've had your virgin already – you know that's not the best offer."

"Let me go and she lives," Yassir growled through his clenched teeth. He still had the gun pointed with both hands at Camille. Edwin Hoff would not have his arms around his neck again. Metaphorically or physically. It made him seethe to have to bargain with Edwin. There would be no more dealing.

Bound on the floor, al Hamzami unleashed a torrent of Arabic. "Go back! Find the Leader. He wants to see you. You can make me proud again." But Arabic was as clear as English to both Edwin and Camille.

"Who wants to see you?" Camille said. Edwin flipped Yassir onto his back.

"I know what you are about," Edwin hissed. "I know what you did, and what you are going to do next. Never assume I am gone. I will always be watching you."

Yassir made a quick move. He broke Edwin's grip. He whipped a chair at his legs, then grabbed the shade off a bedside lamp and smashed the bulb. He jabbed the jagged glass toward Edwin, keeping more than an arm's length of distance. Then Yassir, as he leaped backwards onto the double bed, flipped back and was on his feet, and out the window. They heard the sound of rusty metal straining until he reached the ground.

At 3:32 p.m. on Thursday September 13, 2001, a call came in to the FBI dispatcher. A woman said, "This is Camille Henderson. I'm at 86 Hays Street in Cambridge."

Within two minutes sirens whipped red bands of light at the location on Hays Street. The team wore bulletproof vests, their guns drawn. The group at the front door with the battering ram found force unnecessary. It was unlocked. When they crept upstairs, and down the hall, they found their most wanted, Camille Henderson, presiding over a bound and seething mastermind who would be fully capable, if asked persuasively, of providing details of the failed plank of the 9-11 attack.

CHAPTER 5

At 3:55 p.m., Hudson was sitting in the Cambridge Coffee House, still in possession of Edwin's hot Blackberry. People trickled in for a late afternoon boost. There were only three other full tables. Hudson scanned the floor. Between the scattered crumbs, flecks of paper from straw wrappers and dust balls caught in a shaft of sunlight, he watched the shoes. There were sneakers. Black lace ups. Loafers. Red flats. Heels.

But no blue shoes. As Hudson watched the door revolve, in walked a pair of worn jogging sneakers with a familiar face. It was Kyle Figby, the former classmate of Edwin's and CTO of a database start-up in Kendall Square, and his wife Meredith. Kyle's company had raised a little money and buzz, a bit limp compared to the D6 rocket. The one who had sent Edwin that backward compliment of congratulations on the IPO. Meredith was an executive secretary at one of the biotech companies in the Square. She often had an unfortunate choice of clothing, and perhaps more unfortunately, it was always assembled to make an impression. Today was no exception. She wore black and electric blue striped trousers with matching high heels and a fluffy black top. The black frames of her rectangular glasses pinched her nose to make the effect complete. She carried shopping bags.

"Too bad credit cards don't need a license," Hudson thought, ducking under his paper. Too late. Kyle spotted him and sauntered over. In his faded grey Reeboks.

"So, about Edwin," he began. "God, how awful."

"Yes," said Hudson. "It is awful." Kyle was blocking his view of the door.

"Strange, isn't it," Kyle continued. "He was so young, and came out of the blocks so fast. I'm a little older and our company isn't so fast, but you never know. It's kinda like that old tale, the Tortoise and the Hare."

Hudson looked at Kyle with disgust. Was this man so tortured by envy that he was in fact gloating about Edwin's untimely demise? Implying that Edwin, by dying at the hand of murderers, had "lost" and Figby had "won"? Hudson felt sick.

"Well, you should come by some time," said Kyle, after Hudson's glare made him step back. "I'd love to tell you about what we're doing now. We could use someone like you. D6 probably won't be around for much longer."

"See you later, Kyle," Hudson said, looking down at his paper. He flipped a page. But no one came in while Kyle took two cups from the barista to the back of the shop where Meredith saved a table. A woman walked in next.

Hudson grinned, began humming softly. "When a man loves a woman, can't keep his mind on nothing else." She was a dark beauty, her black spiky hair striking against her deep blue eyes. He watched her move toward the back of the shop. She placed a stack of books on a table all the way in the back corner, and then stood in line. She looked at the menu, shifting her weight from her left foot to her right. Above the menu, the clock's long hand held the 59th minute.

"What do I want, what do I want?" she said. Just as the second hand pulled the minute hand in line, and elsewhere in Cambridge four carillon bells rang from a clock tower, she said. "Okay. I know what I want. A skinny quad cappuccino."

Just then the door swung open again. A young woman joined the line. Black shoes. "Oh, hello, Officer Marly!" said the new arrival.

"Nadia, hi!" said Marly, looking around the shop. "What a surprise."

"I should say," said Nadia. "I was just about to call you! It turns out we did take a short run of silver and blue for our logo. It was a mistake, but we did do it after all!"

"Really?" said Marly. "I'd like to see what it looks like. Just for my own, you know, marketing knowledge."

"I assumed you would," said Nadia. "There were just six shirts made. And we were out of the regulars so the new employees oriented that day got them. I suppose they are kind of collector's items now."

"Probably," said Marly, her eyes moving past Nadia's shoulder.

Hudson appeared. "Nadia, how are you? Hey you got a minute? I need to ask you a few questions since I've been out for a few days."

"Oh, hi Hudson," she said, looking back at Marly. "Oh gosh! Are you here for…." she nodded in the direction of Hudson.

"No," said Marly. "I'm just getting a cup of coffee. Hello, Mr. Davenport."

Hudson nodded at Marly, and led Nadia by the elbow to his corner. Marly leaned on the pickup shelf, waiting for the barista to drop the fourth espresso into her cup of super leaded coffee.

"Just a minute, Hudson," Nadia said. She was back at Marly's side, waving a piece of paper at her. "These are the names and contact numbers of the people who oriented on silver logo day. Hope it helps you. And please, please feel free to ask me any questions at all you may have in the future about brand identification." Then Nadia backpedaled and rejoined Hudson around the corner of the coffee bar.

Marly opened the paper. One name leapt at her. But it made no sense whatsoever. She was back to square one. It had to be another company with a silver logo on blue fabric. She just was missing something important.

Over Nadia's shoulder, Hudson watched people leave the coffee bar except Marly, in the back corner. Kyle held the door for his shockingly dressed wife.

Nadia was eager to leave. "I hope…I hope everything works out for you."

"Thanks, Nadia," Hudson said. Then no one remained except Marly on one side and him on the other. Hudson's hopes fell. The leak clearly had given Edwin a dead end.

But as Nadia pushed one side of the revolving door, another person entered. Wearing blue shoes. Blue shoes that matched her shocking striped trousers that squeaked as she pressed through the coffee tables to join Marly in the back of the shop.

Meredith Figby sat down opposite Marly. She leaned back, crossing her arms and legs. "I wasn't expecting someone like you," she said.

"Likewise," said Marly. The body language was not good. She needed to dispel her quarry's suspicions. "Look, less conversation is more here."

"Yes," said Meredith. "How do you want to do this?"

"Same way as before is fine," Marly said.

"Good," said Meredith. "Show me, then I show you, then we swap."

Marly pulled out the suede satchel from her purse. "Taste one, if you want."

Meredith looked at her somewhat strangely, then peered into the Ziploc bag like a child in a candy store with the proprietor's paper sack. She selected a small clear stone and put it between her teeth. Then she spat it into her palm. Before she raised it to the light, she looked around.

"Okay. Now I show you," said Meredith, pulling from her purse a tube of lipstick. She opened the cap. "I wouldn't taste that, if I were you."

Marly picked up the lipstick. She studied the etching on the crystal: ".001".

"Don't lose this one," said Meredith. "There were only two. That's why the price went up ten million. But I deserve it. It's not easy getting this away from the labs."

"But you are better than them," said Marly.

"So it seems," she said, tipping her chair back casually. "At least twice as good. You know, in hazmat suits, if you just keep your eyes down, you can get in places maybe you shouldn't really be. If you watched very closely when they typed in access codes."

"Impressive," said Marly. She pulled out a thin wallet out of her pocket.

"Cash on top? Bonus!" said Meredith.

"More bling, I'm afraid," Marly said. Her badge flashed in the light. "Meredith Figby, you are under arrest. You have the right to remain silent…"

Flashing strobe lights distorted the coffee shop. Police cars screeched and swarmed. Twelve people in hazmat suits evacuated the coffee shop and surrounded Marly and Meredith Figby. A figure with thin white gloves gingerly put the vial in a box with eight inches of white foam padding encasing an indentation the size of the vial.

Captain Brath entered the coffee shop. "How did you know? Peters is still at his desk flipping through phone books."

"Reliable sources," Marly said. Brath put his hand on her shoulder.

Marly looked around for Hudson. He was gone. But what Nadia had written on that white piece of paper meant Marly had no choice but to track him down.

CHAPTER 6

The piece of note paper curled like a cigarette in Marly's hand. She rolled it back and forth. It did not make sense. It was not possible. The pieces did not fit.

Her phone rang. "Detective Marly, it's SFPD here. I got the tapes from SFO. The story checks out. A young guy was late for the plane, came bursting down the ramp, and put up a fuss to get on and make sure he made that red-eye."

Her heart sunk. What Walker had told her was true. Hudson had been seen with the victim, and MIA during the time of her death, barely making it to the flight. As soon as he sent her the copy of the video, she would have to meet with the DA. The case was not strong enough, but there was too much to ignore.

Twenty minutes later, the file completed downloading. Marly clicked "play" and Apple Computer's QuickTime program began buffering the video. It was slow and jerky, but detailed enough. There was the man sprinting down the ramp from security. He was sweaty and breathing hard when he got there. There was no audio, but she could see his arms waving and eyes glaring at the stewardesses, who reluctantly pulled back the rope and allowed him to thunder down the gangway out of sight, into the plane.

The film made Marly gasp. She gripped the little paper cigarette in her closed fist. Now it all made sense. No matter how appealing he was, there was no denying it. She had her Esplanade Murderer. So she would nail him to the wall.

"Get me the DA," she said into her phone, voice cool as an April lake, ice still on its edges.

CHAPTER 7

EDWIN
7:00 P.M, BOSTON, MA

The man sat on his motorcycle idling in the no-parking spot outside the Starbucks coffee shop on Charles Street. He wore a Kevlar jacket, scuffed Nikes, blue jeans that needed a wash, and a helmet. The visor was half open.

Edwin would keep moving. He would not sleep for more than two hours at a time, usually sitting up with his back against whatever was there: a tree, a chimney, a cave wall. He had to remove himself completely and quickly. Fortunately he knew just where to go. It was a place he had planned for, a side perk of the boundless financial successes he had enjoyed in this high tech romp.

Hudson emerged from the shop with two cups. "Venti coffee, four sugars," said Hudson, offering Edwin a preposterously tall cup.

Edwin pulled off the helmet for a moment. His hair was now bright red and so were the webs where his fingers met his palm. The dye job was hasty. He blew across the surface of the coffee and took a sip.

He fingered the change Hudson gave him. "Four-fifty for a cup of coffee! Obstreperous! But good, good. Thanks," Edwin said.

"So the vial is back in the right hands, or rather, vault," said Hudson. "Unbelievable. Figby's wife!"

"Figby's wife?" said Edwin. For a moment he was off the battlefield, back in back in the playground of competitive classes and

321

start-up companies, where he had just begun to learn the intrigue of gossip.

"Yep," said Hudson. "Trading seeds of destruction for diamonds."

"It's always been this way," said Edwin. "Any criminal, any country, any time. The ones who will sell out their country and their people do it for ego and money. She couldn't stand sitting by while the rest of the world leapfrogged them. She wanted to be driving the flashy cars, wearing the jewels. She wanted Figby to be on the Top Ten techie list, on the Boston billionaire's ranking instead of an ordinary smart PhD working on hard but trivial projects with the occasional original part of an idea. Money and ego."

Hudson frowned. "Are you sure you can't just come in, tell people you are okay?"

Edwin shook his red head firmly. His jaw was set. "No. This was an unplanned stop. I have to do something now. I have to go."

"Where are you going?" Hudson asked. Edwin swallowed the last of the coffee. "You just don't understand. People are really wrecked about you. They are trying to process it, and can't. You just – you just …died. That was it. And that's just the people at work. I can't even imagine how your family feels. You've got to let them know."

Edwin saw tears slide in Hudson's brown eyes. "No. And let me be clear. Again. If anyone thinks you know what happened to me, or where I am, you will be dead. For real. This is not your business. Don't make it your business. You have a mission to do. Save D6. Get your XTC deal done. Make it happen." Edwin put the helmet on.

"Wait," said Hudson, holding out the Blackberry. "Do not forget this again."

Edwin picked up the black piece of plastic from China. Then he dropped it on the cement. With a boyish smile, he crushed the device beneath his heel.

"What the –, " Hudson gasped. "Do you know what I went through to get that thing back? Don't you need it? To talk with your ASP?"

"Nope," Edwin said. "I just needed to be sure no one could find it on you. Now go save D6. Bye. And Slacker…thanks." The visor closed, the engine kicked to life and Edwin drove around the corner down Charles St.

Hudson was smiling as he walked the other way down Charles Street until he heard the shots. They sounded like an engine backfiring. But the pops came too fast, too close together. People were screaming. It was the spray of machine gun fire.

Hudson bolted for Beacon St. "No!" he cried. "Please, no."

When Hudson rounded the corner he saw a motorcycle on its side, wheels tattered from gunfire. He looked for the rider, who would have been flung truck lengths when the bullets ripped the tires off his bike, when the cement rims bit the pavement. Hudson saw a small crowd gathering. He pushed through the crowd. At its center was a dark bloodstain.

"What happened?" he asked.

"I don't know!" gasped an older lady. Her dog yapped at the end of his narrow leash. "There was a bang-bang, like that! Then the poor driver! He flew and landed. We rushed to him. He was not moving."

"Where is he?" shouted Hudson.

"Some man in dirty rags took him down there! I've never seen anything like it," she said, pointing down a road leading in to the flats of Beacon Hill.

Hudson ran through construction frames that filled the narrow sidewalk beside brownstones. Who was he pursuing? A Samaritan? Unlikely. A bystander would have waited for an ambulance. Hudson knew he was chasing the ASP hit squad, come to prove a rogue dead.

At the next corner, Hudson stopped outside the old Episcopal church. Its brick walls blended into the tight neighborhood, spires reaching above it. Looking in every direction, he saw no one. Then he looked down. Blood spread in opposite arcs around the steel rim of a sewer grate.

Hudson knew then two things. One, he would never see Edwin Hoff again. And two, he would work for him for the rest of his life. He would imagine whether Edwin would approve of his actions. Would he bark at him for being behind, or be proud of the way he cleared out the doubts, saw his goal, and reached for it? He could tell others what he learned. How Edwin always gave it everything he had. Then more. How they could too.

Edwin awoke to pitch blackness. His adrenaline kicked in immediately as his eyes sought sensation. There was no difference between opening and closing his eyes. He took inventory with his other senses. Gravel prickled under his back. He could hear distant sounds of rumbling, it seemed, from every direction. Traffic?

Somewhere water dripped on iron, ringing dimly as it slipped around and dropped off landing in a wet thud. He listened hard for something else. Breath. Before he gave away that he was conscious, he wanted to know if he was being watched. Was he captive or sheltered?

There were no sounds other than his own halted breath. Very slowly, he stretched his toes in his shoes. He flexed his thigh muscles. One felt like fire, and was tight in a strange direction. Something clamped down in the opposite direction of his sinew. One leg was bound. Edwin stretched his neck. No pain.

He had not seen the shooter as he came fast around the corner of Charles and Beacon Street. But the edge of the Public Garden was a risk; he had known it would be. The wall was thick with foliage and off the common path. Pedestrians focused on making way for the row of cute bronze ducklings from the children's book, not the lumps of humanity under the bushes at the edge of the park. It was an ideal sniper nest.

He could feel the fire start in his leg, how hard it was to grip the bike even for that second before the front tires shredded and tore the bike out from under him. Then everything went dark. Now here he lay. In the dark, flat on his back, with free hands and feet, and a bind on his thigh.

"Don't move," muttered a gravelly voice. The man coughed slightly.

Edwin decided to speak. "What happened?"

"They got you. Nearly," the man said.

"Who?" Edwin heard feet scuffling on gravel. A rock struck flint; a flame caught a pile of dry grass, sticks crackled. Edwin could see a small circle of light that showed a dirt floor, low curved crumbling brick walls. He could see the man moving near a pile of dark objects. He turned toward Edwin with a dirty plastic bottle.

"You are hit," he said. "I'm going to put this on your leg."

Edwin looked down and saw his jeans were shredded. A dark stain stretched on either side of duct tape that ringed his thigh like a tourniquet. The man deftly tore the tape from Edwin's leg. Edwin watched the fluid foam over his bloody leg."

"There are two holes; bullets went through. Lucky." The man's voice was growing smoother. Edwin could not see his face, but as he watched the man work, he recognized the approach. Field triage. Which made him watch the man all the more closely.

"Where did you come from?"

"Saw some guys in position. Watching a friend of mine having a cup of coffee. So I watched them."

"Well, thanks," said Edwin. "You know Hudson Davenport?"

"Who?" The man said. When he pulled a roll of duct tape from the ground and lifted his wrist to tear off a binding piece, and when the blue fleece sleeve slipped an inch lower, Edwin saw the tattoo. Then he looked down and saw the dirt caked in black creases on the man's filthy feet. One foot was missing two toes; the other missing one. Then Edwin understood why this man had just saved Edwin's life.

Now they were even.

"We've met," Edwin said quietly. The man twisted his wrist. He knew what Edwin had seen. Only those in the force recognized the location and the tiny tattoo, the sword over the left shoulder. "Bonaire. The docks. You are Lennox Alida. I was on your...recovery mission." Edwin saw the moments below the deck. Thrashing in the water. The severed toes falling in red plumes to the ocean floor. Drawing sharks. The bags of blood caking the red sand.

"Yes," he said. "You gave me a chance. Now you can try."

"What happened to you?" Edwin said. "You had a...woman. A baby coming. They closed your case. Mission accomplished."

The man's eyes flashed as he looked up. "Yeah, well, it didn't work out."

"You broke up?" Edwin said.

"No. They took them. You can never leave ASP. You can never live – not with anyone else, anyway. No matter what. They clean up after you."

"Why are you here? In Boston?" Edwin said.

"One day I saw your face in some magazines I was using for insulation. I never forget a face come to kill me. Especially not one come to kill me and let me go. I thought you might need help one day. Maybe I return the favor."

"Where are we?" Edwin said, rubbing his leg.

"Below the church. It's an old tunnel that used to feed the patriots with muskets and powder, while the British were controlling the governor's office. Leads to the river."

"I need to get to Concord without being seen," Edwin said. "The private airfield near the river. And you need me to get away from you fast."

CHAPTER 1

JAMESON
9:00 A.M., CAMBRIDGE, MA

The ends of the long maple table were rounded, giving everyone between them the sense that they were part of an extended circle. Their boss, Jameson Callaghan sat at one end. His boss, the Chairman of the Board, Sterling Davenport, sat at the other.

Board meetings allowed a brief glimpse to Jameson's management team of what he must have been like coming up. Knowing the goals of his superiors. Preparing detailed presentations to meet them. Usually Jameson focused down, absorbing uncertainty around his people. He fanned the good attributes, squelched the less productive ones, with the goal of creating a frictionless environment so his team could work well.

It was Jameson's job to prepare the Board for more bad news. First the tragedy of losing their north star; now the sales numbers were going to miss. Badly.

"Q3 will be several million short," Jameson opened. He thought about the Wall Street Journal article. It would probably hit the front page, bottom fold. Jameson's profile in speckles. Everyone at the table knew what missing the quarter meant in these fragile times. With Edwin's death. The dot com balloon puckered on the floor.

First, any value left in the stock price would crater. Freaked-out day traders would dump it. Nervous fund managers would see it fall and sell the last of their large holdings. Maybe a share of D6 would be worth a few pennies.

That would just be the day after they reported earnings. Long term consequences were worse. If the stock stayed below a dollar for too long, the NASDAQ would delist the stock. Then all D6 shares would have no value whatsoever. Customers would cancel. They only wanted to buy from survivors. With less revenue, D6 would have less money to pay salaries. There would be more layoffs. There was no fat left; the next cuts would take more bone. Limbs. And heads. First, Big Mac's. Next, Jameson's.

"There is one long shot out there," Jameson said, when the numbers were plain. He spoke surely, giving bad news clearly and standing behind it.

"Which is?" Sterling asked coldly.

"XTC," Jameson said. "Hudson is 'left seat' but he's been preoccupied." Jameson never, ever threw anyone under the bus. He never saw it produce a gain. Ever.

Down the long table Sterling crossed his legs casually. He leaned back. Rocking ever so lightly, his chair swiveled slightly to the side. He looked like a man who had overindulged on dinner, chewing lazily on a cigar. He could almost see the glowing embers dropping off the tip with each slide Jameson showed.

"So who is leading XTC, for the moment?" Sterling said.

Jameson nodded to a young man perched nervously on the edge of his seat against the back wall. He rose to his feet, pressing up on the cane that rode at his side where others clipped their cell phones.

"M-me, sir," said Walker Green "But Hudson will be back before it's too late."

"It already is too late," snapped Sterling. "Do you have paper from them? A term sheet? How about a call set up with the decision maker?"

"Ah, I know Hudson was supposed to have a call with the director of product management tomorrow, but–"

"Tomorrow? With a product manager? And you think he'll get from a phone call to a closed deal in the next two weeks?" Sterling stared down the table. "Jameson, why didn't you see to this deal personally? Your quarter hinges on it." It was a rare act to dress down his leader in public. Jameson knew what it meant: Sterling was dismantling him.

"Indeed," said Jameson. "I have a lot of confidence in Hudson. He can get it done."

"You know nothing about my son," said Sterling stiffly. No one moved.

Walker added eagerly, "We also had a really good meeting earlier this month with the business development manager, when Hudson and I were out in the Bay Area. He said he would totally recommend a deal to his bosses. I'll put a lot more time into it when I relocate out there next week." He waved the crutch. "Can't deal with the ice."

"Uh huh," said Sterling dubiously. "Well, it's pretty simple. Either we get XTC done in two weeks, or D6 misses the quarter. A miss, on top of losing Edwin, will be the tipping point. That will be it, friends. We reap what we sow." Sterling held Jameson's gaze.

Jameson smiled through thin lips. "So, team. Let's make it happen. Big Mac, you've got a lot of contacts there from your old days running sales. Walker, come with me. Let's figure out how we close this deal in two weeks."

What went through Jameson's mind next was this: If they missed the quarter, he'd be gone within weeks. What would he have then? Not family: Belle was all he ever really had. Not his fortune: it hinged on D6 shares. He would not ever have the belief that he had been done wrong at SAC. And his reputation? Gone. Forever, if someone got a whiff of his link to Maggie Rice the night she was killed. What would be left of Jameson Callaghan? He felt like he was watching a speck of light grow very small just before it went out.

CHAPTER 2

HUDSON AND MARLY
6:00 P.M., CAMBRIDGE, MA

On the steps outside Sterling's home, Jameson prepared his wide smile. Then he rang the bell.

"Jameson," Sterling said. "What are you doing here?"

"Grace asked me to come," Jameson said.

"Oh," Sterling backed up. "Well, come in. Hudson is here too, with a friend."

Sterling led Jameson into the red room where Grace sat in her usual chair by the fireplace, in this season a backdrop to a coffee table laden with art magazines and books. On another pair of chairs sat Hudson and a woman with black spiky hair, sharp blue eyes.

"This is Christine Marly," he said. "She's a recovering lawyer."

This evening Officer Marly wore a black dress, covered with a loosely tailored blazer. She left her office clothes behind but her pockets were full. This was about to become a business meeting.

"Nice to meet you," said Marly, holding her hand out to Jameson. Clearly she did not want to acknowledge that they had already met. Or how.

"Well," said Sterling. "This looks like a party, of sorts. I should get drinks."

On his way to the kitchen, the doorbell rang again. A frown crossed Sterling's face. He opened the door to four men. The two closest to the door wore suits; the two behind them wore windbreakers with FBI above the left side of the chest. They held rifles.

"Tom Davis, Securities Exchange Commission," said one in a suit. "We're looking for Jameson Callaghan."

Sterling smiled. Let out a huge sigh. "He's this way, officers. This way."

The four men entered the foyer, following Sterling to the red room where Jameson, Grace, Hudson and Marly were gathered.

"Sterling Davenport?" Davis asked, turning to the host.

"Yes," said Sterling. "Welcome."

Tom Davis faced him. "Sterling Davenport, you are under arrest for the crimes of bribery, insider trading and obstruction of justice. You have the right to remain silent...." He continued the Miranda warnings steadily though Sterling began to shout.

"What? No – you want Jameson Callaghan! He's the one who did it. He's the one who shorted D6 stock and sold on inside information about the bad quarter."

"Dad, stop," Hudson said. "Be quiet."

"I won't be quiet!" Sterling raged. "You have it all wrong."

"I'll call your lawyer," Hudson said. "Just stop talking."

Here Marly stepped in. "Mr. Davenport, we know about the Shearwater file. We know the Shearwater Company is your corporation, that its purpose is to short D6 stock, and pay Richard MacIntyre to delay sales to miss the quarter. We know you paid Maggie Rice to make it look like Mr. Callaghan made an illegal trade. We know you paid Walker Green to take pictures of them leaving together, to trash his reputation."

"What does Maggie have to do with this?" said Hudson.

Sterling looked from face to face. He was smart enough to know it was over.

"She wasn't supposed to die," Sterling said. "She was supposed to bring down Jameson's reputation, accuse him of creating a hostile work environment. Then Hudson – you get in the middle and get tagged for her murder. I had to protect you. It was easy to help make it look like Jameson did. Maybe he did do it. Where was Jameson the night Maggie died? He drove her home. Maybe he killed her too. How do you know he didn't?"

"Because he was here," Grace said.

"What?" Sterling gasped.

"We were looking at old pictures," she said. "Of Hudson."

Hudson was confused. He shook his head. "So who killed her?"

"I was in D.C. the tenth, drove back that terrible morning of the eleventh. I don't know what happened to her," Sterling said.

"Why Dad?" Hudson pleaded. "Why do all this? You and Jameson are friends!"

"So it was you," Sterling said softly. Hudson looked at the floor. "You found the file last night on my desk. When you were in here. You turned me in. Makes my heart swell. You know, I wish I could say I was proud of my own son."

"Dad, please," Hudson begged.

"A father should be proud. How do you feel, Jameson?" Sterling sneered.

"Go easy now, Sterling," cautioned Grace. She slipped her arm into Hudson's.

"What's going on?" Hudson said.

Marly touched his elbow. "Maybe you should talk with your mom. In private."

"Oh come now Grace," Sterling spewed. "Don't be shy. Really, demureness is not your nature. Never has been. Jameson. I think I hear your crystal cracking."

Grace said nothing. The officers were in no hurry to remove Sterling, now that his hands were cuffed and his mouth was open. One had pressed a recording device.

Jameson looked at Hudson. He had tried to rehearse the words but they never came together smoothly. He thought for a moment of Edwin. The man, though twenty years younger, had taught him. Edwin would have let the facts speak without softeners. Get the worst out first. Then deal. With everything. So nothing lingers unsaid, nothing festers, nothing can come up on the brink of a deal to blow it up. Even if it breaks glass.

Jameson took a deep breath and said, "Thirty years ago we went on a sailing trip. Your mother, Sterling, me and another woman. She left. She got sick. Sick of the water and sick of having to sit two feet away in the cockpit and watching me watch Grace, not believing what I made up when she caught me. She had to hear me laugh like a school girl when Grace made a joke. Then it was just the three of us for four more days. Sterling went ashore to get provisions. He left us on the boat alone for hours. It felt like a dare."

Hudson looked with incredulity at his mother. He was amazed to see her face lift, as if she was happy to feel a warm memory.

Jameson's lips worked nervously, curling against his teeth as he pressed on.

"When we left the boat, your mother was pregnant. She and Sterling were planning to get married; they did. Later I met my wife. We left things as they were."

Hudson's jaw hung open. "I don't believe it."

"It's true," said Sterling. "And because of complications when you were born, Grace could not have any more children. So she never had any of my children. So this was our deal. I got you. You are my son. But I waited. And waited. And waited for the right moment. Jameson screwed me out of my future. I would screw him out of his past. At the end of his career, take away everything he had built – his career, his reputation, his money, maybe his freedom. Things that could never be rebuilt – he would not have the time or opportunity even to try to repair. Then D6 came along. Flashy enough to get a lot of press, small enough to manipulate for my purposes. So I pitched Jameson on the opportunity when he was weak and vulnerable. It was perfect. But then he started wheedling into your life. He hired you. Started spending more time with you than I did."

Sterling turned to Jameson. "So you thought you could have your past and a fresh future. No responsibilities for children, and an heir. It was time to sink the ship."

Hudson stared at Jameson Callaghan. Now he saw in the older man hair that held his own wave, the same chestnut hue between the sprays of salt, their similar stature. And his own name – did his mother intend the parallel to the name of the man whose "son" he in fact was?

Hudson turned on Jameson. "And what, you learned you were going to be a father and just backed out? Had a son and walked away?"

Jameson looked down. The facts were what they were. "Yes. I'd like to change that."

"And you get to screw my Dad over again? Bonus," Hudson said.

Jameson said nothing. The facts, looked at plainly, showed his intense selfishness. But that was the base they had to build on.

Then Hudson turned on Sterling. "And you? You paid Big Mac to tank the quarter? Sit on XTC – my deal? Make me look like a loser who can't get anything done? Wipe us all out financially? You have no idea the world of financial trouble I'm in."

"I can make you whole," Sterling said. "Money is no issue."

"No!" Hudson shouted. "I'll take care of it by myself."

Hudson was building into a rage. He wanted to feel like he could make something happen instead of clinging like a speck on a rug taken outside for a beating. His mother had betrayed him, choosing for her convenience who his father should have been, overlooking entirely her own contribution to who it actually was. His biological father had glided away. The only person who actually had stood by him, who had every reason not to, was standing in the restraints of federal and local police because he had turned that fidelity into a blind and ill-fated vengeance.

It was too much to sort out. Hudson left the Red Room and slammed the heavy front door of the Davenport home behind him. He started walking, fast, then running hard toward Harvard Square where he could catch the T back to Boston, the other side of the river. He had to settle his mind. He had to find a way to channel this much heat and anger into what he had to do next.

Marly excused herself from the Davenport's troubled home. With the folded piece of paper still in her pocket, and the images on the video surveillance from the departure gate at San Francisco Airport, she could not lose track of Hudson now. She watched him get in a cab. She followed in another one, all the way back to his apartment.

Marly knew who had killed Maggie Rice. What she did not know yet, exactly, was whether her plan to catch him would work.

As the sun was gilding the MIT dome on the western side of the river, she watched Hudson reappear on his steps in shorts, a t-shirt and running shoes. In the alley behind the row of brownstones on Marlborough Street, Marly stepped behind a parked black SUV. She pulled the black dress over her head. Beneath it she wore a tight spandex running tank top and Lycra shorts. She pulled a pair of running shoes out of her small backpack and stuffed her jacket and dress and flats inside it. Then she broke into a fast run over the uneven brick sidewalk, down to the bridge over Storrow Drive to the Esplanade.

It was dark when she reached the river. The Canada geese were huddled together near the pond. The children had long since left the playground. A rollerblader zoomed past her. Occasionally another jogger passed. Marly passed the Hatch Shell where the Pops gave free concerts in the summer, but it was dark. She jogged up the steps to the Salt and Pepper Bridge and glanced around for her old friend,

Mr. Squibbs. He could have been any of the lumps she saw under their disheveled blankets.

Marly felt the wind hit her on the bridge toward Kendall Square, where hours earlier her career trajectory had broken wide open with the takedown of a key and failed component of the 9-11 plan. But she was not done yet. She had to catch the Esplanade killer. Which was why she was out here. Not without fear.

She padded past MIT, then back across the Mass Ave bridge into Boston. She was beginning to tire on her second lap around, when she saw Hudson sitting on a bench. Just where she thought he would be. She ran on.

The path veered through a patch of trees, which made it a particularly dark and lonely section of the course at night. Near where they found Maggie Rice's body. This was when she heard footsteps. A faster jogger would overtake her. She moved to the right to give the runner room, but then in the dark her senses pricked. He was not maintaining his pace. He was too close.

Then a hard pipe hit her full across the back, knocking her to the ground. A man gripped her by the strong elastic straps of her top and dragged her off the path. Her face was down in the dirt. Marly twisted, reached and grabbed his ears as tightly as she could, tearing one from his scalp. Her thumbs went into his eyes and he screeched with pain. Then she was on top of him, jamming his head into the ground.

"Okay Marly," Hudson said. "You can stop now. We've got him." He was standing behind her, his hands gently on her shoulder as she straddled the attacker. Hudson had fallen in to pace behind her as soon as she passed him. As they had planned.

Marly pulled two zip ties out of her sock and secured them tightly around the man's hands and feet. She knew exactly who she would see when she flipped him over. And she had known instantly what he hit her with: his magic wand.

"Walker Green," she said, tossing the collapsible cane to Hudson. "You are under arrest for assault and battery, for the murder of Maggie Rice, and you can expect another charge for the murder at the San Francisco Marina.

"Why, Walker?" Hudson asked. "Why'd you have to kill her?"

Walker grinned. "Can you believe it? My mother named me 'Walker' of all things, then left me with legs that don't work most of the time. It's all right – she hit me enough it was a pleasure to see her go."

The three sat on the ground, breathing hard, as the police lights swirled down the access road toward them. Walker felt like talking.

"This disease – my immune system is supposed to protect me – just like she was." He laughed bitterly. "Instead it attacks my muscles, what should be strong about me. So when I have my legs, I use them. Payback's a bitch."

"But Maggie isn't your mother," Hudson said. "She's just an innocent girl."

Walker shrugged. "She would have been somebody's someday."

Sirens flared as police cars reached them. Several officers cuffed and stuffed Walker into a car. He put up no resistance.

Later that night, Marly and Hudson sat on his roof deck with a glass of white wine.

"Multiple Sclerosis can come and go," she explained. "My friend Vanessa is his doctor. She said he could be lucky. So when he has an attack, he needs a cane. But when he's fine, he can run. No one knows when except him. There's power in that."

"How did you figure it out?" Hudson asked.

"Physical evidence matched from both murders – a strange combination of colors in the belly fluff the rapist left. I traced it to your company logo. But it was only a limited edition. Nadia gave me a list of everyone who got those shirts. Walker was one of six. Only Walker was in San Francisco at the time of the murder. And the surveillance video showed only Walker running, no cane in sight, to catch your flight back to Boston."

Hudson was quiet. "How did he get linked up with my dad?"

"Just luck. He worked at his charity to benefit abandoned children. I guess your dad spotted a guy who he thought would quietly take a few pictures for a buck."

"My dad – Sterling – damn it, he's still my dad – didn't think he'd kill Maggie?"

"No. Your dad may be vengeful but he's not a murderer. He did not know how twisted Walker was. This was just an unfortunate coincidence. Bad luck," she said.

"But what about those pictures of Jameson with Maggie the night she died?"

"Grace put an end to that theory," Marly said.

Hudson gulped his wine. "Now I just have to figure out how to close this XTC deal in two weeks." Because if he did not come up with $200,000 in cash for J.D. Sullivan by October 1, Marly might just be looking at another grisly victim. But Hudson had a powerful ability to compartmentalize, particularly when a beautiful woman was sitting next to him.

"Do you like Jimmy Buffett?" he said, refilling Marly's glass.

CHAPTER 3

JAMESON
10:00 P.M., CONCORD, MA

Jameson sat alone at the end of the diving board of his pool. His bare feet dipped into the water, sending the ripples marching, even rows of energy until the formation lapsed. He tapped the surface, sent the waves. They crashed into each other, sent waves backwards.

How much did one really control, anyway? He thought. They had tried to control paternity – Jameson, Sterling and Grace – to return fatherhood of Hudson to Sterling. He told himself it was his biggest act of generosity. But it was what most deeply shamed Jameson, because he was guilty. He had pursued Grace, even though she was engaged to his best friend –in part, because she was – he had to admit. And then there would be a permanent testament to his competitiveness, his need to please himself above friendship.

It was Sterling who would live up to his name. He took in the child and raised him as his own. He forgave the love of his life, who shared hers with another, then sought a well-financed perfect life with him. But he adored the boy. He would do anything for the boy. He did.

Jameson's mind flashed to Edwin. It was becoming annoying how plain facts produced themselves on their own, more and more so since Edwin had died. As if thinking of him, which was always in Jameson's mind, could conjure his voice.

He said it aloud. "Grace never wanted to leave Sterling. And, I never asked her to. Because I did not want her to."

Because although she was beautiful, and the charmer and the star among their college friends, he just really needed to win her over. Just once. After that, they both knew the charge was gone. Even if the consequences were only beginning to gestate.

Then he had met Belle. And she did flip him. Wow. When no one else was looking. They just clicked, broadly, deeply and truly. It was a bond that made him better than the playboy he had been. She strengthened him where he was weak. He did the same for her. But a child never came so they pursued their careers together. They explored the world together. They were partners in every sense of the word.

Then she died. And Jameson's eyes glazed over too. Every morning he woke up to the brief moment of consciousness that it might not have happened. Then it hit him like a four by four across the chest, took his air and flattened him back on the pillow.

Was it fate? Or choice? Was it his choice not to do his duty to Grace – and their son – all those years ago, so he could meet the right woman? Or a controlling fate that knew Grace did not really want him, but one day, Belle would.

That was when the elephant in the pool reared its trunk.

In the distracted days since Tuesday, Jameson had not let himself pause very long on this simple fact: he was supposed to have been on that plane. With all those innocent people. With Edwin. He should have met Belle again, he hoped, in that place where his thoughts slipped out of logic into faith, a place better equipped to handle concepts of loss, and eternity.

But Jameson got stuck in the suburbs, thanks to a vandal with uncanny timing.

"Lucky Jameson," he muttered. "Someone just did not want me on that plane, I guess. So it's fate, then." He dangled his legs in the pool, deciding where to send the waves. Then he jumped in. The water closed over his head, cool, and cleansing. The buoyancy felt good. The water muffled his voice. He was alone without feeling it. But he could still hear his own words in the bubbles.

"Someone did not want me on that plane."

Jameson's feet found the cement floor of the pool. He pushed to the surface, gulping in deep breaths of air. Who knew he would be on that plane? Just Maggie Rice. And Edwin Hoff.

"We can talk about it on the plane," Jameson had told Edwin. He remembered the way Edwin had paused at the door. Briefly. *"Fine,"* was all Edwin had said. Subject closed.

Dripping wet, Jameson dashed through the pool house to the garage. He had kept the four slashed tires for insurance purposes. He pulled one over and examined the slash. It was incredibly thin. It was not a normal knife, or a tack. Something had made that slash with a blade so fine, so long and so sharp that it had not even pulled at the sticky rubber.

He had seen a blade like that before. He had seen a blade like that go through the duct tape in a motivational mock attack that Edwin would playfully deposit on his most trusted employees to sharpen them, remind them what their job was,

The thoughts tumbled over one another. Jameson laughed, a full happy, laugh, for the first time in a long while. A force certainly did not want him on that plane.

Edwin had known something. Maybe, just maybe, somewhere, Edwin was still in control. At least, Jameson thought, he could believe that.

CHAPTER 3

AHMED
6:00 P.M., CAMBRIDGE, MA

Ahmed Farzi closed the door to his interior cube. He placed a magnetic board the size of a candy bar across the seal, and then pressed a button in his pocket. Until he pressed it again, the door would remain locked. He did not want to be interrupted.

It was sunset, time for the day's fifth prayer. He laid out his rug pointing east and sank down to his knees. He stretched his arms forward and prayed. As he recited the familiar words, he sought the total submission to the will of Allah, through which to achieve peace with himself, with the Creator, with all He created. To be a pure Muslim.

Then Ahmed set to work. To work for the hereafter as if he would die tomorrow and to work in this life as if he would live forever. Or perhaps find himself somewhere in between. To always seek the middle. Moderation was key.

The Blackberry on his desk began to whistle. Ahmed looked at it. He picked it up. He clicked a series of keys and pressed it to his ear.

"Yes?"

"Dear," said an elderly lady. "How are you holding up?"

"Fine, Head. Thank you," said Ahmed.

"It is a big loss. But it was his time. But I know how closely you have worked together. You have been partners for so long."

"Yes," said Ahmed. "But we all know that change will come."

340

"Of course," she said. There was a long pause. "Where is his gear, then?"

"I would think he left it with the Extraction team? No?" Ahmed said.

"Yes, quite," said the elderly woman. "That would be proper procedure. Lovely to chat dear. We'll be in touch." The line clicked off.

Ahmed put the phone down. He took out the battery. Took out the chip. He put each piece in a separate drawer. Then Ahmed sat down and clicked keys. He pressed a button, and the corkboard stuck with pins and a chaotic mosaic of notes and sticky pads slid up. A large black monitor moved forward on silent hydraulics.

He had waited a long time for this moment. He pushed a series of buttons. A green bar lit up. The system was now on. Then Ahmed Farzi, or Zed, as some of his colleagues liked to call him, having taken care of everything from A to Z, went home to honor and attend to his wife and children.

Thousands of miles away, the heavy seas rose and rolled through the immense cement posts that anchored the oil rig to the bottom of the ocean floor. Atop four massive pinions rested an abandoned steel platform and tall pumping frames that had once been home to ten men trying to drill oil from the shelf below the sea. When the supplies appeared to be tapped, the rig was abandoned. But it had been built so solidly the structure stayed in place despite tropical storms or hurricanes that tried to rip it from the sea floor. The big oil company that built it wrote it off as lost, a sunken rig. Then Mariner's Law took over: finders, keepers.

The rig was the world's smallest sovereign nation. Papers had been filed declaring it so. It could not be invaded without an act of war. Its tax status was generous. A prince ruled over it.

After many years of darkness, this day the lights came on. Row after row of square windows illuminated along the residential structure where a small kitchen, lavatory and several bunk rooms lay.

High atop the drilling frame, a man sat calmly in the ruffling breeze. He felt the electric hum kick in, the slightest buzz traveling up through the frame.

He was working on something new. He lifted his hands out in front of him, then he beat the air and lifted off into the breeze as the jacket spread layers of fabric under his arms. They caught the air and lifted him. He circled, rose, then plummeted in a spiral, eyes focused down on the white caps on the sea. Just before impact, he pulled back and spread his arms. The resistance from this sudden expanse of fabric pressed against the air molecules caught him, held him vertically. As he scraped his feet over the wave, two sea bass caught on his Nikes. The magnets had been optimized to sense even the trace heavy metals that now filled the fish flesh everywhere.

He caught another thermal wave and rose back up to his throne on the oil rig. He clutched a rail with one arm and leaned back against it. He tore at the fish with his teeth. Sushi in the sunshine.

He liked to read during lunch. He pulled from his pocket the tattered striped green paper bag. Lula's parting gift. He drew out the small, square volume. By now he must have read it a hundred times.

Howl by Allan Ginsburg, was an astonishing poem.

CHAPTER 1

HUDSON
2:00 P.M., BOSTON, MA

It seemed everything had changed in the past three weeks, but the seasons continued their effortless adaptation, unaffected by the spikes of human tragedy. The Public Garden rolled from lush green grasses and shady green umbrellas of leaves, tourists with dripping ice cream cones, to a place where crisp air carried the scent of wood charring. Nature's balance held the gentle hint that human order would also, eventually, be restored.

Hudson held Marly's hand in the deep pocket of his Barbour coat as they left the Oak Room of the Ritz Carlton. It was late afternoon. The best burger in town and afternoon glass of wine left them lazy, sybaritic.

"So how's your – how's Sterling?" Marly asked.

"Dad's doing okay, considering," Hudson said, letting go a long sigh.

"Understandable. These injuries stay with you," she said.

"Yeah. But he's still my dad, you know? Jameson always knew about me, yet what did he do about it? Nothing! All my life. Until he had no one else. Then he decides he wants family. Even if it blows up everyone else."

Marly held his fingers in the deep coat pocket. The leaves crackled as their shoes scraped through them. "I can understand why a man would need to know his son. Particularly later in life, when he's measuring his impact on the world. What he'll leave behind."

"Maybe. I don't know. All I do know is that the man who raised me is my father, even if he's gotten himself into a bad situation," said Hudson. "So he's okay inside. The food's not great. It's hard to see him. You have to get on a list. They lose it. Soon he'll be in a room where we can at least give him a hug."

Hudson and Marly had begun to spend a lot of time together. In Hudson's light touch, his easy humor, the way his receptors seemed tuned to find pleasure, to offer it, Marly felt a new way; not tight, worried, and always on the verge of venting a long held fury.

Hudson felt the magnetism of Marly: how she was so driven, always drawn toward her future and her goals. Her direction challenged him to think about his own, to consider putting goals in place, and to push.

"I'm having a premonition," he said, scuffing a stray line of leaves on the path.

"A premonition? Of?" said Marly, puzzled.

"It's very clear," he said. His smile held her on the line as he slowly reeled her in.

"What is it?" she giggled.

"My premonition is that you are going to end up in a leaf pile," he said.

"Is that a meta–?" Before she could complete the thought Hudson had scooped her into his arms and carried them both backward into a pile of auburn leaves on the grass.

Marly laughed. "Remind me to have more faith in your powers of prescience."

Hudson kneeled in front of her and plucked a leaf out of her hair. He kissed her.

"I gotta go," he said. "I would love to love to love to take you home, make you dinner –"

"Your dish?" she said. Hudson's bachelor repertoire, for all the professional appliances in his kitchen, was one meal. His freezer was stocked with sausage. His pantry held jars of tomato sauce and bags of pasta. Not much else.

"Yes, my dish," he said. "There's a special sauce in it, you know. Or perhaps you could do it better. Maybe you should give it a try and I'll see how it compares."

She smiled. "I'm sure I'd never make it as good."

"So I'd love to make it good for you...and later with you...," he smiled. Then his face grew serious. "But I have somewhere I have to be."

"You're going to California? XTC?"

Hudson nodded. "I have to get them to sign this deal by Sunday night. If I do – we make the quarter no matter what Big Mac did. We save D6. Edwin's company."

"It's almost as if he knew, somehow," she said sadly.

Hudson was quiet. He had not told her exactly how he had gotten out of the motel room. Some unknown hero took out the terrorists. Maybe it was an internal battle gone wrong, he had suggested. Like the mafia. Lots of murder, but usually confined to its own warriors. She had not pressed him on it.

"Who knows," said Hudson, pulling her to her feet. "I just know it's my job now."

Two hours later he boarded a 767 American Airlines jet to San Jose after a very slow security line, in which nearly every toiletry with any fluid in it or sharp edge – nail clipper, scissors, razor blade – was confiscated. Hudson sat in business class, row 9J. The same type of plane Edwin had flown on, three weeks earlier. He buckled himself in to just about the same seat and looked around.

What had Edwin seen? What had he noticed? Now, Hudson did not feel terror when he thought about Edwin's experience. He knew now that Edwin had not been caught unaware. That he knew full well who sat in the first two rows of first class, in the aisle across from him in business class, and immediately behind him. He was not surprised by the sudden, coordinated movement; he did not lurch awake from a stolen nap to a horror unfolding before his intense open eyes. He was not murdered on that plane.

Instead Edwin had had a plan. He had watched the criminals closely while they had no idea who was sitting in their midst, or what he had planned for them. He executed that mission, and two of the terrorists, while succeeding in disrupting the most destructive element of the 9-11 plot. He had saved the New York Metro area from widespread pneumonic plague. And then he had done so much more.

Hudson wondered where Edwin was now, what he was preparing to do next, somewhere, sometime, in a way no one else could. Now it was Hudson who sat in business class going on an important sales call for D6. He was surrounded by a new group of fliers: a troop of vigilant passengers. Those brave enough to get on a plane found their fight instincts kicked in. None would be caught unaware. They eyed every person boarding, stared down anyone with dark hair, dark skin. Men with long beards and turbans were held at the gate, frisked. Women prepared to step out of their heels, grab and jab at any terrorist who tried to take over this flight. People carried hardcover books they could smash on an attacker's head.

Soon the stewardesses would bring plastic cups and plastic ware to the first class and business class customers. Gone was the glass. Gone were the real knives and forks. As soon as they finished serving, they would push the cart sideways across the galley, blocking the newly reinforced, and locked, cockpit door with another physical barrier. Someone on the plane was a U.S. Marshall in plain clothes, armed.

They took the knives, but they let everyone keep their pens. Pens that could put out an eye or more. This was Hudson's weapon of choice. He rolled a special ballpoint pen in his hand. It had been a gift.

Hudson had six hours in flight to figure out how to close an eight million dollar deal with one of the biggest technology companies in America by the end of the day. By the end of the weekend, at the latest. The quarter would close Sunday, September 30, at midnight. Which meant the deal had to be signed, money wired by the close of business. But big meant slow. Big meant no one made a decision unless they were at the top giving orders – the lower downs were charged with executing, not doing new things, not striking out on their own path. Not closing a strategic deal with a small company for an eight million dollar ticket.

It was the only hope for D6. The commission check – five percent – was the only hope for Hudson. He did not want to meet J.D. Sullivan's debt collectors.

Edwin had said "make it happen." So Hudson would.

"How would Edwin have done it?" he muttered to himself. He could hear his own voice but the engines muffled it. "Like a bull." He smiled, imagining Edwin insisting on going to the top technical guy, the CTO, insulting him until the flea bite stung enough to get his attention, then he would downshift, apologize for his brusqueness, then appeal to his academic curiosity about the merits of D6's superior technology and how a strategic partnership would help them leapfrog their competition. He would call any engineer who tried to get in the way "a marketing guy" – the ultimate insult to anyone who went to work in a t-shirt, mined the free vending machines for Mountain Dew and Twix bars, and dangled Star Wars figurines over their cube edge.

"But I can't do the super technical stuff. I'm a joker," he thought. "Edwin's approach would not work for me. They'd stuff me in a can." It was true. Hudson was quick with a joke. He could get most people to laugh, just about any time he wanted to. Edwin called him a glad hander because he handed out a lot of sugar. Made people feel happy for no particular reason. But what use was that?

Hudson flicked on the computer to run through the websites it had cached in its memory. At the very top of XTC management was the CEO, Kamia Kahn. She was a stunning woman, about Jameson's age, whose long black hair showed no sign of grey, and whose dark eyes smiled with genuine confidence.

She was also a woman who, despite having risen far beyond the glass ceiling to reach the top of the technology business, today would have an unpleasant time getting on an airplane. So Hudson bet she would be at headquarters that Friday morning. She was his only hope.

At 6:40 the next morning, Hudson sat in the parking lot near XTC's company soccer fields. Its campus near Palo Alto rivaled the resources of an Ivy League school. There was an outdoor Olympic-size swimming pool, two softball fields, and an indoor gym with weights, yoga studios, basketball courts, and a glass dome over another swimming pool that let the sunlight in to dance on the waves. There was a cafeteria that served only healthy meals, for free. The kitchen ran healthy cooking lessons, and pulled produce from its garden on the premises.

Hudson was sitting in his rental car in the parking lot between XTC's soccer field and the central offices. The whole gambit had to happen before 7:00 a.m.

At 6:47 a.m., the blades of Kamia Kahn's helicopter chopped the air. Hudson smiled. He had predicted three things correctly. First, that the CEO, who lived in Tiburon, on the northern side of the Golden Gate Bridge, would not tolerate two hours of traffic to get to work. Second, that helicopters would land on the soccer fields instead of at the nearby airport. Third, that it would be her habit to get to work before anyone else. She would set the standard. Lead by example.

The parking lot occupied the space between the playing fields and the main executive office building of XTC. On the first floor of the building, a sign with a familiar green and white logo filled the window. But the Starbucks was still unlit. For another thirteen minutes.

The blades lowered until he could no longer see them cutting through the air behind the eucalyptus trees that edged the field. Momentarily, a woman with glistening black hair pushed through the branches. She was shorter than Hudson had imagined. She carried a slim black leather briefcase in one hand. Her other hand was empty.

"Okay," Hudson breathed. "Be the hero or be the goat."

Hudson opened the door to his rental car and stepped out. Kamia Kahn wore a dark red suit with a long jacket and a cream blouse that fell open at the neck. She wore a scarf over her hair.

"Excuse me, Ms. Kahn," Hudson said, stepping in with her quick pace.

"Hello," she said, smiling, but continuing to move. She was a sort of mini rock star, her fan base concentrated on this campus. But the techniques of dealing with strangers were the same: smile genuinely and keep moving. Take their hand if you must. Never let them take yours. Never stop moving.

But Hudson kept pace with her. He held two coffees in his hand as they approached the building. It was now 6:51 a.m. The Starbucks would open in nine minutes.

"My name is Hudson Davenport. I work at D6," he said.

"Nice to meet you, Hudson," she said. "All the way from Cambridge? Hope you have a nice time on the right coast." Her pace quickened.

"I was hoping I could talk to you for a few minutes," Hudson said.

"I'm sorry – I do have a busy day," said the CEO of XTC. "Would you make an appointment with my office?"

"Goat," Hudson thought. Then he caught Kamia eyeing the coffee shop, which was still closed.

"I flew here to give you the rare gift that's in this cup," Hudson said with a grin.

Kamia regarded the well-dressed young man. His wavy brown hair was crisply parted. His suit fit him well. His white shirt was pressed. His computer bag had the D6 logo. The corners of his mouth moved back and forth, as if barely keeping hold of a good joke. His brown eyes laughed.

"He's probably not a lunatic," she thought. "There's something rather delicious about him."

"Did you?" she said aloud, eyebrow raised. "What's that gift?"

Hooked! Hudson's grin broke wide. "Yes. In this cup are twelve and a half minutes."

"Twelve and a half minutes? How about ounces of dark roast?" she smiled.

"Eight minutes until the shop opens. Two to stand in line. Two more for them to make it," Hudson said.

"That's only twelve minutes," she said.

"Thirty seconds to add sugar and stir. I already put it in for you. And a dusting of chocolate," he said.

"You flew all the way out from Boston to give me twelve minutes?"

"And a half," he said. Kamia laughed. That was when Hudson knew he had her. Edwin taught him that if you inspire someone to create, you own them. You inspire someone to dare to reach further; you give them a tour through their day, through their life, with more air, more depth, more colors, more sound, and more sensation.

It turned out the same was true of laughter. You make someone laugh, you give them something: you make them feel good. So they give you a little gift back: gratitude. Which means you have a better chance to persuade.

"I thought if I gave you back time in your day – even twelve and a half minutes – that you might give me the time of day," Hudson said.

Kamia Kahn laughed fully. It was so nice to have a pleasant surprise first thing in the morning. The guy was a delight. It would actually be fun to listen to him as she walked up to her office.

"I only need seven minutes," said Hudson. "That way you're still ahead."

"I'll give you seven and a half," she smiled, taking the coffee from his outstretched hand. "Walk with me."

"So," he began. "D6 has a technology called Interfaces. They create a way for any electronic device to become a node of the Internet and connect to a decentralized system that makes digital pulses fly through the Internet."

"I know the technology. MIT genius again, right?"

"Yes. Originally it was a distributed math problem – how to make the right decision about matching up A and B when information is incomplete at any given moment. Our founder, Edwin Hoff, came up with it."

"Yes," she said. "I heard…I never had the chance to meet him. I'm so sorry for your loss."

"Thank you," said Hudson. A voice in his head piped in. Use everything at your disposal to reach your goal. Everything. Even sympathy. So Hudson said, "This was Edwin's vision. That all of XTC's hardware appliances – TVs, telephones, refrigerators, house alarms – anything that plugs in to the wall and operates on digital impulse – embed D6 Interfaces."

"Then all eleven million of XTC's appliances become their own grid, another layer of the Internet," she said.

"Not just any layer, not just any grid. This deal would bring the Internet literally into the hands of your customers, through your devices. All of them. Where your customers could then drive," Hudson spun the vision.

"Our hardware would control the new operating system," she mused.

"Exactly!" Hudson said. "Think of the software that could be built for it. Around your formats. Your security systems."

Kamia sipped her coffee. "I know, actually. Our technologists have been looking at D6 for a while. Let's just say the strategy has occurred to us. So what's the price to license Interfaces for embedding across our devices."

Then Hudson saw how a great senior executive made her coin: having the courage and vision to chart a new course. Less capable people in the positions of power mimicked bold strokes, with ill-considered reasons, only to reap disaster. But true leaders saw negatives with clear eyes, and still found ways to go firmly forward where boldness was required.

"Ten million for a perpetual license," said Hudson. "Twenty percent a year in upgrade and support."

Kamia whistled. "Rich," she said dubiously.

Be candid, said the voice. Honesty clears out the clutter. Makes progress faster.

"I'll be straight with you," said Hudson. "This deal is very important to our quarter. Very. It needs to happen today. So the terms can be very sweet."

"Eight million. And an exclusive deal," she said.

Keep the tension, said the voice. Remind her that you can help her with her competition. Let her realize that if she won't let you help her business, you'll have to help her competition.

"I can't do an exclusive," Hudson said. "It would not be natural for our business model. But, I can guarantee you will be first if we get this done this afternoon."

"You have someone over at Standard Appliance – Jameson's old house – negotiating this same deal, today don't you?" Kamia said. "Seeing as it's so important to your quarter."

Candor early bought him her expectation that he was being candid now. Hudson shrugged. Then he said, "This deal is a category killer. Whoever is first will leapfrog the competition. And we're small. We can't do multiple big deals simultaneously. Whoever is first will suck up all of our resources. So first is effectively exclusive."

Kamia picked up her phone. "Ravi? It's Kamia. Would you bring your team to the conference room? I want you to hear what this clever fellow from D6 has to say. We may have an extraordinary opportunity today."

Over the next six hours, Hudson found himself at the whiteboard, mimicking how he had seen Edwin draw the smiling faces to represent people holding appliances with D6 Interfaces, scribbling lines between all of their devices as connections came to light. He painted the future on the border of the whiteboard – listing application after application as the XTC team saw its vision fulfilled, and how it would enter and own this next generation of technology where plugs in the wall became two-way feeds to and from the devices they already knew so well how to place in people's hands.

It must have happened at a certain point, but he could not tell exactly when, that Hudson was no longer just responding to the voice piping in advice in his head; he was in his own groove, doing it his way, with the voice becoming paint on his palate.

In parallel, lawyers drafted deal documents. Hudson kept his eye on the clock. The deal teams worked late Friday night. They appeared Saturday before 9:00 a.m. and continued on Sunday. Sunday September 30, 2001. The last day of the quarter.

He would just make it: if they could convince the technologists their silver bullets actually flew when fired. If the lawyers did not raise the specter of risk too high. If no one ever guessed just how close to the precipice D6 was. They just might do it.

Hudson sat in a small conference room with a glass window facing the western ridge where he could review the deal documents on the phone with the lawyers who were redlining them in Boston. Fog had crept in from the cold Pacific and was billowing up over the dense green crest, spilling down into the valley like dollops of whipped cream.

It was 8:30 p.m. Which meant 11:30 p.m. on the East Coast. Nearly close of business on Sunday, September 30, 2001. In thirty minutes he would know if he had saved his own neck; if he were the hero or the goat. The one who brought in the needed deal that would save D6, and prove Edwin's vision, or the goat, the one who failed, the one the group would gather against and vent their angry spleen upon. Their fury at the quarter lost, D6 down an irreversible spiral to Chapter 11, the vision lost. And the man.

In less than thirty minutes Hudson would know if he had to face J.D. Sullivan's friends with an empty wallet.

All was going smoothly. But this was what made Hudson worry: every promising deal he had worked on had either fallen apart before it came together at the end, or just stayed in tattered pages in the recycling bin.

There was a knock at the door. An older man with grey hair that matched the pin stripes in his suit smiled warmly.

"Hudson Davenport?" he said. Hudson nodded.

"I'm Dennis Waller, the General Counsel," he said. "Kamia asked me to come talk to you while she made a phone call."

"Yes?" said Hudson. He did not like the sound of this. The coach was about to turn into a pumpkin and important decision makers seemed to be slipping quietly away. As if a decision had been made, and more important ones were filling her mind even as the clock neared twelve.

Dennis hoisted his trousers and sat down, crossed one leg over the other. Then crossed one arm over the other. "I'll be honest. We're concerned about the viability of D6. It's a big price of entry. And if you go under, our eight million goes too. Then our strategy is out there, so bidding for the piece parts of what's left of D6 becomes a price war. It's bad for us. It would be better to wait and see how things go next quarter. You guys do well, then we can do this same deal just a few months from now. You don't, we help you create some value for all the hard work people have put in out of the piece parts but we don't telegraph it to the world. See? It's a win-win." The man offered a friendly smile.

"Better to be a vulture, you mean," said Hudson. "This deal is sweet already."

"My guess is next quarter it'll get sweeter," he said, his red wattle waggling. "Anyway, hell of a Hail Mary, coming all the way out here. The gimmick with time in a coffee cup. I'll have to remember that one." Hudson flinched when the older man patted his shoulder and left the conference room.

"So, goat then," Hudson said. The voice in his head had been quiet for much of the evening as he had swung along on his own momentum. But as he sat in the stillness, his momentum stalled. When there was nowhere left to go, he heard this:

"Never be the one to say you are done."

Hudson thought about pulling on those oars when his arms were useless sticks full of lactic acid. How Edwin's must have been too. How his neck bled. How he pulled as if every stroke was the first fresh one. Kept pulling.

At 8:56 p.m., Hudson stood up. He tossed his limp paper cup in the trash. He would not just sit in the conference room and let this deal go die. He had four minutes before the clock struck midnight on the East Coast.

By now Hudson knew where the corner office was. He could see Kamia inside, on the phone, leaning back, her heels on her desk. She was laughing.

"Can I help you?" asked her gatekeeper assistant.

"I need to see Ms. Kahn," said Hudson. The clock on the assistant's desk clicked to 8:59. "Please. It's urgent."

"She's on the phone," said the assistant.

"It can't wait," said Hudson. "I know everyone says that, but if it gets to —"

The clock ticked 9:00 p.m. A chime went. Witching time on the East Coast.

"Nine?" said the assistant.

"Midnight," Hudson's shoulders fell. The third quarter was over. They had missed. "Meh-eh," he bleated.

"Excuse me?" said the assistant.

"Nothing," said Hudson. He thought of J.D. and the men with thick necks who would be knocking on his door tomorrow. His lungs began to heave. He lurched to his feet.

But then he saw Kamia smile through the glass panels of her office door. She waved him in. "I want you to listen to this," she said to him, pressing speaker phone. Then to the phone, "Jameson?"

"Kamia," boomed a familiar voice. Hudson now listened to it for notes of his own. He heard history between the two, Jameson Callaghan and Kamia Khan. That generation of technology leaders was small – the industry started with only a few companies, so nearly all of the best heads of the dot coms had crossed paths before. Apparently so had Jameson and Kamia.

"I'm here with Hudson Davenport," Kamia continued seamlessly. "You've got quite a guy here." There was a pause. Ever so slight. Kamia would never have noticed it. But Hudson did. Jameson did.

"Yes," Jameson said. "Very true."

"Did the fax reach you?" she said. "And the wire?"

"Yes, thank you. Both have been received," he said.

"As I told you earlier, we look forward to doing business with you."

"It's done? The deal is done?" Hudson said, leaping to his feet.

Kamia smiled. "I had a few concerns, so I just called Jameson directly. He assured me D6 is sound and will be sounder. And, if not, we have right of first refusal on any auctioned assets of D6. Win-win," she said.

"But Waller just told me the deal was dead," Hudson said.

Kamia smiled. "That's his job. He's supposed to give all the reasons it should be. Mine is to judge the risk and take it. Around here, the bias is in favor of action. So we acted. Thanks to your tall skinny latte, D6 now has eight million more dollars in your third quarter revenues. And you, my friend, have a hefty commission check waiting. What do you get, five percent? What are you going to do with four hundred thousand dollars?"

"Buy an old watch," said Hudson. "And maybe put something in the bank."

CHAPTER 1

CAMILLE AND MARLY
10:00 A.M., CAIRO, EGYPT

The Visiting Professor of English at Cairo University selected a small table in the back corner of the patio. She sat with her back to the tea house's glass wall. A scarf covered her hair. She wore a light linen jacket over an ankle length skirt. The fabric actually helped keep her cool, a shield against the sun. It discreetly covered her beautiful shape. Tennis three times a week had drawn her core muscles up, straightened her neck and added half an inch to her height through naturally straighter posture. A wisp of auburn peeked under her scarf. Her makeup was very light. Her lips brightened with soft rose gloss. Her cheeks carried a natural blush, and, in the heat, the color rose.

The Professor watched the passing crowd as the teapot, cup and saucer, bowl of lemon slices, cream and sugar sticks were delivered by a man who bowed.

"May I bring you anything else while you wait?" he asked in English.

The woman responded in Arabic. "No, thank you." She waited two minutes more before holding the teapot's handle and top and maneuvering both to pour an arc of steaming brown liquid, thick as her little finger, into the cup. She listened to the strains of conversation going on around her. She listened for two particular words. The verbal Bona Fides were "Tour Group."

Tea outside on a glorious afternoon, thought Camille. Surrounded by the people and culture she adored, who made her feel at home. The new job had its perks. Much better than being locked inside all day with books, the computer, telegraphs and printouts.

A woman crossed the street toward the café. She too wore a headscarf, but it could not contain her raven hair that framed her face with a gentle bob. Camille heard her say to the shop owner, "Do you speak English? Is this the Café Paradiso? I'm afraid I'm terribly lost. I've been to three others and I must find my tour group."

"No," said the shop owner. "I'm sorry it is not."

Camille's orders had been specific. She stood up with a smile and recited, "Are you American? Perhaps I can help you find your tour group."

"Oh! Thank you," said the American. "So nice to see a friendly face. I might as well have a cup of tea while I'm here. Then I'll just have to get back to the hotel somehow. They told us not to travel on our own." Tea was delivered shortly.

Marly spoke in low tones. "How's your tennis?"

Camille nodded. "I have a regular partner now. Her name is Mira Galoub."

"Galoub? Like the construction empire?" said Marly.

"She's one of his wives," Camille said. "Third or fourth, I think."

"How does she play?" Marly asked.

"Very well," Camille said. "Very well indeed."

"I always found tennis a challenge. It's always about the handle, finding the right grip," Marly said. Handle was the trade term for how one got a hold of someone to spill the beans on their country, their friends, even their spouses. It was the intelligence officer's job to land in a foreign country, assume a solid cover for status, then get to know people who would be close enough to the people who knew. Then get a handle on them.

"Mira has a good grip," said Camille. "Health is very important to her – it's why she plays. Her mother is quite sick – cancer - she is afraid it will get her too. So she wants to be in the best shape possible. Her mother would have such a different outcome if she lived in the U.S. Of course, they are here."

"Mmm," said Marly. "I wish someone could help her."

"Yes, so does she," said Camille. "Well, I must be off now. I have to teach a class in thirty minutes." Then she pulled a small street map out of her purse and put it on the table, dragging her index finger across it. "Just walk down here, turn here, then here. Follow this line straight back this way and you will be at the hotels. Good luck." Camille left the café. Marly picked up the map and, looking like a lost tourist, ambled through the streets of Cairo.

Later, back to her hotel. Marly ran the map across the scanner. The flowery images that looked like tourist attractions ballooned on the screen to reveal the tiny photographic images that lay embedded within them. Magnified x 4000, the microscopic dots showed photographs of a man from different angles meeting with several others, then several pages of a document. One showed a reporting structure. One showed a budget. One showed a project planning schedule that would indicate, by the green and red bars, that they were basically on schedule and half way through.

Marly's superiors in the FBI's Counterterror Division would be pleased with this cross-departmental communication with the CIA. And the pictures were good. One could easily see Galoub and identify his associates. They had picked up a lot of noise in the U.S. about Galoub construction and its charitable funding of young people abroad. The org chart showed how each silo reported to him, though operated independently. The budget was $26 million. Maybe they were just building a bridge. Or maybe they were doing something else. But what exactly the plan was, and when they were going to do it, would depend on a few more games of tennis.

CHAPTER 2

EDWIN
12:00 P.M., SOMEWHERE IN THE CARIBBEAN

No had noticed, that Friday evening in September, the small skiff puttering down the river after dark. The two men dangled lures along the gunnels. No one had recognized the man limping toward the small helicopter on the private airway. The flight restrictions had lifted.

The whip of the blades had felt like an army. Edwin had only their company as the plane lifted off Hanscom's private runway, gained altitude, and flew southeast over the ocean for hours. Eventually, the early dawn light showed the black silhouette of the drilling rig that appeared out of the sea, just where the flight instruments indicated it should.

Its prince was arriving home. His mission now was clear. Edwin would heal, quickly. And from this perch, he would watch. He would determine when and where to fight his own war on the terrorists that were threatening the world he had loved being a part of, even for such a short time. He was an entrepreneur again. When necessary, he would re-enter the world, and build a team with whoever was around. Edwin could bring out the hero in anyone.

Edwin went first to the small house. Ahmed/Zed had built the network and shielded it behind thousands of other IP addresses. Thanks to his brilliance, Edwin was on the grid, but invisible. He could see out, but no one could see in.

Edwin tapped into a military satellite feed focused on the hills of Pakistan. A screen showed a small line of people marching along the edge of a hillside. Men dressed in robes that blended with the tan dusty cliffs. Except for one man, who wore a dark western suit. He walked just behind the guide.

Edwin poured a cup of steaming coffee while he watched the monitor, and registered every single step of the one he had let go. Once. It had been a worthwhile trade at the time. But it was a deficit he would not allow to linger for long.

It was as Edwin had always said. Ali – Yassir – was a genius. His intellect, if ever combined with passion instead of the apathy that always circled his feet at D6, would make him a force to reckon with.

CrossPathz was working well. Ahmed's data feed, linking satellites, Homeland Security feeds, driver's license applications, commercial licenses for trucks, planes, supplies of nitrogen, ATM machines worldwide, and other trends, filtered into Edwin's program and began to predict where dangerous affiliations were growing, showing where to slot individual people in precise geographic locations.

Raptor was on duty. But attachment had changed Edwin Hoff. It was not only Lula. There was also Ahmed. Sterling. Jameson. Michael James. Nancy. Hudson. The thousand people who fed their families because of him. Even Camille. Instead of feeling like the outsider, in his cover life he had created a real world, and he was its core heat. He was attached to all of them. And it was fabulous.

Whatever commands Ali would send, Edwin would know. He would see planning for the next attack begin; he would know when it would happen. When the time was right, Edwin would leave his floating nation and go wherever necessary to take Ali and his evil cells out of business. Edwin would settle in the hot spot. With whatever people he found there, from whatever walks of life, Edwin would make a team of them. He would give them direction, teach them to focus, and set their hair on fire.

EPILOGUE

The convoy was four cars deep, enough to show respect without too much risk. A man with dark hair and flashing white teeth sat in the black car. The dust was everywhere. He purposely wore a tie with his dark suit and white shirt: the tie, the symbol of the west that made Middle Eastern leaders leave shirt buttons uncovered. It was, after all, why he had been chosen. But he regretted the dark color; the way it trapped the heat and showed the dust accumulating in the moist creases.

"You make me very proud," Yassir heard his uncle's words, though he was very far away, locked under a mountain somewhere in Nevada. "To think, this is where everything has been leading, for twenty-five years. And we are now here."

"I am honored," Yassir had said.

The convoy stopped. "We walk from here," announced the Head, who along with two flanks of ten each, shouldered Kalashnikov rifles. They wound along a steep path where caves appeared in the jagged cliffs, all but invisible until they were on top of them. After nearly an hour, the leader stopped.

He motioned to Yassir. "He has asked for only you."

Yassir ducked through the dark opening. In the distance, he could see the light of oil lamps bouncing off the walls. The ground was surprisingly even under his feet and free of the loose rock that had scraped his shoes. The man with the long beard and white robes sat with crossed legs on the floor. His feet were bare.

"The Dust King," thought Yassir. "Living in squalor in a cave. And all this could be mine." He remembered the down comforter over his bed in New Haven. Napping with Camille under its warm pockets of air, the clanging radiators bringing the heat on dark afternoons. Across the courtyard the dining hall opened, offering daily Jell-O and steak "with au jus."

The leader considered Yassir. His cold eyes shone light to a very small part of the world and pitched blackness to the rest. Yassir kneeled and pressed his torso to the ground, nearly as low as he bent in prayer five times a day for god. The comparison in his mind made him rise, ever so slightly. He hoped this was not noticed.

"Yes," said the leader. "You are ready, then?"

"Yes, if it is Allah's will," said Yassir, peering up at him.

"I must go now. They are after me. So it is time for my successor to take my place. Someone western, with better access to a world of assets to fund our business. Someone they will not suspect."

"I am ready," said Yassir.

"You have no…liabilities," he said.

Yassir paused, covering it with humility. "Only that I am but a man," he said.

"Then it is done," said the leader. He waved to a man in the shadows of the cave. "Notify the media group. My successor has been chosen. Bow to him."

AUTHOR'S NOTE

All people, entities and events in this book are fictional and do not represent any real person, entity or event. It is also true that the character Edwin Hoff, though wholly fictional, was inspired by Danny Lewin, the founder of Akamai Technologies, Inc. Danny was a genius, a demanding entrepreneur and a twenty-eight year old who titans of academia and industry chose to follow. Before launching one of the most successful technology companies in the dot com craze, Danny had been a Captain in the Counter Terror unit of one of the world's most elite commando units: the Israeli Defense Force's Sayeret Matkal. He made new things happen, and he had unique methods to make others reach as far as he did.

After the military, Danny Lewin studied at The Technion - Israel Institute of Technology, and then went to MIT to pursue a PhD in mathematics. He co-founded Akamai Technologies in 1998 to speed up the Internet by using special algorithms to deliver web pages, applications, and videos across the Internet quickly and reliably. Akamai went public in October 1999, then one of the most successful IPO's ever. Its stock peaked at $345.50/share on January 3, 2000. With only a few million dollars in revenue, the company was worth $30 billion dollars. But a few months later, the dot com bubble burst. Akamai stock plummeted; customers went out of business; and the nascent company had to evolve quickly or perish.

Despite the crash, on July 1, 2001, Enterprise Systems Journal published its "Power 100" list of the most influential people in

Information Technology. Danny Lewin was No. 7. Steve Ballmer, CEO of Microsoft, was No. 6 , and the founders of Oracle and Intel followed Danny.

Two months later, Danny boarded a flight in Boston for a sales call in Los Angeles. On September 11, 2001, he was seated in business class on Flight 11, in front of one hijacker; across from two. His loss, at 31, is a staggering tragedy for everyone who knew him. It is also a profound loss for the many more people who never did, and for the challenges he never tackled.

But there could not have been a person better trained to respond to the horrific acts Danny must have seen, opening his eyes from a rare rest. Members of the Sayeret Matkal trained to kill terrorists with their bare hands; they specialized in deep cover. Later, the government found that Danny had fought to defend the stewardesses and cockpit from the hijackers. That they cut his throat.

I deeply wish that Danny had had a different reason to be on that plane, with a different result. The First Secret of Edwin Hoff is that hopeful fantasy. But this curious fact is true: on September 10th, 2001, Danny packed up his office. I saw him put his master's thesis in a box. He gave away the Lucite trinkets, awards for each stage of success in the company he started. No one knows why.

On September 11, 2001, the high number of attempted telephone calls swamped telephone networks. But websites using Akamai – like Yahoo.com and CNN.com – could still deliver the crucial news. Ironically, that tragic day, Akamai's network handled its highest load and was among the world's most reliable communications technologies.

As America struggled to absorb 9-11, the technology market shook. Akamai stock peaked in January 2000 at $345.50 per share, but by October 2002, that share was worth fifty-four cents. But ten years later, Akamai has survived. Led by many of the same people who started the company with Danny and committed to carry out his vision, today Akamai is a profitable, thriving company that makes the Internet work better. Today, one out of every five web pages that you see comes through Akamai's network – Danny's invention. Today, at Akamai headquarters, on the engineering floor, there is a conference room. In it is a whiteboard that no one touches. It is covered on both sides with red, green, and blue marks.

ACKNOWLEDGMENTS

First, I would like to thank my agent, Josh Getzler, and the outstanding team at the Hannigan Salky Getzler Agency, for understanding the essence of Edwin Hoff and for inventing and pursuing an entrepreneurial strategy for the series that he would applaud. Josh's vision, editorial guidance, unflagging professionalism and good humor make him a joy to work with. I am also grateful to the exceptional Maddie Raffel at HSG who, with sound judgment and sharp execution, made the book happen on its tight but essential timeline. It is exciting and fun to work with them to make the most of all opportunities in the shifting shape of today's publishing industry.

For their helpful advice in researching this book, I would like to thank by name, but cannot, several former operatives in the CIA. I am grateful for their prudent guidance. I would also like to thank Attia Linnard, for helping me understand more about the history of Pakistani immigration to the U.S. and what it is like to worship in a mosque. And many thanks also go to Julie Callaghan, for her advice on the title, her steadfast enthusiasm, and to her and Alisa Kapoor for bidding up the opportunity to name a character at the school auction.

I would also like to thank Paul Sagan for recruiting me to the rocket ride of Akamai Technologies, Inc., and for his mentorship and friendship. Working at Akamai placed me in the fascinating moment of our economic history which inspired this book and lit my passion for entrepreneurial endeavors.

I will be forever grateful to Danny Lewin for showing me how to make big goals happen. I share the deep grief that so many feel at his tragic loss, much too soon. Those who had the chance to work with Danny lived smaller lives before knowing him; we know how to live much larger ones now.

I am so thankful for my family and friends. To my father, James, for seeing the path forward - with this project and so many others - and for giving me the courage to take it. And my mother, Phoebe, for sharing her thrill of the first read of an early draft, which her candid constructive comments made believable. Both of you helped greatly. To my large and supportive family – Juliet and Christopher, Phoebe C. and Todd, Vanessa and Bruce, Christine and Anton, Bonnie and John, and my aunts and uncles and cousins on both sides of the pond - who offer love and support so strong that it makes first steps possible. And to my friends who inspire me by their example and urge me on with encouragement and delight – Dan, Eric, Jamie W, Jamie W (there are 2!), Jean, Kristen, and Lauren, and many others. Thank you.

Dash's enthusiastic welcome and warm wag helped me write in the pre-dawn hours, and Elmo often bought us a few more paragraphs.

And finally, I thank my husband Julian, my creative partner in the adventure of our lives, and extraordinary inventor with an uncanny knack for seeing the "bigadia" in books and technology. As with all of our beloved start-ups, these words reached the page because of you.

ABOUT THE AUTHOR

A.B. Bourne worked closely with Danny Lewin at Akamai Technologies on strategic deals with IBM and Oracle, and managed Akamai's IPO, raising $234 million in 1999. The author graduated from Yale College and the University of Michigan Law School and practiced law in Boston. She lives in Massachusetts with her family, consulting for start-up technology companies and writing *The Second Secret of Edwin Hoff*.

Made in the USA
Lexington, KY
11 February 2012